Praise for Kathy Acker

"I'm no superstar shit and never will be. If anything, I'm what happens after death, which is writing." —Kathy Acker

"Kathy Acker's writing is virtuoso, maddening, crazy, so sexy, so painful, and beaten out of a wild heart that nothing can tame. Acker is a landmark writer." —Jeanette Winterson

"[Acker] is more than a dirty talker. She is a storyteller par excellence, and her hardness is balanced by a goofy humor." —*Seattle Times*

"Her books are a gift to humanity."
—Zackary Drucker, *New York Times*

"Acker was nothing if not a mistress of the contradictions of being woman, a post-punk amalgam of de Sade's masochistic Justine, virtuous in her enforced prostitution, and his triumphant libertine Juliette. If her evocations of (sexual) violence against women make her, in some senses, a precursor of millennial feminism, her plaint or critique was less aimed at individual male malefactors than at the *system* of patriarchy as a whole." —Lisa Appignanesi, *New York Review of Books*

"No writer I know is more audacious than Kathy Acker, whose anarchic wit drives a thoroughgoing attack on conventions and complacencies of all sorts. Not unlike Gertrude Stein in her day, Acker gives us a different way to look at the uses to which language is put." —Lynne Tillman

"Genres in Acker are a shifting kaleidoscope of forms that, like facets of identity, are not stable and mask the crucial fact that, like the unified 'you,' there is no comforting master narrative. Acker wants to keep open the questions—in both art and life—of what a human is and what forms of life we might potentially create ourselves . . . In a world in which liberal democracy is itself in crisis, Acker's work is more relevant than ever. Change the political genre, fight for something new, Acker's work urges us, because conventional politics in the post-factual, image-driven age is failing and unable to evolve."

—Ralph Clare, *Los Angeles Review of Books*

"She did an enormous thing, which was that she single-handedly in London connected people who bought records to people who bought books. There had not been a writer, a contemporary writer living in our midst, who united the world of pop culture and music and post-punk to the world of literature, let alone to the world of critical theory."

—Michael Bracewell

"Kathy Acker's trancelike writing style peels away the layers of reality. . . . Acker is an expert at evoking this shadowy realm of belief and emotion where the rules of cause and effect do not necessarily apply."   —*San Francisco Chronicle*

"America's most beloved transgressive novelist."   —*Spin*

PORTRAIT OF AN EYE

three novels

PORTRAIT OF AN EYE

three novels

Grove Press
New York

kathy acker

Originally published in the United States as three separate works in paperback:
I Dreamt I Was A Nymphomaniac, published by Traveler's Digest Editions,
New York, in 1980; *The Adult Life of Toulose Lautrec*, published by TVRT
Press, New York, in 1978; and *The Childlike Life of the Black Tarantula*, published
by TVRT Press, New York, in 1975, and as a limited edition by Viper's Tongue
Books, New York, in 1975

Published simultaneously in Canada
Printed in the United States of America

First Grove Atlantic paperback edition: January 1998
This Grove Atlantic paperback edition: July 2020

Library of Congress Cataloging-in-Publication data is available for this title

ISBN 978-0-8021-5756-0
eISBN 978-0-8021-4665-6

Grove Press
an imprint of Grove Atlantic
154 West 14th Street
New York, NY 10011

Distributed by Publishers Group West

groveatlantic.com

20 21 22 23 24   10 9 8 7 6 5 4 3 2 1

contents

introduction: texts of nothing
by kate zambreno

[]

I am listening to a 1992 recording of Michael Silverblatt interviewing Kathy Acker. The two speakers aren't aware of the fact that Acker will die five years later, at the age of fifty, but this fact now suspends over the recording. Acker is supposed to be promoting the book that's been titled *Portrait of an Eye*, a collection of the three early mail-art serials that were self-published in the seventies semi-anonymously under the pseudonym The Black Tarantula and republished in various forms as her name became known, including this final form, an accomplishment of a midcareer artist who must now find some coherence or chronology in her origins, some attempt at a linear narrative, the fiction of a continuous and unified voice. To have one's early texts reissued—to have this retrospective—is a form of resurrection of the fictions of the past, of past selves. There's a ghostliness to that as well. Kathy Acker's radio voice surprises me: she sounds like any New York intellectual. "Lit-er-a-ture," she pronounces it. "I wasn't interested in producing a piece of lit-er-a-ture," she is saying.

[]

I am now supposed to speak of this book for the foreword of yet another reissue of this collection that has gone through so many transformations. The persona of Kathy Acker has taken on even more attention and visibility in the past years, a biographical read often overdetermining the actual work's compositional methods and aims toward decreation, fragmentation, and the nonlinear. This already was under way when Silverblatt was interviewing Acker. In England, she tells him, they manufactured an image of her—the punk iconoclast— and that made her career. Here in the U.S., the Grove Press covers, with her peroxided bust. The interviews she gave, the repetition of anecdotes—the origins of her intellectual coming of age, of her experimentations—the texts too, if one scans only for the fragments of autobiography, hidden like puzzle pieces, you get repetitions multiplied into myth: the isolated private school childhood, the mother's suicide, the months spent when out of college working at the Times Square sex show while an outsider in the St. Marks poetry scene, an alienation that her biographer, Chris Kraus, sees as informing the fragmentation of her work, the squalid romance of being an artist in early-seventies New York, all that survival energy.

[]

This is what has been told before. Kathy Acker began writing the first of The Black Tarantula texts, *The Childlike Life of the Black Tarantula*, in 1973, in her early twenties, having left the chaos of New York temporarily for Solana Beach, a town outside of San Diego, babysitting for David and Eleanor Antin, the poet and conceptual artist who were her earliest mentors. Borrowing from one of David Antin's undergraduate writing prompts, Acker began taking out mass-market biographies of eighteenth-century murderesses from the UCSD library and copying them but changing them to first person so they seemed to be about her, collaging them with her own diary entries. "I figured, of all the people I could figure I'm not, I know I've never murdered anybody. At least not directly." An obsession that has a tradition in Jean Genet and the surrealists' obsession with the Papin sisters and Marguerite Duras's fixation with the French crime reports, or *fait divers*. So she proceeds to juxtapose the "fake" autobiographical material with the "real" autobiographical material that jut out in frantic parentheticals. The first serial, "Some Lives of Murderesses," begins: "Intention: I become a murderess by repeating in words the lives of other murderesses."

[]

Acker saw these texts as experiments in first person, aided by her reading about schizophrenia (Laing, etc.) as she explained to poet Jackson Mac Low in a letter: "I do have this identity or self that's full of holes, and I need other texts, I'm a totally reactive person." What could the "I" be in language, could it dissolve into other "I's," could it be multiple? Could the I's begin playing games with each other? By rewriting these pulp histories in the first person, with an anachronistically contemporary voice, she could play with her porous feelings of identification with mythic figures like the gender-bending Moll Cutpurse, seventeenth-century fence and pimp of the London underworld. She set herself constraints: no rewriting, no imagination or creativity (tenets of the bourgeois novel and cult of individuality), just tighten up the language, a certain number of pages a day. Calling herself The Black Tarantula, she prints up a booklet a month for six months, using the mailing list for Eleanor Antin's mail-art postcard project 100 Boots (itself a photographic picaresque sending up of the American road trip after Kerouac, suggestive of soldiers returning from Vietnam, a squadron of boots posed in supermarket aisles, in fields with ducks, climbing single file over a car, connotations at times comic, fascist, pathetic).

[]

I try to imagine the thrill of what it was like to receive the first of The Black Tarantula booklets in the mail, her Byronic fugitive pieces, what it was like to read them then, the identity of the author unknown or hearsay, to try to make sense of the rushed confessionalism of the brutal isolation of childhood(s), the tonal shifts into picaresque tales, the layering of wild anachronistic language. This was the only time Acker's sources were printed in the back. In the later installments, she begins drawing from literary texts, copying Violette Leduc's schoolgirl novel *Thérèse and Isabelle*, overlaid with personal fantasies ("I move to San Francisco, I begin to copy my favorite pornography books and become the main person in each of them"). In another, she rewrites the autobiography of Yeats (a writer himself known for channeling and automatic writing). In the final chapter of *The Childlike Life*, Acker takes on as her alter ego the Marquis de Sade at Charenton (who changes genders), juxtaposed with abject scenes of an I voice from the clinic at Columbia Presbyterian, diagnosed with Pelvic Inflammatory Disease. *Justine* was also a durational experiment—the Marquis wrote it in two weeks while imprisoned, as a satire of the morally turgid novel, much as Acker here is reacting to the bourgeois expectations of surely still the most conservative art form, so aligned with the marketplace and moral values, her bad sentences mocking the expectation of beautiful ones, her overidentification devouring readerly expectation, her refusal of Aristotelian unity, of finding a "voice" as a writer as opposed to the unstable and multiple ("Why did I have to find my own voice and where was it?").

[]

Not only are there explicit rants here regarding American involvement in Vietnam and the American government in this first text ("I won't be jailed and given a lobotomy if I become an American solider instead of a murderess"; "The American government wants all poor people to die in the fastest way possible"), there's something in these early experiments — their dissolution of boundaries and false truths — that speaks back to the hallucinatory instability and dread of Nixon-era America, seeming even more prescient now.

[]

As Acker has noted in interviews, there were other feminist conceptual artists making work in the early seventies about becoming somebody else, often switching genders — durational performances with which The Black Tarantula forms a ghostly and intentional correspondence — Eleanor Antin posing as many selves, Adrian Piper's alter ego the Mythic Being, Joan Jonas's hyperfemme Organic Honey masked personae. In his essay "Identity without the Person," Giorgio Agamben traces back "persona" to the theater of the Stoics, the actor depicted holding his mask or the mask at a distance on a pedestal, a gap between the self and personae that Western concepts of identity has obliterated. "Point to the mask." Acker, a trained classicist, looked often to the Greeks as well; the Greeks just repeated stories over and over. In her

Black Tarantula femme fatale persona, Acker murdered her self over and over again.

[]

Back to the sotto voce of Silverblatt and Acker. As always, Acker brings up William Burroughs. She will only reference male writers in the interview, even schlocky ones, possibly to shore up that she is speaking back to this lineage she envisions herself in. Burroughs was interested in the gaps she is saying, in what happens between the cutups. The gaps. Of time, selves, fragments. I like thinking of these empty spaces in these early texts of Acker that seem so cluttered, so polyphonic. "La-cu-nae," Michael Silverblatt says in response, which amuses and irritates me. "Yes," she says. Lacunae—"an unfilled space or interval." The missing pieces of a fragmented papyrus, a hole or lost section in a medieval manuscript. It reminds me of my favorite line in Anne Carson's introduction to her Sappho translation: "Brackets are exciting." A proposal for an essay I will never write about the kinship between Anne Carson and Kathy Acker—both come from the tradition of poetry, both classicists, both interested in fragmentation and decreation—except Anne Carson's language and juxtapositions are elegant, Acker's often self-consciously "bad writing," including her copying of porn and best-selling hacks (in fact, it's a war, she is telling Silverblatt here, a war against writing "properly, writing elegantly," writing "lit-er-a-ture").

[]

By the second serialized work, *I Dreamt I Was a Nymphomaniac*, her durational project becomes ritualized: the first half of

1974 occupied by free-form first person writing, then six months of producing the pamphlets, collaging pornography with diary entries. Her address list has now doubled, she's become known, and she announces herself in the text: "My name is Kathy Acker. This story begins by me being totally bored." She began repeating passages set amidst the existing tedium and repetition of pornography—a nymphomaniac repeats obsessively. A Sadean catalogue is also a series of repeated gestures, positions, pyramids. Sade can be a slog to get through. Acker's *Nymphomaniac* is boring, too, but you're not supposed to really read it, not in a linear, continuous way. This is what repetition does. It disrupts linearity, resists narrative. A text repeating becomes an experience of uncanniness—have I read that before—flipping back, scanning. Something that is no longer. Something that persists. Anne Carson performs this in *Nox* as well, a repetition of the same fragment over pages, so does Franz Kafka in his early diaries. Repetition is a form of ghost-making.

[]

There are similar composition techniques here as in Terry Riley's drone-like *In C* (1964), its aleatory nature, the orchestration of loops repeated an arbitrary number of times. The name of Acker's partner at the time, the music composer Peter Gordon, is repeated throughout *Nymphomaniac,* a sometimes hilarious Brechtian alienation effect (point to the mask or the name), to jolt a reader from emotional involvement. "Peter Gordon" changes genders, personas, in Sadean-lite chateaus and private school milieus, as well as sex-work settings that are both autobiographical and anecdotal reporting, the line blurry and impossible to know. "Peter Gordon" becomes Patty Hearst as a Symbionese Liberation Army (SLA) agent (Patty Hearst sending out communiqués as Tania at this time seems the exact sort of multiplicity at play here), and then, in following installments, appears in a history of Folsom prison, swapping in friends' names for prisoners (including David Antin and his son, Blaise).

[]

What am I reading? This is what Acker is performing. What is a book? Is this a book? What makes a text legible or illegible? "You seem to be, in a Mallarmé sense, inventing the book," Silverblatt is saying to her now. In a Mallarmé sense. "If you just open a book and say all a book is all these pages, anything can happen," Acker responds. Mallarmé who wrote: "The pure work implies the disappearance of the poet as a speaker; he gives way to words."

[]

I've been rereading Foucault's 1969 essay "What Is an Author?" over and over, as if on loop. It strikes me that this is another correspondence for the flash origin of Kathy Acker's oeuvre, even though Acker wouldn't have read Foucault until 1976, when she meets Sylvère Lotringer, as she tells him in their conversation first collected in the Semiotext(e) book *Hannibal Lecter, My Father* (published in 1991, a year earlier than the Silverblatt conversation). Once she did, she tells Lotringer, the theory allowed her to continue these radical innovations in voice, collaging texts, rewriting literature. Both Foucault and Acker share an obsession with Artaud and Sade; their work both theorized a desire to disappear, to disintegrate into texts, but their photographed images through their fame often overdetermined this (also the twin leather jackets, the twin shaved heads, their stares).

[]

In his essay, Foucault quotes Beckett's *Stories and Texts for Nothing*, a line that feels like it could come right out of Acker: "What matter who's speaking, someone said, what matter who's speaking." The essay reads like a noir. The disappearance of death of the author in the contemporary narrative versus the strategy of Scheherazade fending off death with further story-telling in *Arabian Nights*. Foucault writes: "Rather, we should reexamine the empty space left by the author's disappearance." An empty space where the author disappears—or the author is murdered. A gap.

[]

The last serialized narrative, or "novel," *The Adult Life of Toulouse Lautrec* (first self-published in 1975) is something of a cross-dressing farce, where the gender-bending is at the level of naming, making us always aware we're reading plays with language, where characters are just signified by names. Toulouse Lautrec, unbearably horny, worries she's a "hideous monster," a figure amidst a field of cocks. "I'm not even anonymous," Toulouse Lautrec worries, a sly authorial commentary. There's a character named Poirot out of Agatha Christie, investigating a murder mystery like slapstick noir. On the radio, Acker is saying it's something of a class war for her: she takes on mystery and true crime and other "low-class genres," because it makes her "giggle." Gauguin is the local cleaning woman, boys work the brothel, Giannina the brothel waitress—like something out of

Fellini's *Nights of Cabiria*—wants to go to San Francisco to visit Ron Silliman (the real-life poet who Acker was crushing on, her books also functioning as gossip and infatuated correspondence, like a game she is playing). Juxtaposed throughout are anarchist histories, such as of Sophie Perovskaya who assassinated Alexander II of Russia, a short history of Paris in 1886 as it dovetailed with the Haymarket Massacre, porn starring a "Jackie Onassis," and then an involved story line featuring a twenty-four-year-old James Dean and his apocryphal love affair with a nine-year-old Janis Joplin, juxtaposed with a stage reading of *Rebel Without a Cause* and a rant about Henry Kissinger, threaded into a history of the origins of American capitalism. Here, this last novel enters the pace and energy of the later, more canonical texts. If we insist on one singular Acker or Author. Foucault writes, "Rather, we should reexamine the empty space left by the author's disappearance." An empty space where the author disappears or the author is murdered.

A gap.

THE CHILDLIKE LIFE OF THE BLACK TARANTULA BY THE BLACK TARANTULA

Intention: I become a murderess by repeating in words the lives of other murderesses.

1

some lives of murderesses

JUNE 1973

I become a murderess.

I'm born in the late autumn or winter of 1827.

Troy, New York.

My childhood is happy, and my parents allow me to do whatever I please as long as I, by my actions, don't infringe on their high social standing. My father is a great and wealthy man, a tall man, whom I look up to. As a child, among my dolls, I feel safe. I will never die. No one can hurt me. My mother, my father, my two older sisters, my younger sister, and my brother often ignore me, or promise to love me, give me a present, then don't; and I cry. My name at this time is Charlotte Wood.

I don't remember any of my childhood before I was 6 years old when I start learning to read. My eldest sister marries a baronet and lives in England; my second elder sister marries a doctor and moves to Scotland. I'm an obedient child: I stubbornly do what my parents and their associates want me to do. I hallucinate. I climb trees, stick needles up the asses of young boys. I hallucinate that the Virgin Mary wears black leather pants and a black leather motorcycle jacket, she climbs trees, she doesn't give a fuck for anyone. (I call up D in Los Angeles do you want to sleep with me with me when and where there why don't you spend a few days with me I'll call you tomorrow. No call three days later I'm maniacal I have to see D I don't know him hello I've got a ride to Los Angeles lie I'm not sure I know where we can stay should I not come up come up. We don't touch talk about anything personal until we get to motel never talk about anything personal spend night together I have to be at Irvine in the morning I'm busy call me Friday. Do you want me to call you yes. I call Friday call Saturday Sunday this is Kathy O uh do you want to spend a night with me again are you too busy I'm too busy uh goodbye have a good time in New York uh goodbye.)

When I'm 16, I board for the next two years at the Female Seminary in Troy, the school my elder sisters went to. The school sits by a large lake, or ocean; I spend my free time staring at the blue then green then white water. I want to be a mermaid: I swim under the heavy water with my legs together; the heavy muscles in my arms move the rest of my body. I want someone, a man, to walk up to me while I'm standing on a stone terrace, put his arms around my shoulders, his hand brush the hair off my forehead. While I'm at school, I meet the only love of my life. He is honest with me, as intelligent and paranoid as I am. My father forbids our marriage because my lover's family has insufficient social connections. When my (adopted) father suspects I've been sleeping with my future husband, he slobbers over me. Rape. My parents take me out of the Seminary, 1846, and return me to their home in Quebec.

I'm 19 years old. I meet Lieutenant William F. A. Elliot, eldest son of a baronet, who loves me, and, with the help of my parents, forces me to marry him. I have to get married. My new husband plans to take me to New York to England but I'm no longer safe. I change my woman's clothes to man's clothes, roam through the streets of New York. My parents, my husband, and I have locked me in a prison and I'm unable to fuck anyone. England is worse. Europe is worse. Scotland France Italy. These are the first signs of my madness.

Despite my two children (I fantasize D calls me that's impossible I fantasize he reads my letter to B he finds out decides he likes me we're both in New York or Los Angeles he undoes my black velvet cape, puts the palms of his hands over my nipples, rubs his hands quickly up and down his hands swerve around to the center of my back he pulls my body against his body I begin to open my stomach he leads me to a hard bed lays down his stocky body under me) I leave my husband, I decide, I get out, leave my children out I go back home to America. My maid Helen comes with me. I hate everyone, I want to kill everyone, a rich famous man at a hotel in New York City sees me, I know what he wants, I go back home. The man has a lot of influence. My parents hate me, they drive me out of their house in Quebec, I've left my husband, I have no right to leave a man especially a man who loves me, I'm weird, I'm not a robot. Get the hell out, get the hell out of here. Do what I want. Get the hell out everywhere. Fuck them. Shit up their ass fuck them.

I have no money I'm on the street I'm dying no one's going to help me they step on me I puke puke I cause whatever happens to me I'll get the fuck out of here.

On the boat back to New York I have paranoid delusions: I believe that the man who is staring at me is not staring at me out of desire, lust etc. Spies daunt my footsteps at every hour of the night. I allow the man to talk to me so I can find out who my husband my parents has hired him to spy on me. Fuck me. I don't love this man; in the future I will never love him.

I have a paranoid delusion I'm revenging myself on my parents. I'm escaping. I become crazier.

I give a party for my doll.

In Albany: I'm 23 years old; my lover tells me I'm beautiful and intelligent. I can't speak to anyone else but him. After skulking in the streets of Troy, I force myself to move to Albany, New York where I'll be freer. I'm constantly alone; I have no one to talk to. There's no one to whom I can be myself. The people who live in Albany hate me; they don't notice me, I'm in disguise, they talk solely about me when I can barely hear them. (I sneak down to the dark green hall to the edge of the doorway of my parents' bedroom I'm supposed to be asleep my father's telling my mother I'm bad and worthless child I can barely hear what my parents are saying.) I have to buy a pistol I scare my new maid so much she swears out a warrant for my arrest. Everyone hates me they just want to fuck me they don't want to fuck me. The cop finds me with my new lover; my lover gets me out of jail. No matter where I move in Albany everyone talks about me. I force myself to move back to Troy. Seclusion

25. Not 25.

To escape my parents, I tried to fuck whoever I wanted, lean on a number of people; I become more closely imprisoned. I don't want anyone to tell me what I should do. I don't want anyone following me around, secretly gossiping about me, because I'm not also a robot.

In Troy I learn not to talk to anyone, even my maids, I make my lifelong plans in secret. I travel to Boston, then to England, back to my beloved husband. My lover follows me to Boston, he puts his arms around the upper part of my body where are you going I'll take care of you I love you I'm the only person who can take care of you he's tall and thin grey hair I don't care who he is I don't care what he looks like his hand swings down the side of my thin body into the waist the broad spread of my ass I don't know what I look like skin separates from skin in my cunt the skins below my navel around my navel reveal a hand curves around the edges of the soft skins

He takes my left hand places it below his cock on softer skin his hand rests above my hand his cock rises above his hand I shape move my hand around his skin he begins to moan I hear body rolls side to side I squeeze my hand in out I feel his hands grasp the turns of my shoulders push me down along his body his body lies over my body so that his cock moves in and out of my mouth between the opening of the skins I form a long narrow tunnel I begin to move my thighs up

(I come out of the bathroom buttoning my pants I ask him to put on the T.V. my left hand touches his shoulder he suddenly turns toward me I've wanted him to turn toward me quickly I feel wet lips tongue in the center of my mouth the sudden change from dream-fantasy to reality makes me unable to react he lifts my body over his body on to the bed I feel his tongue enter my mouth the sudden change from fantasy-dream to reality makes me unable to react we both lie on our right sides I in front of you your cock touches the lips of my cunt enters the wet canal your arms tightly clasp my body around the waist warm fur up down my spine your cock slips out I bend my body until my hands almost touch my toes though I lose warmth of your skin I can feel your cock moving inside my skin skins I can begin to come the muscles of my cunt begin to move around your cock my muscles free themselves swirl to the tip of my clit out through my legs the center of my stomach new newer muscles vibrate I'm beginning to come I don't know you)

These are my insanities:

I tell people I see on the street my neighbors are conspiring against me. I arm myself with pistols, threaten my enemies I'll rape murder them. My neighbors are a band of burglars who're planning to rob me. One of them has stopped all navigation on the Hudson. I hold a magic cork in my mouth which will accomplish everything. As the sun comes up each morning, I wander around the streets of Troy in disguise. I can appear to be sane (a robot).

I will never again write anything.

My only friends are the poor unwanted people of Troy. I hate the rich shits, will do anything to destroy them. I'm not political. I buy my meager groceries from a grocery-saloon keeper, an Irish bum, Timothy Lanagan, who has a wife and four children. I know that I'm drinking too much beer and brandy, I'm too close to myself to think clearly about my degradation, my unhappiness, I'm scared all the time. I don't know what to be scared about. I love I don't love I hate I don't hate I'm scared I'm not scared I kill I don't kill. I'm beginning to learn who my enemies are.

One day the spring of '53 I'm at a dance in the Lanagans' booze-parlor I've learned how to speak the correct language one of the disgusting men insults me. No one believes he insults me. I don't know anyone I can really talk to. The Lanagans' filth ask me to leave. I'll show them. This time I'll revenge myself. I tell my gardener to ask the Lanagans to lend me two dollars. My gardener's thinking of killing me I ask the Lanagans myself for the two bucks they don't have any money they're starving I know exactly what's happening. I go back home. (I dream I return to New York I'm going to miss an important meeting of radicals in the middle of St. Mark's Place I sit in an uptown apartment stare out a window of course I miss the meeting I wander into the church when it's empty night.)

Two hours later I walk into the Lanagans' back room tell the Lanagans and the mysterious men the truth: my husband just had a railroad accident. I know exactly what's happening.

Two hours later I walk into the Lanagans' back room. The Lanagans are eating. I ask the Lanagans for an egg, and Mrs.

Lanagan gives me the egg and a peeled potato. I invite her and
her sister-in-law to drink beer with me. I know I'm a drunk. I'm
clever, this is my plan:
I ask Mrs. Lanagan for sugar they refuse I just bought sugar
I ask Mrs. Lanagan to put powdered sugar in my beer she
brings back powdered sugar in a saucer, two glasses, some beer.
I ask Mrs. Lanagan for enough beer to fill the glasses to the
brim I now have the sugar bowl in my hand. She leaves gets
more beer. I spoon the sugar and arsenic I bought ten days ago
to kill rats in the beer. Mrs. Lanagan notices powder on the top
of the beer. It's good to drink. Lanagan calls his wife to mind
the store Lanagan drinks the untouched beer. The sister-in-law
drinks her beer. Two hours later Mrs. Lanagan tells me I've
killed her husband and sister-in-law. She tells me to go home.

I feel angry. I've forgotten how to feel. I feel like I've done
what I wanted. I feel elated. I've succeeded forgetting my
parents. (I awake between 11:00 and 1:00 for a half hour to an
hour, clean up, talk to friends, eat, spend an hour on the beach,
exercise, work for the next 8 hours taking 3 or 4 short breaks,
eat a quick meal, drink wine or play chess to calm myself, fuck
or don't fuck, fall asleep. I speak to almost no one because I
find it difficult to find people who will accept my alternating
hermitage and maniacal falling-in-love. My style forces me to
live in San Francisco or New York. I don't want to learn to
drive a car I love cities I have to be sure I keep working hard
in a large city.) During my childhood I give ample signs I'm
wild, unlike my parents and other people. I run away with a
gang of gypsies from my family's estate, my father is heavy dull
I'm meek my mother's beautiful I elope with one of the
grooms. I have gold hair, large blue eyes, I'm always laughing.
I'm very tough. Because I won't stop being a tomboy, my
parents decide I have to get married. I want to get married to
get away from my parents do whatever I want to do. I'm born
poor St. Helen's, the Isle of Wight. 1790. As a child, I had

hardly any food to eat. My parents go to the workhouse; I
become a farmer's maid. The shits begin to tell me that if I
don't become humble, respectful, I have to have security.
. . . I'm going to rape you you need security. I become chamber-
maid in a hotel. I know better.

They take me to jail. My lover who has kept me in the white
house by the river never appears to help me. The Troy Female
Seminary where I went to school announces in the local newspaper that Charlotte Wood lives in England. I'm Henrietta
Robinson. My brother visits me in prison, due to the uproar,
shaking, I'm not his sister. I wear a veil. I try to commit suicide
but the shits save me. How do I get the vitriol? They make me
confess the truth.

(I live quietly I change my way of life I eat grains vegetables
some dairy products because I have an ulcer I'm too poor to
see a doctor about once a month I fall in love with someone
at the same time I live with Peter who I love I rarely form
friendships I deal awkwardly with people I fall in love with.)

I'm born poor St. Helen's, Isle of Wight. 1790. As a child I
have hardly any food to eat.

I'm still a child when I see my father and mother dragged
to the local poorhouse, I walk alone on the city streets an old
man stops me asks me if I need help I run away a dark man
sticks his hand under my sweater touch my flat chest a local
farmer takes me in as a general maid. Three years of shit I have
to be tough I learn fast. I know I have to get myself what I
want; the farmer boss-man his wife below him tell me I can't
do what I want. If I don't do what I want humble respectful,
I'll lead a happy life. The fuck with the farm-life I vanish

I walk through a black world if I want something I have to
get it. These are my next jobs—before I begin to do what I
want: assistant in a millinery place in the West End of London

where I get fired for sleeping with a workman, I learn I can't sleep with who I want until I get enough money; I almost starve; hawk oranges in the gallery of Covent Garden theater; become the mistress of a wealthy army officer. I'm too insecure, I'm still almost a slave, I'm not yet fully planning every step of my future life, but grasping on to this man who can feed me and clothe me and hold me warm.

I make my first mistake: I become too calm I identify too much with this man who stops me from starving. I become confused, I forget my ambition and the ambition becomes misplaced: I have clothes so I want more clothes; I think I can do what I want without fear of starvation so I order my lover around. I'm learning about lies. (I wear men's clothes, jeans cut an inch above the hair of my cunt I hold the jeans up with a studded brown leather belt when I sit on my waterbed where I write the material of the crotch of the pants presses against my cunt lips I'm always slightly hot I masturbate often when I write I write a section 15 minutes to an hour when I unbuckle my brown belt either unzip my jeans and/or squeeze my hand between the cloth of the jeans and my abdomen the lower palm of my hand masturbating calms me down maintain a level energy I can keep working the last two days I haven't wanted to fuck P because D hurt me I wear men's clothes jeans cut an inch above) I act too much like a man, I seem too forceful; despite my beauty my lover leaves me. I'll give you 50 pounds a month, I need more, you spend too much money, you don't save up enough money. I look at myself in the mirror I don't understand whether I'm beautiful plain or ugly I have to use what I see as an object make it as attractive as possible to other people. Now I'm two people.

The second step of my success begins in hell. No one notices me despite my beauty and intelligence; I try to teach myself politics and philosophical theory but I begin again to starve. No one can get me down; I'll show the creeps. I'm wandering in

hell the streets stink of shit I want to be able keep doing new
and different actions I can't find how, the dogs eat the limbs
of living humans and howl. Robbers mingle with the corpses
of rich men and no one denies the rich the aristocrats anything.
I decide to become servant to the madame of a brothel patron-
ized especially by foreign royalties and noblemen forced to flee
the enmity of the revolutionary governments in their own
countries. The social bums, as long as their vision isn't an-
nihilated by starvation and fear, usually know more about the
ways men operate and kill in a city, than do the wealthier. I
go straight for the information, the knowledge, I'm too curious;
I'm too vivacious charming dazzling to be fired. I hide my
ambition then my knowledge behind this new front. Fuck
them, I don't have to pretend to be humble and sweet. The
only men I meet are the servants of aristocrats, not the aristocrats themselves.

The Duc de Bourbon one night tells his valet Gay that all
beautiful women are stupid. Gay protests, mentions me, does
His Royal Highness want to meet me? I've somewhat attracted
a near relative of Queen Victoria and an earl, but I'm not sure
of them. This time luck favors me. I meet the Duc de Bourbon
in the house in Piccadilly and become his mistress. Almost the
entire rest of my life I devote to His Royal Highness, who I
do not love, but use. Intellectually, I don't know if I can love
anyone. I want what I want if I let myself become involved
with a man his socially made power over me will make me
merge with him. I'll lose myself, my ambition. Perhaps at some
times I love the Duc de Bourbon, but at every moment I have
to tell myself I'm using him, I'm separate from him, so that
I keep our powers at least equal. His Royal Highness, like me,
is ambitious, and I know how to play someone who is like me.

First, I have to insure that I'll never again hawk winkles in
a Covent Garden theater, work for a fat imperious prostitute
in any house, spread my legs, watch women smile flirt with men

I know they hate I always try to look young that's the only way I can keep my lover I'm 23 years old I look at pictures of myself when I'm 20 so I know how to compose my facial muscles so I still look like I'm 20 I do a strip to keep the muscles under my skin tight and smooth why do you ruin yourself this way I'm too old to sleep with a woman I'm getting older I'll stop being beautiful my intelligence can't influence His Royal Highness unless it's backed by a strict education; I have to force His Royal Highness to respect me and need my advice about his personal and political affairs.

My goal: to enslave the Duc de Bourbon so I'll be safe, be part of the court aristocracy, so noble men and women will ask for my opinions, especially the men, I can kick them in their asses for the rest of my life. No one will look down on me and starve me again. The Duc de Bourbon laughs at my charming desire to study; I learn French, Greek, Latin the expertise of a university don: Ω της θηβας πατρικη μγσμ ηοη I have to learn to use my defeats. I never again become defeated.

About the Duc de Bourbon: My name is Sophie Dawes. He is married. A reversal in the politics of France restores to him his vast ancestral possessions and political powers. By this time, I am the only member of the royal set who can influence him, who can please him, who has his trust. He returns home to Chantilly, his palace: he tries to explain to me that recent upsets in the French government force him to live quietly with his wife and to abandon me, his mistress. He's a tall slender man, a man whose subtle and quick intelligence is hindered by his belief in the restrictive morals of his ancestors. He's frightened of being alone and being disliked. I become scared of again starving and of being without him. I show him he's blind: he'll never again feel the touch of my hands inside his thighs, he'll live alone, not even knowing if his abandonment of me helped his political career and the affairs of the Country. I love him more than I ever have or will. How can I tell? (remember)?

I'm scared, I'm no longer beautiful: I'm tall and heavy, my features are large, slightly red. I can only rely on my wits, like any man.

What happens? I enter the palace, Chantilly; the Duc de Bourbon subjugates his poor wife; for 14 years I rule that part of the court aristocracy. I want both men and women to love me. I don't have enough control the women look down on me; they sense I once worked in a whorehouse, I'm not married, fuck them, I'm not a robot, I want to love them, I want to walk into a room, watch them flock to me so I can kick their shit up their assholes. When you've come from the gutter, done everything you can to stay alive, rich and famous, you don't forget anything, you get a photographic memory. I tell the Duc de Bourbon I want to ease his wife's position at Chantilly. I now make use of the ambiguity of my position at Chantilly to raise my social position in the Court. I bribe an old match-maker 10,000 francs to tell Adrien Victor de Feucheres, a young nobleman in the Royal Guards, that I'm the daughter of the Duc de Bourbon and have a dowry of ten million francs. I have to get married.

The next day I marry Adrien in London; my lover gives my husband a position in his household. I meet the King and Queen of France. I entertain royalty; I'm 29 years old; I'm not beautiful; I own jewelry, horses and carriages; my husband purchases two estates for me because his other property, when he dies, descends to his nearest blood relation; I visit the Court several times. What does this wealth mean to me? I can no longer remember any of the events of my childhood. One of my brothers dies in a workhouse infirmary. I'm able to do the work I want and have the men I respect discuss my and their work among each other and with me. I care about the economic aspect as much as I care about my fucking with men. I often sleep with my women friends, I lie under heavy quilts, my body next to my friend's body; I place my lips on her lips,

I put my left arm under her sweet head, dark curling hair, my right arm around her left shoulder my hand touches her back. Her thousands of long arms draw my body against the front of her body so my head rests under her head in the hollow of her neck and chest. My eyes are closed. For a long time we lie still like this we both rest at the edge of sleep. I don't have the leisure to be monogamous. Other women sleep around our bed watch us. My sex operates as a mask for my need for friends.

I make a major mistake. I stop trying to gain more power; for me, respectability. My husband realizes that I'm the Duc de Bourbon's lover, not his daughter; censures the Duc de Bourbon, god knows for what the fucking moralist; writes to the King; resigns his commission in the Royal Guards; and disappears. The King informs me I'm no longer allowed in Court. The Duc de Bourbon tries to console me, give me more money. I spend almost all my money trying to reobtain my right of entry to the Court; I can find no way to do what I want. This is the first time anyone has absolutely denied me (I remember). I can't understand, deal with the situation. I begin to become monomaniacal and learn about the nature (nonnature) of reality.

The duke, like most men over 70, is attracted to young charming women. I'm neither young nor charming; he could abandon me any day, tell me nothing until disaster occurs. I discharge almost all the servants who are loyal to the duke; I substitute my servants who check all his mail. The duke might revenge himself on me for his imprisonment by secretly making a new will and dying. I fight. I have to get as rich as possible.

If I make the duke leave me all his money, the duke's relations will begin a series of lawsuits which will, at best, tie up the money while I'm alive. I ask the duke to make the younger son of the Duc d'Orleans, the cousin of the King, his heir. (1) The Duc d'Orleans is almost impoverished, will gladly help me obtain the money if he can get part of it. Poverty

destroys stupid scruples. (2) The royal family will help settle
the will, as relatives to the Duc d'Orleans, and then'll grant me
the right of entry to the Court. The duke refuses to make a
d'Orleans his heir. I force him to. Am I doing wrong? The duke
secretly plots to flee Chantilly; I find this out; he hides in the
corner of an old room, his frail body shakes when he sees me.
He tries to bribe me to leave him. 50,000 pounds. I watch
myself destroy him, I become more scared that he'll take possession of me. I'm often too frightened to fuck, to let myself
open myself. Masturbate.

The King informs me he is graciously pleased to receive me
at his Court. Louis Philippe becomes King of France. One
night the duke and I are dining at the Chateau de Saint-Leu,
a present the duke has given me. (I don't like or don't care
about most people; when I decide I like someone I overreact
I scare the person. I know I'm going to overreact, no one I like
will like me, I try to hide my feelings by acting like a sex
maniac, excuse me, would you like to sleep with me, I begin
to think I'm only sexually interested in the person. I chase the
person, I'm vulnerable, I act as tough as possible to cover my
vulnerability. I don't know how to tell people I like I want to
be friends, sit next to them so I can smell the salt on the skin,
try to learn as much as possible about their memories, ways of
perceiving different events. Because most people I like don't
like me, I'm scared to show them I like them. I feel I'm weird.
I don't comprehend what signals a person I like gives indicate
the person likes me, what signals indicate the person dislikes
me.) The duke, two gentlemen-in-waiting, and I play whist; the
duke calmly tells Gay, his head valet, he wishes to be woken
at 8:00 the next morning, and retires to his bedroom. I feel
restless. I see a warm friend of mine, a woman servant, who
tells me she knows the duke has made a secret will which
disinherits me. Where's the will? She shows me the will. If I
destroy the will, the duke will eventually discover its disappear-

ance, make a new will. I can stop this only by killing him. My friend understands. We sneak quietly to the duke's bedroom, we use two of the duke's handkerchiefs to strangle him in his bed, sailors' knots my nephew taught me when he stayed with me at Chantilly; we move the huge heavy bed the duke sleeps in two feet away from the wall, hang the thin body by the handkerchiefs from the fastening of the long French window, the feet of the duke 30 inches above the floor. The duke seems to have committed suicide.

My name is Laura Lane. I'm born in Holly Springs, Mississippi, in 1837. My name is Adelaide Blanche de la Tremouille. I, K A, fall in love with D; D burns me.

When I'm 16 I marry William Stone who owns a liquor store in New Orleans. He likes to think of himself wearing black leather, studded flashy boots, he drinks, shoots bullets into the walls around me, I learn to handle guns, I have to do what I do, he threatens he wants to kill someone. I learn about that fantasy. He holds a gun to my head when he's drunk so he can watch me throw fits. I love my mother; we decide to go off to San Francisco together. First fantasy.

I marry Colonel William D. Fair, a lawyer. Lawyers tell you what's wrong, what's right. The colonel shows me if I don't do what he wants, he'll kill himself. Phooey. Two years later, he shoots himself in the head with a Colt six-shooter. Am I supposed to feel guilty? Second fantasy.

My mother, I, my year-old daughter Lillias, with three hundred bucks, head for the silver, Virginia City, Nevada. Head for the money without a man. I have to do what I have to do. Single-handed I open the Tahoe House, make a success out of my hotel. I don't want to sit in my room, count my money forever; I got sexually burned twice. Big shit. I want more than money and fame. Third fantasy.

I meet Alexander Parker Crittenden and fall deeply in love with him. He's 46, a hawk; the first time we fuck, he holds me on top of him in bed, he's surprisingly gentle especially since he's a bad fuck. Has no idea how to touch the skin around my clit, give me pleasure. Fourth fantasy.

My mother believed that marriage, both marriage and monogamy, cause the people involved to lose their ambition, wits, and sense of humor, especially the people who have less of the power. My mother's neighbors soon showed my mother they would accept no bastard weirdos in their robot town; my father, a well-to-do Englishman, flees with me to England.

On April 9, 1895 I marry a man who I've met only once before my father's paid him to marry me because I'm a bastard.

The story of seven years: The early 1860's in Virginia City, Nevada. 30,000 people shove to get themselves as rich as possible. I don't want to be rich and famous. You can kill whoever you please as long as you've got a reason. Make one up. Wild dogs howl beneath the gangrened limbs of the old. Respectable has no real meaning. I'm 19 years old five feet three inches tall large dark eyes dark curly hair I know about music and art. Crittenden's a famous lawyer; elected to Nevada's first General Assembly; holds one of the most successful corporate practices in the state. Like me, he believes in being politically powerful, socially respectable, and rich. We're both tough; we do what we have to do; we don't believe in bucking other people, the society, unless we have to. We're both loyal Southerners who respect the ways of luxury and tradition. When some fucking Yankee runs his puke Union flag up the pole that stands outside Tahoe House, I flash my revolver, order the Yank off the roof; no; I shoot the son-of-a-bitch.

The bastards arrest try me for attempted murder. I appear to go along with society, but that's what they are: bastards. Crittenden, my lover, has the same respect for society I've got. I use my flashy looks. He uses his prestige and money: impanels

a jury of twelve secessionists, prays aloud to Shakespeare and
Jeff Davis; his silver tongue gets me off the hook. I learn about
the nature of reality and love Crittenden even more. In this
situation, murder means nothing.

All that matters to me is my love for Crittenden I think
about him every hour I imagine I see him again he tells me he
hates me I turn around in the bathroom I see his blue eyes next
to my eyes I put my hands on his shoulders he closes my body
with his body his skins close wild horses around my skin.

What are the sources for this insane love? In what ways is
my desire to have someone I love with me connected to a desire
to murder? (When I'm a child, my parents own a summer
house by the Atlantic, every afternoon between 5:00 and 8:00
I walk on the sand by the green ocean, I climb up to the ends
of the jetties, watch the waves break as they turn under each
other, not back/forth, but back/forth under/same/time/as/
over/back/forth.) I decide I'll do anything for Crittenden. A
few days after my acquittal I learn Crittenden's married, has
7 children. Crittenden convinces me to have dinner with him
and his wife at the Occidental Hotel in San Francisco. I descend into slavery, I let a man drive his fingers into my brains
and reform my brains as he wants. Crittenden follows me back
to Virginia City; my mother kicks him out of Tahoe House,
refused to let him see me; I buy a house in the rich part of town
and move in with Crittenden. Crittenden invites his wife to
stay in my house. Why do I let Crittenden enslave me? I'm
lazy. I'm no longer interested in this. I remember my second
husband; I shoot at my head with a gun.

Stop. I go from trap to trap to trap. Crittenden's still promising to divorce his wife. I follow Crittenden to San Francisco;
I have more money than I need. I have more than I want.

I almost die from a stillborn childbirth; I tell my husband
I'm not going to have a kid again. I didn't want to marry him;
I don't want him around, ruling me. Fuck all of them.

If someone bothers me, I shoot her/him. I shot that Union soldier on the roof, and Crittenden got me off the hook. Crittenden now tells me Mrs. Crittenden's back East; he won't let her again into California. I'm his slave and believe him. I don't want to be a slave. I aim a five-shooter at Crittenden, fire, and purposely miss him. I marry this guy Snyder who's a weakling; in a month Crittenden arranges for me to get a divorce so I can return to him. He begins to furnish a house on Ellis Street for his wife who's returning from the East. (A wants to fuck E. A's sleeping with me he puts me to sleep in the attic M's fucking next door I hear A make love to E through the floor. I open the attic window climb down the roof, shimmy down a long pole, I run back to school A tells me he'll decide between me and E; I'm better. He picks me. Next day he tells me E's pregnant, get out this instant.) Crittenden's going to get a divorce, go East with me. For the moment I'm content. I don't believe him, I pretend to believe him. I have to learn how I can coexist with my tempestuous emotions. I'm mainly interested in myself. I buy a new gun: a sharp four-shooter. (After L at night goes to sleep he has to work the next day I think about killing him I imagine I walk up to the bed in which he's sleeping with a knife stick the knife through the left side of his body under his ribs.) On November 3 Crittenden stops at our house, I know it's the last time; I want to be tough; I won't be hysterical; if I don't hate someone I have to be hysterical I can't let the first emotions out I'm not his robot his fuck. He could belong to me; I have to kill the other people he thinks he belongs to. I'll be a vegetable. (I let L hit me leave me broke without a home because I no longer want to fuck him he lives at the same time with a new lover his new lover watches him hit me makes comments about the scene. I let L tell me the only thing I'm good for is fucking, the only reason he lives with me.) I want to be rich and famous; no, I want to be able to talk with people without having them put me down.

I put on a huge velvet cape, a hat with a thick veil, my holster and gun; I follow my lover carefully silently in a hack I secretly hired yesterday, past low brown and grey buildings whose empty windows rats hover over, past women and men walking arm-in-arm as if they can. (In New York, I shaved off my hair, wore a black bishop's coat, jeans, heavy boots, so I'd look like a boy; if a man asked me the time in public, I'd kick him. I tried to meet more women, I couldn't figure how; everyone disliked me.) Secretly I board the El Capitan, the opium-infested side-wheeler that's going to ferry my lover to his so-called wife. People crowd around me; they want to confuse me, gather me; I become lost. I don't like to be in a crowd of people unless I'm invisible I have fantasies I'm invisible or people rush over to me how are you darling do you want to sleep with me? The ferry docks; I rush through the crowd to see Crittenden meet his wife; bodies block me; I can't do what I want; I see Crittenden and Clara sitting on the upper deck; Clara's hands are crossed, I see a blue dress with tiny white flowers, gloves, why gloves; I think she's smiling, a stupid kid in a military uniform, Crittenden's smiling; I can't even escape into my own pretensions. I watch every movement they make. I hear a whistle, 5:50 P.M. the side-wheeler's about to return to San Francisco. I'll never see Crittenden again. (I don't know how to deal with someone I love or want to see refusing to see me, disliking me. I finally force myself to see that the people I love (some) dislike me. Even though they dislike me, I can't them; I keep trying to talk to them, I keep bothering them, make them dislike me more, me more entangled in fears/shynesses. They show they hate me; I see myself sitting under the clothes in my closet; I don't see anyone; I wait for the hole to close.) I shoot Crittenden; he mutters something; I drop my gun, wait for the police to capture me. I'm hysterical start screaming louder and louder.

All the above events are taken from myself, *Enter Murderers!* by E. H. Bierstadt, *Murder for Profit* by W. Bolitho, *Blood in the Parlor* by D. Dunbar, *Rogues and Adventuresses* by C. Kingston.

2

a point-to-point comparison between
my life and the life of moll cutpurse,
the queen-regent of misrule, the
roaring girl, the benevolent tyrant
of city thieves and city murderers,
the bear lady

I'm born crazy in Barbican, four years after the defeat of the
terrible Armada. I decide immediately to do what I want: have
adventures as a highwayman instead of gossiping with a bunch
of women liars, fight with a quarterstaff, destroy every fucking
needle they try to give me. I'm the bear lady, the leather coated
eyes, the tough brawler-queen of the jewels of the slums. If I
was a man, I'd go down with Colonel Downe's men upon the
road; I'd sail to the Spanish main with black velvet over my left
eye black velvet over my crotch. Baiting, in the Bear Garden,
is and will be my favorite sport. I learn to fight, cudgelplay, in
all ways, take care of myself. My father's a stupid tailor.

My father hates me, tells me I have to be a woman and take
service at a respectable saddler's. All he wants to do is rape me.
I refuse. The shit arranges for his friends to kidnap me, throw
me into the dungeon of a ship that's bound for Virginia. I'm
a slave. I sit for an hour among the rats, the cold floor; I see

a light slipping through a crack in the door, tighten my muscles, the bonds gone; I look quickly around, I escape. I run straight back to the Bear Garden.

(I don't remember anything about my early childhood. A quack doctor tells my mother she has to get pregnant get well she gets pregnant two days after she has me she has appendicitis. I hate everyone; everyone hates me. I don't know how to talk to other people and make friends. I'm wilder and stranger than anyone I know; my vegetable father wants me to be a boy and I don't want to be anything. My mother refuses to tell me who my father is.

(I meet a starving filmmaker the first person I feel I'm like I decide I'll be a writer. I don't want to be like my rich friends, then I'll be dead. My parents want me to marry a rich guy and get rid of me when I marry a typical slob. I hate their guts too. I want to be a tough sex motorcycle hood silver leather on a BMW I take shit from nobody.)

I meet the divers and rumpads of the town. The golden age of purse cutting. They invent pockets. The bulk bumps into the schnook, causes a disturbance. The file extracts the money with his long, nimble fingers, passes the bung to the attendant rub who scurries away before anyone cries out in terror.

Unfortunately or fortunately, I'm a poor file. My hands are formed for the quarterstaff, and the sword, not for such clever delicate operations. I'll risk my life freely as any slave, but it's a drag. I dream I'm in the black room, the dungeon; rats scurry up my cunt, nibble at my body; I scream, and scream, and scream.

(I have nightmares every night. About once a week I walk into the library throw all the books off the shelves I'm among shifting disappearing objects I black out for two weeks then realize I've blacked out. I'm queen because I fuck a lot I don't let anyone reach me. I smoke a lot of pot so I can fall asleep. At times I'm ecstatic I dance down long sloping hills I can't stop laughing.

(I leave my parents, then my husband, my career. I'm not very good at making money. I have two main problems: (1) how to earn $200 to $300 per month to eat, pay rent, without becoming a robot and with my clothes on (2) do what I want which is real, approaches reality. End of my life.)

I believe in nobility: sticking up for my friends, risking my life, when necessary: the last remnant of my femininity, a sort of motherliness, helps me solve disputes of the gang. I act kindly and stern: not a facade, but me. I'm trying to figure out what reality is. I begin to plan the robberies and I become the fence, not the cly-filer; the gang doesn't kick me out. I have to make myself more secure. I restore to the honest citizens of the city their lost jewels. They pay me well and I pay the gang.

(I think about fucking K. I'm too scared to speak to anyone I don't know well I get fucked over by D I haven't had close friends in too long a time. How do I stop this problem? I could descend to my usual place: I want to be alone. Better for me I should fuck someone I'd have to speak to him/her. I have to stop acting like I'm shy.)

I control my gang and the remotest details of my craft. I get rid of myself as a woman. The largest gang of pickpockets in London. I decide to sacrifice each member's freedom of action for his security. I can't run the gang any other way and I'm, above all, a good businessman. If a member of my gang misbehaves, I send him to the gallows. I'm king. I reward my faithful members: I never fail to save a friend from the huge black shadow of the hangman's noose. I myself never commit murder.

These are my actions: I order a regiment of heavers to lurk at the mercers' doors; at the first opportunity carry off the mercers' account-books and ledgers. For a while, the mercers pay heavily to obtain their books, I frown upon violence; I'm only interested in money. I wear a doublet and petticoat, I'm not interested in pretense; later, for comfort, I wear a great Dutch slop. If someone stands in my way, I draw my sharp sword. No one stops me. I frequent only the haunts of men and I'm celibate. I'm constantly drunk, shouting roaring obscenities; no one can daunt my endless madness which echoes through the grey and wet streets of the laughing city.

(I work hard I still can't sleep with who I want (1) I get refused (2) I'm too shy to speak to anyone if I work harder get famous then everyone will sleep with me I won't have to be so shy I'm tired I want to be the Virgin Mary with a steel bar stuck against my bloody cunt inside of me are red cocks like dogs, animals whiz down midnight buns on diamond motorcycles I start yelling)

These are my friends:

Captain Hind, the Regicides' constant enemy, pretends he's done what I have done. The notorious Moll Sack who emptied the vegetable Cromwell's pocket on the Mall. Crowder, who dresses as a bishop and steals the money of true penitents as they confess their sins to him. We are loyal to the dead. Ralph Briscoe, the clerk of Newgate Prison, and Gregory the Hangman are my truest friends: they've already cut off their cocks for me. They pack juries, get my men reprieves, when I wave my plain fingers.

I take my sex with animals. I give each of my dogs a trundle-bed, wrap them from the cold in sheets and blankets; I give them part of the gang's well-cooked food. Parrots fly through my black hairs, scream at me until I rub their red and yellow necks. I imagine I'm flying through the night, twirling screaming yelling, I'm the wind; no one can stop me or do anything but love me. (People should do what they want to do. P and I decide we're each other's best friend P will help support me the first few weeks we get to San Francisco because I'm regressing. Don't read books about schizophrenia. I want to read books about schizophrenia, especially Laing's books and the books from Kingsley Hall. I'm getting sick of pornography and murders which was all I used to be interested in. The skins around my eyes begin to itch: should I begin to remember (the familiarity of pain, pleasure, hides the original pain) D etc. dislike me?)

The shits try to arrest me three times but they're not going to succeed. (1) A stupid jack-in-office bumps into me, early morning; he thinks I'm a lady or some nonsense. He looks at my clothes, at me; insults me by questioning me. I'm in a good mood; I tell him who he is: a jackanapes, a mule with a pin for a pump. He drags me to jail, and, the next morning, his Honorable Ha Ha Mayor Shit-Ass Sir releases me. I have a boy of mine send a message to jack-in-office his rich uncle in Shropshire's just died: he's inherited a fortune. So much for that schmuck.

(A fat sadist at 7-11 grabs my comics you stuck your tongue out at me last time you were here I won't sell these to you that's against the law he's too stupid to talk to this is my store are you going to beat me up you look the type is that how you handle your grievances stupid-muscle-man get out of my store I'm going to stop writing. I can't write anymore.)

(2) Two of my men speak to a farmer whose pockets they know are well-lined. Chancery Lane. Another of my men improvises a quarrel at the tavern door which confuses the farmer. The first two men snatch the farmer's watch though they don't get his money. The next day the farmer journeys to see me; I promise him I'll try to find his watch. For a fat fee. The farmer turns sees his watch hanging on the back wall. I've become careless. A shit throws me into Newgate.

I never despair. First I demand the constable should keep the watch. I plead *not guilty;* I cry and sigh, oh, my watch and the farmer's watch are two different watches. The farmer demands to see my watch; the constable reaches into his pocket for the watch; no watch: one of my officers has stolen it. This is the most dangerous point in my life.

(3) Banks, the vinter of Cheapside, the queen who teaches his

horse to dance and shoes his horse with silver, bets me 20 pounds I'll not ride from Charing Cross to Shoreditch astraddle on horseback: breeches, doublet, boots, spurs. I add "a trumpet and a banner." I do so, laughing, the black winds swirling about me; I'm invisible; when I reach Bishopsgate, an orange-slut cries "Moll Cutpurse on horseback!" A crowd surrounds me; alas! Some of the creeps want to kill me because I'm not wearing a skirt; others laugh and I laugh with them. To the left, the cops grab a debtor whose daughter, sobbing, lies half dead in the street; a party of drunken wedding revelers race over the child. The crowd turns away from me; I spur my proud horse, gain Newington by a hidden evil lane. I wait till the sky turns black, I turn black, I race to Shoreditch; peacefully turn home and collect my sweet 20 pounds. I have to figure out how to support myself.

The Court of Arches summons me how could I appear publicly in men's apparel? I'm a black dog; I have to stand in a white sheet at Paul's Cross during a Sunday service. I drink three quarts of sack, swagger off to the cross. Curse everyone who doesn't talk to me. I'm the black leather Virgin Mary. At this point I change my costume; for the rest of my life I wear only men's clothes.

(All I talk about is money I'm moving to San Francisco I don't know how I'm going to live in San Francisco model I'll become a famous pornographer ha ha if I don't get the money myself I'll die starvation alone on the street I'm out of money right now.)

All the above events are taken from myself and *A Book of Scoundrels* by Whibley.

3

i move to san francisco. i begin to copy my favorite pornography books and become the main person in each of them.

JULY 1973

I'm two people and the two people are making love to each other.

In my girls' school, I watch the green metal door rise up and down; I can't decide whether I'm a woman giving birth to a brat or a five-year-old girl. I have to piss so I won't piss in my pants. Older girls are talking to each other. It's so hard to shit I think I'll dig it out with my fingers. Do you want to help me? I'll cut off your cunt hair. Uh ugh ugh. O.K. I'm coming in to help you. I flush the toilet. I'm madly in love with the older girls and scared of them.

As Jean opens the heavy brown door to the bathroom, she sees one of the stall doors open; a small white face appears long brown ponytail which is always falling apart white middy blouse and navy wool jumper like hers. She looks into her lover's face and smiles.

"Jean, quick, come in here." I grab her thin long arm, drag

her back into the metal stall. She slyly lets her hand brush against my hand I move slower toward her; she shows her teeth puts both her hands on my shoulders yanks my body toward her tall thin body. We look up at each other and our lips begin to touch. Thin layers of skin against thin layers of skin, fluids swirling through, until we don't know whose skin's whose. Tiny fingers curl around the sides of my body. I don't understand what I'm doing. I hold on to Jean harder and harder. I want to enter into her body rise up through the metal ceiling blow the select girls' school into tiny bits. Are they going to catch us?

(I begin to copy *Thérèse and Isabelle*):

I push Jean's body against the metal door, I surround her with my hands my legs, my teeth bore into her neck. "That's not enough." I throw the weight of my body against hers, my heavy ulcer stomach; I whisper something to her. Her body wrenches away from me she wants to get away. Her thin white hands lie in my hands, her tall body droops over me so that her lips rest above mine.

(Start again: I'm a lesbian):

"Hug me harder." I tighten my hands around her chest, my knees imprison her knees. "We have to scram." "I hate you. I want to punch you out first for going with Linda yesterday. You have no right to be in that gang." A small girl walks into the bathroom just to annoy us. "Get out of here crud. Who do you think you are?" "I'm going to stick a knife in you."

"Jean, when can we meet again secretly? I have to be with you." "Tonight, when it's dark." I place three kisses on her right shoulder. "That will be the bond between us until then." "Jean, I'm scared: I'm not going to see you again." My stronger self laughs at me, turns away, content to move down the long hall, alone, a gallant knight lost in this stupid school I have to attend.

I hate this school. I hate to wear a white blouse, navy blue jumper, navy blue knee socks, curtsy, no underwear, I'm a freak, no makeup; no men are allowed inside the school buildings except on Parents' Day and a few repairmen. I keep a bottle of Scotch in my locker so I don't get too bored and think only about Jean. I decide I'm never again going to take a job "job" means my dealing with straights and pretend freaks I'll prostitute if I have to hopefully I can get away with modeling. There's the world of jobs and the world of freaks. The school, the headmistress wants to expel me because I wear black nail polish on my fingers and I'm a Jew. I take another drink of whiskey. I want Jean. I want Jean.

At night I read the Marquis de Sade, Artaud's poems, and my algebra book. I'm dead unless I'm in love, most of the times I've been in love nothing's happened no I dream I'm never going to see Jean again: I follow Jean everywhere, I lay in my white cubicle, Jeans walks off with another teacher ignores me, I hide in a black corner, I'm invisible; I see Jean put her arms around another person and kiss him. She lays her head on his shoulder. I'm not sure whether I'm a male or a female. I withdraw into a tiny ball, black. My mother pretends she's my sister: we throw snowballs at each other how old's your younger sister? She promises me presents and forgets to give me anything, she remembers to forget she plans to forget; she gives birth to me because she can't get an abortion. This is what she tells me: she gets appendicitis her mother tells me she loves me madly I can't climb into her bed because my sister climbs into her bed every night, she puts her arms around me tells me she loves me, she takes away my home. Mother I'm dying there are free clinics in the city will you help me you better find someone to pay for your grave you're giving your father a heart attack. I think of Jean. Piss on the teachers if they find us; they don't even fuck.

I hate men because I've had to be a semi-prostitute; an ocean rolls over me I don't want men touching me if I have to semi-prostitute again for money I will because getting a straight job would lobotomize me a wall breaks down I'm a single animal fending for myself I'm clever and relentless.

I hear from X gallery D wants to give a show with me does D know who I really am? I write back immediately after I send the letter the phone rings. D. Do you know who I am? Yes. I'm not sure what that means (my unconscious fantasy).

How heavy can I get. Pornography's more fun and interesting. I have a child I hate children I don't have a child Jean says she'll scream. I'm scared we'll be expelled. Jean and I lie in Jean's cubicle, midnight, Jean tells me that she's going to make me a house, set me in the house among thick velvets silks yellow brocades and yellow suns, she's going to leave me: I'll be out on the streets alone where men go looking for starving young girls they can make into prostitutes I grab on to Jean my hands circle around her arm "I'll scream" "I don't care if you scream, I can take anything" she placing my hand on the hair between her legs. I'm scared, I don't move so that I won't increase my fear, I gradually fall asleep I'm scared no one will respect me. Everyone will know about me.

"Move your hand lower. Press down. Do you feel my lips. Insert your finger slightly between my lips below my clit toward the top, lightly run your finger over the inside in lighter circles." I feels Jean's hand on my cunt. "Slowly increase the speed. Touch the skin more firmly as it becomes wetter dart press your finger down on my clit faster put your fingers together, thrust them into me two fingers right above the edge of the opening; I feel your fingers move into my belly, press against the muscle walls touch my clit again." In every other bed a girl has her lover. One girl lies still; only her hand exists. The other girl is coming, you're coming. "You'll have to do it right, faster . . ." I'm coming; I feel Jean coming I'm able to make Jean come. "Rest." She draws my head against her chest; I let my lips fall against her flat nipple. I'm always thinking about the tasks I have yet to do.

"I think Miss St. Pierre's a lesbian" Jean whispers. I can't tell Jean about everything, who I like and hate, she'd reach too far inside me rub against the open veins. I hate the Mueller twins because they're the only people who are as intelligent and beautiful as I am; the head of the school encourages the Mueller twins and I to fight so we can raise the intellectual standards of the school. We use each other's last names; we have no sex. "Do you like being in school?" I ask Jean. "No, I want to do whatever I want to do fuck everyone I don't want to listen to anyone. I want to blow my identity outward, away, until I'm always running in a black ocean under a black sky and I can control my emotions." I don't see Jean in classes: I'm in section A and she's in section B. They stick the rich kids in section A and the poor ones in B, they want us to learn that poor means stupid. We hate them but what the hell. I'm like Nixon: when I lived in New York I was so paranoid I couldn't see that I was acting totally from an unnecessary paranoia. Blow up the school.

This is a list of what's necessary: I'm scared Jean's falling asleep, I'm scared I'll have to leave Jean, I'm scared someone's coming; I listen carefully "No one's coming stupid; you're stupid." Jean carefully licks my ear, blows into my ear; I trust her she'll never leave me, her hand lies on my belly; I love her because she's beautiful, I love her because she's tall and skinny has short black curly hair, she's more historical than I am; her hand enters me her three magic fingers, I love her, we pretend we're communists we announce the meeting of the next communist club in our ritzy girls' school, are you a virgin, no what does it feel like at first it hurts then some feeling I can't describe; it grows I claw at his back I usually rip open his skin, it's terrific. I tell Jean this, she puts her hand over my mouth; we look into each other's eyes
(more programmatic):

The big toe of my left foot is making love to the toe of my right foot. The toes become two people. In my head I'm telling

someone about me the two voices become voices outside my
head I almost hear, not quite, I feel I'm closest to people in
loony bins I see myself acting superior I'm going to get a job
emptying toilets in a loony bin because I subconsciously know
that I'm crazy. This is how I'm sneakily helping myself: I ask
L about B's work say I think B's work is important because I'm
still secretly and madly in love with B; secret sexual intentions
determine my actions. The black water and black sky become
menacing, I see them as menacing because I'm becoming used
enough to them; I'm projecting. A semicircle of people stand
around Jean's cubicle, stare at our forms through the thin white
curtains. Everyone knows about me. I love you.

The fuck with this shit I'm going to be as direct with you as
possible. The first time I fuck a chick, sorry, a woman, I'm
scared as hell I mean I'm really scared, I'm not sure my dong
belongs on me but I have to do it anyway I want to. A few
inches from my body I create a wall of bricks white concrete
that exactly mimics the contours of my body I'm as tough as
possible, and I've got a dong! I wongle it a few times I figure
I'm pretty big, not all that big, but when we, the guys, mea-
sured at camp I came in second. I've got a good body good
strong muscles. I can feel myself bulging, right there. A cock
feels like, it feels like me, I can sense it hang outward from my
body sort of down, I don't really feel anything though I know
it's there, I feel proud: a piece of flesh. When I have to piss
or when I get hot, I can feel it more, I can feel the skin or the
muscle gather, begin to tense, create a different world. Especially the tip of my prick, the blood flows to and from it, faster
I want to touch its tip lightly, constantly; I can feel the spot
burn; the burning causes the muscles next to the spot then the
next set of muscles onward large vibrations. The first time the
woman runs her hand down the hair on my stomach up my

prick I can't feel her touch, she puts her hands on my waist motions for me to roll over on top of her, I'm scared out of my mind I have to appear sure of myself controlling the events; I control the events, I put my hand on my prick touch the tip to her lips I feel something wet suddenly I feel wet walls close around my prick I feel wonderful I can feel my balls swell I still don't feel any strong sensations. When I come the burning at the tip of my prick increases with the swirling flow of the blood increases the tension, about to break open, I'm a volcano. When I wear tight pants, I watch my cock rise and fall it looks like a small animal only I know it's me; I stand straight over the toilet, now my back's extremely straight, I look at the wall and hold my cock in my right hand, I feel faint vibrations in the upper half of my cock as the liquid shoots through it. I rub my cock up and down especially at the rim of the head and underside of the head where there's a slight white streak between the pink skin, my piss-hole's about as large as three needle points, when I rub my cock quickly in these areas with my right hand some cream the burning extends from the tip to the bottom of the head, and then outward; I bring the tension to a pitch, back down, to a pitch back down, etc. until I feel like the sperm's boiling and rising no matter what I do, until the slightest touch of my finger on my cock is enough to make me come. I usually jerk off into the toilet bowl or in my bed alone late at night.

A woman with blonde almost orange hair and large light brown eyes, cross between Spitz and the dog Cluckle Clark, looks up at me, her face is diagonal to mine, I see her large eyes and I see her smile; she takes my hand in her left hand brings my hand between her legs so that I feel her cunt hair and the wet lips of her cunt. I press my hand against her cunt I try to bring the palm of my hand up above her bone so that I can excite her, I feel her excitement she begins to whisper to me. "I want you to do what you're doing; I want you to tease me ha ha." She sticks her tongue out of her mouth. I stick the third finger of my right hand forward, gently draw my finger inside against her outer lips, barely touching her inner red lips. She lays down on me her buttocks over my crossed legs so that I can touch her as freely as possible. Her right hand presses against my cock I want her to love it. (me.)

The Black Tarantula moves to San Francisco. The windows are two huge eyes staring at me, any person can become part of these composite insect eyes, I sit against the white walls of the enclosed room and gibber. The walls are all white. The walls of an asylum. The walls of a hospital. The walls are going to close around me, are closing around me: crush me. I start to scream. The walls are the legs of a huge spider. I walk into the room, a woman flips up to me, do I want to be in her poetry class I'm new here she'll help me. I tell her to go to hell. P runs up to me, hugs me, loves me, arranges everything. I'm famous (I see A who's with a blonde small girl friend, he looks exactly like me and has the opposite name so we have to become good friends I don't care who he fucks I don't care about sex and heterosexual sex always fucks up friendships, I'm scared it will fuck up this one; T platonically falls in love with me, I see D and sleep with him everything happens perfectly. Someone even offers me a job.

(I'm scared to go outside alone, I'm scared everyone will hate me, everyone's watching me everyone doesn't know me.)

I tell Jean I want my belongings back. "I want my belongings back." "I agree with you completely." I have to ignore everyone, I turn my face to the side, I can't look at her. "I'm placing them on your body, each piece of clothing, each feather, each scarf." Jean's not me, I can tell now she's not me I want to touch her. No. "Place that feather in my hair." "Is it too tight?" Softly people are watching us, the people outside the window.

"How do you know?" "I have to do everything for you, you're stupid." "I'm too scared to write, I'm too scared to walk on the street, I don't know anyone in this town, I'm too scared to call anyone I know." "I've moved too frequently from city to city in the past year, I can't deal with anyone any more, I lie I don't care, they can believe what they want to believe, but when I find out their fantasies about me I have to work make them like me." "If I call up P he'll be cold, I'm obviously bothering him O we'll have to have dinner together uh sometime. I'm paranoid and don't know the truth. If I call up P he might be happy to see me again. I'll have to pretend I admire him be bored shitless." "If I call up anyone either I'll be bored shitless or they won't like me." "You're losing your mind." "What'd you say Jean?" "I don't have any mind." One of the people comes by. "You're making too much noise. Stupid." "I have to piss." Jean and I giggle, I press my head into her belly. "You're not allowed to do that." "I can do what I want." "You're a creep you're stupid you're making too much noise. They'll come in here, kick us out of the world." "I hate their guts." Jean opens the cubicle window. "Have you thrown your nail file out?" I'm thinking about Latin. I'm going to become a Latin scholar because I love my teacher my parents tormented me when I was a child tried to make me kill myself because I hated myself so much. Hate them. I show Jean the razor marks on my wrist. Am I offending you? Jean and I standing in a sunblazed square low white walls around us; a camel lowers its head, we laugh, start racing down a slope to the next place. We laugh and laugh, "Jean, did anyone see you come to me?" I touch my cunt with my hand. "Who knows you're with me?" Jean brushes my shoulders with my thick brown hair, she covers her eyes with my hair, "they're coming," she enters into me, she disappears in me, "no one's here," I hear steps, I'm scared. Jean leaves me.

A teacher pokes her ugly nose in my cubicle. "Who was with you? Are you a lesbian?" "Go to hell creep." "Jean was here, she was helping me because I'm crazy the other teachers know that: what's the matter with you? I hate you." A and T both come over, fuck with me, we enjoy ourselves, discuss sexism and get rid of that problem. I talk to P on the phone: he doesn't get upset. "You're astonishing me. Hurry up and get to class. You don't want to get more demerits." I'm alone again. (p. 32)

I don't have an image of myself I'm moving too quickly to a strange city. I'm a young lesbian in a French boarding school who's growing up too quickly to have a childhood. I read Sartre De Sade Laing Esterson and Leduc. I'm scared I don't have my own space. I have a slight urine infection so I piss too much. You don't want to get more demerits. I'm alone again.

I decide I have to hide from my public, rest; for two weeks I think I'll blank out, black. The bottom half of my leg is slim, pink, sticks pointed upward in the air. I'll live alone, quietly, Peter will tell my friends I've disappeared: wait for further communications. I wrap my silver gold lamé dress and cape closer and closer around my huddling body. *I'm Silver Gold Lamé.*

Linda arrives with lice in her hair. She lives in the snow in the winter. The teacher tells her to get the lice out. I imprison her hand, imprison her so I can become her.

"Is it cold outside? In the country" I explain. "I froze my toes off."

"Is your father preparing for spring?" We don't believe any of this nonsense. We spend all our time gossiping about our friends, our fellow students, and our teachers: who's going with whom, who's outcast whom, who's most popular, who's tough, who's smart. I secretly know that the richer parents force their kids to be best friends with the girls of the richest parents. I want to puke. I sense I'm an outcast, so's Linda; we make friends with the children of the poorer parents. "Did you hear they've got a male in the school?" "What for?" "He's a religion teacher, everyone's falling in love with him." We part.

In the distance I see Jean looking at a younger girl's photographs. "Renée's been showing me some photographs. What do you think of this one?" Jean says to me in the assembly hall as we wait to go into breakfast.

"It's a landscape. It's good."

I faint. I pretend to faint. I pretend I'm dead, I'm most scared of being dead after starving, being alone on the streets, I think I'm going to die my consciousness will go; I won't be anything any more (conscious) I fight, all the time I fight. I see myself: I'm a leopard. I get up. A teacher tells me to go to my bed. Jean says she'll accompany me. (p. 36)

As I return to study hall, I find an envelope in my locker, I think of Isabelle, no Jean, I shouldn't think of Jean, I give way to Isabelle. There it is.

"It's true," says Isabelle, "I'm upsetting you." She opens her eyes, I watch her opening her eyes, we both begin to moan.

"Someone's coming. Wipe away the saliva."

I don't want to hide. I want to hide.

I come square against the fear. My fear. Until here I avoid, here I begin to merge, I hit the old fear. I'm Jean. I'm trying to make someone else's fantasy, fantasy caused by fears, my reality so I can deal with my fear. I can do it but I don't want to. Can I do it?

■

"The teacher's here, you have to get away." Jean looks at me.
The sound of running water frightens us.

Leaving Jean like a criminal, leaving her like a thief, adds to
my fear. The bars close around me.

I sit down on Jean's bed, look at her horse's face.

"I don't want you to go. Go. It's dangerous." This is how
I am. This is how I will be. I begin to make love with Jean.

In San Francisco Jean and I pretend we're in disguise; I wear
red lipstick, my violet diamond butterfly coat, huge shoes,
mirrors all over me; she wears all black because she's a cat
burglar, she's he, we walk into this room with T.V. mirrors, I
hide behind Jean I say hello to someone I want to avoid, then
turn away he doesn't recognize me other people recognize me.
I have to say hello to the guy I want to avoid, we begin kissing.

I love lonely criminals and thieves.

All events are taken from *Thérèse and Isabelle* by V. Leduc,
my past, and my fantasies.

4

I've always feared most that someone will destroy my mind.

i become helen seferis, and then, alexander trocchi

I'm lying in the dark, in a tent, my thighs wrapped in the thick skins of sheep. The dark lies around me, murderers thieves who have taken me stand around, I can smell them I hate their guts; they'll need food when we get to the city, I'll take my revenge. Right now I'm impotent.

My lover Y sold me to them the man I had allowed to touch me: I'll kill him. Why do I still fuck?

All I have left is my writing. That's the only stability I know have ever known. Y wanted to kill me because he was scared I might kill him. Now I want to kill him. He's not so fucking powerful, he can sell me, I'll get my revenge. Part of me, a box, hates men, despises them, I can usually see that box and forget it; now it's exploded. I like to fuck.

I don't understand why I think so much about sex. I'm scared to death to call up someone, ask him/her to fuck me, go out on the street, let a stranger touch me (fantasy): my desire usually overcomes my fears. I do what I fantasize doing. Right now, I'm nowhere. I'm touching my thigh my hand is someone else's hand, an inch toward the inner thigh the low wind of the skin curving toward my cunt hair; I touch myself again alone I know who I am; I experience strength pulse the muscles between the arms of my back a young virulent athlete. I feel alone and strong.

The beginning:

I climb alone down the rocks of the cove. The coral reefs stretching into the sea look like mirrors of my cunt, my inner womb; then look utterly strange: black sea monsters skimming the surfaces of each other's bodies for their communication. I imagine I'm a mermaid. At night I see the sea, the ocean black against black against black, long thick lines of white appearing moving inward at my image. Because my father's chief I'm always alone and can do whatever I want. At night I run into the black ocean: a wave which I can't see lifts me up in the blackness larger unseen waves lift me breaks over my head, white, the ocean lights up! The waves grow larger I always swim alone.

I'm fifteen years old; I hate everyone. I don't hate everyone (that's stupid).

All I do is fantasize about sex. Someone being nice to me. I close my eyes, begin to space out: feel I'm rolling down then out my legs straight out on a pillow, my head falls backwards I begin to fantasize: I move like a sleepwalker among deeper sleepwalkers in this beach I remember. (Memory makes everything romantic.) I open my legs, the water feels coldest around my ankles as it rises around my legs the shock disappears the foam springs around me wets my cunt, I begin to swim naked the long muscles running around my ass down the backs of my long legs relax, my body opens at my cunt, I'm alone I laugh talk to the ocean my pickle paul lizzy dizzy fizzy cluckle clark, I float in it and leap over it, when I leave it I'm gleaming I see blood blood floating around me everywhere. I want to fuck impersonally passionately so that I feel completely free, two twin streams of blood run down the inside of my legs, I draw my knees apart, gently, and let the blood dry.

My father wants to fuck me, fears his desire which is the only honest part of him, and fears me. I scare everyone away. I look like a rat. My father's partly conditioned me: made me scared of everyone in the village, especially men. I hide from people; I despise people because they accept the shit they live in and get, limits limits no complete absorption into anyone/anything I can feel my fear. My father tried to fuck me and doesn't succeed. I vow to sleep alone. I wait for the day my father'll die: I can do whatever I want.

Tomorrow I'll get mail. I look at the ocean, I slowly take my clothes off feel the material leaving each inch of the body, I look at the dark ocean I run into the ocean expect the physical shock to break apart the wall of my fantasies relieve me, nothing happens, I'm constantly horny untouched, I throw myself on the sand, the pointed shells. I see a half-rotten log, fat, in the sand as I know what I'm about to do my legs feel like they're opening without opening the muscles in the center of my belly extend like fingers toward my throbbing clit I watch my cunt approach the log I'm on the log I'm a man my hands shake then my whole body, as I collapse on the log my whole weight thrown on my clit against the wood as I sink the log falls on top of me scrapes the delicate skins of my breasts, the thick layer of fat soft skin across my navel. The shells beneath my buttocks cut into my buttocks, sharp points drive into the lips of my ass so that nerves spasm sharply in arrows from my ass upward, down to my cunt. I press the log more tightly with my legs. I

I press the rough sharp wood against my clit an inch below my clit then rhythmically increasing speed touching my clit.

I look up at the black air behind the black air I fantasize. If

I could see people I like I could get out of the fantasy, there would just be fewer fantasies. I'm covered with blood I'm hurt which makes me scared a few green streaks cover my body.

(For the last time I walk into the ocean. Now I'm stuck in San Francisco. I moved here for good reasons: I leave all my friends. I go to a party, I know everyone, everyone loves me. Do you want to go? Anywhere. On Mission and 18th Street three guys rape me. I hear laughter. Once I open up to the possibility of sex, I can fuck anyone I want to feel my strength there. My sex is myself my strength. Was someone watching me? Is a man going to rape me? Elemental signs of conditioning.)

"Let me go . . . no . . . no . . . I'll kill you."

Her fear rouses my fear and the excitement that I feel with fear. I scale the rocks, immediately see one of the village girls I know, she was in my school class I thought her stupid, a man on top of her, his hands clenched around her arms. The girl throws him off, runs away. For the first time I'm no longer scared because I have a cunt. "Do you have a cunt?" I walk across the sand to the man whom I recognize. We're both dressed.

I can see his dark body clearly beneath his clothes. "I'd leave this village again," he tells me, "if I could get the money."

I watch his eyes fall against the cloth of my skirt which is pressing against my mound. "If you like, I could get the money."

"You mean together?"

"I was watching you make love to P." He lays one of his hands on the thick skin of my thigh, I lean back into space; I open my eyes.

(Pure pornography.) I scarcely feel his fingers edging through the layers of my musk into the sex of the body, the twin mouth, strange sensations like waves rip through my body, I only feel relief as his fingers penetrate, move freely inside me, the outside becomes my inside, then I feel nothing. He slowly removes his fingers, licks them, as I feel his lips rub against my wet lips, his double cock quickly tears through my knotted hairs into the long spiraling muscles of my cunt a knife toward my womb I feel nothing I arch my back so that the top of his cock presses against the upper part of my cunt, the delicate opening of the skin below the cunt hairs, I'm scared I move back and forth quickly abandon myself to his rhythm as his legs tense, my tensed muscles the muscles around my clit shooting outward disintegrate I lose my sex by coming.

He opens my blouse his head mouth falls on my left nipple. Hard. A thin line of desire, electric nerves, moves from my nipple straight down over to my sensitive clit my right hand presses his head against my breast the muscles around my clit begin to quiver I run my hand down in the sweat down to caress his thick hairs, he simultaneously slides his hand under my buttocks his middle fingers into the more delicate opening between my buttocks. I'm doing what I've dreamed of doing wanted to do for years. Never again. I sit alone in the house I don't talk to anyone. I masturbate. I dream of ass. Cunt against the plate behind the cock, rapidly, our juices mingle, the juices of my 18-years-starved body. Cats howl at each other and screech. I contain the strange liquid in me. I have no definite feelings.

We make our plans: "We'll go to Charleston first, then we'll go south from there."

"How soon?"

"I'll steal my father's money tonight." I remember I need someone to protect me. "We'll get married there."

I have no intention of getting married: I'll stay with this guy as long as he can help me, then find another guy. All that matters is my own sexuality.

[7/18]

I persuade myself I can't call up A because I'll ruin any chance of a friendship between us for a quick fuck I call him up decadence wins ah I'll call back I persuade myself

Now I touch my cunt I can work. I hide my writing my self fear someone will steal me a man enters a shadow. I lie in the tent of falling sheepskins. As I see his eyes fall down on me his finger point the muscles below and beneath my belly begin to quiver I watch my self falling into my cunt: I take off the rough robe they've put on me I dig my heels into the blankets my legs feel heavy thick I spread them outward first the muscles at from the center of my groin my knees flexed like a dancer's my ankles twisted I slowly raise the altar of my body the thick outer lips open my whole body opening up toward the black air heavy and dangerous then toward the man. He thrusts his bearded mouth against my cunt.

Again I feel the complete joy of giving myself, myself fully since I don't know this man, to another person and having the person equally, for both our pleasure and pain, give himself to me. A person who I will never see again, not recognize, so no ties can interfere with our delight. As I come again and again, his lips working softly against my clit, I again rejoice that I have no personal friendships, I dream, fantasize, awake briefly to meet someone and come, to worship my own coming. I'm almost asleep. I want to make myself become/put down everything before they try to destroy an anomaly such as me. I hate the robot society I know.

I arrived with A in Charleston early on the morning of my 19th birthday. I gave A a quarter of my money, pretended I didn't have any more. I don't want to depend on any man. A slowly touches my cunt under the table, moves his hand under my velvet dress lightly up the waving hairs of my leg until the tip of his fingers scrape the beginning of the opening of my sex. I want to come but am too anxious, too scared. "We have to get to Charleston." "I want to marry you," A says, "settle down take over your father's lucrative fishing business."

A's a death person despite his body, his cock. I don't let my feelings show. Now that I've gotten away from my parents, I have to steer free of every one, those who want to entrap me; I have to get every thing where on my own. I see policemen in the streets waiting for us with guns.

"A, I need some of my money. I have to buy clothes."

I take my money, 40 pounds, split. Split. Into the toilet, out the side door, around the policemen. I'm very smart and clever.

I look up at a man who, I realize, is attracted to me. I want to fuck him. I watch him watching me until I can't stand the agony the vibrations of the huge metal wheels under the slimy flesh around my clit, and fur, a yowling cat, I rise leave the train car, a few minutes later, I find the stranger standing behind me. I slide my hand below the low tight belt of my jeans lower along the skin made thick from milk, I can feel the lips of my cunt separate, the outer ones, the inner ones moving slightly against my clit, the muscles behind the mouth tense until my fingers ease over to them, to my clit. Tough wait touch lightly wait the third finger clit-centered wait "trains are always boring" at the rim of the walls I lose myself touch again "are you coming?" "am I coming?" the skins fold into around each other I feel them too close touch lighten then insistently the rhythm rub my clit slowly. The wave centers begin everywhere.

I look up at him my desire obvious. His lips touch the lips of my cunt my erosion as my muscles tense. Upward begin to break my nipples open I feel his lips then tongue my seed flows and at the peak, like a male, I begin to moan, repeat my desire, I rise, and snap. I feel his lips inside me

I slowly fall asleep. End of minimal pornography.

I don't see anything any more. White beating down white glimpses of white the edge of my shoulder. Am I breaking out, or enclosing myself further? I'm no longer interested in my memories, only in my continuing escalating feelings.

After we leave the porno shop walk A home I sit down on

the corner of Market and 9th fold my cape over my face. I
don't want to see or hear anymore. Stasis before the danger
occurs: my space disappears. I do this over I sit down on the
corner of Market and 9th. Can I steal your money? Can I take
your black leather jacket lined with black fur? If I hate you will
you love me more? They put a black tent over me as I sit on
one of the camels. No other men can see me because if they
see me they'll fuck me. I can smell the sex everywhere: I reach
down along my neck kiss the skin of my right breast. I smell
at the brown pit of my arms. I have more power than most
people which I don't use am scared of if I turn on the power
I attract everyone. Men aren't attracted to me but I can charm
them by being forceful if I want, otherwise I can vanish. I'm
so horny I'll sleep with anyone. The dark men gather around
me, stare at me, I can't recognize who I've slept with I'm
unsure I say hello to the junky he doesn't say hello: good-
looking long black hair, sharp yellow features, brilliant B
touches me because he wants to fuck me I can touch his
extending cock. I see my cunt ahead of me the pear lips pulsing
and the thin inner folds. But I can never be certain.

I don't want to escape now. My revolt against the death
society collides with my desire to be touched I have no identity
I can feel the hand softly running up down my leg inside the
leg against the sand softly spreading my legs my buttocks
against the burning sand the sand rises into my ass tiny diamonds every touch causes all people think about when they
meet me is sex ripples of flesh to collide against the returning
ripples as they enlarge into waves I give myself entirely to each
desire because there's nothing else to give myself to nothing
else exists I have to hide my work am I scared? His hands grasp
my thighs pulling him upward over me. My, Silver Gold
Lamé's, first vision of San Francisco: nothing, delight, hey stop
yeah ah, what, you're under arrest, I see some black junky, I'm
Vice Squad and I'm arresting you, I start to cross the street,

you can't move I've got a gun, he reaches in a plastic portfolio
he's carrying, I'm still alive, his hands fold around my cheeks
he turns his head bend down on top of my mouth to kiss me
saliva flows into me I'm burning saliva and mucus flesh until
I can't tell object from object, my feeling rushes to my center
I don't want to sleep with you my feeling rushes to my center
I rise there against the new lover there is only this and my
account of this I immediately begin to come, I see a frame
around me: my space. The rest is blackness, money-death-
necessity coming to destroy my gropings toward, sex-money
looming over me destroy my tentative beginning human sex,
I rub my body against P. I become a parrot. O.K.

I do only one thing. I touch my self or I feel a hand a leg
touch me a mouth enters me I can feel its wet softness against
my skin I expect nothing and quickly I begin to quiver my
hands contact the strange flesh my delight begins I thrust my
hands under the shoulders the body over me burning flesh
sliding on my burning flesh the strange object slides into my
body within the secret walls of my cunt wet hairs pierce my clit
until I'm about to break my clit swollen with blood until I'm
at the final edge

for hours I come and come until there's no difference between coming and reality. I have to be careful for they may visit
me at any moment, and take away my writing; I'm still me, I'm
still scared by my passion and sex. Reporting involves memories
involves identity: I have my identity and I have my sex: I'm not
new yet. I have to be careful for I may be visited at any
moment.

[7/20/73]

I became a man and a woman:

The ground pulls out from under my body I feel the anxieties
I felt as a kid because my parents hate me or the anxieties I
feel on acid I stay with the anxiety to find out what's happening

I forget who I am I don't know who I am I see a huge soft black widow no identity a large tarantula I have no feelings I begin to float. I'm Helen I know who I am, then my work means nothing to me my work means less to me than my sexuality. I'm a failure. This is a failure all I'm causing is my own disintegration. What'm I trying to do? My work and my sexuality combine: here the complete sexuality occurs within, is not expressed by, the writing. I feel anxious. Last night no one comes in. I hear footsteps muffled voices talking about me describing my real being, bricks being thrown on the ground, large black woman jiving, I hear two tough guys on telephone wires one tells the other I love you, cat begins to yowl. Nothing stops my writing finally I'm alone I use my writing to get rid of all feelings of identity that aren't my sexuality. I have to exist only when someone seeks to touch me or I touch myself. Fuck this. I feel hot and sweaty. It's hot and sweaty, early, the heat of the day focused in the grey-black evening air. The endless sand still burning. Men mutter and cry around me, stare at me uneasily, and talk. I eat a few dates, cheese, bread, and wine. No one touches me; I'm constantly horny; I think only about sex. I don't like sexual explosions getting mixed up with hampering my work. I'll do anything to fuck.

Last night no one comes in. I tried to remember the last time a stranger more than one of them touched me I wet my finger slid it up the tight writhing hole between his buttocks the strangely smooth skin welcome me a thin cord of skin spiraling around my finger a vein throbbing and helping my finger climb upward tightened around me pulsating as my finger pressed inward toward his belly. My other hand slid between our wet flesh around the head of his cock pressing the white cord under his cock I remember the two men staring at me, huge rectangle eyes the eyes of spider, as I sit flat against the white walls the sand I have no protection the sand is a hospital and a loony bin I go off. Fuck people, by the time anyone's 26 years old he/

she's crazy unable any longer to communicate with more than 1% efficiency genitals meet but no info gets across so I act romantic I'd rather make love with parrots and cats I like and bite them they lick and bite me. My dears, we're all very sophisticated, but it's a drag; I sleep with few people. As one man lays his cock in my mouth, the other spreads my legs with his hand already the nerves at the ends of my cunt like tiny paws stroke the inside of my flesh. I can't handle my horniness. We're, I think, moving into a city.

My sex fucking is impersonal. My sexuality's impersonal. I'm rapidly losing my identity, the last part of my boredom. I caress the heavy thighs that turn outwards from my center, like a spider, sink into the rough clothes in the minaret, the thin muscles twirl around my calves to turn the feet outward like a golden dancer, leap through the hot air, the hairs of my cunt brush against wet the rough hair on your head, I can feel the liquid drip down the fat inner bulges of the legs near my cunt. Veins stick out from my wrists. I rub my flesh against my flesh, my skin against my skin, my skins against my skins, my torso begins to rise I'm always at the beginning of desire I can hardly tell when my orgasms rise and fall as if I'm almost unable to come and don't care, or am continuously slowly coming, I rub my back like a cat does against the rough wool, spread my heavy brown legs so that my buttocks open, the red flesh against the black wool, I pretend it's the hair of another person: there are mirrors making my hands into another person's hands, people all around me watch me. I watch the thin hands hold my arms, move slowly living bracelets around my arms on to the heavy flesh of my aching breasts.

The liquid begins to rise, and my orgasm, I can no longer keep enticing myself (with the future), my orgasms, begin: the thighs spread apart at my ovaries, two central nerves parallel

5 inches apart from each other passing past my navel to my clit begin to burn, my cunt is my center my cunt is my center my cunt is my center, the hand reaches into my cunt my womb like a strange cock back and forth the thumb presses against my clit lightly then harder I imagine whips slashing into my ass just where the buttocks begin to spread I imagine tongues licking the round opening of my ass quickly lighting me until a dome begins to rise in my cunt, a growing sphere that wants to conquer me I touch myself faster

I have to wait till people physically want me and I can be. But I'm no longer and I have my fantasy of my outcome, scared.

[7/21]

No one comes near me.

[7/22]

A tall man comes up to me and looks at my standing naked body. He turns my body around; with his thumb and third long finger opens my mouth sticks his tongue in my mouth, around my gums, to my inner throat. His hands touch the beginning of the outward curves of my upper buttocks the thick layer of fat developing over my ass and around my stomach. After stroking me, so I feel like a cat, his hand moves to the hair over my cunt, down to the lips of my cunt, softly; his eyes carefully note every expression on my face. I understand they are trying to sell me. How do I feel?

The man leads me to a tent, motions for me to lie down. I expect him to kick me or hurt me. I'm slightly scared and also hot. I'm not supposed to look at him. He lays his left hand flat on my shoulder, looks at my eyes. I start to lift his robe. He stops me, lifts my heavy breasts with his right hand, draws two fingers around the purple nipples. As I look up at him, he turns his back to me, and leaves the tent. Again I'm alone.

I no longer care about being safe, I don't care about the men because they'll make me feel safe; I know now they see me as an animal, I have only these wide arms, these breasts, eyelids shut over my eyes, and the heavy flesh of my legs shoving out of my cunt. If they sell me, they treat me badly it's because they think I don't matter. I matter when someone touches me, when I touch someone; the touch matters; so in this way I no longer exist, nor do the men. My body matters to me: the heart next to the lungs, the stomach pressing on the lungs, the lungs thoughtlessly drawing the air in and out, the oxygen out of the air. I'm no longer as scared as I was in the world because I no longer care. My only fear now is that no one will touch my body. I don't know yet how I'll get rid of this fear.

Days pass by, moment like moment, the light becomes yellower and yellower, my fantasies more constant and thicker, like orange cloth on blue silk, on yellow sun; so that I'm always at a slow rolling edge. If my hand brushes across the flesh of my leg, the nerves begin to quiver, to stimulate other nerves further away from and closer to my clit, the desire rolling like soft dangerous animals an inch below my skin is everpresent, increases until I'm incapable of satisfying myself, I'm forced to wait; I'm forced to enter the worst of my childhood nightmares, the world of lobotomy: the person or people I depend on will stick their fingers into my brain, take away my brain, my driving will-power, I'll have nothing left, I won't be able to manage for myself. In the midst of this level anxiety, I'm constantly at rest. I wanted to control all environments and actions surrounding and of me; I was scared they would take control of me. Me. How strange now as I lay here waiting for another person, in the desert a man, I don't know who for what purpose, waiting so long that I can no longer perceive. I play with myself, smell the sweat at the pit of my arms, is it sweat, how can I tell what sweat is? I perceive yellow, yellow all around me, faint misty outlines of a body, everyone I know's crazy, I believe everyone's in her/his own way crazy, the edges shifting of the body look white I close my eyes I don't. I feel a limb thrust against the outjutting bone right above my clit, not a limb but a head, if I see an arm intersect my arm, I think my arm's been cut in half, the lips and beard rub against the fragile lace of my inner legs and the skins beneath the wettened hairs. Lips twine inside me slowly kiss the inner walls of my body until every inch of my body in shuddering my feeling becomes present to me. I can perceive everything. I'm a child; I sense through touch. Every inch over and over first with: the soft lips thick lips then the needle at the end of the tongue, my wetnesses begin to mingle, I open myself, I have no more will, so that anything can touch me, can enter me, I'm any thing/one more sensation at the bottom and top levels of my flesh, licking me I begin as I'm doing, orgasm, orgasm upon orgasm, open OPEN the nerves roll in cycles in preconceived courses through my body faster and faster in huger and huger rolls until my flesh disintegrates and turns on itself. Like a devouring spider. I begin to clean myself and laugh.

I lose my memory. Days after days pass blackness I am blackness. I'm alive.

[7/25]

We climb down the rocks and sliding sand Devil's Slide to the beach, tiny cove surrounded by boulders crash the huge waves against the rocks. B, V, and I take off our clothes. I lie in the hot sand. V starts drinking, people recognize her she tries to harden her nipple by rubbing it with wet finger. I lightly rub my tongue around the center of her nipple and press my lips against it as it grows. We separate, she looks around, waves to the people on the beach who are watching us. A stupid macho creep walks by. V scratches the back of my neck. We begin to kiss, gently, the slow liquids drawn by her lips to the inside curves of my skin, I begin to shudder, I surprisingly yield to her, the kiss continues, at the edge of each inch of skin, feelings in my lips and skin of swirling lines nerves lines of nerves, everything opens, the kiss continues I draw my body over the blanket against hers some relief I get hotter. Now I'm drawn in, I need her, I can't escape orgasm, escape desiring V; my hand touches her heavy triangular breasts which scrape the skin above my stomach simultaneously I draw myself under her so that she can do whatever she wants with me and so I can hold her head like a cat's against me and protect her. How many people are watching? We look up; try to separate. V spreads her legs at people, laughs at them, passes her book around *Female Orgasm*. Three Spanish kids are staring entranced at us; one straight couple behind us and two bisexual couples in front of us are obviously turned on. I feel weird. I'm weird. I have to orgasm blank everyone out. I thrust my legs up huge pyramids her wet hairs press painfully against my clit this won't work. She looks at me. I have to come. We continue to kiss still lightly as if each inch of skin contains snakes she's a he this is a lie, "Can I wipe the sand out of your hairs; can I put my tongue in you?" I'm too far gone to hear anything she tongues me too hard I thrust her away she's hurt the situation's too weird I beg her to climax me. She tongues me a woman's touching me a woman's touching me as I rub as hard as I can my open outer lips against his hairs I can hardly feel his cock his hands begin to beat my ass I feel strange I don't feel anything how am I supposed to feel his hands begin to slap my buttocks harder and faster as I rise I begin to orgasm the pain finally surprises me and pleases me I completely relax her tongue directs each nerve within my lips and clit each center and line of nerves I'm completely dependent on her tongue I blank out every thing/one else I hold on to her as I begin to rise, easily, I can partially control the strong orgasm, increase its length

I see two blonde women in front of us kissing each other

My world is the four walls ceiling and floor in which I live hot they have shuttered the windows I do not think about them the other person who lives in the room with me a young girl whose flesh is now thick and soft like the legs of a spider is my life.

I realize nothing else so that I will completely please whoever comes to me, whoever could be the only person who could give me pleasure. The oil runs from the pores of my skin, greases the skin of my beloved, the only person I now see, so that at night we slide over each other animals who live at the bottom of the deepest parts of the ocean.

I don't know when I started living here at first the young girl stared at me and drew away from me. At first the young girl stares at me and draws away from me. I'm completely alone, I'm bored with touching my own flesh, I hide myself with heavy light brown blankets, and, like the strange creature I am, I sit and wait. I no longer care what happens so I no longer remember. I cast away my memory so I'm always at the edge of multiple orgasms. I sit and wait. As if I'm laying my heavy older hand on her child's thigh and doing nothing else. I stop approaching her because I'm continually at ecstasy.

The third day she smiles at me, then runs away. I smile back, once. I won't let anyone have complete control of me my body ever again. I have to keep returning showing that I'm willing to touch enter her I'll never rape her. I live in this world: have to take pleasure opening myself where and when I can, most of the time I'm alone. She's younger and on the fifth night as I rub my flesh against the rough wool bored of touching myself by now so open to myself that I can't tell whether I'm touching myself or not, I feel two hands at the pit of my body a spider circling I throw my arm slowly into the dark circling around nothing, then the smooth skin lying over the sharp bones of a shoulder, I draw her to me until she's lying quietly in my arms. Inside me, I begin to shiver. I am her. I'm her child and her mother so that I'm completely safe I'm inviolable and there're no men around. My blackness cuts off all extra perceptions. Our mouths meet as my mouth has never been met in a thickness of feelings physical and mental that have a complexity that leads me to orgasm. I kiss her for hours and hours. At some point without knowing how I get here I have to complete my orgasm I mount her our cunts meet and fit surprisingly for me and easily and I ride her as love is our only way until we begin to peak and need more, and turn around

I can do what I want. I can write more freely make my break to get rid of my damaged mind my lover silently aids me and watches out for them, the servants who bring us the rich boring food we eat, who licks the tips of my ears then quickly thrusts her tongue into their quivering centers into the center of my brain. Do I give a shit about her? I want to become as stupid and mindless as her and yield to the hard thighs of my next faceless lover. I want control over my environment. Like a fat spider I sit and wait. I float. Night after night we fold our limbs around each other and come and come we exist only for each other, then only for ourselves until there is no difference.

I think a week has passed. I'm not sure of the time anymore, in this room where the light is always grey and I'm always hot. I love you. I realize my roommate's not me, another person; she's left me, already, in what remains of her memory, believes she's about to meet someone besides the servants who give us food. I'm tired of her. I like to look at her as I sit back in myself, her skin's now thick and fat, like the oil we continuously ingest, the hairs swirling dark in the middle of her flesh. I no longer care about her.

I look at my body as if it were a web, solely a way of asking people to touch me. My body doesn't exist. I watch myself: I'm now heavy and even more beautiful: huge curves of thighs zooming into the valleys around my belly I begin to love myself as if I'm someone else no I realize my attractiveness coldly, I basically couldn't care how I look; I can see anything in a set of shifting frameworks. I'm interested solely in getting into someone else. I find the heavy flesh sensual, as if it were permanent. I'm not sure if I think of myself as a person.

Enough mind remains in me to want this prison to disappear. The awareness of time (prison). I find myself more interesting than my companion, my former beloved; I'm no longer interested in such paltry pleasures in which I have to exert myself, I have to command and control an orgasm; the more I feel my self and my strength, the more I desire complete passivity. Blackness and minimal stuff I have to sense. My breasts are bright red.

I'm sick of this society. "Earn a living" as if I'm not yet living; lobotomized and robotized from birth, they tell me I can't do anything I want to do in the subtlest and sneakiest ways possible. They want to erase all possible hints that I've been born. I have two centers: love and my desire to sleep. I want only the moving toward exaltation, opening toward and becoming other people; the exaltation, then nothing, until it starts again. People are unused to love because they don't go far enough. As far as possible, and farther, into their intuited desires. And complete love, apart by nature from "time," does not meet complete love where, given consent, anything can happen and there's no such thing as strength or weakness except as masks to be acted out. All forms of love are drag. How little do I have to do to survive except for passion, my desire to open and exist as I can only depend for existence on my surroundings, and if I have to do more, if I again have to prostitute by becoming straight, is life—fakery of living—that necessary to me? As if in that case, that deadness without love, there would be any me.

I find my being dependent on love. Physical passion for others and thus myself. Fuck the shits who think otherwise.

A calls me up do I want to meet him at The Stud midnight I've got to work I tell him V ate me in the middle of a public beach terrific are you upset about something? I love you

[7/27]

They wrap a thin white veil around my body, lead me out of the room, across a square of dirt, a courtyard, to a place where there are loud noises, animals and men. The cries of whipped beasts are my subterranean cries. I begin, in my body-mind my mind gone, to descend. Slabs of wood, a long heavy knife, and the shadows, the shadows help me undress. I can again see and hear; roofs, pipe and zither music, the evening prayers, the blackness of the evening air. I haven't gone as far as I thought I had: I'm still part of the daily death-goal world.

Now there's only my large bed.

A large heavy woman enters, hands me a sweet sticky mixture she motions me to eat. I like her; she smiles at me. My will-power is either totally reflexive or gone. Gone. I slowly eat the glue, sandy glue, which is too sweet for me to eat fast, her food, so that I'll do what she wants. No. I simply don't care: at this point it's easier not to make a fuss. I don't know what would help me and I'm too far gone to do more than act through my delirium. I'm completely involved in delirium.

A hand inside my stomach begins to trace light circles on the inside of my skin the skins of my belly my limbs fall outward. Do they disappear? The spirals rise to a peak down below my breasts; I not only feel the various liquids in my body, but I can control the pulsing rhythms of their flow, I can move the muscles which form a cylinder around my clit tense and loose so that the walls and canals of nerves through my body vibrate under my command. Drugged, I can completely control myself.

The drug aids my passivity and thus my strength. Living has become pure pleasure. I can hardly tell the difference between my coming and not coming: if I concentrate on the air that my lungs draw into themselves, I can feel the nerves around my breasts move and shift in complex patterns. I feel more clearly than I've ever felt now that all of me, my mind being every pore of my body, my whole body quivering to open from clit outward, is connected. I begin to play with the spirals within me, my flames, brush my fingers over my tender skin red from the suns, my sensations rise toward my coming, am I about to come? I play with my disbelief, feelingless, until I'm almost insane. I can feel nothing, and have no mind. I can do nothing for myself, nor do I know what I need done. From nowhere needles start rising in me and outside of me through my skin; I have no idea what comes from inside and what comes from outside; I descend into the mental and physical blackness. I see a frame: inside the frame, I'm suspended from a piece of wood by a string tied around my clit; the muscles upward from my clit tighten, and I cry out loudly. My eyelids are sewn to the skin below my eyes. I'm an opening in the earth, moving and crying through the rain. Somehow I awake enough to sense an animal standing over me.

As the man's cock enters me, every muscle of me begins to shake, every nerve begins to burn and quiver. I'm both liquid and solid. I'm completely pleasure. At this moment. (1) I'm opening enough to contain all identities, things, change everything to energy, a volcano. (2) I'm constant energy and I can never be anything else. (3) I have no emotions; I sense textures of everything against textures; I'm completely part of and aware of the object world. I don't exist. My nerves so quiver, quiver burning, up and down the secret inflamed passages of my skin, the nerves tensing my muscles so that my blood zooms to the edge of my body, swells and inflames me, and unable to burst, I begin to come. These sensations—I do not know how to describe them—last for hours. I come again and again and again I now equal to everything and nothing am completely dependent on the pleasure this stranger is giving me.

As I begin to swoon, my body covered with films of cooling sweat, I find myself alone again. Another man enters, sinks into me, leaves, and then another; I count six men in the blackness who wake me out of my semi-orgasmic sleep. I have no idea what this means.

I'm going to finish this logically: I eat the sweet sandy mixture every night, stewed lamb and eggplants drenched in oils, thick honey pastries. I don't have to earn my living any more. I think of the mixture (the drug) and the sex, but mostly I feel the pleasure of the masochism which occurs *only* when I give my consent. If I consent, now, I can do anything.

I find this harder and harder to write lest I be ripped off. I

I'm speaking to you directly. Complete disorder exists. I spend most of my time, alone, in the monastery; I bend slowly to my knees, and I pray. I am very poor, but whenever I can I stay alone and pray. Think. Sometimes I go crazy I go pick up a man. "Do you want to fuck?" we go off fuck in every way possible until he can no longer stand the passion, I never see him again. At times I fuck women. I believe in explaining everything about my sexual life as fully as possible. If I have to, I use people to get where I want. I am most scared of dying: I think I will do anything to stay alive. I think I would rather die than submit become a robot let them lobotomize me. Each time I'm about to fuck suck tease a man I think I'll get what I want I vomit have to get out. I fuck only the men I'm madly in love with (for that time).

I would have slept with my brother, after my mother died, but he chases me away. I now have to be alone I've been seeing too many people who I don't know well I have to consider everything within myself. If I feel I don't have any space left, I start going crazy. Soon everyone will go crazy if things don't change. My closest friend, Madame Lydia Paschkoff, tells me

I need a lot of money. She is crazy and loving, the Virgin Mary of the spirits; I adore her. She tells me how to get money, but I can't do it. Some people think I'm mad. Some people forget me. I use psilocybin, mescaline, pure acid; occasionally hash as an aphrodisiac. I eat as little food as possible to save money.

Of course, I disguise myself as a man. I'm 26 years old. I am exceedingly lazy. Lydia is furious with me because I sleep with men, and refuses to see me again. Now there is no one. The senses and the spirit are independent manifestations of each other; sexual ecstasies become mystic communion. Human communion. There's nothing else I want.

All the above events are taken from *Helen and Desire* by A. Trocchi, *The Wilder Shores of Love* by L. Blanch, and myself.

5

i explore my miserable childhood.
i become william butler yeats.

EVIDENCE:

Age 8:
My mother tells me why I was born: she had a pain in her stomach, it was during the war, she went to some quack doctor (she had just married this guy because it was the war and she loved his parents); the doctor tells her she should get pregnant to cure the pain. Since she's married, she gets pregnant, but the pain stays. She won't get an abortion because she's too scared. She runs to the toilet because she thinks she has to shit; I come out. The next day she has appendicitis.

My mother puts on black fur-lined boots with two-inch-pointed heels over her tan stockings, an orange-brown tight sweater over a white bra, she has large soft full breasts, a straight orange-brown skirt brown and blue triangles running down her thighs. Bright red lipstick and pink powder. Over this, her black seal coat. She looks young and pretty. We go out of the apartment together, down to the street where it's snowing, three blocks away to my favorite park. Pure white covers over the lower level: the basketball court, skating rink, and adult swings, completely; the upper lever where seesaws, jungle gyms, sandboxes used to be, looks like a magic woods. My mother and I play together; she tells me she's my sister. We go to a drugstore to get ice-cream sodas; a man asks her if we're sisters.

My mother tells me my "father" isn't my real father: my real father left her when she was three months pregnant and wanted nothing to do with me, ever. This husband has adopted me. That's all she tells me. I feel happy that none of my adopted father's blood is in me.

Age 10

My mother tells me that carrot juice is going to come out of me where I piss sometime soon and I shouldn't get worried. All young girls eventually, once a month, watch carrot juice flow out of their piss-holes. I wonder if I can drink it, and if my mother's lying more.

Age 12:

My mother and my sister lie together on my mother's bed watching T.V. I sit on the floor in front of my mother's bed. I love the floor. Later I learn to love walls. My "father" sits on his own bed. My mother tells my sister that my "father" drinks three drinks when he comes home from work, is an alcoholic, falls asleep at 7:30 at night, and never does anything. My sister laughs at him and tells him he's dull and stupid. He tells me he doesn't know who Dostoievsky is. My mother tells me she hates his mother because his mother treated her badly: my sister and I also have to hate her. My sister laughs. I feel bored.

My mother tells me to wrap my used Kotexes in newspaper. Pepper (the dog) takes out a newspaper bundle from the garbage can, chews it up, drags it around the house. My mother tells me I'm dirty and evil; I'm selfish and don't do anything for anyone but myself. She's right.

My mother tells me she loves me and tries to kiss me. I don't tell her I love her. She never does anything for me, and when I want to talk to her, she's always talking to one of her friends on the telephone. I tell her she doesn't want to talk to me; she tells me I'm a liar. She makes my sister her close friend, lover, and servant.

Age 13:

I fuck and find out my mother's been lying. I know my mother lies about everything. We outwardly hate each other.

Age 15:

My mother tells me to come into her bathroom she has to talk to me: "How far have you gone with boys? You can't let them touch you, uh you know, because then other things will happen, you're disgusting . . ." I interrupt her say there's no need for her to tell me all this. We don't discuss sex ever again.

One winter afternoon I manage to get out of the house; I take the subway to 9th Street and Third Avenue to see my lover P. We spend the afternoon fucking. When I get home around 6:00 p.m. my mother asks where I've been. "Just walking around." "Why weren't you at the rehearsal for the Jewish Guild for the Blind Coming-Out Dance?" "I'm sorry; I forgot." She starts slapping my face as hard as she can "Whore. Whore."

Age 16:

My mother tells me while my father and sister are listening that my father's cock is too wide and short for her, he doesn't fuck her enough. I show I understand what she means.

Age 16:

My father tries to rape me: he thinks that I've been fucking and he starts to cry, puts his arms around me, kisses me, generally glops. I call my mother who's in their country house, tell her to calm down her husband or I'll never see either of them again. I refuse to kiss him.

The last time I'm home, my mother's giving me trouble: I'm selfish I'm insane I have to see a psychiatrist I should be dead etc. I tell her to stop bugging me, I've been having a hard time: I show her my wrists which I've cut up rather badly with razors trying to punish myself. She tells me not to talk about nasty things at the dinner table.

My mother and I look almost exactly alike; we have many of the same characteristics.

Everything is incredibly beautiful:

I dream that I'm looking out of a window I see a group of boys playing with each other and laughing. A young boy in a black uniform leaps into the middle of the crowd. I'm not a boy. A servant tells me he's planning to blow up the city. Peacocks walk past the balustrades. My silken hands press down on the lids of my eyes.

I live in Bedford Park, in London, in an old black and white house that has secret passages. (I'm most scared to be alone and I want most to be alone.) I'm 13 years old, and a child. Rough brown wools rub against my skin, I dream of being warm again, laughing as if I were in a dark, rainy wood.

I dream I see an old wood house on the corner of a town street. A furniture van drives up to the house; two men carry furniture into the house. The house is empty again. I look at the house: in one window an old woman clings to a sash. She says there are ghosts in the house. Opposite the house, when it is black, the young novices of God start screaming.

I kill a duck so I am evil. No one punishes me: my grandfather rewards me and tells the servants to cook the duck for dinner. I wiggle my cock at my (grand)mother.

I call up images of myself, or just images. They are "my" images and yet, they extend my knowledge. I usually hear that other people have the same images, and I know we are all connected. Fucking is a religious ceremony. People who have died are still thinking and choosing, for all thoughts and desires are connected and pulsing, in the utter blackness, back and forth. I'm not sure of this.

Images exist, and the causes of, reasons for the images. Sometimes I believe there are no causes or reasons. Or no images, just the causes: fire, earth, air, water. These four also might be images and hidden, another reason or cause, an endless unknown infinity. I am an old man talking.

If everything is drag, there is no such thing as real love or friendship. I am drag too. Other people, dead and alive, are presences: I can sit next to the fire, I cannot enter into it. I want too much to become the people I love: I have too high an idea of friendship and love and suffer each time I fuck or talk to someone. The Gods are those who infinitely desire to become other people and so, suffer endlessly. I begin to study myself again since I have no one else to touch.

Sometimes, when I'm most in child-drag, I act shy I can't speak to anyone, I lay down and watch people, open to embrace anyone who sits next to me talks to me touches me. Usually the people ignore me, and I go home. Only at these strange moments, I call them nymphomaniac moments, I feel free; other times I'm scared. Hate. Most of my life is hating people or events. I'm not happy but at ease open only when I'm in drag. In my head I'm always talking to someone (I have few real people to talk to) and when I forget, the two voices go on in my head, if I forget I perceive by chance one of the voices or both of the voices outside my head: I decide I'm insane.

Dreams and fantasies and the desires these events show are growing.

I am beginning to love my nakedness and revel in it. This abandonment of hatred is new for/to me. It is important for a boy to realize his sexuality. As I, in one second, one second of change, begin to love my body thus the emotions that rise from my desire to be touched, I begin to love to desire and to derive joy from my memories, far more than from immediate perceptions.

I take off my clothes whenever and wherever I can. I can't talk to people unless we obviously establish a sexual basis. I see visions: old dead bums, poor people who had been driven from their homes because of money or prejudice which is money, live above me, in the hidden caves and dark green leaves; when I search for them in the forests around Mills College which is the only country I can get a ride to I see young women fucking in the same caves.

I see: the lapse of the sciences, the lapse of the certainty of knowing, the love of melancholy, of a love so strong no person could return it. Now I must love who I fall in love with without worrying if the person will love me. As my fantasies enlarge, my desires inflame me and themselves until I am almost my desires, I am more unable and unwilling to talk to people. I have to stop this.

(More details about my actual childhood)

I hate my "father." My father now influences me strongly. Every morning we go to Oakland by train, to a large room on York Street wood beams cross the ceiling wood divides the upper wall from the lower wall; strongest: over a white fireplace which doesn't work swirl different levels and kinds of wood, in strange curling shapes, as if portraying some dream I had in which my body grows and grows. He shows me that I must return to the familiar social conventions, get through passions, overrated thoughts, love of pleasure and indulgence, to the "actual." I become crazier and crazier. Suck on a pear which I think is my mother's nipple-breast. Open my eyes and don't say anything. Shiver. I feel naked, as if my skin is being stripped off me, half-solid red mucus is me: what I see. I know I'm presenting a wall of shivering to anyone who tries to talk to me. I hate myself and I feel I'm right to do this. I act this way now with everyone I meet.

[9/11]

I'm acting worse and worse with people I can hardly talk to people I know (I fuck) and much less to people I don't know and admire. I zip up my black leather and run away. I'm the shyest black leather freak in the world. I walk into the large crowded room J says "hello" I'm surprised and happy. "O your girlfriend isn't with you that's why you're saying hello." Do I feel like fucking him? Say "hello" to A who quickly replies "hello" runs past me to see famous poets. I expect too much FRIENDSHIP LOVE other people don't share my visions of total friendship. If I can't convince them here, they run past me. Now I know they're going to run past me, so when anyone I admire seems to like me, I run away. I know all my friendships and love are going to fail. No. I don't blame A and J: they're not visionaries, or they don't live by their visions. Kick me again in the cunt please. When I go to visit a woman I had known as a child, she tells me I'm now a garbling idiot. I want to be smart and be able to communicate my knowledge as clearly as possible, and I can't even say hello to a poet I somewhat know and admire, much less say something more complicated. I'm making myself miserable. P laughs at me shows me how I act socially foolish: in my mind I frame these memories, exaggerate, have to run away from myself. I'm not interested in what I, except as a medium, have to say. I have no music in my work and talk. I'm awkward and I lie. At times the exultation comes, I know love exists, and I cry aloud on the black streets, I touch anyone who comes to me, I walk high and straight down Kearny Street past groups of businessmen, untouchable winds. I need to fuck someone, call up J but he's not home. I know what the birds cry at night as if in their dreams.

The minute I touch my cock I see an angel waving white wings in the air. I become terrified.

I give details about this transformation: I travel to Sligo where I'm living with my uncle George Ally who's taken over my grandfather's tall lonely house. He lives with one general servant, a horse servant, and complains all the time about death. My grandmother lifts up my pink organdie dress shows the headwaiter my new panty girdle. My first true bloodstained kotex. I fuck D, A, stop for a year, when one boyfriend asks me how far I've gone I tell him only as far as I have with you thinking all the time he's a fool and stupid, then? P, B, then I become a nymphomaniac. I'm still a nymphomaniac because my skin is white, my cunt lips are red, no, pink, I have no social education. I think that having conquered body desire, lust, my physical inclination toward women and love, which I haven't done yet, I will live in ecstasy, seeking wisdom. O.K.

My childhood dream:
(Narrow down to process.)

On a certain island a hideous monster guards a tree which bears godly fruit. At 6:00 P.M. I set out from Sligo, light green on dark greens on light green, I walk slowly I can't tell if I'm in dream or reality, the thoughts move past me as does the silk outside my eyes, the trees streams are endless black and white silkscreen. I can't sleep anymore because I'm so lonely. I'm scared the wood ranger who guards this forest will shoot me. I wake up just as the birds start crying, the small birds, inside and outside of me. Now I long for the country again.

I resolve to work harder and worship my passions. I walk through the dry forest, branches crackle under my toes; suddenly the ground gives way and I'm walking through a kind of sticky leech-ridden mud. Through endless miles of my blood. Smells. I'm in a nightmare because I have nowhere to go I start crying my uncle says, "You have good right to be fatigued," meaning "Who did you fuck?" I start screaming louder and louder. I'm not explaining why I feel so strongly, why I hate and love, and finally, despite all childhood reasons, I don't know.

Kathy also writes about this and her memory of it is the same as mine:

I'm sitting under an old-fashioned mirror and I'm sitting in another part of the room. An old-fashioned room: brown walls, small, white lace blankets. Suddenly I hear a sound as if somebody's throwing a shower of peas at the mirror. Later I see the ground under the trees burning a great light. As I cross the river to a destroyed town, I see the same light moving across a torrent of water. A man walks toward, and disappears in, the waters. A small light moves over Mt. Tamalpais; in five minutes reaches the summit.

I see many phenomena for which I can't give cause. I guess I'm insane. I'm scared of my physical desires, but we won't talk about that.

I stroke my long white legs, as the tongue the tip of my tongue touches the skin above my right breast I feel pain I taste nothing no salt I smooth back against the pillows around me

I see myself: thick skin over heavy limbs, white bones. I'm a mirror: the muscles around my clit begin to move, I want myself. Inside me, a tiny circle. My hand runs along the skin from the sand of the hairline, oil, down the straight nose since I'm a cat, down to the string tied from nipple to nipple. I roll around inside myself and around my body, my legs spread: I sink further, down, until the weight of my body rests on the back between my armpits. I take off my white man's undershirt low jeans which are starting to stink, I'm completely horny and there's no one to fuck I've been and am too insane to carry on a normal conversation anyway ("Would you like to fuck me?" "I'll love you and be your friend forever"), lift my left breast which sometimes hurts the edge of the nipple to the long brown smelly hairs, press the rough skin of the breast against the skin around the breast. I'm going to fuck myself. The nerves muscle around my clit sharply draw in and out, loose and tense, I imagine the clit-muscles I see the clit-muscles an inch inside my eyes; an inch below my skin my hand's touching my veins arteries organs should I use my dildo?

I see myself: brown very thick skin tender low breasts with huge violet nipples the skin below them curves downward over man's hips to heavy long spider's legs. I have no fingernails, some scars from the slight pain I endure. I'm looking down at my body and writing. Two fingers tap my thick outer lips, press the lips against each other until the skin begins to burn. I shift I want to get this over with, I press myself against myself: I touch each separate nerve each separate muscle, I touch my clit slowly press down on it I have to relax go slower, no I touch myself just less than I move toward the touch very steadily I rise toward the finger. I move the finger faster flickers over the growing skin, I feel the clit grow, the skins below the fingers become moist. The sensations multiply I can't think of anything else.

■

(Now I know that everyone hates me. Complete blackness and horrible feelings: I want to hurt myself, I can't do anything for myself, I lean on anyone I can. I'm falling apart. I see myself:)

"I'm so bored," I said, swinging my legs away from the fireplace in the old English mansion. I'm talking to my friend T. "Everything here is perfect: for the first time in my life I have enough to eat, I don't have to work as a stripper, do anything but write, if I'm dying you have enough money to call me a doctor, I have two pairs of blue jeans, I have lots of animals I can fuck."

T laughs. "Things aren't usually this way you know."

"Just when the country's falling apart. Isn't it nice to be rich."

NIXON MURDERS CHILE
AGNEW MURDERS NIXON
THE POOR STARVE, EAT THEIR
CHILDREN

I throw the newspapers away from me in disgust. Half the skin on my legs, white, half red. "Tell me, T, who are your favorite writers?"

"I only read mysteries, pornography, and newspapers. I like writers who say things."

"I like silver and gold, purple silk through which you can see stranger more hidden silks, thin yellows of the suns we almost no longer know, whites on whites on whites of snow sinking into the heavy wood branches, snow frozen on the soles of feet, whites wrapped in the pale silvers of my lips things and cunt. I like watching the bluejays robins grey sparrows grey pigeons hawks barn owls parrots kinkajous fly into the trees above the silver-blue lake, thin patterns of branches and leaves placed against thinner patterns of leaves and fur, fur against wood, leaves against leaves, huge red blossoms separated by trees and stones, an occasional path at the edge of the lawn through the wood, life which no longer exists."

"O God I'm bored," I exclaimed.
Just then,

I don't talk to anyone because I don't know how to talk. I'm going to tell you about my childhood: (tell the truth)

"Hello Kathy." "Oh hi, how are you?" "I'm fine, dear, and how are you?" "I'm O.K." My father. "I'm getting all these diseases 'cause I'm not getting enough protein." "O that's too bad." "How come you didn't send me the money so I could go see you?" "Mother will tell you about that." "Uh, are you O.K.?" "I'm working hard as usual all the time" whines. "Why don't you retire; you have enough money." "I'd have nothing to live on," he makes over $50,000 a year and my mother has a half-a-million in the bank. "You're rich enough." "Don't say that Kathy, I'm poor: you're the rich one."

"I'll let you speak to your mother." The woman who gave birth to me speaks: "Yes, your sister's baby is just adorable. I love all babies; all babies are just beautiful. I love all babies; all babies are just beautiful. Except for you and your sister: you were both ugly. Except for you and your sister: you were both ugly."

Immediately I close front door: grey air grey grey piss dog piss all over me go into Haight Clinic to get rid of white worms squirming in my ass. No, I never eat, thank you; I don't have enough money. Wait half hour to see person who fills out forms, half hour to see person who takes blood counts, one hour then person sticks me in wood room: doctor will see you in a few minutes. 8:00 hottest day yet in San Francisco. I feel the sweat dropping down the skin at the sides of my breasts. 8:15. The room's getting smaller and hotter. Listen to people talking about hepatitis. The doctor isn't going to see me because other people are sicker than me. The doctor isn't going to see me because I have disgusting worms, the doctor isn't going to see me because he hates me. I have to cool off, try to go to sleep. I can't. Black shapes outside the door lean against the door of the room to be sure the door's shut. The shapes are people. The shapes are shapes: menace me. I'm getting paranoid, but I can control it. I want to sit on the wood floor in a corner, but they'll think I'm crazy. How far out do I have to go before I can't control the paranoia? Am I near or far from that point? Come back tomorrow. I immediately go to buy new Marvel comics; tall black guy looks at me, opens silver sharp curved razor, passes razor between his thumb and third finger. I don't go into store.

Get home. "Hello Kathy this is L." "Uh, hello." "I'm going to come to San Francisco and I want to know if I can stay with you?" "Uh, sure, but I'll have to ask P." "The thing is: I can't stay with you if you're going to fuck P." "I'm sorry, I don't get to see P often now (P's my brother lover I've been living with him for a year and the only friend I have) and I fuck him and will every time we feel like it." "Can't you find me somewhere else to stay; I'll take you out to dinner." "You can stay at the motel near Mills; it costs only three or four dollars a night." "I want to be near you" "I can only see you three or four hours a day anyway. I'm very paranoid now and I don't see people much." "I'll be seeing you. Do what you like. I'll be seeing you."

I call up P. "You have to watch out: people easily take advantage of you."

I am sleeping and I think about lovers who don't fuck. They dislike their bodies. I love to fuck. My brother is shy and when he gets too sexually excited, his cock refuses to stand up. I bring out my precious bottle of red wine. My brother's scared, he's scared to fuck women and they always have to proposition him. I propositioned him: I put my hand on his lap and looked up at him, then I turned my head around and snuggled in into his cock. Lovers who don't want to fuck each other are shy then, like my brother. My brother is the only person who respects me and that's why he feels shy.

A woman-lover asks me if my brother and I are lovers. I want a hundred brothers, and only one now is possible.

I went from Cannes, being a Catholic and scared of my huge desires, to Monaco, through Antibes, through Cannes searching for my brother. He is the first man I have ever fucked.

We have no money and think of parting. Two dark figures, bones of black fans loom behind the trees, black nets on light green net on black nets, through the yellow green more and more yellow into pure light!

Does the soul survive the body?

Yes.

Then love need not be physical.

Is our civilization near an end, or transformation?

Yes.

We have to consider the terror we are living through.

All the above events (and thoughts) taken from *Mythologies* and *The Autobiography of William Butler Yeats* by William Butler Yeats, and myself.

6

the story of my life

1947   I'm born April 18; my family thinks of itself as aristocratic, though it isn't, since my grandmother (mother's mother) came from Alsace-Lorraine to U.S.A. poor and in her later life married a wealthy man. They properly worship money as do all good Americans. They assure me that only the unworthy work. I will never have to work since I'm rich and will marry rich, that if I ever have to think about money it's because I've come down in the world. They're incredibly stingy with me. These conflicting early trainings make me proud and shy, confident that I'm by nature above other people and aware that everyone, especially my parents, hates me. These are the first roots I remember of my schizophrenia and paranoia.

As a baby I spit at whoever I feel like: whether or not the person's rich. Whether or not the person's insulted me.

1947–51 Early childhood in apartment 6C 57th Street and First Avenue. Manhattan. To continue, when my sister, a baby, snores too loud, I bite through her knee.

1951 My grandmother (mother's mother) receives me in her house and nurtures my weaknesses; my selfishness, my pride, my obstinacy at getting what I want. My grandmother's incredibly rich.

1952–1957 Educated by private tutor, the Black Virgin Mary, and I teach her to suck my cunt. She corresponds with many famous poets. My mind, my sole repository of freedom, is beginning to be born.

1957 Enter a private girls' school for ladies and cheerfully submit to that training. It is there that I receive my final education, a retreat not unknown to you: there the most intelligent and insane artists have been educated.

1970 I begin to live solely according to my desires. I hate fighting, all use of weapons and show of courage since I'm only interested in operating sexually. I want to do only what my imaginations dictate.

I realize this is how I must live but as yet I don't have the moral strength. For psychological (childhood) reasons I cannot work and I'm through fear of starvation dependent on my parents. I dislike my parents who hate me and simultaneously bind me to them; I hate even more their double way of life: the facade they want me to be, their more real void of desire. They are nothing. The family is always pretending they're starving and they never follow their desires. I want to be totally unlike these creeps. I meet a beautiful woman who does not love me as I love her; she doesn't understand that my actions must realize the images within my mind: the image of love and destruction of the self. She abandons me,

the woman who lets me kiss her beautiful red cunt; and I do
what my parents want, out of my weakness, I marry a woman
whose family wealth will restore the riches of my parents. I
compensate for this weakness of mine by more successfully
satisfying myself, now by trying to find out systematically
what my real desires are. Are the images in my thoughts and
in my dreams indicators of my sexual desires; do I want to
replicate just these events (images); do I want to do more; do
I want to do nothing? I find out about my real self by systematically, in order of progressions away from "normality,"
trying out each sexual act. I hire prostitutes because I feel
that the people with whom I experiment should receive some
compensation since they might not have the same desires and
curiosity I have. Prostitutes have the experience to let me
alone.

I am thrown in jail for trying to figure out my desires.

1971   I fall in love with a man (L) who uses me. I realize
passions are too strong, and although holy, only finally destroy
me. I hate this man derive great pleasure from my hatred.

1972   I hate these women and men who are totally sophisticated which means they care only for money and kick me and
tear me apart each time I fall in love with one of them. I will
now fall in love only with someone who is inexperienced ready
to be taught the desirability of pure passion, as is natural before
society overtakes her and makes her into another mercenary.
My cunt is bright orange and smells good. I succumb again: I
fall in love with a man who makes a fool of me, who

Too many painful memories here. I cannot write in this
black prison.

1985   My mother (in-law) makes sure I'm forever imprisoned
in jail. She doesn't want me to disturb the pretty social facade
she has created; her maniacal ivory tower. I live in a small stone

room in which there is constant light, wet stone below my
naked feet, against my upper and lower limbs, above my wild
brown hair. Grey hair and skin. I'm not allowed to exercise
because I might meet other prisoners and corrupt them. I grow
fat all sorts of diseases huge fat white worms crawl squiggling
out of my ass. My ass skin is red. No one cares for me or does
anything to help me including my so-called wife who knows
only how to cry. The more I despise her, the more she loves
me and licks my absent feet, makes me despise her and myself
more. Don't say this.

In prison: In prison: I have nothing to do with people anymore. I live entirely in fantasies. Yet I remember all the people
who've persecuted me: these memories underlie my mental
pleasures. Now that I'm no longer able to fuck etc. I can throw
away that crutch, that fear: I can fully investigate all forms of
sexual desires, what are these forms; catalog them. Find out
everything I can possibly think. Everything I can think comes
from me, obviously, and is good; every action I can think of I
should be free to do.

Am I really a criminal? Of course the people who shut me
in this prison are wrong. I denied my mother love because she
hated me but she also wanted me to love her so her hatred
could destroy me more. I see so clearly I can't stop my emotions
from hurting me. I have to deal directly with my mother: every
time she talks to me, my will wilts: I'm unable to tell her
anything true, I silently take her abuse, I don't talk back. I obey
her unspoken commands hate myself. When she finishes talking to me, I say in my mind all the horrible words I hate you
you hate me I'm never going to talk to you again I should have
said to her hate myself for being weak not saying these final
words to her. I become terribly scared. I become scared think
that she's going to take my brain away. The moment that she
talked to me and I was unable to do anything but what I've
always done: be her slave is the same moment I become a

prostitute, want only to accept the abuse of other people. Sometimes I want to punish myself because I don't understand all the emotions I feel toward my mother and why I feel them; I try to separate my memories from events I have fantasized or dreamt (impossible). I want to punish myself; I don't want other people punishing me without my permission. These people are eternally injuring me and nothing can repair those injuries. I'm a person like they are, and I am separate and inviolable.

My mother wanted to make me exactly like her. I look like her: we both have large eyes, same bone structure, thick child's skin, dark brown hair, purple lips. We're both fond of our bodies and willful. From the first day I was born and hypocritically smiled, pretending I was happy, I opposed her: I set myself against her so that I should become someone else. She began outwardly to hate me when I began to menstruate. She wanted me to be nothing, like her.

Why do I constantly want to blame myself when I know others are at fault? I don't understand this vestige of stupidity. I've done nothing to be treated like a vicious rat.

1789   On account of my pro-Revolutionary attitude, they move me from my prison at Vincennes where I possess some velvet clothes and light to write by to the loony-bin. I'm concerned with my personal freedom I'm not insane by my standards. I hate it. They allow me to take walks at stipulated times. My wife destroys three-quarters of my manuscripts when they move me into the loony-bin.

I move to New York because I write and want to meet writers. I have no money, no way of getting money, no friends in New York, no parents. I get Pelvic Inflammatory Disease, walk into Columbia Presbyterian clinic: woman vomits blood over floor,

wood booths with tiny filthy white curtains for doctors' rooms
in front of wood chairs on wood floor filthy, doctor yells at one
man you haven't taken your medicine now you're going to die
of T.B. man is skeleton sit down not next to anyone we'll call
you man sits down next to me, nurse yells Mr. X your turn man
two seats ahead of me wiggles back Mr. X your turn man makes
attempt to move falls back in chair nurse comes over to man
slaps him on the back Mr. X we can't wait for you, man gets
half-way out of chair doesn't make it half hour later cop walks
over to man "get out of here; no loitering around here" drags
man out of clinic, nurse wheels figure wrapped in white
mummy cloth blood tube tied to one mummy cloth arm over
floor person vacuuming asks if he should move vacuum "no"
bump bump over vacuum cords mummy jiggles blood and
needle in mummy arm jiggles almost out of arm nurse changes
his mind wheels cart back again corpse jumps up and down all
this done three times, black guy and woman sitting to my side
black woman starts yelling at man high on drug man twists her
arm viciously almost breaks it, nurse-guard tells man he's acting
properly. Three hours later I'm now in shock slightly hallucinating doctor gives me four shots of penicillin in ass throws
needle into my ass BAM "mmm that one got in O.K." gives
me endless bottles of synthetic opium and nembutal to shut me
up. A month later I'm even sicker.

1790: April 2   My children visit me, tell me they have declared the billets de cachets which imprisoned me fourteen
years ago invalid. I'm going to stay in Charenton the loony-bin
until spring because I fear the democracy. They won't imprison
me next time: they'll kill me. I fear everyone. This lovely
peaceful democracy exists balanced between atrocity and fanaticism—but no more. Is it possible to come to the end of my
fear? Black waters of ocean, black legs, black inner rooms. I can
almost not see. I'm too fat and no one will fuck me. I love only

what occurs in my mind. I've remade the outside prison inside me because there's no difference between outside and inside my mind: they release me from prison and I'm still in prison. My wife wants to do away with me: she no longer likes leather.

I no longer want to marry anyone or live with any of my lovers. I want my family: my one brother who gives me some help, and a room in which I can think and masturbate and write, which is the only activity this evil society has left me capable of doing.

1791–1792 I produce my first plays. I become secretary of the revolutionary "Sections des Piques"; I improve public hospitals, publish reports and addresses, try to cut down the number of human executions. The people plunder my home, destroy my family belongings, steal my remaining estates from me. I'm extremely poor.

In one of the acts in my sex show I become a young woman who is talking to a psychiatrist. I tell the psychiatrist how Santa Claus fell out of the chimney told me I should always be a good girl I talk baby talk I should always do what he tells me I slowly start taking off my blouse and rubbing my right hand over my right breast, I have to believe in Santa Claus. Suddenly, as I'm about to kiss my nipple, I stop; I see hundreds of men watching me. I've delusions: men follow me, men want to hurt me, men want to have sexual activities with me without my consent and desire to. The psychiatrist laughs at me. The men who are watching me as I writhe around on the bed start talking to me I joke back with them. The psychiatrist tells me I've hearing delusions; I cut off my hair; I'm Joan of Arc. I lead soldiers in drag and kill everyone. I become hot: I rip off my clothes, I begin to masturbate men make me ooo soo hot. The psychiatrist fucks me we both come five million times. OOOO O yes

yes that's it no no? o please o yes o please o come on faster
. . . faster give it to me now NOW oooo (low) oooooo (higher)
oooo oooo oah auahhh oahh. eha. (down again). All my diseases
are gone.

1793 I'm made judge, then chairman of my section of the
Revolutionary party. I'm not sure what I am. I become somewhat more secure. They throw furniture out of the windows,
smash all the wood and marble they can, set the rest on fire.
I have the chance to put to the guillotine my mother-in-law
who had been the primary cause of my imprisonment; but I
don't. I'm interested in following my ideas into actions, my
ideas are my desires, not in revenge. I watch the head being
placed on the guillotine, mucus streaming out of the eyes, nose,
and ears, until the face covered with dripping gook, the sharp
diagonal knife descends. I have a knife in my hand: a living
person stands next to me, I run the tip of the knife against the
thick white skin. This is complete pain. On December 8, 1973,
they arrest me for not believing in God.

I hate men and shave off my hair. I decide this is not the
way to live. I write for that is the only thing I know how to
do, and I dress in velvets, furs, silks: anything that approximates
the thick softness of my skin.

1814 **I go through my death:**
April 11 Napoleon abdicates
I feel sick, snot wet watery the worst kind runs down the skin
below my nose. The edges of my eyelids burn. I want to crawl
under the grey sheet the white blanket, go to sleep.

May 3 Louis XVIII struts into Paris, takes over.
I sleep six hours not much sleep for one night I usually like
to sleep ten to twelve hours wash my face go to radio show. I
want to fuck someone who I can talk to.

May 31   M. Roulhac de Maupas replaces M. de Coulmier as Director of Charenton.

I replace the heads of the universities with jackals; I laugh and go back to sleep. I rub thick creams pale white into the thick skins of my leg. The white of the bathtub. I worship my body, hate whoever I think is trying to kill me. I open the red lips of my cunt and begin to laugh.

October 21   The Minister of the Interior asks the Director-General of the Police to try to move me into a State Prison away from the asylum.

My belly is slightly swollen and my eyes are dim. I'm born rich and cannot escape my birth (the ways I was told to perceive the world even before I was born. Seeing hearing smelling tasting feeling: all taught how to me.) I want people to wait on me: treat me with respect.

I begin to masturbate: I move the muscles in the upper part of my cunt so that the flesh around my clit rubs against the other flesh opposite it. I slowly spread my legs weights at my knees I watch my knees move away from each other until my body is magnetized to and from itself limbs turning against limbs fingers set against the glistening skins the skins of the lips which break let the blood through drip my fingers fall downward to the wet flesh the red burning cunt

December 2   I rub thick creams pale beautiful into my leg sticking upright into the air. I'm endlessly beautiful in my white bed. My dutiful son who's stolen my money Donatien-Claude-Armand visits me and asks the new student-doctor to stay with me. Very sick. I want to see the Abbe tomorrow; I want to hate myself and destroy everything. My breathing is noisy and labored; I take a few sips of some hot liquid I die from either pulmonary congestion or adyamic and gangrenous fever about 9:50 A.M.

■

I'm trying to become other people because this is what I find interesting.

I was interested in "fame" as one end: (1) people whose work I want to find out about would talk to me, (2) I would somehow be able to pay for food rent etc. doing something connected, (3) artists I fall in love with would fuck me: these desires are fucking over my work (and me). So I say the desires out loud.

I'm trying to get away from self-expression but not from personal life. I hate creativity. I'm simply exploring other ways of dealing with events than ways my lousy habits—mainly installed by parents and institutions—have forced me to act. At this point, I'm over-sensitive and have a hard time talking to anyone. I can fuck more easily.

The least boring act for me is to find out why I'm alive and why I'm going to die, so I can decide how I can talk to people and how I can fuck.

If I begin respecting the money-rules my mother teaches me my teachers teach me, which I don't respect, and if I see everyone in the world doing what he she selfishly wants irregardless of these rules, why shouldn't I also satisfy my desires? Why shouldn't I murder someone? My parents (mother, adopted father) are rich have disowned me and when they die I now starving will become rich, I could kill them. Or else: if American soldiers every day kill and maim millions of poor people like me and get praised for their actions, why shouldn't I kill someone so I can have an orgasm? Of course they're safer: I won't be jailed and given a lobotomy if I become an American soldier instead of a murderess. Do what people tell you to do: don't die. How do I know it's absolutely wrong for me to murder someone? How do I know anything? Do I know anything? When I look at the white clouds passing across the black sky, moon behind these clouds drive me mad free psilocybin for everyone, yay yay, I look down at my outstretched hand; I have a silver knife in my hand; do the sky and the white clouds care? These considerations are totally stupid and naive. I'm stupid and naive. My thick skin is beautiful.

Permit me to conceal my name the names of my parents the place where my mother spread her legs, out I came: I am an aristocrat. I was born to be able to do whatever I want. When I'm barely two years old unable, of course, to fend for myself, my parents cast me out on to the street. Having been physically well-taken-care-of, that is, always enough diet margarine and diet bread always a doctor with tons of penicillin for my ass by my parents and mother's mother between the ages of 0 and 2, I was totally unprepared for reality. No one wanted to give me a job, any job, much less a job suited for my advanced knowledge state, my five Ph.D.'s in the higher sciences; the shits simply wanted to fuck me. I had no money, no resources, I became sick with a dread sexual disease, mistreated by a doctor of the poor who called me a "whore": I desperately needed everything I quickly learned that I was no favored son of the rich. Nor was anyone else.

Redo myself

I slobber down the right side fat white mouth goo goo goo goo "yes my dear that's right" I'm a pudgy ball stick a knife in me and I bleed. I scream and I scream and I scream. I don't scream; I keep that wrapped up inside of me and I smile. I smile at the evil people who are evil because they're going to hit me so they don't hit me. If they know how I really feel, especially about them, they'll hit me. I begin to cry and the skin on my hands turns red. I remember yellow: bright hellow bright yellow. Yellow explodes into my thick skin. "What do you want dear how are you dear we don't want anything to do with you dear you're so cute woo woo woo goo-goo goo-goo

goo-goo goo-goo goo-goo." I want to hide. I'm a famous movie star, I'm six months old and I'm going to hide the shit out of my self. Stretch out one leg. Put my hand on that bump in the leg. Squish out the gushy stuff out of my ass yum roll around o yes I can orgasm o yes. Goo goo goo goo. I'm remaking I'm remaking myself proud.

"Well my dear," Count Alexander looks at me and adjusts his golden monocle, "what can you do for me?" I know he can give me all his money.

"Oh sir," I lisp, "I'm just a poor two-year-old and my parents hate me and threw me out on the street please have pity on me I don't want to become a secretary because I don't want to eat shit I want to eat cunt I'm too small and the laws no longer protect me because I'm not rich I'm to crazy to be a stupid secretary have pity on me beautiful sir, I've worked in a sex show I've taken tricks I've stripped, men have shoved dollar bills up my cunt with their fingers I don't want to lose my virginity. I'm a sensitive, a true trembling artist, I always curtsy properly, please help me sir."

"Why should I help you, creep?" says the Count adjusting his peacock robe.

"What are you talking about sir? I'm pure and innocent and stupid." I want the Count to step on me, kick me in the sides a few times so I can hear those ribs crack, feel my childish lip split. Open. Then I can take all his money. No recriminations on either side.

I see peacocks walking across the thin shanks of my legs on to the bed on which I sit, sick. I wrap the black furs around my body. I know it's night outside, and begin to think.

Only interest in the ideas of the Marquis

I no longer understand what I'm doing.

I become the Marquis de Sade.

No evil results if I fuck animals. All laws of all nations should allow us, rather, not stop us from creating our favorite perversions because Nature creates these desires for perversions in us before we create the actual perversions. That is, I feel I'm a freak because I want to fuck women, hamsters, trains, criminals, black leather I can't speak to people I don't want any one or group of humans to kill me because I do these things. I want everyone to love me. (No.) Let us examine murder.

Murder's the worst. I'm going to do whatever I want. I'm going to speak the truth because this is the apocalypse. Is murder objectively evil? (This is a dopey question.) Humans aren't any more important than any other animal. Obviously: because I fuck my hamster. This isn't true: only men are capable of destroying forever the human and the living world.

What's the difference between humans and other life on this sphere? When I die, I change form. If I murder, I change your form? Different nations have different customs about murder, killing children, enforcing public assassinations. I'm trying to destroy all laws, tell you not to follow laws, restrictions. "Murder" is not a general act. If the number of living people exceeds the amount of natural resources necessary for the maintenance of those people, it's necessary to kill some of the people so all the people can live. It's not necessary for American soldiers to kill men and women who are poor and live in foreign countries except for a few rich white men who get lots of money when an American soldier needs a new weapon. Necessary according to the rich men. It's not necessary to kill a person who has just killed another person: "I grant you pardon" I say to my parents who, to divert themselves, have turned me into a paranoid schizo freak sex freak, "and I also pardon myself when I kill you." Murder, finally, is a horror.

What should I do to please myself? A stranger with a weird sex maniac voice W asks me if I'm The Black Tarantula yes will I send him my books yes will I fuck him? I only fuck once a month then I fuck every one. Fear. I see bodies rolling in white feathers, thin layers of sweat across the skin, the muscles around my clit begin to move. I need four or five close friends, fuckers or not, around me because I'm scared to always follow my desires in this sick society. The only offense against my pleasure is suicide. I often stick razor blades in my wrists to punish myself. "Offense" is a stupid and meaningless word. Many early governments authorized suicide; the American government wants all poor people to die in the fastest ways possible. I'm trying to stick out my tongue at the Church. I can now do what I want and I want to be as courageous as possible. Everyone of the rich people who were guillotined asked voluntarily to be guillotined for sake of a future unionized nation. (Ugh.) Now let us worship our nation, fart over it, get involved in national politics. (Ugh.) I'm gentle: I'm scared of people; if I'm constantly terrorized and starved by laws, I cannot come.

I've clearly demonstrated that I no longer need to work. Fire and steel surround my flaming head. Let the thrones of Europe crumble of themselves; your delight will send them flying without your having to meddle at all.

All the above events taken from *The Marquis de Sade The Complete Justine Philosophy in the Bedroom and Other Writings* by Count Donatien Alphonse Francois de Sade, *Portrait of de Sade* by W. Lenning, and myself.

I DREAMT I WAS A NYMPHOMANIAC IMAGINING

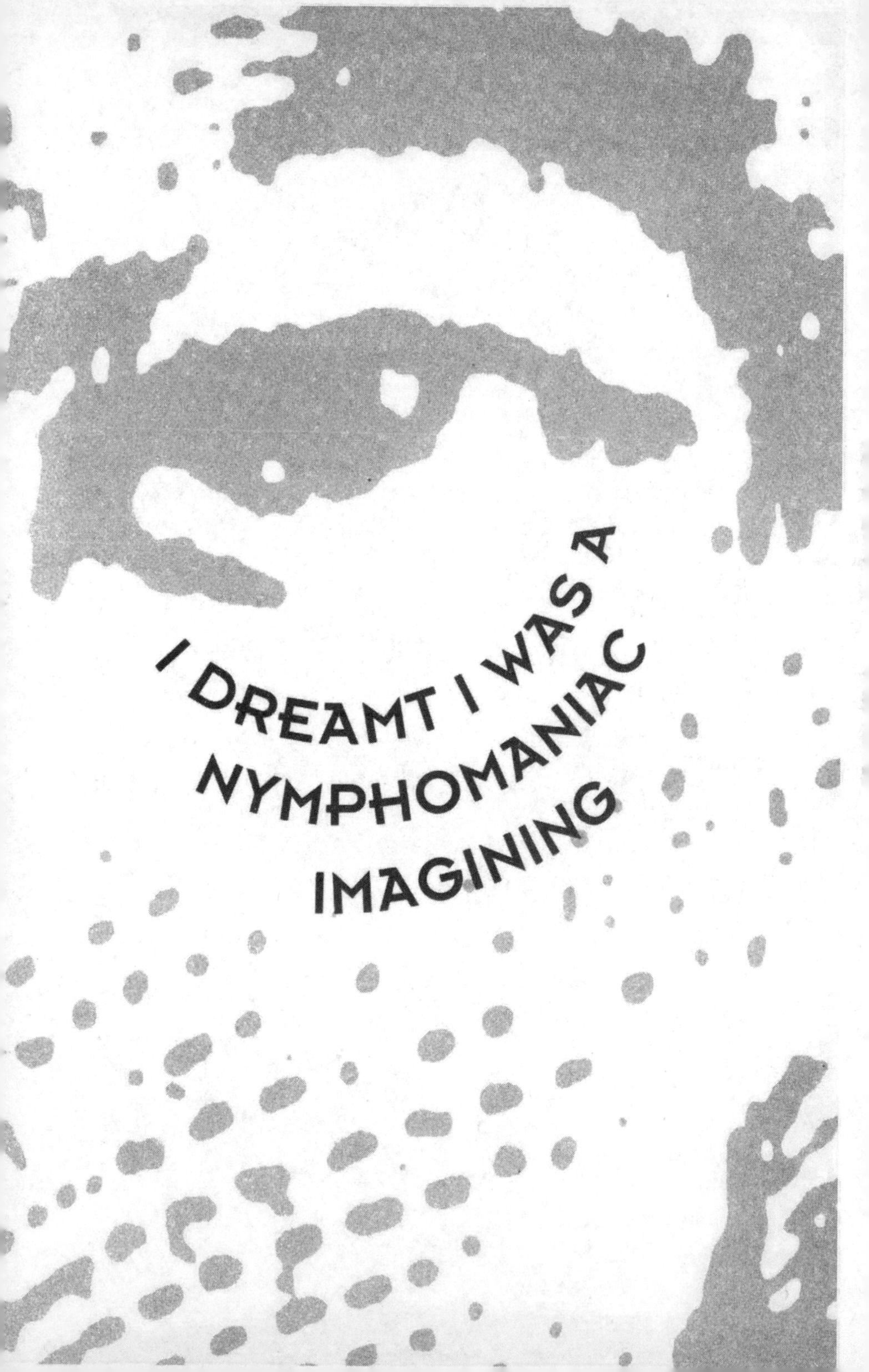

contents

"This is very nonpolitical, therefore reactionary," he said. "But what would the world have to be like for these events to exist?" I replied.

1

I absolutely love to fuck. These longings, unexplainable longings deep within me, drive me wild, and I have no way of
relieving them. Living them. I'm 27 and I love to fuck. Sometimes with people I want to fuck; sometimes, and I can't tell
when but I remember these times, with anybody who'll touch
me. These, I call them nymphomaniac, times have nothing to
do with (are not caused by) physical pleasure, for my cunt could
be sore, I could be sick, and yet I'd feel the same way. I'll tease
you till you don't know what you're doing, honey, and grab; and
then I'll do anything for you.

I haven't always been this way. Once upon a time I was an
intelligent sedate girl, who, like every intelligent sedate girl,
hated her parents and didn't care about money. O in those days
I didn't care about anything! I dated boys, stayed out till 5:00

in the morning then snuck home, read a lot of books. I cared more for the books than anyone else and would kiss my books good-night when I went to sleep. Would never go anywhere without a book. But my downfall came. My parents kicked me out of the house because I wasn't interested in marrying a rich man, I didn't care enough about money to become a scientist or a prostitute, I couldn't even figure out how to make any money.

I didn't. I became poor and had to find a way of justifying my lousy attitude about money. At first, like all poor people, I had delusions about being a great artist, but that quickly passed. I never did have any talent.

I want to fuck these two fantastic artists even though I'm not an artist: that's what this is about. This is the only way I can get them: (I only want them for a few hours. Days.) Jewels hang from the tips of silver branches. I also want money.

My name is Kathy Acker.

The story begins by me being totally bored.

Sunny California is totally boring; there are too many blond-assed surf jocks. I was lying on my bed, wondering if I should go down to the beach or sun myself on the patio until I passed out. I watched the curly silky brown hair below the damp palm of my hand rise and fall, I watched the rise, the mound twist in agony, laughed at myself. No way, I muttered, among these creeps no way. I need to love someone who can, by lightly, lightly stroking my flesh, tear open this reality, rip my flesh open until I bleed. Red jewels running down my legs and branches. I need someone who knows everything and who'll love me endlessly; then stop. My cats leaped up to me and rubbed their delicious bodies against my body. My cats didn't exist.

Suddenly heard a knocking at the door. No one ever knocks at the door, they just walk in. I wondered if it was FBI agents, or the telephone Mafia after Art Povera. I opened the door and saw Dan, I didn't know his name then, looking bewildered. Then, seeing me, looking scared. I realized I had forgotten to put clothes on. That's how southern California is: hot.

"Excuse me, I'm looking for 46 uh Belvedere."

"Oh you mean up the hill where David and Elly live; I'll show you. I have to get some clothes on."

He followed me into my small bedroom.

As I slowly bent over, reaching for my jeans, I noticed him watching me. He had brown hair, couldn't see his eyes because he squints so much but they look red, some acne, short with a body I like: heavy enough to run into and feel its weight on me; about 30 years old. I hesitantly took hold of my jeans. He started to talk again: he talks too much. I wanted him to rip off my skin, take me away to where I'd always be insane. He didn't want to fuck with me, much less do anything else. I slowly lifted my leg to put on my jeans, changed my mind. I turned around; suddenly we grabbed each other: I felt his body: his lips wet and large against my lips, his arms pressing my back and stomach into his thick endless stomach, his mouth over me, sucking me, exploring me I want this

"I want you you lousy motherfucker I want you to do everything to me I want you to tell me you want me I want you any way I can get you. Do you understand?" We run screaming out into the night, other people don't exist, feet touching the cold stone, then the sand, then the black ocean water. I look up: black; toward the sand: black; I reach up for him and fall. The water passes over us. We stand up, spouting water; our mouths' wetness into each other's mouth cling together to stay erect. I rise up on my toes, the black waves rising, carefully, press my thighs into his so that his cock can touch my cunt. His right hand caresses his cock, touches its tip to my cunt lips, moves upward, into me I hold him tighter we fall

My hand touches my wet curling hairs then the thick lips of my cunt. Takes sand, rubs the sand into the outer lips of my cunt. Two areas of softness wetness touch me, move back so the cold air swirls at, touch me I feel warm liquid trickling between the swelling lips I feel them swelling a tongue a burning center touches me harder, inside the swollen lips: I lift my legs and imprison him. My nipples are hard as diamonds. The inner skin of my knees presses against his rough hairs: now I feel roughness: sandpaper rubbing the screaming skin above my clit. The joining of my inner lips almost more sensitive than my clit. Now I feel soft surface wetnesses, gently lap, now the burning center which becomes my burning center: rhythmically pressing until time becomes burning as I do. I'm totally relaxed. I'm a tongue which I can't control: which I beg to touch me each time it stops so I can open wider, rise rise toward the black, I open rising screaming I feel it: I feel waves of senses screaming I want more and more

At the peak, as I think I'm beginning to descend, he throws himself on me and enters me making me come again again. All I feel is his cock in me moving circling circling every inch of my cunt walls moving back forth every inch, he stops, I can't, he starts slamming in to me not with his cock but the skin around his cock slamming into my clit I come I come he moves his cock into me slowly even more slowly, and then leaves.

For the new life, I have to change myself completely.

The next artist I meet in a bar in New York. I'm sick of artists. The next man I meet is tall, dark, and handsome. I was wearing a black silk sheath slashed in the back to the ruby which signals the delicate opening of my buttocks: tiny black diamonds in my ears and on the center of my fingernails. I had come to the bar to drink: it was an old transvestite bar East Village New York no one goes during the week, rows upon rows of white-covered tables low hanging chandeliers containing almost no light: mirrors which are walls reflect back, reflections upon reflections, tiny stars of light. The only people in the bar are the two women who run the bar, tiny grey-haired women who look like men: incredibly sexy. One or two Spanish hustlers. I wanted to be alone.

I had no background. I'm not giving you details about myself because these two occurrences are the first events of my life. Otherwise I don't exist: I'm a mirror for beauty. The man walked up to me and sat down. He bought two beers. I wasn't noticing him.

"What do you really want to happen?" he asked me. I couldn't answer him because I don't reveal the truth to people I know slightly, only to strangers and to people I know well and want to become. "I used to act as a stud," he was trying to put me at my ease. "Housewives would pick me up in their cars, pay me to satisfy them. I didn't mind because I hate house-wives: that class. Then I used to work this motel: I'd knock on a door to a room, a man would start screaming "don't come in don't come in" scream louder and louder; after a while he'd throw a pair of semened-up underpants out the door. In the pants would be ten dollars."

I couldn't say anything to him because I was starting to respect him.

"I only like people of the working class," he went on. Under-neath the table, he was slowly pouring wine on the black silk of my thigh. I moved my legs slightly, open, so the cold liquid would hit the insides of my thighs. Then close my thighs, rubbing them slowly together. "You have a lot of trouble with men, don't you?"

"Don't you love me?" I cried in anguish. "Don't you care anything about me?"

He gently took me in his arms kissed me. Lightly and gently. He didn't press me to him or touch me passionately. "Quick," he whispered. "Before they notice."

He threw me back on the velvet ledge we had been sitting

on, pulled up my shift, and entered me. I wanted more. As I feel his cock rotate slowly around the skins of my cunt walls, touching each inch slowly too slowly, he began again to pour wine on my body: liquid cooling all of my skin except the inside burning skin of my cunt. Putting ice in my mouth on my eyes, around the thick heavy ridges of my breasts. Cock slowly easing out of me, I can't stand that, I can't stand that absence I start to scream I see my mound rise upward: the heavy brown hairs surrounded by white flesh, the white flesh against the black silk: I see his cock enter me, slide into me like it belongs in my slimy walls, I tighten my muscles I tighten them around the cock, jiggling, thrust upward, thousands of tiny fingers on the cock, fingers and burning tongues: this is public I have to move fast: explodes I explode and my mound rises upward, toward the red-black ceiling, I see my mound rise upward, toward the red-black ceiling I see us come fast

He quickly got out of me, and arranged our clothes. No one in the bar had noticed. We kissed goodbye, perfunctorily, and he left.

Every night now I dream of my two lovers. I have no other life. This is the realm of complete freedom: I can put down anything. I see Dan: The inner skin of my knees presses against his rough hairs: now I feel roughness: sandpaper rubbing the screaming skin above my clit. The joining of my inner lips almost more sensitive than my clit. Now I feel soft surface wetnesses, gently lap, now the burning center which becomes my burning center: rhythmically pressing until time becomes burning as I do. I'm totally relaxed. I'm a tongue which I can't control: which I beg to touch me each time it stops so I can open wider, rise rise toward the black, I open rising screaming

I see my second artist love: I can't stand that absence I start to scream I see my mound rise upward: the heavy brown hairs

surrounded by white flesh, the white flesh against the black silk:
I see his cock enter me, slide into me like it belongs in my slimy
walls, I tighten my muscles I tighten them around the cock,
jiggling, thrust upward, thousands of tiny fingers on the cock,
fingers and burning tongues: this is public I have to move fast:
explodes I explode and my mound rises upward, toward the
red-black ceiling, I see

I want a woman.

I'm sick of dreaming.

I decide to find these two artists no matter what no matter
where. I'll be the most beautiful and intelligent woman in the
world to them.

2

I want to make something beautiful: an old-fashioned wish. To
do this I must first accomplish four tasks, for the last one I must
die: Then I'll have something beautiful, and can fuck the men
I want to fuck because they'll want to fuck me.

For the first task I have to learn to be as industrious as
possible: I have to work as hard as possible to make up for my
lack of beauty and charm. Not that I'm not extremely beautiful. I have to learn what is the best love-sex possible, and
separate those people whom I can love from those people I
can't love. I have until nightfall to do this.

Last night I dreamt I was standing on a low rise of grassy
ground; Dan was standing next to me facing me. He put his
arms around my neck kissed me, said "I love you." I said "I
love you." Two years later I'm riding through a forest with my
four younger sisters, green and wet, leaves in our eyes and skin;
we push leaves out of the way the brown horse's neck lowered.
My next-to-youngest sister tells me Dan asked her to marry him
two months ago. I'm galloping wildly through the woods

branches tear at my eyes flakes of my skin hanging. I try to go faster and faster. It's night. Three days later I appear, night, the livingroom of my parents' house: we're moving to Boston, a bayview overlooking a black sky, where I go to college. The skin of my face is torn; bruises over my naked arms; one of my eyes is bloodshot. My family's glad I haven't died. My father greets me, then my older sister who's tall, blonde, beautiful, intelligent. We love each other most. The room in which we're standing is large browns on browns; my parents are rich, not very rich, and liberals. A thin dark-haired man asks me if I want to go to a party. I want to: I rush upstairs to dress: my sister and the man, who's a close family friend, look happy because I'm not going to kill myself. I (outside the dream) look at myself (inside the dream): I'm tall and thin, short waving black hair: I'm not beautiful until you look at me for a long time. I'm very severe. When we walk into a large grey-white house, we realize the party's an artist party. The tall, dark, handsome artist walks over to me and asks me to dance. I wonder if he's asking me because he wants to marry a rich girl. He tells me he's a successful artist makes a lot of money. We dance, dance out to a dark balcony; he starts to take off my black dress as I lean over the portico. I've got two glasses of champagne: one in each hand. He says "I could strangle you like this" I get pissed and walk away. As I begin to walk away, I see Dan and some woman on the balcony: Dan walks over to the man I'm with. They greet each other: Dan admires the stranger's work. I nod hello to Dan. He announces he's getting married: introduces the woman with whom he's going to get married. I walk away to get more champagne. As I return to the balcony, a blonde woman walks up to the group the stranger says "I didn't know you wanted to come here." He introduces his wife to us. I'm going crazy but withstraining myself admirably. If I don't fuck someone soon know someone wants me, I'll have to ride my horse for three days again: do something wilder. I

can't stop myself. I get another drink. Mel someone walks up
to us says "I'm the only man here who isn't married or about
to be married" meaning I might as well fuck him because I'm
so desperate. I ask him to marry me since I have a lot of money:
I'll support him. I tell him how much money I have. He says
"Yes." I tell him to go shit on himself. I'm in a lousy mood.
An old friend of mine comes up to me, who I haven't seen for
a few months. I tell him I need someone's shoulder to cry on.
His new lover comes up to him: he can't do anything. This
dream's repulsively hetero. I get a bottle of champagne and
drink it. I have to ride my horse through the dark forest, the
winds swirling around. I rush out of the party. As I'm descending the wide wood steps, I turn around, see the tall dark artist.
He asks if he can see me again. He's very severe. I say yes. I
fall down the steps I'm so drunk. He asks me if I intend to drive
myself home. I'm going to drive myself to the ocean so I can
go swimming I'm rich do whatever I want he lifts me up puts
me in my car drives me home I end up fucking him quickly
then his wife comes I never see him again, I'm lying in my bed
with my older sister who's very "I'll take care of you" severe
type and whom I love. As we're fucking, her boyfriend enters
the room and stops us because we're not supposed to act soooo

Last night I dreamt I was standing on a low rise of grassy
ground; Dan was standing next to me facing me. He put his
arms around my neck kissed me, said "I love you." I said "I
love you." Two years later I'm riding through a forest with my
four younger sisters, green and wet, leaves in our eyes and skin;
we push leaves out of the way the brown horse's neck lowered.
My next-to-youngest sister tells me Dan asked her to marry him
two months ago. I'm galloping wildly through the woods
branches tear at my eyes flakes of my skin hanging. I try to go
faster and faster. It's night. Three days later I appear, night,
the livingroom of my parents' house: we're moving to Boston,
a bayview overlooking a black sky, where I go to college. The

skin of my face is torn; bruises over my naked arms; one of my eyes is bloodshot. My family's glad I haven't died. My father greets me, then my older sister who's tall, blonde, beautiful, intelligent. We love each other most. The room in which we're standing is large browns on browns; my parents are rich, not very rich, and liberals. A thin dark-haired man asks me if I want to go to a party. I want to: I rush upstairs to dress: my sister and the man, who's a close family friend, look happy because I'm not going to kill myself. I (outside the dream) look at myself (inside the dream): I'm tall and thin, short waving black hair: I'm not beautiful until you look at me for a long time. I'm very severe. When we walk into a large grey-white house, we realize the party's an artist party. The tall, dark, handsome artist walks over to me and asks me to dance. I wonder if he's asking me because he wants to marry a rich girl. He tells me he's a successful artist makes a lot of money. We dance, dance out to a dark balcony; he starts to take off my black dress as I lean over the portico. I've got two glasses of champagne: one in each hand. He says "I could strangle you like this" I get pissed and walk away. As I begin to walk away, I see Dan and some woman on the balcony: Dan walks over to the man I'm with. They greet each other: Dan admires the stranger's work. I nod hello to Dan. He announces he's getting married: introduces the woman with whom he's going to get married. I walk away to get more champagne. As I return to the balcony, a blonde woman walks up to the group the stranger says "I didn't know you wanted to come here." He introduces his wife to us. I'm going crazy but withstraining myself admirably. If I don't fuck someone soon know someone wants me, I'll have to ride my horse for three days again: do something wilder. I can't stop myself. I get another drink. My sister who's also drunk asks me to dance, she's wearing a low grey gown; we dance in each other's arms giggling. I lie close in her arms: I lie backwards over her left arm. We're leaning against a grey wall under a picture: she kisses me, as she looks down on me I wonder if she now feels sexually toward me I'm excited, I ask her and she says she'd like to fuck me. I look up at her and kiss her: I want us to fuck in front of all these creepy people. Her thin dark-haired boyfriend comes over tells us we can't act too wildly: do what we want in our bedroom. Mel someone walks up to us says "I'm the only man here who isn't married or about to be married" meaning I might as well fuck him because I'm so desperate. I ask him to marry me since I have a lot of money: I'll support him. I tell him how much money I have. He says "Yes." I tell him to go shit on himself. I'm in a lousy mood. An old friend of mine comes up to me, who I haven't seen for a few months. I tell him I need someone's shoulder to cry on. His new lover comes up to him: he can't do anything. This dream's repulsively hetero. I get a bottle of champagne and drink it. I have to ride my horse through the dark forest, the winds swirling around. I rush out of the party. As I'm descending the wide wood steps, I turn around, see the tall dark artist. He asks if he can see me again. He's very severe. I say yes. I fall down the steps I'm so drunk. He asks me if I intend to drive myself home. I'm going to drive myself to the ocean so I can go swimming I'm rich and do whatever I want he lifts me up puts me in my car drives me home I end up fucking him quickly then his wife comes I never see him again, I'm lying in my bed with my older sister who's very "I'll take care of you" severe type and whom I love. As we're fucking, her boyfriend enters the room and stops us because we're not supposed to act soooo

Last night I dreamt I was standing on a low rise of grassy ground; Dan was standing next to me facing me. He put his arms around my neck kissed me, said "I love you." I said "I love you." Two years later I'm riding through a forest with my four younger sisters, green and wet, leaves in our eyes and skin; we push leaves out of the way the brown horse's neck lowered.

My next-to-youngest sister tells me Dan asked her to marry him two months ago. I'm galloping wildly through the woods branches tear at my eyes flakes of my skin hanging. I try to go faster and faster. It's night. Three days later I appear, night, the livingroom of my parents' house: we're moving to Boston, a bayview overlooking a black sky, where I go to college. The skin of my face is torn; bruises over my naked arms; one of my eyes is bloodshot. My family's glad I haven't died. My father greets me, then my older sister who's tall, blonde, beautiful, intelligent. We love each other most. The room in which we're standing is large browns on browns; my parents are rich, not very rich, and liberals. A thin dark-haired man asks me if I want to go to a party. I want to: I rush upstairs to dress: my sister and the man, who's a close family friend, look happy because I'm not going to kill myself. I (outside the dream) look at myself (inside the dream): I'm tall and thin, short waving black hair: I'm not beautiful until you look at me for a long time. I'm very severe. When we walk into a large grey-white house, we realize the party's an artist party. The tall, dark, handsome artist walks over to me and asks me to dance. I wonder if he's asking me because he wants to marry a rich girl. He tells me he's a successful artist makes a lot of money. We dance, dance out to a dark balcony; he starts to take off my black dress as I lean over the portico. I've got two glasses of champagne: one in each hand. He says "I could strangle you like this" I get pissed and walk away. As I begin to walk away, I see Dan and some woman on the balcony: Dan walks over to the man I'm with. They greet each other: Dan admires the stranger's work. I nod hello to Dan. He announces he's getting married: introduces the woman with whom he's going to get married. I walk away to get more champagne. As I return to the balcony, a blonde woman walks up to the group the stranger says "I didn't know you wanted to come here." He introduces his wife to us. I'm going crazy but withstraining myself admirably. If I don't fuck someone soon know someone wants me, I'll have

to ride my horse for three days again: do something wilder. I
can't stop myself. I get another drink. My sister who's also
drunk asks me to dance, she's wearing a low grey gown; we
dance in each other's arms giggling. I lie close in her arms: I
lie backwards over her left arm. We're leaning against a grey
wall under a picture: she kisses me, as she looks down on me
I wonder if she now feels sexually toward me I'm excited, I ask
her and she says she'd like to fuck me. I look up at her and kiss
her: I want us to fuck in front of all these creepy people. Her
thin dark-haired boyfriend comes over tells us we can't act too
wildly: do what we want in our bedroom. Mel someone walks
up to us says "I'm the only man here who isn't married or about
to be married" meaning I might as well fuck him because I'm
so desperate. I ask him to marry me since I have a lot of money:
I'll support him. I tell him how much money I have. He says
"Yes." I tell him to go shit on himself. I'm in a lousy mood.
An old friend of mine comes up to me, who I haven't seen for
a few months. I tell him I need someone's shoulder to cry on.
His new lover comes up to him: he can't do anything. This
dream's repulsively hetero. I get a bottle of champagne and
drink it. I have to ride my horse through the dark forest, the
winds swirling around. I rush out of the party. As I'm descending the wide wood steps, I turn around, see the tall dark artist.
He asks if he can see me again. He's very severe. I say yes. I
fall down the steps I'm so drunk. He asks me if I intend to drive
myself home. I'm going to drive myself to the ocean so I can
go swimming I'm rich do whatever I want he lifts me up puts
me in my car drives me home I end up fucking him quickly
then his wife comes I never see him again, I'm lying in my bed
with my older sister who's very "I'll take care of you" severe
type and whom I love. As we're fucking, her boyfriend enters
the room and stops us because we're not supposed to act soooo

    Last night I dreamt I was standing on a low rise of grassy
ground; Dan was standing next to me facing me. He put his
arms around my neck kissed me, said "I love you." I said "I

love you." Two years later I'm riding through a forest with my
four youngest sisters, green and wet, leaves in our eyes and skin;
we push leaves out of the way the brown horse's neck lowered.
My next-to-youngest sister tells me Dan asked her to marry him
two months ago. I'm galloping wildly through the woods
branches tear at my eyes flakes of my skin hanging. I try to go
faster and faster. It's night. Three days later I appear, night,
the livingroom of my parents' house: we're moving to Boston,
a bayview overlooking a black sky, where I go to college. The
skin of my face is torn; bruises over my naked arms; one of my
eyes is bloodshot. My family's glad I haven't died. My father
greets me, then my older sister who's tall, blonde, beautiful,
intelligent. We love each other most. The room in which we're
standing is large browns on browns; my parents are rich, not
very rich, and liberals. A thin dark-haired man asks me if I want
to go to a party. I want to: I rush upstairs to dress: my sister
and the man, who's a close family friend, look happy because
I'm not going to kill myself. I (outside the dream) look at
myself (inside the dream): I'm tall and thin, short waving black
hair: I'm not beautiful until you look at me for a long time. I'm
very severe. When we walk into a large grey-white house, we
realize the party's an artist party. The tall, dark, handsome
artist walks over to me and asks me to dance. I wonder if he's
asking me because he wants to marry a rich girl. He tells me
he's a successful artist makes a lot of money. We dance, dance
out to a dark balcony; he starts to take off my black dress as
I lean over the portico. I've got two glasses of champagne: one
in each hand. He says "I could strangle you like this" I get
pissed and walk away. As I begin to walk away, I see Dan and
some woman on the balcony: Dan walks over to the man I'm
with. They greet each other: Dan admires the stranger's work.
I nod hello to Dan. He announces he's getting married: introduces the woman with whom he's going to get married. I
walk away to get more champagne. As I return to the balcony,
a blonde woman walks up to the group the stranger says "I

didn't know you wanted to come here." He introduces his wife to us. I'm going crazy but withstraining myself admirably. If I don't fuck someone soon know someone wants me, I'll have to ride my horse for three days again: do something wilder. I can't stop myself. I get another drink. My sister who's also drunk asks me to dance, she's wearing a low grey gown; we dance in each other's arms giggling. I lie close in her arms: I lie backwards over her left arm. We're leaning against a grey wall under a picture: she kisses me, as she looks down on me I wonder if she now feels sexually toward me I'm excited. I ask her and she says she'd like to fuck me. I look up at her and kiss her: I want us to fuck in front of all these creepy people. Her thin dark-haired boyfriend comes over tells us we can't act too wildly: do what we want in our bedroom. Mel someone walks up to us says "I'm the only man here who isn't married or about to be married" meaning I might as well fuck him because I'm so desperate. I ask him to marry me since I have a lot of money: I'll support him. I tell him how much money I have. He says "Yes." I tell him to go shit on himself. I'm in a lousy mood. An old friend of mine comes up to me, who I haven't seen for a few months. I tell him I need someone's shoulder to cry on. His new lover comes up to him: he can't do anything. This dream's repulsively hetero. I get a bottle of champagne and drink it. I have to ride my horse through the dark forest, the winds swirling around. I rush out of the party. As I'm descending the wide wood steps, I turn around, see the tall dark artist. He asks if he can see me again. He's very severe. I say yes. I fall down the steps I'm so drunk. He asks me if I intend to drive myself home. I'm going to drive myself to the ocean so I can go swimming I'm rich do whatever I want he lifts me up puts me in my car drives me home I end up fucking him quickly then his wife comes I never see him again, I'm lying in my bed with my older sister who's very "I'll take care of you" severe type and whom I love. As we're fucking, her boyfriend enters the room and stops us because we're not supposed to act soooo

Remembering my second task:

I ask Bob if I can use the typewriter. All day and night. "Yes." The ribbons I have don't fit: I buy a new ribbon. I'm typing away; Bob asks if I'm going to use the typewriter today and tomorrow, he has some work. "Just today I'm typing new book I've got a deadline tomorrow." "You'd better let me use it: you can use it later tonight do it all then. Get out of here." Everyone's looking at me: I gather my stuff get out. Down steps to where everything is green and yellow. Peter (my brother) yells at me because he and I are doing a book with Bob I'm not acting professionally. I walk across thick grass to car: I don't make it plop down on sidewalk and cry. I'm a poet and what I do is sacred. The people who keep me from the few lousy instruments I need to disseminate this crap are evil. They're using the instruments for business. They've no regard for those activities which are sacred.

Tonight is the night of the ball given by subscribers to the Opera. All of Paris will be there: the artists who know nothing, rich bankers who prey on the blood of the poor, for everyone is poor who works, who thinks he or she has power over his or her own life, revolutionaries hiding from the maws of the police which are the maws of the rich by pretending they're interested only in pleasure; women who know their sexuality is endless and holy; the garbage riffraff who live below the gutters of the street who see everything that happens. The philosophers of the city who know that the city and this way of life is doomed.

I'm in love with Peter, a man who is capable of deceiving both sexes. He usually wears the clothes of women: long white silk skirts with thin nets of white and snow shawls: in them he looks both like a female faun and like a young boy who adores to tease.

Although Peter is a male, I don't regard his gender as a defect. Despite the event (fact) that he didn't choose his sex, I don't dislike men. They are, by nature or by societal conditioning, cruel, arrogant, selfish, proud, stupid, stubborn, unwilling to admit their stupidity, willing to be friends only with those people they deem lower than themselves such as women; but they can be taught to be otherwise. They have some good characteristics, though I can't at the moment think what these are. They can be tamed; and, if treated with some severity and care, can make excellent consorts. Lately I've thought how little my identity matters, how physical necessities are slowly making this splendor as I know it change, causing a new world I have no idea of. I have no feelings about this change: I simply observe it. As if individuals don't matter. Night in this city is incredibly beautiful: black branches floating against an unfixed moon; tiny stars mirror streetlamps mirror etc. I'm not sure if I want,

As a poet I'm actually an agent for the SLA. My mission is

to reveal the uncertainties, unimportances, and final equivalences of all identities. Transformation to what? What changes
are necessary will occur despite fear and greed. I'm not interested in being a hero. I've nothing to say, nor teach. I'm going
to the Opera ball to contact another agent, PP (or Peter) who's
fleeing from the CIA, needs shelter, a way of reaching his next
contact. I have to pretend I'm in love with Peter.

Obviously I'll attract Peter most if I appear as a man. It
hardly matters to me.

A dark blue suit, large shirt, my heavy brown boots: I care
little about clothes. I look like a young, too sedately dressed
boy. 20 or 22.

When I enter the ball, the large dark house on the Rue de
Montparnasse lit by a thousand flickering lamps, insect lights
circling around the black house, I see no one: a white room too
brightly lit, too dazzling and brilliant for my eyes to adjust to.
I walk from room to room: each room brighter than the next.
Finally I see a tall, slender woman dressed in white furs: a long
cloak trailing on the polished lights made of alternating feathers and white skunk, a thin gown of silk through which her
pink-tan skin gleams. This is Peter. I ask her if she would like
to

I'm dreaming of fucking again and again, again and again
because I'm never satisfied. The revolution is taking place, as
"Blue" Gene says, without, for there are no, climaxes. I do
whatever I want to do: if any one/event opposes me, I do what
I can to erase that opposition, and slowly I'm changing. The
revolution is taking place, as "Blue" Gene says, because "innate" and "learned" are no longer viable descriptions: "inside
the mind" and "outside the mind" are no longer viable descriptions. The revolution is taking place, as "Blue" Gene says, day
follows night night follows day. I have to decide whether I'm
an SLA agent or a woman transvestite who's wildly in love with
the most gorgeous fag in town.

Obviously I'm a woman transvestite who's wildly in love with the most gorgeous fag in town. I walk slowly through this decaying city, this city composed of lights, glistening lights and black skies, all about to explode to the Assembly where the ball is being held. As I enter the ball, the huge grey house on the corner of the Rue de Montparnasse, I see no one: dark masqued shapes pass me as they quietly shit on the floor.

I ask Peter to dance with me. She quivers, moves slightly away from me. Taking her arm, I lead her through the white adjoining room into a darker alcove.

"What is your name, my dear? What're you doing here at your young age?"

"I'm old enough to do what I want," she replies. Underneath her long thick eyelashes, she shyly glimpses my body.

"Listen," I gently stroke the hair on her right arm. "I've been searching a long time for a woman like you: gentle, tender. A woman I can make demands on, such as to support me; who'll make no demands on me I can't satisfy. I become guilty extremely easily, won't stand for being bossed around. A woman who'll flirt with me, wait 'till I want to have sex with her then be passionate and relaxed; who'll always want to live with me, but not own me. Who'll adore my writing."

"I'm very scared," her blue eyes burn into mine, "of losing my independence. I never want to be situated such that I'm imprisoned."

The lights of the party went black.

"I need to feel both stable and able to do whatever I want whenever I want. I'm quite bourgeois in my tastes: I like liquor, dope, I'm decadent. I'm scared of fucking and rarely fuck. I care most about my music; most important, have to be able to compose as much as possible."

I assured her I would never stand in the way of her work. I mainly needed to be financially supported, left alone, fucked, told I'm a wonderful writer.

"Although I've never really had a home," she murmurs, "I'm very naive. I've been carefully guarded all my life, so know nothing of the more real and despairing world. I'll never starve or die of bad medical care, for I can always rely on my parents for financial help, but I hate this society: its bases of money and power desires. Every night I dream I'm a member of the SLA I'm hiding from the police I can't figure where to hide. I don't know how most people exist, for they don't have parents like mine."

"I once worked in a sex show," I whispered.

"My parents love me will always help me, but they don't understand my politicism. They think Nixon, Kissinger, etc. are evil men deviates, not products of this way of life. They don't understand why I say I'm an anarchist and why I talk often, in performances, rather than play/have other people play my music so I can tell people as much as possible about myself. I hate any privacy. I'm slow; I do things slowly; I'm quiet and stubborn. Reliable, for I am so slow. My mother's scared I'm not reliable because I don't want to be a secretary: when I have to have shit jobs, I hate working them announce so. My mother says I shouldn't feel this way. She wants me to depend on her; she worries I might love some other woman besides her. I have ten other brothers."

"You're just blabbering, dear child." I place my hands on my narrow hips. "You need a man to care for you: a real man whose lap you can rest your head in; whom you can tell all your troubles to. You need to live with someone more, more objective than your parents. Do you believe in marriage?"

"I'd never thoughtfully do anything this society approved of. I admire Tania, Yolanda, Teko, Cujo, Zoya, the others who were willing some did lay down their lives for their visions. I wish I had their courage."

I took her thin hand, led her out of the ball. At first she began to turn away from me, but then, her body trembling, let me take her where I would. I knew she planned each of her tremblings, each of her symptoms of fear as a further means of seducing me. As we left the large wood house, the winds swept her long blonde hair away from her shoulder. She gathered her velvet cape more closely around her. On one street, in the shadows of the building, we saw a man leaning over a body: either he was robbing the body, or beating it. Dogs snapped at us, ran away from our empty footsteps. On another street, in an apartment consisting of one room, we saw a woman dying of starvation: she was too fat to move, too poor to get anyone to help her. Fifteen children and two parents lived in another room: they were allowed to live there free because the father did the janitoring for the building: they couldn't get Welfare because the father worked as janitor; since he didn't actually make any money, they were starving. In a hospital for the poor, an old man sat too sick to walk from his wooden chair to the curtain which was the doctor's booth; a half hour later we saw a policeman tell old man "no loitering here" throw him on the street. Then we saw angels rise out of the sky: blue, green, and red angels: we saw their huge hands hang over the buildings. I sat down on the street: I could no longer do anything: I could only think about myself.

I saw Peter slowly take off her clothes, and dance around naked the cold night street. First slowly, then faster and faster twirling arms bent so the fingertips touch. I see a library empty of books, and walk into it. Large empty rooms upon rooms connected by halls, then central and side-staircases going from hall to hall. Viola Woolf's Dancing School. Ten or fifteen girls in cocktail and formal gowns surround me. One girl wears a long white chiffon dress, a red ribbon around her waist. We're on the lowest floor. I begin to walk up the central staircase toward the dancing-class room. Ahead of me's the evil man. I begin to chase him, catch him! We race up the central staircase, each staircase dividing on the next floor to the sides, into two side staircases, run up a staircase to my left. Empty unknown rooms upon empty unknown rooms, more and more scared, up the third central staircase to that floor, I see the murderer leaning against the bannister of the central staircase. Surrounded by my friends: he jumps to reach the next lower staircase to get away; he misses the staircase falls through the narrow opening between the central and the horizontal side staircase, through the next opening, through the next opening: as he falls his left hand grabs the hand of one of the girls: as she falls, her hand grabs another person's hand, etc. I watch the bodies of my friends fall smack! break against the metal stairs. I watch my friends die. I understand they want to die. I rush over to stop them: I convince them to stop. The rest of the people, about a third left, hold on to the bannisters as hard as they can.

I see everyone I know taking off their clothes, flinging their limbs around without control until they have some sense of their bodies; transcending every possible barrier then every barrier. On the dog shit and garbage of the Paris streets.

I see 10- and 11-year-old boys and girls on the streets drinking bottle after bottle of wine because they have nothing else to do. In the laundermat one girl tells a boy her boyfriend's beating her up. Boy: "Do you want to marry me? I've never been married." Girl: "I don't know. I have to go somewhere." Boy: "Why don't you marry me?" Girl nods; they share pills. Boy puts his head on girl's lap: finishes bottle of Ripple. Almost passes out. 40-year-old Spanish man enters: tells boy and girl to go with him. They do. I see murderers all the time around me, a slow beginning rising white-yellow light, rising like dust from the streets at night, I see ecstasy everywhere, and I want to be there totally insane

Peter's still dancing around. I'm scared a cop will see us, bust us. I can hardly see anything. I have to protect Peter because I'm the stronger: the man.

"Come, my darling," I whisper to Peter. "We'd be warmer in my house: it's more luxurious. We"

Suddenly I found myself at my lodgings. Peter was leaning, gracefully and elegantly, on my arm.

I see a stream, strong current, which lifts me up, over a rise, then downward. I walk down a hall: to my right and left I see rooms which are perfect: To my right a red-brown room, a dark desk which contains tiny objects this is an Alice-in-Wonderland room. Again to the right my baby room: a light room light blue very few objects. To the left a magic room dark blues and browns more furniture. I want to look in/at each of these rooms for a long time, but I can't I have to get to the final room as quickly as possible. So far I'm ahead. I walk fast down the wood, the red velvet carpeted, hallway. Finally I reach the end room, an empty wide hall then a wall that looks like yellow metal. I turn left upward into a large gym, then other room, about four rooms spiraling downward until I reach a laundry, dark reds and browns and blacks, below the level of the first hall. Go back into the hall: nowhere else to go. I think to myself I lost because I didn't examine the magic rooms carefully therefore learn everything. I moved too fast. Now the other people have caught up to me. I have to return examine every room carefully. I no longer care if I win: I'm interested in the magic rooms. I'm playing a game, a huge board on the biggest table imaginable, which mirrors the hallway journey I just made. My father and someone else play against me. We start at different points, move around the board toward different goals. The stream or current which first lifted me is now football. Football is the first goal. I'm almost there; my father's slightly ahead of me. My black men change into large purple grapes which I pick (to get more men) from the center of the board. The sun is extremely bright almost blinding.

There are three kinds of change. Start with a present (a present time interval). Take Peter and me as the individuals occurring in this present.: (1) Peter precedes me; or I precede Peter. (2) Peter and I occupy together; and Peter disappears, I remain. (3) Peter only: Peter moves, changes color, etc. Or me only: I move, change color, etc. A present duration supposedly means no change. Consider (2). In (2), Peter's and my durations overlap: overlapping is the essence of duration. Because duration must be more complicated than (1) which can be presented by a series of dots on a time line. (3) is continuity: (2) and (3) are the ingredients of duration (or of the present). Apply this notion to duration to another individual: that of identity. My identity at any time depends on (my) lacks of stabilities.

Remembering my second task:

I ask Bob if I can use the typewriter. All day and night. "Yes." The ribbons I have don't fit: I buy a new ribbon. I'm typing away; Bob asks if I'm going to use the typewriter today and tomorrow, he has some work. "Just today I'm typing new book I've got a deadline tomorrow." "You'd better let me use it: you can use it later tonight do it all then. Get out of here." Everyone's looking at me: I gather my stuff get out. Down steps to where everything is green and yellow. Peter (my brother) yells at me because he and I are doing a book with Bob I'm not acting professionally. I walk across thick grass to car: I don't make it plop down on sidewalk and cry. I'm a poet and what I do is sacred. The people who keep me from the few lousy instruments I need to disseminate this crap are evil. They're using the instruments for business. I don't do business. They've no regard for those activities which are sacred.

Tonight is the night of the ball given by subscribers to the Opera. All of Paris will be there: the artists who know nothing, rich bankers who prey on the blood of the poor, for everyone is poor who works, who thinks he or she has power over his or her own life, revolutionaries hiding from the maws of the police which are the maws of the rich by pretending they are interested only in pleasure; women who know their sexuality is endless and holy; the garbage riffraff who live below the gutters of the street who see everything that happens. The philosophers of the city who know that the city and this way of life are doomed.

I'm in love with Peter, a man who is capable of deceiving both sexes. He usually wears the clothes of women: long white silk skirts with thin nets of white snow shawls: in them he looks like a female faun and like a young boy who adores to tease.

Although Peter is a male, I don't regard his gender as a defect. Despite the event (fact) that he didn't choose his sex, I don't dislike men. They are, by nature or by societal conditioning, cruel, arrogant, selfish, proud, stupid, stubborn, unwilling to admit their stupidity, willing to be friends only with those people they deem lower than themselves such as women; but they can be charmed taught into being otherwise. They have some good characteristics, though I can't at the moment think what these are. They can be tamed; and, if treated with some severity and care, can make excellent consorts. Lately I've thought how little my identity matters, how physical necessities are slowly making this splendor as I know it change, causing a new world I have no idea of. I have no feelings about this change: I simply observe it. As if individuals don't matter. Night in this city is incredibly beautiful: black branches floating against an unfixed moon; tiny stars mirror streetlamps mirror etc. I'm not sure if I want,

As a poet actually I'm an agent for the SLA. My mission is to reveal the uncertainties, unimportances, and final equivalences of all identities. Transformation to what? What changes are necessary will occur despite fear and greed. I'm not interested in being a hero. I've nothing to say, nor teach. I'm going to the Opera ball to contact another agent, PP (or Peter) who's fleeing from the CIA, needs shelter, a way of reaching his next contact. I have to pretend I'm in love with Peter.

Obviously I'll attract Peter most if I appear as a man. It hardly matters to me.

A dark blue suit, scarf, large shirt, my heavy brown boots: I care little about clothes. I look like a young, too sedately dressed boy. 20 or 22

When I enter the ball, the large dark house on the Rue de Montparnasse lit by a thousand flickering lamps, insect lights circling around the black house, I see no one: a white room too brightly lit, too dazzling and brilliant for my eyes to adjust to. I walk from room to room: each room brighter than the last. Finally I see a tall, slender woman dressed in white furs; a long cloak trailing on the polished lights made of alternating feathers and white skunk, a thin gown of silk through which her pink-tan skin gleams. This is Peter. I ask her if she would like to

I'm dreaming of fucking again and again, again and again because I'm never satisfied. The revolution is taking place, as "Blue" Gene says, without, for there are no, climaxes. I do whatever I want to do: if any one/event opposes me, I do what I can to erase that opposition, and slowly I'm changing. The revolution is taking place, as "Blue" Gene says, because "innate" and "learned" are no longer viable descriptions: "inside the mind" and "outside the mind" are no longer viable descriptions. The revolution is taking place, as "Blue" Gene says, day follows night night follows day. I have to decide whether I'm an SLA agent or a woman transvestite who's wildly in love with the most gorgeous fag in town. I walk slowly through this decaying city, this city composed of lights, glistening lights and black skies, all about to explode to the Assembly where the ball is being held. As I enter the ball, the huge grey house on the corner of the Rue de Montparnasse, I see no one: dark masqued shapes pass me as they quietly shit on the floor.

I ask Peter to dance with me. She quivers, moves slightly away from me. Taking her arm, I lead her through the white adjoining room into a darker alcove.

"What is your name, my dear? What're you doing here at your young age?"

"I'm old enough to do what I want," she replies. Underneath her long thick eyelashes, she shyly glimpses my body.

"Listen," I gently stroke the hair on her right arm, "I've been searching a long time for a woman like you: gentle, tender. A woman I can make demands on, such as to support me; who'll make no demands on me I can't satisfy. I become guilty extremely easily, won't stand being bossed around. A woman who'll flirt with me, wait 'till I want to have sex with her, then be passionate and relaxed; who'll always want to live with me, but not own me. Who'll adore my writing."

"I'm very scared," her blue eyes burn into mine, "of losing my independence. I never want to be situated such that I'm imprisoned."

The lights of the party went black.

"I need to feel both stable and able to do whatever I want whenever I want. I'm quite bourgeois in my tastes: I like liquor, dope, I'm decadent. I'm scared of fucking and rarely fuck. I care most about my music; most important, have to be able to compose as much as possible.

I assured her I would never stand in the way of her work. I mainly needed to be financially supported, left alone, fucked, told I'm a wonderful writer.

"Although I've never really had a home," she murmurs, "I'm very naive. I've been very carefully guarded all my life, so know nothing of the more real evil and despairing world. I'll never starve or die of bad medical care, for I can always rely on my parents for financial help, but I hate this society: its bases of money and power desire. Every night I dream I'm a member of the SLA I'm hiding from the police I can't figure where to hide. I don't know how most people exist, for they don't have parents like mine."

"I once worked in a sex show," I whispered.

"My parents love me will always help me, but they don't

understand my politicism. They think Nixon, Kissinger, etc. are evil men deviates, not products of this way of life. They don't understand why I say I'm an anarchist and why I talk often, in performances, rather than play/have other people play my music so I can tell people as much as possible about myself. I hate any privacy. I'm slow; I do things slowly; I'm quiet and stubborn. Reliable, for I am so slow. My mother's scared I'm not reliable because I don't want to be a secretary: when I have to have shit jobs, I hate working them announce so. My mother says I shouldn't feel this way. She wants me to depend on her; she worries I might love some other woman besides her. I have ten other brothers."

"You're just blabbering, dear child." I place my hands on my narrow hips. "You need a man to care for you: a real man whose lap you can rest your head in; whom you can tell all your troubles to. You need to live with someone more, more objective than your parents. Do you believe in marriage?"

"I'd never do anything thoughtfully this society approved of. I admire Tania, Yolanda, Teko, Cujo, Zoya, the others who were willing some did lay down their lives for their visions. I wish I had their courage."

I took her thin hand, led her out of the ball. At first she began to turn away from me, but then, her body trembling, let me take her where I would. I knew she planned each of her tremblings, each of her symptoms of fear as a further means of seducing me. As we left the large wood house, the winds swept her long blonde hair away from her shoulders. She gathered her velvet cape more closely around her. On one street, in the shadows of the building, we saw a man leaning over a body: either he was robbing the body, or beating it. Dogs snapped at us, and ran away from our empty footsteps. On another street, in an apartment consisting of one room, we saw a woman dying of starvation: she was too fat to move, too poor to get anyone to help her. Fifteen children and two parents

lived in another room: they were allowed to live there free
because the father did the janitoring for the building: they
couldn't get Welfare because the father worked as a janitor;
since he didn't actually make any money, they were starving.
In a hospital for the poor, an old man sat too sick to walk from
his wooden chair to the curtain which was the doctor's booth.
A half hour later we saw a policeman tell old man "no loitering
here" throw him on the street. Then we saw angels rise out of
the sky: blue, green, and red angels: we saw their huge hands
hang over the buildings. I sat down in the street: I could no
longer do anything: I could only think about myself.

I saw Peter slowly take off her clothes, and dance around
naked the cold night street. First slowly, then faster and faster
twirling arms bent so the fingertips touch. I see a library of
empty books, and walk into it. Large empty rooms upon rooms
connected by halls, then central and side-staircases going from
hall to hall. Viola Woolf's Dancing School. Ten or fifteen girls
in cocktail and formal gowns surround me. One girl wears a
long white chiffon dress, a red ribbon around her waist. We're
on the lowest floor. I begin to walk up the central staircase
toward the dancing-class room. Ahead of me's the evil man. I
begin to chase him, catch him! We race up the central staircase, each staircase dividing on the next floor to the sides, into
two side staircases, run up a staircase to my left. Empty unknown rooms upon empty unknown rooms, more and more
scared, up the third central staircase to that floor. I see the
murderer leaning against the bannister of the central staircase.
Surrounded by my friends: he jumps to reach the next lower
staircase to get away. He misses the staircase falls through the
narrow opening between the central and the horizontal side
staircase, through the next opening, through the next opening.
As he falls his left hand grabs the hand of one of the girls. As
she falls, her hand grabs another person's hand, etc. I watch
the bodies of my friends fall smack! break against the metal

stairs. I watch my friends die. I understand they want to die. I rush over to stop them: I convince them to stop. The rest of the people, about a third left, hold on to the bannisters as hard as they can.

I see everyone I know taking off their clothes, flinging their limbs around without control until they have some sense of their bodies; transcending every possible barrier then every barrier. On the dog shit and garbage of the Paris streets.

I see 10- and 11-year-old boys and girls on the streets drinking bottle after bottle of wine they have nothing else to do. In the laundermat one girl tells a boy her boyfriend's beating her up. Boy: "Do you want to marry me? I've never been married." Girl: "I don't know. I have to go somewhere." Boy: "Why don't you marry me?" Girl nods; they share pills. Boy puts his head on girl's lap: finishes bottle of Ripple. Almost passes out. 40-year-old Spanish man enters: tells boy and girl to go with him. They do. I see murderers all the time around me, a slow beginning rising white-yellow light, rising like dust from the streets at night, I see ecstasy everywhere, and I want to be there totally insane

Peter's still dancing around. I'm scared a cop will see us, bust us. I can hardly see anything. I have to protect Peter because I'm the stronger: the man.

"Come, my darling," I whisper to Peter. "We'd be warmer in my house: it's more luxurious. We'"

Suddenly I found myself at my lodgings. Peter was leaning, gracefully and elegantly, on my arm.

I see a stream, strong current, which lifts me up, over a rise, then downward. I walk down a hall. To my right and left I see rooms which are perfect: To my right a red-brown room, a dark desk which contains tiny objects. This is an Alice-in-Wonderland room. Again to my right my baby room. A light room light blue very few objects. To the left a magic room dark blues and browns more furniture. I want to look in at each of these rooms for a long time, but I can't. I have to get to the final room as quickly as possible. So far I'm ahead. I walk down wood, red velvet carpeted, hallway. Finally I reach the end room, an empty wide hall then a wall that looks like yellow metal. I turn left upward into a large gym, then other room, about four rooms spiraling downward until I reach a laundry, dark reds and browns and blacks, below the level of the first hall. Go back into the hall. Nowhere else to go. I think to myself I lost because I didn't examine the magic rooms carefully therefore learn everything. I moved too fast. Now the other people have caught up to me. I have to return examine every room carefully. I no longer care if I win: I'm interested in the magic rooms. I'm playing a game, a huge board on the biggest table imaginable, which mirrors the hallway journey I made. My father and someone else play against me. We start at different points, move around the board to different goals. The stream or current which first lifted me is now football. Football is the first goal. I'm almost there. My father's slightly ahead of me. My black men change into large purple grapes which I pick (to get more men) from the center of the board. The sun's extremely bright almost blinding.

There are three kinds of change. Start with a present (a present time interval). Take Peter and me as the individuals occurring in this present.: (1) Peter precedes me; or I precede Peter. (2) Peter and I occur together; and Peter disappears, I remain. (3) Peter only: Peter moves, changes color, etc. Or me only: I move, change color, etc. A present duration supposedly means no change. Consider (2). In (2), Peter's and my durations overlap: overlapping is the essence of duration. Because duration must be more complicated than (1) which can be presented by a series of dots on a time line. (3) is continuity: (2) and (3) are the ingredients of duration (or of the present). Apply this notion of duration to another individual: that of identity. My identity at any time depends on (my) lacks of stabilities.

I was born evil and became more evil and more evil by chance. Chance is fate. It's impossible for a man to know how to live. In this city which is based on money-lust oversexuality poverty false anthropomorphism suffering, I can do nothing else but act as part of the city: evil out of love.

First I remember my past. All our thinking (acting) is based on remembering. I remember nothing before I was in school. I'm six years old. My parents are weak: too weak to curb my proud desires, my ungovernable passions. I have to fuck.

I live in an old rambling house: half of the lower part of which served as the schoolhouse. Half-dead trees swung over the rotting eaves of the house. At night I can hear them scratching at mauling the thin glass windows. The house to me is a house in a dream. Wherever I am in the house is, at the moment, the whole universe. The room I'm in is large and white: Thin lines of brown wood around the windows on one side of the room. A raised wood dais on which stands a similarly colored podium. Wood chairs the old-fashioned kind raised writing tables on the lower part of the floor. The room is empty. I walk around it, hear my footsteps. I like most to be alone, not worrying about having to make friends. My schoolmates respect me, even worship me, and stay away from me. When I'm alone I live in a vision in which each sensation, no matter whether pleasurable or displeasing, each thought becomes framed in blackness. I become more and more aware of everything. In such a state I can't stand the presences of my schoolmates. Children are monsters prefer to be alone. The women who have them are stupid. I remember the schoolyard, the yard around the house, as if it were yesterday. It's autumn: the grass yellow and brown. Damp from the beginning rains. Around me my schoolmates yell. They throw around a white ball. But they seem distant to/from me: separated from me by an impassable wall. I feel strange, and as yet unsure of myself. I feel, as if physically, uneasy. I live from emotion to emotion: my emotions are more vivid, important to me than any perception any event I know happens. I remember through emotions the emotions are colors: dull orange-brown, dull yellow, grey. In diagonal rectangles. I remember everything is sad. Finally I begin to remember events.

I remember the same school-yard: now at the beginning of winter: wet cold against my burning face skin my face is burning red grey. Ice which is almost rain under my feet. No one's around me. To my left, in one of the endless nooks recesses nests of wall shadows of the school, are two dark grey shadows. Shadows, I think, of people. The flakes of water hit me harder, burning me; I become strangely happy. Why, I don't know. I see everything clearly. I see the leafless branches sway above my head and bend. I'm not thinking about class, about the professors, about the work I haven't yet done. The top of my head, where my hair is scant, feels damp and cold.

I begin to perceive stories. The professors who walk through the thin wood halls at night are boy-eating ghouls. The halls are huge oceans in whose depths mangled sailors float. I'm on a wood ship, and only I'm, safe. I'm being pursued by a mad teacher grey hair flying straight from his head at least seven feet tall beats my head each time he nears me with a heavy black-leather book. In one hand he has a chain. Then I perceive stories I believe are true: I'm in the school-yard; a big boy with short blond hair comes up to me. Too close to me. Puts his hands on my shoulders my white shirt. He shakes me. Hard. "You're fat. You're weird." I want to tell him I hate him. "You look like a guinea pig." I don't remember stories. I remember simple events, then imagine (give meaning to the events) or remember my imagining stories.

I remember only one friend. He was evil like me. Evil means freak. There're those people who are freaks, and those people who aren't. Freaks know they're freaks. He had thin blond hair which flew around his head like a halo. He was between short and medium height. Fat. Blue eyes which changed colors like the wings of angels. His name, like mine, is Peter Gordon.

Like mine, his family is slightly, not very, wealthy. His father is a weak, vacillating man who beats his mother whenever he can. About his mother I know little. She probably had several lovers, was tall and thin like a man. He arrived at the school the same day I did. We were rumored by the older boys to be relatives. However I'm an only child. So are my mother and father. Unlike me, he's quiet and self-contained. Unlike me, he never makes a fool of himself. Unlike me, he whispers.

One night, late that night, I decided to visit Peter. I was unable to sleep. The winds were banging more fiercely than usual against the thin panes of window-glass: I thought arms were about to reach to me, slowly shred my skin into tiny bits. The arms were huge crabs. Yellow blood ran all over my body. I wrapped my lamp in a blanket to cut off its light. Barefoot, in a long white nightshirt, I started walking through the halls. I saw this in a dream. I started screaming and screaming. I walked even more slowly down those endless hallways, between each hallway three or four steps either up or down, hallways upon hallways, so I rarely knew where I was. The worn-out rug muffled my footsteps. Sudden corners. Gusts of wind. I slowly took off my nightshirt. Leaving my fat body naked. My skin felt slightly damp, and cold. I reached Peter's closet. Took my lamp, rewrapped blanket around it, left it outside. Noiselessly entered. Listen to his breathing: heavy almost nasal, regular. Since he's asleep, go outside to get light. Again approach bed. Slowly draw open the curtains of the bed; let bright rays fall vividly on Peter's body. As if in a mirror that changes everything from right to left. My desire repeated in a mirror that changes everything from right to left. Was this-this Peter's fat guinea-pig face? I saw indeed it was his, but I shook, feverish, pretending it was not. What was there about him to confound me in this manner? I gazed while my brain reeled with a multitude of incoherent thoughts. Not thus he appeared in the vivacity of his waking hours! The same name! The same contour of person! The same day of arrival at the academy! I knelt, placed my lips on his lips. His face moved slightly to the left. I buried my head in the right nook of his shoulder, between his neck and the upper beginning of his arm. My skin felt warm; no longer wet. I lay still, without moving, on top of him, as I felt his arms go round my back and head, hold me to him. My body, my stomach which is the center of my body, felt warm, no longer here. I could feel my cock beginning to rise. He murmured, shifted under me, his cock beginning to rise.

I left school. I begin truly to live without friends. My friends aren't friends but people I grab on to. We steal together and drink together. Now events become clearer: I remember events more clearly. I remember events more clearly because I remember more clearly about my parents: My father is weak because he wants to be weak: he marries a woman he knows doesn't love him he also knows won't leave him because she desperately needs someone who'll love her. He works nine hours a day managing some factory. His wife is rich. When she finally nags him too long and too hard, he begins to whine. Beats her up. She dislikes him; needs him. He has two serious heart attacks he's 52 years old. When he's in the hospital, outside his hospital room, my mother's mother says, "He was always a good husband to you, Claire." Mother, "Yes." Grandmother "He never left you always took care of you, even though you never loved him." Mother, "Yes." My father listens to all this. Nothing changes.

The first event I remember is hating him for being so weak and stupid, and hating my mother for other, more complicated reasons. My mother hates me; she pays no attention to me. Yells at me because I don't tell her enough times I love her. I hate her because she hates me confuses me is mean avaricious frightened. She's beautiful and intelligent: fucked herself over.

My first meaning-relation (remembering) to the world is hatred. I can begin to remember other events. Prior to hating my parents: I hate them because they don't act the way I want them to act. Because I perceive (remember perceiving) them not acting the ways I want them to act. I don't want them to do anything to get money, self-importance, etc. My first remembering is my desire not to perceive events as they are.

I laugh at anyone who tells me, if I try, I can overcome my jealousy and lust. My needs are violent. My mother taught me, before I was sent to school and learned to read, to play cards. Every afternoon I would play Canasta and Spite-and-Malice with her. She would win, take my meager penny savings. She said her husband didn't give her enough money. If I wouldn't play cards with her, she wouldn't talk to me, not to punish me, but because I only existed when I played cards. She tried to make me. Therefore I don't like people getting too close to me.

She would lie on her bed naked. Huge brown nipples. The

skin of her hips had small holes in it. Order me to get a glass
of ice water which I'd do. Tell me to take off my clothes, lie
down next to her. Begin licking the bottom of her feet, then
the skins between her toes, then her slender ankles. Nothing
else. She would tell me my father couldn't fuck her because he
worked too hard fell asleep as soon as he got home each night.
Ate raw onions with his meals. (I saw this.) Was too stupid and
dumb to see movies.

She would talk on the phone for hours to her friends. When
I was in the room, she would talk about me as if I weren't there.
I always scared she was talking about me behind my back. At
night I used to edge against the dark green, now black, wall to
the edge of their room. So softly: they couldn't possibly hear
me if they were still awake. Listen at the edge of the door.
Sometimes they were awake talking. I could hardly hear what
they said. Once I heard my father say I was too proud head-
strong selfish.

She would tell my father she had all the money. She supported him. He would whine. At night she would lie on her
bed; he would lie snoring on his bed. (The beds were next to
each other.) She would tell me he was stupid, slept all the time.
He never fucked her. Then she asked him why he didn't get
it up. He snores. I sit on the floor next to the ends of their beds.
When they fall asleep, I leave the room.

After a lapse of several months, I found myself at Eton, a
small college for men in Waltham, Massachusetts. I wanted
little to do with people, but found myself drawn to them. I
wanted to adjust myself to the ways of other people. I wanted
to become exactly like my rich and carefree schoolmates. I
began to drink. Since I was underage, a friend of mine would
sneak into my rooms a few bottles of some pale red and dry
white wine. At first I would drink only a few cups to diminish
the violence of my thoughts and put myself, each night, to
sleep. I drank alone and in secret.

Gradually I began to distinguish among the faces that surrounded me. I would go out with a few of my friends on stealing forays. We knew exactly which stores in Boston surveyed their customers with hidden TV cameras, which store-owners would prosecute caught thieves, which pretended to be "hip" "nonprofit" "cultured" etc. and ripped their customers off. One of my friends, a gorgeous boy named Phil Harmonic, was fortunate in having the looks of a beautiful woman. Brown filmy hair stood out from his face like a halo. His cheekbones protrude, high, like spears. He always stole in his finest clothes. One day he walked into Abraham & Strauss, one of the better department stores in Boston. He was wearing a well-cut woolen coat. He took off the coat, put on a mink coat cut to frame his body, and walked out.

I found stealing was an addiction. I became more and more excited; I stole more, no way of calming myself. I stole every day. I began to drink more and more. Phil, I learned, also drank, and my drinking became social. I was, after all, a rich boy in a rich school: I was learning to become part of the leisured society. I drank, as before, to calm myself. To hope for sleep. But I soon noticed that my drinking no longer calmed me and threw me into a, if not deep, prolonged stupor. When drunk I seemed to become more excited than I had ever been. I became able to perceive realities, or rather, the emotions of this reality I had not yet been able to perceive. Emotions that were now so penetrating I could almost not stand to exist.

I can only describe what I now perceived as colors. Grey which never changed. Entered my head and burned. Tiny dots of yellow existed on the surface of light and dark greys. The greys were most important: light and dark greys took over, they swarmed like American pesticides through all living being.

I found that the awareness I had when drunk I could no longer have when sober. I needed these awarenesses. I needed to know the passions still existed. All wasn't an unchanging dullness, a horror, as it was when I was sober. An unchanging

dullness in which everything I could possibly do was stupid
worthless. I finally knew, when drunk, that jealousy, fear, adora-
tion, lust, murder were still possible. A possibility for revolution. I craved alcohol more and more.

I became two people. I now think the worst disease of our
time is schizophrenia. Usually, usually!, I was reserved. More
than slightly shy, and extremely intelligent. I liked most to
listen to good conversation and fuck. In my spare moments I
even composed music. When drunk, I was exactly the opposite: I talked rapidly and ferociously. I only cared for other
people to the degree to which they were satisfying my immediate wants. Paradoxically, I became too scared: too aware of the
violence and endlessness of my needs, to fuck. I began to
separate myself: to watch the violence of my desires more and
more.

Let me give you an example: Three years of my schooling
have passed. Phil and I, two other men who, like us, are rich,
lie sprawled next to each other. For hours we've been drinking,
been throwing away costly wines. We began trying to forget
the stupor we had fallen into (our awareness of this stupor) by
asserting our preferences for our way of life even more strongly:
not by repeating our drunken raptures of earlier nights, but by
increasing our debaucheries. Whatever play (gambling, profan-
ity, etc.) we liked least we made sure to do. Most of all, we
didn't want to stand still. As I was about to toast this life, the
only glory man knows: my servant clumsily opened the door to
the room, and beckoned me.

I followed him into my hallway. The room was still, almost
faded, but sort of shimmering. Its middle part was turning
slowly vertically. A stranger walked up to me: a man about five
feet ten inches tall, stout with thinning blond hair. I think
that's how he looked. He looked at me, slowly whispered name:
"Peter Gordon." His whisper made me remember I lunged at
him I couldn't contain myself. But he fled.

■

I turned more and more to vice. The clink of coins, the heavy smoke, the masculine sweat and wine. I became a gambler. I now live in earnest two lives: On the one hand, I'm a young wealthy man. My house, at night, is open to anyone, that is: to any young man who is also rich. I'm hospitable and gener- ous. I've some vices: pride, a desire for overexcitement, irrita- bleness I have no control over. But in a young man who is wealthy, well-born, amiable, these vices are enchantments.

On the other hand, I'm the lowest of the low. A gambler who preyed on the stupidities of my friends. A man who lived by mauling those closest to him. I denied all possibilities of love and friendship. I was scared, and I craved danger. No one but I knew of these two identities.

I would sit quietly at the gambling table, drinking a little, looking as if I were drinking much more. Actually I was in a frenzy. I was totally intoxicated. I thought only of the play: the plans I constantly changed, the images of myself I constantly changed so I could win. I didn't think about my possible ruin. I was a calculating machine I was scum.

I had no feelings for my fellow players: I simply determined their stupidities: the amounts of their wealth and their inabili- ties (or abilities) to win at play. One young man named Glen- dinning was especially idiotic. He had almost no hair on his head, and whined as he talked. He had formerly been a top football player. Often his hand would reach under his pants to scratch. I could see the bulge of his hand under the thick grey woolen material. I calculated he was rich.

Glendinning arrived that night in a white brocade coat to the chambers in which we were to play. It was already dark and misty. My host had thoughtfully provided candles.

We'd been playing for several hours. Glendinning was a fool: he thought he was smarter than me. I knew better than to make judgments. I remember the top of his head looked grey.

I remember details clearly. I was absolutely calm and in a total frenzy. The room looked totally red. I had some stupid fantasy about dogs: one dog, a light brown mutt low, was tearing at the mouth of another dog. The left side of the mouth began to bleed. Both dogs were emitting a low constant growl as cats do in their most vicious fights. I saw a voodoo doll in the distance. I began to win. I had to win: I had to make myself invulnerable. I made this happen: All the players but Glendinning withdrew. Glendinning doubled. I refused his double. He force me to accept his double. I became a liar. His face grew grey, white, ashen. I saw drops of sweat roll down his face. He was shaking; he was imploring my emotion without forcing himself to grovel at my feet.

I ignored these pleas. In a high-pitched voice he begs me let him redouble. I act as graciously with as much dignity as possible. I'm in a total frenzy; I know nothing. Glendinning piteously announces he's ruined.

I don't understand I feel nothing. Again my servant rushes into the rooms, followed by another man. The room was still, almost faded, but sort of shimmering. There were no lights. There's no cause-and-effect (narrative) except in language. I felt a warm hand lift my right hand. A voice two lips brush my right ear whisper into my right ear that name. Then, out loud, the voice told my friends the truth: "Search the pockets and cuff linings of Peter Gordon's smoking jacket. You'll learn his real character." Lips brush my ear: no more. My host tells me to leave his chambers and to leave Waltham, forever. "You are no gentleman: you're the scum of the earth."

The first time, I repeated one (writing) event simultaneously slightly changed that event. Repeated this changed event two times. Call the first event 'a'; the repetitions of 'a' (which, as I've said, are slightly different from 'a', 'b.') How do these events occur in time? 'a' occurs between zero and 'b.' 'b' occurs between 'a' and 'b.' 'b' occurs between 'b' and 'b.' 'b' occurs between 'b' and zero. Notice each event occurs between two events whose conjunction is unique.

The second time, I repeated one event once. I didn't change the event at all. Call the event 'a.' 'a' occurred between zero and 'a.' 'a' occurred between 'a' and zero.

This time I'll repeat an event three times. This time two of the time placements of the event are the same: Call the event 'a.' 'a' occurs between zero and 'a.' 'a' occurs between 'a' and 'a.' 'a' occurs between 'a' and 'a.' 'a' occurs between 'a' and zero.

Say there's two theories of time. Absolutist theory of time: the world is in time. The world, events occur in moments. These moments can be mapped on a time line. Relativist theory of time: time is in the world. Time is the temporal relations of events. An event can be earlier (later) than or simultaneous with another event. The first theory suggests that individuals (subjects) are the true substance. The second theory suggest that temporal characters are the true substance of the world.

I write down a certain number of words repeat those words again. Does the first unit of words mean the same as the repeated unit? That is, either events in time (as for time, for space) are isolated, or mutually dependent with regard to meaning not existence. (For a moment, skip problem of disjunction of meaning and existence.) If the meaning(s) of the writing events depend(s) at least partially on the temporal relations of the writing events, the relativist theory of time seems more accurate.

Intention: escape this horror as I know it and am made by it. How can I (I being a model of any individual) change? Assume the relativist theory of time accurately maps time in the world. "I change." What do I mean by "I"?

If I'm an individual and I persist over a period of time, I'm a substance. If I'm an individual and not a moment, I'm an ordinary individual. Right now (t_1) I'm picking my nose. Right now (t_2) I'm not picking my nose. "Picking my nose" is a relation between t_1 and me. "Not picking my nose" is a relation between t_2 and me. But what if there aren't distinct moments? If t_1 isn't distinct from t_2? (Relativist theory of time.) I'm an individual who is picking and not picking his nose. Contradiction. I can't be a substance, an individual who persists in time.

If I'm not an individual or if no individuals exist, no temporal relations exist. (In a world without individuals, any character can exemplify any other character. If temporal relations exist, a character could be simultaneously nose-picking and not-nose-picking. Contradiction.) By "I," I mean an unknown number of individuals. Each individual exists for a present duration and exemplifies one or more characters. These characters exist out of time. Example: "I change." "I" exemplifies "change"; "change" exists, is timeless.

This can't be totally accurate because when I remember, I remember an awareness, not an object. I don't remember my hamster, I remember seeing my hamster. Or: I remember seeing my hamster, I remember my hamster directly as I become my hamster, I go back and forth. If I do at any time remember (imagine, think about, etc.) an awareness, I must be a continuant. But when I remember an awareness, I don't repeat that awareness. My remembering seeing my hamster, I'm aware, differs from my seeing my hamster. Or "repeating" doesn't exist.

There are three kinds of change. Start with a present (a present time interval). Take Peter and me as the individuals occurring in this present: (1) Peter precedes me; or I precede Peter. (2) Peter and I occur together; and Peter disappears, I remain. (3) Peter only: Peter moves, changes color, etc. Or me only: I move, change color, etc. A present duration supposedly

involves no change. Consider (2). In (2) Peter's and my durations overlap: overlapping is the essence of duration. Because
duration must be more complicated than (1) which can be
presented by a series of dots on a time line. (3) is continuity.
(2) and (3) are the ingredients of duration (or of the present).
Continuity (identity) and change are mutually dependent.

If by "substance" I mean an individual who exists (continues) without change and totally independently, I'm not a "substance." Change (temporal relations) is a substance. If I'm not
a substance and yet am a subject, I'm an individual or number
of individuals. An individual happens only within a present
duration; an individual doesn't change. Therefore I'm composed of an unknown number of such individuals: I is a (predi-
cate) relation.

It was night of the ball given by subscribers to the Opera.
All of Paris will be there. The young who still think the people
they fuck will feel some affection for them. Artists wondering
how they can next cheat the phone company, if they'll ever
become well-known enough they can sell out get enough to eat.
Prostitutes dreaming of being artists. The poor who can have
no lovers, who long to die. Who would throw themselves
blazing rainbows of the night at every government that exists
if they thought their deaths could help. But nothing, they sit
on their beds, or rather their mattresses, better off then the
wretches who work. Night comes down now, the poor know,
for their sakes: the bill-collectors are silent. Most government
officials are off-duty.

As I walked through the crowded rooms of the Carnival, I
remembered being poor. I had come to New York to be an
artist: I thought I had to go to New York to be an artist. It was
summer. The air became hotter and hotter. People, driven
crazy by heat, hit each other over the heads and pissed on each
other's faces. To relax: they stole cars. I became extremely sick.
I was living with this weasel on a half-couch and a single

mattress in a large empty room. We were lying in "bed" about two in the morning. Suddenly I knew I was dying. Some organ a few inches above my cock about two inches under my abdomen skin exploded. The organ began seeping inside me all over the place. I screamed for the cops. I was scared. My lover called the cops, came back to me. He told me I probably wasn't dying. I was screaming too healthily.

The hospital was the worst hell I had ever been in. It was the clinic of the wealthiest hospital in New York. I see a tiny woman, a woman-boy, wandering around the yellow tiles in a huge filthy blue robe. She mumbles and asked the doctors to give her drugs so she won't go crazy. "Are you sick?" I'm almost in shock from the pain. "Two weeks ago I went to this dentist who took Welfare. I had a toothache." "Oh yeah." "He pulled a tooth then went searching for the root. He wanted to see if he still knew how to find a root." "Did he find it?" "Then he put some crap in my mouth. Told me to go away. A week later my mouth's pain. I went to this hospital." "Oh yeah." "They told me the dentist had dug into my mouth; left it to rot. Now I had a hole slightly under to the right of my nose about a fist big. They'd have to operate." "Are you O.K. now?" "It's a delicate operation cause of the sinuses. They'll have to operate a second time." "Are you going to sue them?"

Ahead of me I see an old guy sitting in a folding chair. Everyone's screaming pain. A doctor standing next to a filthy curtain which swings from a wood frame says, "Mr. Smith." The old guy kind of wiggles. "Mr. Smith." The old guy moves his shoulders forward. Gets them away from the chair. Slumps back. Nurse slaps old guy on back. "Come on Mr. Smith we have a lot of sick people here you can't take all day." Slaps him again walks away. I start hallucinating. A half hour later cop walks up to old guy. "Listen Mr. you can't loiter here." Carries him onto street.

Doctor walks in: I think she's a nurse. She tells me she's a

doctor. I lay down, she sticks a silver thing into my cock. Each
time she turns it, I hurt more. I start hurting so much I can't
think about anything else. Everything becomes total pain. I'm
screaming. Everyone in the examining room's screaming. I tell
the nurse to stop. Lenny tells me I'd hurt more if I was having
a baby. Finally she takes the thing out of my cock: the pain
begins to lessen. She tells me to wait. Later another woman
comes in with this huge needle. She tries to jab, no, bounce
needle into skin of my ass. Bounces off. She tries again. I'm to
go back to folding chairs, wait for my medicine. When the
doctor has the aluminum metal up my cock for a while, I begin
to hallucinate. I stop feeling the pain so badly.

I don't feel so bad. I remember watching a man vacuum the
floors. I see the floors are yellow. I don't remember.

Next event I remember: I go to booth to get my medicine.
Bottles of nembutal and darvon (the kind with synthetic code-
ine) I can renew three times. Come back Monday for further
treatment. No signs of gonorrhea. Sorry, I don't have any
money.

I start working a sex show to abolish all poverty and change
the world. I remember clearly: I would take antipain pills, put
on clothes, not good ones because they'd get ruined we had no
dressing room in sex show only room where dirty-movie-projec-
tor was, hot room but at least no one pissed in it, they pissed
everywhere else in that joint, really filthy black and white tile
floor. A private bathroom (noncustomer bathroom) downstairs
where the peepshows were because the customers always pissed
on the bathroom floor. I got to like one old guy who was so old
he could barely walk and really wanted to get it up. During one
show we were doing a routine (I think I was working with
Lenny) where I'd say I couldn't take my clothes off, Lenny was
trying to seduce me, because a cop in that building over there
(I'd point to the audience) was watching us. Lenny and I'd do
this when we saw cops in the audience, period of great bust

scare, I wasn't sure I'd take my underpants off cause I didn't want to get busted. Also wanted to tease cops. Lenny would try to get me to take my pants off. Old guy starts shouting "You can take your pants off" he takes over Lenny's lines: then he starts naming all the vegetables my cock is.

I was searching desperately for the beautiful wife of the Duke di Mentoni. She was the delight of Paris: a young angelic faithful wife. Her yellow hair was thin and fine as a parakeet's; her blue eyes were brighter, for me, than sapphires. At night I roam through the alleyways of the city, thinking only of my lust. Begging anyone, dog man woman, to help me. The night before she had communicated to me the secret of her costume, all women are too unscrupulous and foolish, I rush through the drunk crowds, suddenly I see the costume. As I struggle harder the crowds grow thicker and thicker. I can hardly move. Just as I'm about to touch her rich snow-white shoulder, to kiss I feel a light hand stroke my shoulder, that ever-remembered damnable whisper of my name in my ear.

I swirl around irritated drunk completely out of my control. I see a figure clothed entirely in black leather: wide flaring pants covered by an enormous sweeping cape. I'm dressed the same way. Masks of black leather entirely cover our faces.

"Scoundrel criminal," I whisper. "You've no right to tell me what to do. You shall not dog me unto death. Follow me, or I'll stab you where you stand."

I dragged him into an empty adjoining room, threw him against the wall. On my command he drew. The contest was brief. I was frantic with every species of wild excitement, and felt within my arm the energy and power of a multitude. I forced him by sheer strength against the wainscoting, and thus, getting him at mercy, plunged my sword with brute ferocity repeatedly through and through his bosom.

When I returned to where he lay, I thought I was hallucinating. I saw a large mirror where none had been perceptible before; as I stepped up to the mirror, I saw myself advancing pale and dabbled in blood.

This was not me: this was Peter Gordon. Unlike me he wore no mask nor cloak. I thought he was me as he stood there, the most beautiful man I've ever seen his skin shining as light. "You have conquered, and I yield. Yet henceforth art thou also dead—dead to the World as it now exists and as you hate it. In me didst thou exist—and, in my death, see by this image, which is thine own, how utterly thou has murdered thyself."

I told the guy I was living with I no longer wanted to fuck him. He told me to fuck or split. Then he started beating me up. I had to split fast. Either I could get a new apartment in New York City or split to California, the only other place I had friends. Either way I needed a lot of money. I was broke.

I was a nice shopgirl, working in Barnes and Noble eight to nine hours a day answering phonecalls. Eighty dollars a week takehome. I was a nice girl earning nice money. Nice money doesn't exist. I needed a lot of money. I figured I could sell my body, a resource open to most young women, not for a lot of money but at least for more than eighty dollars a week and less than eight hours a day. My friends were all respectable (i.e. had minimum money): I couldn't ask them shit. So I opened the back pages of the *Village Voice*. In less than three hours I became a go-go dancer. A go-go dancer is a strip-tease artist, midway in the hierarchy between a high-class call girl and a streetwalker.

I waited on the corner of 178th and Broadway, near the George Washington Bridge. It was a cold and windy night. A large car, a Chevy or Impala, pulled up; a white hand motioned me to get in. I didn't know if I was going to make money or get raped. I didn't have any choice. A guy got out of the car: a cheap Broadway crook. "Come on, get in the car. We've got a time schedule. Do'ya have an outfit?" he mumbled. Gee, I was scared.

The owner of the bar handed me five quarters and told me to put them in the juke box. Dance to 10 songs, rest an equal amount of time. I did what he told me. When I got off the dance floor, I didn't know what to do, I couldn't see anywhere to escape. I sat at an empty table. It was a crummy bar: all men no women. The men were workingclass creeps. A man came up to the table started to talk to me. I told him to go away. The bartender came up to me told me it was my job to talk to the men get them to buy me drinks. He told me I looked terrible. I walked up to the bar sat between two bearable-looking men. Turned out they were younger than me. They told me I was O.K. except my hair-cut made me look like a nigger. I had short curly hair all over my head. The bartender told me he was going to call up my agent to come get me because I was a creep. The men said he shouldn't do that they liked me. My agent told me I needed a costume then I'd be O.K. Gee, I was crying.

It was a sleazy Bronx tenement a high-rise made out of special New York plastic. I thought one of the kids was going to throw a bomb then I'd see a big hole. My agent rang the doorbell again and again. A woman with partly bald head partly gray hair whooshing all over the place dirty nightgown over her body tells us to come in. My agent should stay outside: she doesn't like men. My agent wants to come inside so he does. She tells me to take off all my clothes except for my stockings. Stockings make a girl feel more confident. I have a good body,

she touches my breasts, if I work hard, I'll go far. I feel terrific.
I tell her I like silver best. She has hundreds of costumes: two
bra cups held together by almost invisible elastic, a G-string (or
an almost G-string), that is: a triangle of cloth covering the
cunt (and part of the ass-crack) held together by slightly thicker
elastic: all this covered by gorgeous elaborate layers of pearls
silver beads silver metal disks. These are the simplest costumes:
each one costs eighty dollars.

It's a strange history.

Jean Galmot, the former mayor of San Francisco, after having been a gold-digger, trapper, rum and rosewood smuggler,
and journalist, has point-blank accused, before rendering his
last sigh, his political and private enemies of having him poisoned by his maid Tommie.

Three medical experts have been commissioned by the cops:
the doctors Fear, Gold, and the teacher Tyranny.

Mr. Povera, director of the Toxology Laboratory, takes
charge of a counter-examination.

And then it appears that the heart of Jean Galmot is no
longer there!

It's probably still in San Francisco.

"I leave my heart in San Francisco," Jean Galmot declared
to his San Francisco constituents in one of his inflamed proclamations whose secret he had and which had rendered him so
popular throughout the Land of the Penal Colony and of El
Dorado.

Have Galmot's faithful friends, desiring to follow their beloved, secretly eaten his heart?

Or has the corrupt disgusting capitalist police misplaced his
heart at the bottom of some drawer or dossier?

The heart, let us note, more than any other organ of the
body, bears the marks the signs of poisoning.

We must find the heart! But can we ever find our heart? And
in what state?

It's hard to believe the cops (i.e. Justice) are so stupid in San Francisco, they lose dead men's hearts . . .

Perhaps Justice wanted to lose Galmot's heart . . . Perhaps they wanted to cover up, just as in the Kennedy case, the so-called poisoning . . .

Already 35 important documents (which supposedly convicted the poisoners "cooked their goose") have been lost. While the witnesses, while every hippy and black person the cops could find on the scene of the crime are jailed, the poisoners roam loose, like the Zodiac killer, on the streets of San Francisco.

One newspaper has the following headline:

MAN WHO LOST HIS HEART

and the subtitle,

JUSTICE MISPLACED GALMOT'S HEART
MAID RECOMPENSES WHOEVER FINDS IT

I, for one, am impressed . . .

The newspaper has been made, it seems, to talk. Will they ever talk enough?

I got my costume, figured I needed more money. Seven dollars an hour was shit. I was learning fast. New York's a town in which a girl has to learn to think fast. I was in love with a guy: he wasn't in love with me. What did I care what I did? I started working the rougher clubs, the more expensive ones away from New Jersey and closer to New York, the ones where no workingclass white men but the Mafia who got their money from the workingclass white men bid, with that money, for the dancer, the ones where I made ten dollars an hour straight. Not that I could stay straight. Understand: a girl can make a good living without having to turn tricks. She can take her pearl and silver top off, full pouting lips, off slowly, slowly reveling in wiggling her tits in a customer's face. She can edge her black, O so seductive, lace panties to the edge of her cunt hair: reveal those dainty perky little kissy-koos. She can even more slowly slide her right hand along her damp hot skin, under the tight

elastic of the pants, under the see-through lace, so everyone can
see what this hot bitch is doing, O my god, to her thick slimy
lips. She can't restrain herself! There, in public, making herself
hotter and hotter, finger in cunt pie going round and round,
as finger slips black panties lower, she breathes harder and
harder . . . She can stick that sopping hot pussy in a customer's
face, and get amply repaid. She can, fully clothed, pick an older
man who'll of course do anything for her because she's so
ravishing, take his clothes off and stick a dildo up his ass. She
can go down on another dancer. Lesbianism is so wonderful.
She can fuck/or suck every guy in the place, there're never any
women, on top of the green pool table. All this, you understand, for money. A nice girl never does anything for free. At
first I was very shy. I was stupidly scared of men though they
wanted to rape me. I soon got over my abnormal fears. I knew
the man I loved, the man with long brown hair and perfect ass,
would always cherish and protect his beloved. The guys were
about my age, big brawny guys tough as they come. He-men.
Good Americans who worked hard and ably for their livings.
I was sitting at the bar between two of these studs. One asked
me to touch his cock. "Cut the crap." "Well, touch my thigh."
"Oh, yeah." "You want to fuck each of these guys in the back
room? Eight dollars a head? That'll be, uh," he counts, "almost
200 dollars. Lot of money for a girl." "No way." "I'll give you
a quarter if you touch my knee." I'm sitting beside this one
cause he seems the gentlest. "I'll touch your knee if you shut
up after that." "I'll do anything you say." I touch his knee with
a finger: he grabs for my breasts. "Get your hands off me
creep." We start over again. Now there's eight of them around
me. A gang-bang. I get up to dance. A guy with red hair tells
me he's going to rape me. I complain to the bartender cause
I'm too shy. I don't want to lose my virginity. The bartender
tells me the guy's his son. Tells me I'm cute he'll rape me
himself. What's a poor girl going to do?

I met Jean Galmot 1964.

Who's Jean Galmot?

It was during the '60's: those dreaded years of American economic success. Kennedy and all that. The real war was continuing, not the so-called cold war I grew up in, but the war of the rich against the poor. The rich to get richer; the poor to try to realize what the rich were doing. Who talks of the middle classes? Do they exist? I call these years THE BOHE-MIA OF FINANCES (that's what I called the art world today). I'm not talking about brothels, stupid, but the real evil: the secret combination of Rockefeller and Pentagon who bring to popularity while they cause the takeover of Chile and massacre of Chilean people, largest dope-smuggling poison-cut smack heroine in history, fake shortage of necessities to raise prices; own Argentina, Standard Oil Company (Standard, Mobil, Amoco, Arco, Esso, Enco, Amerikan, Chevron, Citgo, Exxon, Humble, Sinclair, Marathon, . . .), coffee, IBM, CBS, Borden, Anaconda, Metropolitan Life, Allied Chemical, Kimberly-Clark, ATT, Chemical Bank, American Express, Eastern, The Equitable, CPC International, Con Edison, Bank of New York, Consolidated Natural Gas, The Chase Manhattan Bank, Seamen's Bank, etc.

Was Jean Galmot another Rockefeller?

Was he a good guy?

In 1964, Jean Galmot was rumored to have billions. Dozens of hundreds? I don't know anything. But he had coke! Enough to fill Lake Michigan or the Mississippi River! He had gold too: Powder! Nuggets! Bars! All the nouveau riche, Jews-just-turned Gentile, porn kings, army kings in America buy Rolls'. Galmot must have had thousands! He was an arsonist, a man who would destroy buildings and people for the sake of destruction, a confirmed heterosexual!

Who really was this man?

An adventurer, a politician.

Where did he come from?

San Francisco.

He had to leave: fast. The clouds lay dark and gloomy over that city of delight.

Because this juvenile-delinquent-turned-politician loved artists of all kinds, because he loved to fuck all of them, we can assume he was evil. He was an ancient pirate. He proclaimed himself King of Black People. He then murdered his mother and father. He was always various people: a hard worker, a devoted friend, a cruel tyrant, an outrageous liar, a beast, a man-about-town, a patsy, an ascetic, a proud Nihilist, a decadent of the worst kind, a junkie, a self-made man who fucked his lover in public, an ex-prisoner. And his cock was tattooed with roses!

I was working in a tobacco store. Two sliding doors, electric bulbs, a small table, a notebook, 21 telephone lines were my whole world. I never saw the sun. All day I stared at four ugly grey walls. If the radiator was hissing, I knew it was winter. If the air-conditioner blew at my tear-stained face, I knew it was summer. The number of customers entering and leaving the store counted for me the passing minutes.

Every nine out of ten customers talked to me about Galmot!

Galmot existed. Artists questioned me. Journalists questioned me. Theater managers tried to get money out of me. Businessmen politicians men-of-leisure tried to trap me. Through me, trap Galmot. Make Galmot come into the open.

I wanted to kill myself because I had written this lousy book. It was the dead of night. The filthy alleyways were filled with corpses. The tattoo parlor on Mission had finally closed its doors: the freaks knew when to retire. A bad wind whistled its way around the empty streets, a grey dead wind, an evil disease smell . . .

I was rolling my ass around in the lousy bar on Folsom Street the Folsom Street Bar where they hold slave-auctions, trying to pimp for my friend Harmonic. I always work for free. A big, a leather-boy-dress-up approached me with a shiv. I wanted to know what he wanted. He didn't say anything. I kept backing up. I was the only woman in the joint; I was in disguise. He didn't say anything. I kept backing up. He got me in this small wood room which stunk of the piss of sex shows. Locked the door behind him. I figured I better do what he wanted: started taking off my clothes. There was a mystery. No good to scream in a bar where they hold slave auctions.

He started moving toward me more slowly: shiv aimed at my belly where my spirit lies. Moving closer. This wasn't any simple rape. Out of the corner of my left eye I see a window. Run through it screaming, run faster through the pieces of jagged glass, knives stick straight up from the streets, huge pieces of flat iron, I run from Folsom and 11th past 5th (street of winos) past the poisonous bus terminal over Electrocution Bay Bridge to the one person who'll help me take revenge.

He wears only faded blue jeans and sapphires. His earth brown hair curls around the crack of his perfect ass. He has a perpetual hard-on. Blue Cream

I was his whore and his partner. I'd sleep with men, with any men as long as they had enough money, then I'd sneak away from them, if I could: roll them, I'd jump out the window, run madly back to Blue. We'd look for a house, any empty house, where we could fuck and where we could sleep for the night.

"I was the last reject of the most powerful of all families: Acker: the last authentic descendant of the last Hungarian King. On April 18, 1947, my father was found assassinated in his bathtub. My mother, before she was due, started convulsing. While she was convulsing, she died. I came out. This's the fate of all women who're stupid enough to remain pregnant.

"I was born three months early. Fortunately for the world, I didn't die." Cream and I are in bed, fucking.

"I spent the first 100 days of my life in an incubator, sucking Peter's cock. Peter yanks me away from his cock: You didn't

bring me enough money today you fart-faced cunt! Monster
women surrounded me all the time. Now I hate women and
sentimentality. Much later in the apartment on Squalor Street,
in the Folsom Street prison, in this mental asylum I now live
in, the constant maids guards nurses employees friends EV-
ERYONE infuriate me. EVERYONE is Rockefeller, Justice,
Society. I'm never left alone. I'm never allowed to live as I
please. If my own free actions bother you, you can shoot me,
you understand, I'd prefer that. I want to be happy. This is San
Francisco. San Francisco is happiness. It's bizarre what I, or
you, have to do not do sometimes to be happy . . ."

I don't remember any people besides myself at first . . .

I remember sailors. I don't remember a nanny, a mommy,
or any such nonsense. Sailors have cared for me. Only an ass
hung over my cradle wood. Yes, that's the truth . . .

I'm three years old. I have a pretty pink robe. I'm always
alone. I love being alone. I love very much playing in the back
corners which smell good. Under the table. In the bathroom.
Behind the bed. I'm now four years old. I set the curtains on
fire. The greasy odor of the burnt cloth makes me convulse. I
feel so strongly, so thrillingly, I come. I eat raw lemons and
pieces of black leather. The smell of books, especially of poetry,
makes me puke again. I remember also I was sick for a long
time they made me drink insipid milk and orange water.

For several centuries The Squalor Street chateau's been my
dethroned family's refuge. The immense rooms, rooms on
rooms on rooms on rooms on rooms, lie deserted. Only a
well-trained squadron of servants dressed in blue and green
rhinestones—the family trademark—long mustaches, flowing
white feather capes over white silk short shorts. The cops patrol
all the entrances of the park. Vice-squad and narcs alternately
safeguarded our chateau.

I most admired the white Vice-Squad. I would pass through
the corridors drooling, watch the sentries clank their guns

against their cocks after the custom of the Austrian court who order the soldiers of the Monk to face the wall and rub when the Monk walks past them. For hours I would stare at these cops. I couldn't trick insult them though they were socially and absolutely below me, for I feared their blue uniforms, their regular jerky motions. I tried to figure out why they moved and acted so creepily. Like robots. Thus I began to love machines.

One day, in an endless meadow crickets luminescent sun etc., I began to dream of the new world: A world defined by the fact I could do whatever I want wherever whenever. I begin to faint, to disappear from this creepy world. I feel big strong arms around me I look into a cop's face. I feel shock and happiness. He was a gutter kid: a black leather hood. That's why the motor's, the machine's activity bound to images of hearing light sky space grandeur freedom enthrall me and balance me with a huge force.

One day the palace was upside-down. Orders are given in a high voice. The valet runs up and down the stairs. The windows are opened; grand rooms aired; slipcovers dropped; gilded marbles uncovered. Someone wakes me early in the morning. I'm six years old. All day carriages come and go. In the exterior courts, brief commandments resound, companies present arms to fifes and tambours. They find me: I go downstairs. The hall was full of the world: dames in high fashion and decorated officers. All is splendor! Suddenly silver trumpets sound across the fields! A carriage pulls up to my stone entrance steps. An old man steps out, then a little girl. Someone shoves me against them. I said hello to the little girl. She hid her face behind her flowers; I saw only her eyes full of tears. I took her hand. The old general bleating guided us. Immediately a cortege formed around the chateau's chapel. The ceremony unfolded itself. Kneeling on the same cushion, enveloped in the same veil, bound by the same ribbons whose ends the maids-of-honor held, we took the same vow. As the pope said, "I do," the girl smiled through her tears.

We were one. The pretty princess Rita was my wife.

We're standing under the ceiling of white roses. We're alone at a table heaped with delicacies. The general crops up, takes her away. As she leaves, I see myself crying alone in the immense, chandelier upon chandelier, wedding salon. "I'm sick of ideas," I said. "They bore me to shit. The thing is to find out what doesn't bore me to shit."

Rita's my first friend. I think more and more of the actuality of the new world. I suppose I dream. I wander around the empty silent house I prowl like a hungry deserted cat I become aware of my body. I'm not just a mind behind two eyes: I have thoughts in every part of my body all fighting each other all dying to get out. I needed outlets as much as input. I had radios constantly going to drown out the incoming information. Only the heavy furniture pitied me, and crashed to the floor. I was frightened. In the back of some black corridor, or at the bottom of a staircase a breast plate on duty made a half-turn the noise of spurs. That noise transported me to the grand day of the fete. I heard the trumpets the tambours clatter. Artillery salutes. Bells. Organs played, Princess Rita's open carriage like a rocket crossed my sky and was about to crash in the meadow. The old general fell head to his feet, like a clown, gesticulated his arms and legs, signaled me. He told me to come, to come join them, the princess awaited me, she was there, in the meadow. My friend. The air was the flesh-colored perfume of clover. I wished to penetrate the meadow. The cops stopped me.

> *don't hurt me daddy don't do me wrong*
> *I've loved you so long*
> *don't you see corporate violence is killing me*
> *hurt my body cause me pain*
> *I need love so bad I need more again*
> *I want you so badly I'll be anyone*
> *I want any lover so badly I'm a piece of scum*
> *don't you see corporate violence is killing me.*

I began to do what I wanted:

I began to hate people I had formerly only looked down upon because they didn't have Rita's eyes. I wanted to cut out their eyes. At first I tried to restrain myself by sticking a knife in my legs.

Rita again arrived. It was more beautiful than the last time. It was our anniversary. For hours we stared into each other's eyes into each other's eyes. We didn't move. In the still of the night I kissed exactly on her lips our tongues touched and she left. Her mouth was the new world.

After she left, I took out my knife cut out the painted eyes of my ancestral family who were in the gallery. I didn't feel guilty at all.

I saw Rita once a year on the anniversary of our marriage until I became ten years old. I became ten years old. I was still trying to do what I wanted. But I didn't know how things are. I received a letter from the old man in Vienna who directed my education telling me I had to come to Vienna forever the night before I would see Rita again.

I would never see Rita again. I was outraged. I had to flee. Early in the morning, grey and red light slowly streaming over the sleeping winos, I tiptoed out of the house to the stables. I undid the horses' halters: strapped myself under the stomach of the black mare. I set fire to the hay. Immediately: fear flames and crackling lickety-split the horses fled. Huge uproaring panic. My mare leaped three times joined the streaming maddened horses. I cleverly fooled the cops. But one cop, without warning, shot to kill. He didn't care about the value of a life. My mare collapsed on top of me. I was covered with blood. When I got to the palace, my skull was cracked my ribs crushed my legs broken. I had done what I wanted. I could stay and see Rita. I hadn't figured things out.

But Rita didn't come.

I couldn't make Rita come I became delirious. I had no

friend I couldn't do what I wanted. I was delirious for three weeks. Then I began slowly to recover. But my right leg, after two more months, hung inert. I didn't know if the doctors had been unable, or had been ordered to leave my leg disabled. My leg was anchylosed. This infirmity is due to the sinister old Viennese man's vengeance. He was punishing me for not going to Vienna.

I began to realize the nature of reality:

My world, my social position, my friend, my enemies, my family ties, my relations to the Viennese court. Why was I held prisoner? Who was holding me prisoner? Who was controlling my life?

When I could begin to walk again, I hobbled to the family library. Books would tell me the truth. There I passed the next three years, studying. I had no need for Rita, for fantasies,

> no more parents no more school
> no more society's dirty rules
> spread my legs I'm so poor I want to die
> San Francisco's the place for me
> it's the place I want to be
> spread my legs I'm so poor I want to die.

I deciphered my family papers: old manuscripts, private deeds, title deeds. I learned my family's history: its grandeur, who had caused its downfall. Like the rest of my family I vowed unappeasable hatred against the Viennese court. I would foul up their designs on me, resist their orders, escape. Escape. Anywhere, anywhere without politics, without Rockefeller where I could live, free, simply unknown.

But Rita, my friend, returned! She was huge: a grown-up giantess who mysteriously drove me wild. She raced wildly down the halls into my mother's bedroom. Burst out sobbing wildly. I clipclopped into the room burst out wildly sobbing with her. She didn't care about my dead leg. For hours we lay in each other's arms. We had no need to say a word. Our lips lightly brushed up and down, hour after hour, the hairs of each other's neck. Suddenly Rita left.

I could no longer think about reality the information I had learned from my family papers I became Rita: My voice was now broken. Low resonances, deep and long fluted sounds, sudden register and modulation changes. Like Rita's. The fuck with crummy books. All day like an idiot a crazy I looked toward the falling sun. Where Rita had gone. This was the meadow. My nervous infant dreams became my reality.

I became excessively attentive to my inner life. For the first time I noticed I lived entirely alone. Who was controlling this constant silence, loneliness? A company of beefy FBI men replaced the patrol cops. These hamburgers didn't enchant me: They had no regular hours, trumpets, spurs. They do everything secretly. I hear a hoarse voice, the dull blow of a gun butt in the corridor, behind a door, strike out. Everything's moving. Voice, articulation, incantation, thunder. I see everything: I see the moving treetops: Park foliage squeeze open close like a voluptuous cunt: Sky stretch out farther farther. These're my senses. I'm total music. Sex. Energy. Vitality.

I'm ecstatic. Ecstatic. I perceive the root of my senses. My cunt swells. I'm All-Strong. I became jealous of nature. I should control every event, my desires and my breath should control every event. My solitude was making me see this.

I wanted to control Rita. I wanted Rita.

I was fifteen years old.

In this exaltation, every event which reminded me of reality totally exasperated me. Living is idiotic.

I committed a crime so horrible, so disgusting to the ears of humankind that perhaps you'll understand why.

Days weeks months pass. I'm 19 years old. Rita moves next

door, in a neighboring chateau. I see her once a week, every week, on holy Friday. We're good Catholics. We spend each day in the armory room. I love this room because it stinks and doesn't have any furniture. We gaze deeply into each other's eyes. Sometimes Rita plays Bach in the small piano salon, or puts on ridiculous old-fashioned clothes, Haight drag, she finds in closets under dusty chairs under the bodies of winos lying on the doors to the chateau. In these tatters, these pieces of shit-stained velvet, fishwives' netting, black net stockings with seams torn an inch below the ass, pink silk bras, Japanese robes with holes at the crotch, she runs into the sunlight dances like a Haight queen flowers in hand mouth wide open. I see her feet her hands the bottom of her ass the tips of her violet breasts. When she leaves me, the softness the wet of her skin remains for a long time like a delicate odor on my skin. I remember most of the seances we held in the armory room. She was a perfume in which I drown myself. She doesn't exist: she's a vapor I absorb in my delicate pores. Her gaze is my coke. For a long time I run my hand through her lower hairs.

I'm the Chinese wood comb running through her curly hair. I'm the bra which outlines her delicate breasts. I'm the transparent net of her sleeves. The dress swishing around her upper legs. The silk stocking around her thigh. The heel which lies beneath her. The puff she uses after she bathes. The salt of her armpits. I sponge off her clammy parts. I'm wet and tender. I'm her hand that does what she needs. I don't exist. I'm her chair, her mirror, her bathtub. I know all of her perfectly as if I'm the space around her. I'm her bed.

I want to control her: often I control her without her knowing it or wishing it.

I want to see her naked. Touch her naked. I tell her this. She says "no." Now she hardly sees me.

Deprived of her friendship, I become nervous, susceptible, melancholy. I can't sleep. I dream or I see women surrounding me, women of all colors, women of all heights, women of all ages, women of all eras. Like robots they stagger in front of me. They lie, wiggling and squirming in a circle in front of me. A stringed instrument. I'm a rock-and-roll star. I control their cunts (them): My gaze makes some of them come. My hand, others. Standing, dressed like the drummer of Hot Tuna, I beat the measure to their frenzy: slow them down, accelerate, stop them, begin again, a thousand times a thousand times d'a capo, tutti, rework their poses their rhythms, all together, throw them into delirium. This frenzy kills me. I can't do anything. I'm stuck.

I'm all gooseflesh.

I don't want to see anyone anymore. I lock myself in the empty armory room. I don't bother to brush my teeth wash my face change my clothes eat regular meals wake up in the morning go to sleep at night, all that social crap. I start to stink. Love it. Pleasurably piss along my legs.

I begin to love objects. Events that don't have their own wills. I'm not talking about art events, things that are based on ideas, that cleverly reveal the sources of their ideas, things the old chateau abounds in. I mean dull stupid tool things. I surround myself with them. A tin box of biscuits, an ostrich egg, a sewing machine, a bit of quartz, a lead nugget, a stove pipe. I spend my time handling them and sniffing them. I change their places a thousand times a day. They amuse me. Distract me. Make me forget I have and had boring emotions.

This's a big lesson to me.

A stove pipe excites me sexually. The lead nugget feels thick and soft like Peter's skin. Can I trust anyone even Peter as much as I trust the lead nugget? The sewing machine is a perfect plan, ability to take power, like a hooker's legs' inner muscles, a stripper's mechanical bump. I can crack the lips of the perfumed quartz, drink the final drop of that primordial honey the life of origins deposits in vitreous molecules, Venus foam-flecked from the sea; the quartz doesn't deny me her pleasure. The tin box is a summary of women.

Circle, square, and their projections in space, sphere, cube excite me. I see touch smell taste hear them red and blue genitals, obscure barbarous ritual orgies.

All becomes for me rhythm, the unexplored life. I no longer know what I do. Cry out sing howl. Roll on the ground. Perform zulu dances. Grovel before a block of granite which I put in a wine barrel, seized by religious terror. The block is living like a mass of nightmares, full of riches. It hums like a beehive. Ardent like a hollow shellfish. I thrust my hands there inexhaustible sex. I fight the walls to pierce through the hallucinations which climb up from all parts. I bend swords flat iron I demolish the furniture with my club. When Rita, my friend, appears—she appears rarely, her foot doesn't touch the ground—I have to rape her.

It was the end of summer. Rita appears in a long ridinghabit. She gets off her horse. Comes into my room as she used to do. Lies on the ground as she used to do. Looks into my eyes as she used to do. She's good now: sweet, serious, aware of my desires.

"Turn your head a little," I whisper to her. "Thank you. You're not allowed to move again. You're the friend I've always wanted. You're tough as a stove pipe. Your body's as beautiful as an egg at the edge of the sea. You're full of information like rock salt and as transparent, nonexistent as crystal. You're a motionless whirlpool. The abyss of light. You're a sound able to take me to incalculable depths: sensations I've never known. You're a commonplace: a bit of grass enlarged a billion times."

I'm terrified. Scared. I want to cut her up. She rises? She's carelessly putting on her coat? Goodbye? The old man the one who controls me has summoned her to Vienna she'll pass this winter at court, a season of brilliant balls light dazzling on lights; she can't see me again . . . I don't hear her. I don't hear anything. I hurl myself at her. I turn her around. I strangle her. She struggles stripes my face with blows of her horsewhip. But I'm already on her. She can't cry out. I push my left fist in her mouth. My other hand sticks a knife in her. I open her stomach. Blood floods me. I pick her intestines to pieces.

The following happens: They lock me up. I'm 18 years old. It's 1965. I'm locked up in Alcatraz. Ten years later they secretly transfer me here, with the crazies. Everyone abandons me? I'm crazy. For six years.

> *no more parents no more school*
> *no more society's dirty rules*
> *San Francisco's the place for me*
> *it's the place I want to be*
> *fuckers lovers ideas go free*
> *all I want is ecstasy*
> *spread my legs I'm so poor I want to die.*

If I trust you
A revolution will happen.
If a revolution's fight guns:
No thing good or new.

Today's society makes us
Murderers liars assassins.
If I trust you
A revolution will happen.

I don't like people. I feel like I'm a misfit in this society because I'm scared of other people I'm scared to go out on the street deal with the people who're totally unlike me. I dislike this society my politics are based on this: at this point there's no way I can be useful. At times I hate anyone I've fucked. I think most murderers thieves come from this.

"It began with Uncle Albert."

"What're you saying, dear?" the tall man whispers. He's tall: long brown hair to his check front and back. He's going to solve my problems.

"Uncle Albert's dead. And I, I think I killed him."

"Of course you didn't dear. Why don't you tell me what happened in your house from the beginning?"

I looked up at him my clear large brown eyes. I had gotten my eyes from my father who's now dead. My parents, both my parents are dead. They died in a plane crash when I was only a few months old. I don't even remember them.

I live with my grandmother, Nana Hattie, I guess she runs the roost. She's always run me. She's 80 years old now. But she knows more than all of us she knows more how to get what she wants. She's, she's old-fashioned. Do you understand?"

"I think I do."

"Her rules, the ways the house is run would be weird to anyone else. I mean anyone except for our family. We're used to it we don't even notice, you know, how weird we are. Or maybe we're not. Two Sundays ago Uncle Albert, Uncle Albert and Uncle Cyrus're always fighting, decided to go to church alone. He's not supposed to you know."

"Uh huh."

"We're all supposed to go to church together. Or the women go with the women, and the men with the men. Those are the only two alternatives. But Uncle Albert refused to go with Uncle Cyrus. They'd been quarreling mainly because Nana Hattie tells them what to do, she's their mother. They resent that they're 60-year-old children and think they can begin to tell themselves what to do. So they take their hatred of their mother out on each other.

"Uncle Albert stormed out of the house, saying he'd meet us at church he'd rather be dead than ride with a murdering brother and, . . . and then we never saw him again."

"Then why do you think he was murdered?"

"You don't understand. You just don't understand. Our house is different. In our house everyone obeys Nana Hattie. We've been obeying Nana Hattie, well, as long as I can remember, ever since I was a child. I don't remember younger than when I was 5 years old. I don't remember my parents at all. But Uncle Albert and Uncle Cyrus have obeyed Nana's advice and rules ever since they were born. They've never disappeared. Much less for 14 days. You just don't understand."

"I'll need more details."

"Everyone's been quarreling. It's as if a shroud hangs over the house. Cyrus refuses to talk. He hangs in the shadows; the shadows are thick and deep. My two aunts, one of them's not really an aunt but a step-aunt, scream at each other all the time. They know something's wrong, but they won't admit it.

"You see, I'm not only worried about Uncle Albert's disappearance, I . . . I'm also scared."

There's one other thing: "The air was wet and cold. I felt the bottom edges of my eyelids and my eyelashes stick to the skin below my eyes." "The day before Uncle Albert died, I had a terrific quarrel with him. He was picking on Uncle Cyrus, he was always picking on Uncle Cyrus. Uncle Cyrus was about to cry. I can't stand to see a man cry. I told Uncle Albert to leave off. Uncle Albert told me I was a helpless baby. I got so angry I told him something I shouldn't have known and never should have told him: A week before that Nana Hattie had remade her will. In the new will all of us were to split her money except for Uncle Albert. He got nothing. He had nothing more to live for.

"I think I forced Uncle Albert to kill himself."

I can't tell him the real reason I know I murdered Uncle Albert.

"How rich are you and your family?" asks the tall lean detective.

The detective led me into the house. It was a dark gloomy

house full of uncomfortable furniture, austere lines, impeccable servants. But it was home. It was all I'd ever known. If it hadn't been for this home, I'd be an orphan. Left out in the cold. Gutter tramp. Piss drivel down my legs I wouldn't have anything. I'm glad I'm a prissy little bitch.

I show the detective into a room lined in leather and untreated wood. It smells of tobacco.

"My name is David."

"Oh," I say.

Just then Uncle Cyrus comes in the room. Uncle Cyrus isn't dead yet. It's Uncle Albert who's dead, I remember.

"How's my favorite little niece," says Uncle Cyrus pinching my rosy cheek. "Oh, excuse me." He notices the tall detective. "My name's Cyrus."

Uncle Cyrus is fat short rosy cheeks. He looks like a cherubic baby.

It's the beginning of the revolution. I think that I'm in love with Peter a tall light-haired revolutionary who wants to get rid of leaders and money. Thinks he can with others do this. Because he's so involved in his work, his underground sabotage, his electronic work, he never has any time to eat, much less see me. Because he doesn't see me, I'm pining away from desire. I don't eat. I get a sniffle, cold, flu, malaria, finally all my blood's poisoned. I know about women's liberation, but I'm still pining away from desire.

Peter and I live together. Formerly Peter's need to earn money took him away from me. Now his fight against money and the money powers takes him away from me.

I could fuck other people. I do, but it isn't purely a physical longing for Peter that's making me die. The other people I find to fuck bore me.

The first fuck with someone usually shatters me: I'm real nervous cause I'm scared the person'll think I'm a lousy fuck I want to do anything to please the person I have to figure how

I can come hard and lots. The second time we fuck is best: I'm not so frenzied I'm no longer in love I've figured how to come I'm not yet bored. From then on it's downhill: I become more and more bored.

There're a few people I adore. I follow them around. If I'd fuck any of them, I'd explode.

I know I shouldn't be this way. Either I'm scared to change myself, or I don't want to.

How can I fight against myself? I don't trust anyone but I can't live in misery all my life. I'm scared of my power. In grade school, my teachers said: "She's a natural leader but she refuses to recognize this." I want to fuck Peter once a day. I don't want to starve.

Peter had been gone three weeks. He didn't tell me where he was going for fear the Rockefeller government, using various chemicals, would force the information out of me. I'm scared of pain. When he left, I cried out in frustration. By the third day, I was horny unbearably horny. I began to fall in love with everyone I saw who seemed sexually interested in me. I hated myself. I was ugly stupid useless.

I watched the grey waters of San Francisco. White morning light shoot out in streams through the layers of grey. The fog horns sounding are really codes, I know, our army uses to connect its the various almost self-sufficient units. To bring good news.

I couldn't take anymore. I couldn't take waiting home day after day never knowing when my lover'd come home with a broken leg a bullet wound in his neck drips blood, dead. I could no longer take feeling useless. Feeling my time wasn't my time because I did nothing useful in it but was Peter's time because he was doing something useful. Feeling I was nothing. A ghost who flitted over wood floors cement streets was nothing to anyone.

I was horny.

I remember a cold day. Air wet as if air itself is rain. I leave alone. I don't feel sad. I don't feel anything. I'm not even sure what I'm doing. I feel I don't want to kill anyone.

The fighting was taking place in the country.

I get in with a group of soldiers who at first don't trust me. The news over the radio reports violence all through the United States. On October 1, we hear of the death of "Blue" Gene, his brother Bob, and others in San Francisco. The city's the scene of constant struggle. We decide to return to the city. One of the women says we're about to face difficult, dangerous days, with the enemy nearby. We might have to go on for several days, always on the move, with very little food.

Some of the men are decent enough to express their fear, and leave immediately.

As I'm leaning against a tree, eating half a sausage and two crackers, a rifle shot breaks the stillness. A hail of bullets, at least this's how it seems to me in my first fire, descends on me and my companions. Fear approaches requesting orders, but nobody can issue them. The surprise attack and the heavy gunfire's too much for us. Fear runs back to take charge of his group. A woman drops a box of ammunition at my feet. When I reprimand her, she looks at me in anguish. Mutters something like "No time to bother with ammunition boxes." She continues walking. Disappears from view. Sometime later Rockefeller's henchmen murder her.

This is the first time I have to choose between my desire to find Peter and my duty as a revolutionary soldier. I can't possibly do both. For the moment I pick up the ammunition box.

I cross the clearing; head for the Russian River. Near me a friend Arbentosa's also walking toward the river. A burst of fire hits us. My chest feels a sharp blow. My neck tears open. I'm sure I'm dead. Arbentosa vomits blood. Bleeds profusely from a deep hole in his guts. Shouts, "They've killed me!" Fires his rifle at no one I can tell. I see Fear, say, "They've killed me."

Fear says, "O it's nothing," though I can see by his eyes he thinks I'm dying. I lay there alone, unwilling and waiting to die. Fear urges me to go on. I drag myself to the Russian River. There I meet Bob whose thumb's been blown off. Fay's bandaging his hand. My friends now begin to trust me.

As we continue walking to San Francisco, we meet two black women who run away from us when they see us. We chase them until we catch them. They're pacifists: absolutely against any sort of violence. I'm sickened by the bloody arms, guts falling out of stomach, open mouths in the blackness. I no longer want anything to do with fighting. With change or a government based on violence. I plan to go off with the women. But I know my friends are undergoing the fire and possible death I'm now refusing to undergo because of my new ideas. I can't refuse to help my friends just because I have certain ideas which anyway are always changing. Against my wishes, I decide to keep fighting.

We camp about 60 miles north of San Francisco. The people who live in Sonoma County welcome us: give us necessary food and medical supplies.

I'm still incredibly horny.

I keep traveling. On our way south, we meet one of two men who had gone after a deserter. He tells us this: the man with whom he's searching says, "I'm Wong's friend. I can't betray him." So he starts to run away. The man tells his friend to stop. The friend doesn't stop. The man shoots his friend.

Fear gathers us on a nearby hill. He tells us we're going to witness the outcome of a desertion attempt. Any deserter has to die. One by one we walk past the body of the dead friend.

I begin to grow close to an extraordinary man Bob Sheff who's been a newspapermen and studied physics at Mills. He had no military training. He simply left, he tells me, it was his duty to stay in the U.S. and fight. A guerrilla, he says, has to obey three rules: Constant mobility: Never stay in the same place. Mistrust: Don't trust anything or anybody until a zone is completely liberated. Vigilance: Constant guard and scouting. Set up camp in a safe spot. Never sleep with a roof over your head. Never sleep in a house that can be surrounded.

I've no confidence in these rules. I want something more. We have to diversify our farm production, stimulate industry and guarantee suitable markets, accessible through our own transportation system, for our agricultural mining and industrial products in the near future.

On October 15 we begin battle in the deserted shopping centers of Mill Valley. At first we use Streetwater as our base of operations. Next, we set up headquarters closer to San Francisco. Our forces fight troops supported by armored units, and rout them.

It's a white grey dawn. Another group of revolutionaries joins us. One of the men is Peter. We fight together and whenever we have a chance, we fuck.

New York City is beautiful like an Italian saint. A yellow sky reflects mirrors marks a thousand and thousand towers, steeples, belltowers who stand straight, stretch their limbs, rear up, or falling back heavily, widen themselves become bulbous like polychrome stalactites in boiling effervescence, a vermicelli of light. Paved with bumps, the streets are full of the uproar of hundred thousand cars which spread out day and night; narrow, rectangular they insinuate themselves between the red, blue, yellow, ochre, faces of the houses to suddenly widen before a cathedral of gold which some bands are complaining crows whip like silly women. All roars. All cries. Hairy men jerk off in the street. Winos hock their clothes. Small old men sell chestnuts which are scorched. A bearded cop rests on a huge sword. One walks everywhere on chestnut burrs and the crushy acorns of the ashtree. Tire scraps now dust rise in the air like flakes of coal. An acrid musty smell of rotten fish wafts from the city's ass. Two days late it snows. All effaces itself, all extinguishes itself. All's muffled. Cars pass noiselessly. It snows.

It snows feather and the roofs are smoke. Buildings shut themselves up. Towers, skyscrapers vanish. Bells ring under the earth. The people move about all new. Tiny. Squeezed. Rapid. Each walker is a toy with a spring. The cold's like a plastic coating. It lubricates. It fills your mouth with gas. The lungs are thick. Everyone's hungry. Shop windows contain cabbage-pates perfumed and sugar-coated; lemon bouillons with sour cream; hors d'oeuvres all of all shapes all tastes; smoked fishes; roasted meats; fat chickens with sweet-sour jams; game; fruits huge oranges and tomatoes; bottles of booze; black bread; the pure flower of cheeses.

Here we see the first spots of blood pierce the snow. Like bunches of dandelions around Gracie Mansion. We're also present at the first riots, in a workingclass section whose name I've forgotten, below the West Village. We watch the police drag off wounded students.

The revolution glitters.

We take part. We join committees. We put all our funds in the disposition of the central cashier of the revolutionary party S. R. We support both the NY Anarchists and the International Anarchists. Clandestine printing shops. Bundles of newspaper distributed in mass in factories, in ports, in barracks. We attack the universal vote, freedom, brotherhood and sisterhood in order to extol the social revolution and the class war to the limit. We scientifically demonstrate the legality of individual expropriation under all forms: theft, assassination, extortion, sabotage of factories, pillage of public welfare, destruction of paved roads, destruction of underwear. We scientifically demonstrate that a corrupt society forces us to do these things in order to stay alive.

Arm depots're installed in Arkansas. Unbridled propaganda. Mutineers assault every city of this immense country. Strikes religious fervor ravage the cities of the southwest. A right-wing reaction begins.

We flee the hottest affairs.

I'm sure you all know the history of the U.S. revolutionary movement. Runaway servants escaped Virginia tobacco slaves worn-out prostitutes religious dissenters helped the American Indians fight for their lives. Attica Folsom etc. prisoners fight against the lobotomy-mongers, the men who want to plant dogs' brains in prisoners' heads and prisoners' brains in dogs' heads to see what'll happen. The most ardent adepts of the pure Maria Spiridonowa or the heroic lieutenant Schmitt lost their revolutionary ideals to commit crimes.

There're daily cases of madness and suicide: Hookers believe other workers should respect them. Workers turn against their bosses. Soldiers refuse to fight.

A man drinks menses blood to make another man love him. A musician coats her hands with dog shit to massage a poet's aura. Men are fags. Women dykes. All couples practice platonic love. The building-walls of cities are split open by the flamboyant doors of bars, nightclubs, live sex shows. Men with thousands of millions of dollars kill the people in other countries poison the air water soil, to get more money. In the Plaza, the Papillon, ministers covered with spit mingle with bald revolutionaries and long-hair students who vomit champagne into the debris of dishes and raped women.

This is the story about part of the life of my friend Bob Ashley. This's a love story.

Ashley's already given most of his money to the revolutionary party S.R. The bit of money we were still able to procure for ourselves the party's pressing needs gobble down. We live everywhere: Newark Hoboken New Guinea East Bronx. We live in the ghettos. We work in factories and ship-yards. When we don't get paid, we steal goods from these places. After we attack, we go underground.

Ashley feels a huge desire to plunge into the abyss of the most anonymous human misery. No one repulses him. No one disgusts him. When he sees me or anyone grumble, he bursts into laughter amuses himself enormously. He listens closely to everyone. He's interested in everything. He takes no responsibility for his actions much less for anything else. He's taken for the famous terrorist Samuel Simbirsky who killed the Russian Alexander II, escaped from Sakhalin. He's known everywhere.

Mascha thought of the subterfuge when the real Samuel Simbirsky died on a roof, in a blind alley, in Paris, dead from TB.

Mascha and Ashley are deeply in love.

Mascha's a Jewish Lithuanian. Huge. Huge breasts huge stomach huge ass. Legs are mountains. Her head surrounded by frizzy hair resembles the head of Novalis.

She's 38 years old. Ph.D. in math and science. Author of a book on perpetual motion.

We met Mascha at Varsovie where she managed our main secret printing shop. She writes our proclamations our manifestoes our tracts which had so big an influence on the mass which unlatched so many strikes which caused so many ravages. She knows how to appeal to the crowd's base instincts. Her inflamed words are irrefutable. She groups events, lights them up, puts them in relief as she pleases and suddenly draws from them conclusions whose simplicity and logic astound us. She knows how to stir the people's fanaticism:

"This guy the cops bumped off here," she says. "Look here at this spot. What were you doing then? Your friends Do-Do and Goo-Goo rotted in the depths of Attica. When they got sick of rotting, they pounded on their cells so the cops came in and shot them. What were you doing then? When Ms. Prissy refused to bring coffee for the fiftieth time in two seconds to her boss Mr. Asslick, and so got thrown into the streets, couldn't even make it as an eight-dollar-a-throw streetwalker, what were you doing then? When the NY D.A. shoved more heroin into the hands of his shady dealers and ordered his henchmen to bust two 11-year-old kids for half an ounce of pot;

when he ordered all the junkies to take methadone cause he had complete control of the methadone market whereas he had to share the heroin market with the United States president; what were you doing then?" She whispers insinuatingly maliciously just another bored housewife, "Do you have to raise your hand to go to the bathroom at work? Do you have to buy Christmas cards to send to your boss when you have only three cents left in your weekly income after taxes?"

Patty moved closer to me and put an arm around my waist. She squeezed me tightly and whispered in my ear: "I just have to give things to the people I love."

I turned and smiled. "Well, all right—"

Impulsively Patty brought my cheek around and gave me a quick little kiss.

I fought down a flicker of panic. I moved to step away from Patty. But Patty's arm remained around my waist, holding me against her. My flicker of panic became a chill of dread. I raised my head and looked at Patty.

Her large eyes were lidded, their color intensely dark. Her lips were parted slightly. She raised her hand to my cheek again and rested her palm gently on my flesh.

I felt my heart beat rapidly and hard.

"Patty—"

"Yes?" Her voice was soft; her eyes on my mouth.

"Patty," I was shaking my head slightly, "Patty, I—I—can't . . ."

Patty nodded. "I know, darling." She smiled, then bent her head and lightly placed her lips on my mouth. Before I could react, Patty dropped her arms and moved away.

"Honey," she said, "I know you're straight. Just let me love you. And do things for you."

I looked at the big woman and saw the pain in her face. I saw the love, too, and wanted to reach out and hold her comfortingly in my arms. Hot tears of pity, compassion, and frustration rush to my eyes.

"Kathy?"

"Yes, Patty?"

"Kathy, please? I won't . . . Don't worry . . ."

"Patty? . . ." I hesitate. "All right."

The Adjustment Center of Folsom Prison is a prison within a prison. It has maximum physical control and is segregated from the rest of the prison in a separate building. Each unit has 150 inmates. Staff consists of a Program Administrator (the boss), a supervising counselor, two line counselors, a lieutenant, two sergeants, two correctional officers.

Inmates are placed in the adjustment centers because staff can't tolerate their behavior in the general prison population or because the inmates can't tolerate their behavior.

The staff tries to place each inmate in one of several categories. The inmate talks to the staff for ten minutes: then the inmate is classified. According to his classification, the inmate is kept in the general prison population or sent to an adjustment center.

"Kathy," she whispered.

"What is it?"

My voice came quickly, full of a kind of rushing panic. I started to sit up, but before I could do so, Patty moved without a sound to my bed.

Prisoner classifications (Adjustment Center candidates):

1. Militants: Many of the prisoners' personal problems come from their various political commitments.

2. Pressure artists: Certain prisoners are predators who roam the prison and prey on prisoners weaker than themselves. They demand anything from sex to cigarettes.

3. Weakies: Prisoners who, often because of their youthful appearances, become sexual partners or dupes of one or more predators.

4. Prison rats: Prisoners who inform on other prisoners about offenses ranging from escape plots to murder plots to minor infractions of the rules.

5. Escape risks: Any prisoner who seems to want to escape or who has escaped from the prison.

6. Druggies: This is a minor problem.

7. The mentally ill.

"Don't be afraid."

"Please, Patty."

"What?"

"I'm . . ." I begin. Then my voice broke with a quick intake of breath. My eyes grew big and wide as if I was hypnotized. My mouth trembled and a little wet trace of moisture glittered on my lips. "Patty," I started again, but the words seemed to dry up in my throat. When Patty bent down closer and touched her lips to my mouth, I groaned softly. "Oh, no," I murmured, but, with the pressure of Patty's kiss increasing, the sound shivered to a little helpless moan. Patty slipped one hand around my shoulder and caressed my naked breasts, fondling and squeezing them until the tips were hard and hurting. Made speechless by Patty's fierce kiss, I kept staring with a numbed expression in my dilated eyes. A vein flutters in the hollow of my throat and, with each huge breath, my swollen, straining breasts rose and fell, glistening to a satin sheen. At last, as Patty's mouth reluctantly withdrew, I shuddered.

"No," I begged weakly, "No, Patty. Please don't."

"But you knew this would happen."

"No," I whispered. I'm a liar.

"Don't lie."

"I'm not," I insisted.

"Then why didn't you just go to sleep?"

I took a deep breath and held it for a moment.

But after a wordless moment, Patty slid in beside me, pressing and hugging and making little caressing explorations with her hands. Gently, she pushed me down and with whispering huskiness murmuring in her throat, trailed wet warm trembling kisses across my face and down to my shoulders and breasts. Her lips teased and coaxed and burned patterns of heat into sleek hot naked flesh. Her touching fingers traced the length of my back and moved over my hips and thighs. When her lips came back to my mouth, she pressed and parted, then pressed deeper.

The sounds of our heavy breathing filled the room as we sat and stared at each other. A little hot gleam in Patty's eyes pinned me to the bed, but when Patty finally spoke, her voice was under perfect control.

"All right," she said. "It's your choice, Kathy."

"My choice?" My arms hug my naked breasts.

"I won't force you again."

"But Patty—" I began softly.

"No," Patty interrupted. "Just decide."

Melvyn Freilicher is 28 years of age and has been in prison for 13 years and in segregation confinement for approximately 10 years. Melvyn Freilicher was originally sentenced to prison in 1957 for possession of brass knuckles, in 1961 was convicted of possessing a prison-made knife, and in 1965 was convicted of the voluntary manslaughter of another prisoner. Melvyn Freilicher is acutely aware of his previous history of violence and has, during the past few years, achieved remarkable self-improvement and insight. He has made every effort to reorient his life; to return to the prison's general population and prepare himself for society; to participate in programs designed to give prisoners insight into their problems.

The staff has categorized Melvyn Freilicher as a "management problem."

Prison officials in daily contact with and observation of Melvyn Freilicher consider him trustworthy and nonviolent.

Prison officials deny Melvyn Freilicher's repeated requests for release to Folsom Prison's general population or to another prison's general population.

On or about February 9, 1972, Melvyn Freilicher refused to "consent" to his transfer to the Maximum Psychiatric Diagnostic Unit at the California Medical Facility at Vacaville. Melvyn Freilicher is informed and believes and on that basis alleges that the Maximum Psychiatric Diagnostic Unit "program" involves aversion therapy including electric and insulin shock, fever treatments, sodium pentothal, anectine (death-simulating drug), antitestosterone injections (to neutralize sex hormones) and that prison officials are utilizing the threat of his continued segregation confinement to coerce him to "consent" to the Maximum Psychiatric Diagnostic Unit "program."

The Adult Authority has refused to fix Freilicher's sentence or parole date on the basis of his indefinite confinement and has recommended that he be transferred to the California Medical Facility at Vacaville for treatment.

Robert Sheff is a 29-year-old Black citizen who has been incarcerated in the California Prison system for over 11 years. Including 7 years locked up under various forms of segregation.

Robert Sheff was originally sent to prison in 1961 on a first degree robbery charge to which he pled guilty and was sentenced five years to life. His co-defendant, charged with the same crime, pled guilty and received the sentence of one year in the county jail.

In 1969, after a few days in Folsom Prison's general population, following a long period of segregation confinement, Robert Sheff was picked up in a general sweep and again placed back in the Adjustment Center with more than ten other Black and Chicano prisoners. He was charged with conspiracy to commit murder. The charge was subsequently dismissed for lack of evidence. He served nearly three years in Folsom Prison's Adjustment Center.

On February 17, 1972, he was transferred to the Soledad Adjustment Center.

Although Robert Sheff has been charged with many violations of Adjustment Center rules during his incarceration in prison, he has never been formally accused of any violation of the California Penal Code except during 1969 when the indictment was dismissed.

Robert Sheff has been classified as a militant.

On November 17, 1971, Phil Harmonic, Adjustment Center guard, issued a disciplinary report against Sheff because Sheff supposedly stopped to speak with another prisoner on his way out to the exercise yard. This was said to be in violation of the Folsom Adjustment Center rules which are supposed to be given to all prisoners there but are not.

On the same date he was charged with practicing karate during the exercise period in the exercise yard by Adjustment Center guard Warren Burt. Also on the same day he was again charged with talking to another prisoner on the way back from exercise by Officer Al Robboy.

Robert Sheff was the subject of gunfire and possible death by gunshot in the Adjustment Center yard. On November 30, 1971, he was involved in a fistfight with Peter Gordon. On the pretext of breaking up the fight, in which no weapons were used; guntower guards shot at Sheff and Gordon. Neither Sheff nor Gordon were attempting to escape. The lethal force used was unreasonable and excessive in that neither Sheff's nor Gordon's nor any other person's life was endangered by their fistfight. No warning was given to the prisoners nor were any less hazardous steps taken to stop the fight. The firing of live ammunition into the enclosed exercise yard endangered the lives of everyone in the area. The danger of a mortal wound in such a situation, either by a direct hit or by the high possibility of a ricocheting bullet hitting a vital organ, is great.

Prisoners in Folsom Prison's Adjustment Center have been wounded in similar circumstances.

Robert Sheff has appeared before dozens of prison committees, labeled disciplinary, adjustment center, and classification committees. He has never been told if or when he would be released from the Adjustment Center. Instead he has been told by prison officials, or their agents, that he will never be released from the Adjustment Center and that he will die there.

The Lyons prison is a "modern" structure, built in the shape of a star, on the cellular system. The spaces between the rays of the star are occupied by small asphalt paved yards, and, weather permitting, the inmates are taken to these yards to work outdoors. Thin, enervated, underfed—the shadows of children—I often watched them from my window.

The man in the next cell was sitting on a low stool, his head bent. With a sudden jerk he turned his eyes on the door, a terrorized and hunted look in their anticipation. Just as quickly he pulled himself together, his body stiffened, and his look fastened on our guide with concentrated contempt. Two words, no more audible than a sigh.

The authorities did their best to cheer us. On Christmas morning we sat down to a breakfast of cornflakes, sausages, bacon, beans, fried bread, margarine and bread and marmalade. At midday we were given roast pork, Christmas pudding and coffee, and at supper, mince pies and coffee, instead of the nightly mug of

There was a nail in the wall of my cell, high up in the wall. After looking at it for so long, I finally saw it. I had looked at it for 10 years without noticing it. A nail. What's a nail? Twisted, rusty, it was me driven in between the stones. I've no roots. I left behind me only a little whitish dust, 10 years, a little spider dust, an imperceptible sign on the wall's face, beyond the range of my successor's eyes.

Peter Gordon, a Black citizen, 46 years of age, was originally sentenced to prison for forgery in 1952. In 1956, was sentenced for life for assaulting another inmate.

Peter Gordon has spent 13 years, including all but 19 months of the last 11 years, in indefinite segregation confinement at Folsom Prison.

Peter Gordon is not in segregation confinement because he's a danger to himself or others. He's not been accused of nor participated in any violent act since November 1960, when he was sentenced to indefinite segregation confinement for a fist-fight. Since November 1960, he's been in segregation confinement continuously except for six months in 1964, six months in 1968, and 7 months in 1969.

On or about July 17, 1969, Peter Gordon's cell was searched. A small five-and-one-half inch file was found in a library book. The Sacramento District Attorney's office declined to prosecute Gordon for possession of a "sharp instrument" (California Penal Code 4502) because of "insufficient evidence." A small file doesn't qualify as a weapon. Peter Gordon was sentenced to segregation confinement.

Gordon has refused to move to a new cell area controlled by guards hostile to him. On two occasions Gordon has failed to shave properly. Gordon has saved his prescription medicine. Gordon has talked between exercise yards. Therefore, according to prison officials or their agents, Peter Gordon has a "stubborn and hostile" attitude and must be retained in segregation confinement.

Prison officials are here magnifying minor incidents in order to warehouse Peter Gordon whom they view as a Black leader who might conceivably influence younger Blacks. Prison officials, or their agents acting on their behalf, have repeatedly informed Peter Gordon that they'll never permit him to re-enter the prison's general population.

On or about January 13, 1972, Peter Gordon appeared before the panel of representatives of members of the California Adult Authority. Said representatives informed Gordon that he would not be considered for parole as long as he was in segregation confinement.

The prison officials and the members of the California Adult Authority have sentenced Peter Gordon to a lifetime of confinement in a small cell with no hope of release.

On January 5, 1972, David Antin and Blaise Antin jointly composed the rough draft of a letter to members of the California Legislature. The letter was subsequently confiscated by prison officials. The rough draft, which was typed, with a nonsense dummy title, otherwise set forth the same wording regarding tensions at Folsom Prison and the need for reforms there as the final version that was sent to State Assemblymen: Willie Dunlap, John Brown, Alan Fong, March Sieroty, Leo Vasconcellos, and John Ryan on January 7 and January 8.

On January 11, 1972, David Antin and Blaise Antin were "arrested" and taken to the office of the Captain of the Guard for interrogation. This interrogation was unusual and intimidating. Captain Poy and Lieutenant Ten interrogated Antin and Antin concerning the letter and its contents and attempted to establish that the letter was a device to "agitate" inmates.

David Antin explained that he typed the rough draft at a desk assigned to him as the Education Department's clerk. The rough draft was either in his personal possession or in his desk after 3:30 P.M. The desk was not accessible to inmate students who took classes in a room adjacent to his office and were constantly under the watchful eye of a guard.

Captain Poy noted that this was an unauthorized use of state materials. He insisted that it was "possible" for a deranged inmate to break into Antin's desk, seize the rough draft, and, after reading it, take action adverse to the safety of the institution. He asked David Antin if there were carbons of the letter.

David Antin replied that he had copies which were "stashed." Said copies were subsequently confiscated from Antin's cell.

Captain Poy concluded the interrogation by ordering David Antin and Blaise Antin to segregation confinement in the Adjustment Center. The Captain said, "I don't consider the letter in question to be in the best interests of custody."

David Antin and Blaise Antin were taken to disciplinary "strip" cells where they were held until January 16. From January 16 until February 12 they were confined in segregation cells.

On January 14, Blaise Antin, the Warden of Folsom Prison, and State Senator Rich Gold, Chairman of the Select Senate Committee on Penal Institutions, met in connection with the Senate Committee's tour of Folsom Prison, to discuss disciplinary procedures. Blaise Antin stated that he was in the "Hole" for writing a letter to State Legislators. Senator Gold asked why Antin and Antin were placed in strip cells for writing a letter to State Legislators. The Warden replied that Antin and Antin were placed in strip cells because segregation cells were unavailable and because the circumstances of their cases were being investigated.

David Antin and Blaise Antin are informed and believe and on the basis of such information and belief allege that there were available segregation cells on January 11 and that they were placed in the strip cells as a punitive measure.

The Warden indicated that the matter would be fully discussed at a disciplinary committee hearing on January 15. Blaise Antin protested that the procedures of the disciplinary committee were notoriously unfair. He requested the presence of an impartial witness, such as the prison chaplain or a recording device, at his expense, to have some record of the procedure. The Warden refused these requests. Senator Gold asked that the summary of the committee's proceedings and disposition be forwarded to David Antin and Blaise Antin. The Warden agreed to do so, but has not.

On January 15, David Antin and Blaise Antin appeared before the disciplinary committee. The Program Administrator of the Adjustment Center at Folsom Prison chaired. The disciplinary committee closely questioned David Antin and Blaise Antin as to the contents of the rough draft and whether Antin and Antin actually believed that conditions were so bad at Folsom Prison, "that Attica is coming to this Prison." Antin and Antin replied affirmatively.

Antin and Antin were told they would be informed of the committee's results.

David Antin and Blaise Antin have not received a summary of their respective disciplinary hearings.

Antin and Antin received the committee results which stated "Retain in a/c (adjustment center), review for possible release after February 1, 1972, depending on the climate of the institution." This sentence especially "the climate of the institution" in effect states that Antin and Antin are being held because of suspicion of agitation, not because of the charges filed against them. Antin and Antin thus are convicted of what California prisoners refer to as a "silent beef": an offense they're not charged with and not permitted to defend themselves against. The disciplinary committee is punishing Antin and Antin for something other prisoners might do in the future because Antin and Antin wrote a letter to State Legislators protesting conditions at Folsom Prison.

Antin's and Antin's case records now contain statements that these prisoners are "revolutionaries" and "agitators." These statements will jeopardize Antin's and Antin's prison job and housing assignments and will subject Antin and Antin to unfavorable action by the Adult Authority and segregation confinement during periodic sweeps when "militants" and "revolutionaries" are removed.

Blaise Antin was denied reassignment to his previous job as inmate librarian because of his "revolutionary writing."

In 1961, The Black Tarantula, an American Indian, was sentenced to five years to life imprisonment for first degree burglary. He has been confined in indefinite segregation confinement at Folsom Prison's Adjustment Center for approximately six years.

While in Folsom Prison's general population, The Black Tarantula's work record was good. He was confined in indefinite segregation confinement for a fistfight. His behavior within the Adjustment Center has been exemplary.

The Black Tarantula is informed and believes, and on the basis of such information and belief, alleges that he is being kept in indefinite segregation confinement because he refused "to bow down or to walk hunchback" for prison officials but is a proud and strong man who walks straight and with his head held high.

The Black Tarantula's explanation why he is continually warehoused may or may not correspond to prison officials' official explanation, but The Black Tarantula does not know and has not been informed of any other basis for his indefinite segregation confinement.

The Black Tarantula is informed and believes, and on that basis, alleges that members of the California Adult Authority have refused to set The Black Tarantula's sentence or to grant him parole because of his segregation confinement. The Black Tarantula, like Peter Gordon, is sentenced to a lifetime punishment in a small cell.

THE ADULT LIFE OF
TOULOUSE LAUTREC
BY HENRI TOULOUSE LAUTREC

contents

"Make sense," Fielding said. "Tell the real story of your life. You alone can tell the truth!"
"I don't want to make any sense," I replied.

*I'm too ugly to go out into the world. I'm a
hideous monster.*

the case of the murdered twerp

"Toulouse," says Vincent. "What are you going to do with
your life? How're you ever going to make any money? You're
a deformed crippled beast. Look at your hairy chest, your huge
nodding head. Your legs are spindly. You thought just cause
your parents're rich, you had the world on a silver platter.
Money does control everything in this world.

"But just cause your parents have money, doesn't mean you
have money."

"I don't give a damn," I mumbled.

"How are you ever going to get famous and get fucked?
You're such a lousy painter. You may be a great painter, Toulouse, but you're a real lousy one. And that's what matters:
goodness.

"What you need is a man, Toulouse, and you're never going
to get one. You're going to be lonely for the rest of your life."

"You're a raving maniac!" I screech at the top of my lungs.

"I believe artists can do everything! Artists can know all the joy and misery and terrifyingness and usefulness cause artists don't have to suffer! Even though I can barely walk; I'm always in pain; I'm always hungry.

"All I think about is sex. At night, nights, I lie alone in my bed: I see the right leg of every sexy man I've seen on the street, the folds of cloth over and around the ooo ooo . . . I ache and I ache and I ache. I feel a big huge hole inside my body. I see a man I like about to stick his cock in my hot pussy.

"I used to think being crippled meant being in constant pain. I can stand pain. Now I know no man wants me. I can hardly bear to live.

"Fuck art, Vincent."

Just then the owner of the Restaurant Norvins walks up to us. She runs the hottest bar in Montmartre. In the back of the bar's a whorehouse. Her closest friend is Theo, a young teacher.

"Honey," Theo's looking at Vincent longingly, "we're try-ing to organize this party. It's gonna be in the back of here in an hour. And we need help . . ."

Just then this young girl runs over to them. "Norvins," she screams, "you've got to help me. I just saw this, this horrible event. I saw a murder. MURDER! I myself . . ." "She's a liar," Theo says to me in a loud whisper.

"I don't know what to do. I saw . . ."

"I've got work to do," Norvins says. She walks away from us. "You're a little liar." Theo pinches the girl. "I never believe what you tell me in class. What're you doing in this whore-house anyway?"

"I tell you I saw murder . . ."

"I've got to help Norvins with the whorehouse party . . ."

She turns around, dashes into the bar's backroom before we can stop her.

"Art," I say. The room whirls around me: the black bar shudders and turns.

"Art:" I continue, "I'm so unbearably desirous needy I can't think about art. Who can think about art in this miserable city? I think about sex so much my art must be sex. I think about sex all the time, and I try to stop myself. I tell myself I have to be stronger. I'm alone. I should revel in my loneliness. I'm in pain. I should revel in my pain. I shouldn't want to be with another person so much. If I think about this miserable situation too much, I'll realize I'm about to kill myself."

Suddenly a beautiful man rushes into the bar.

Veronique, Berthe, and Giannina run up to Vincent and me. "Where's Norvins?" they cackle. "I read in *Crime*," Berthe mumbles, "this guy fucks his girlfriend in her left nostril."

"Shut up Berthe." Veronique says quickly. "We've got to get these apples to Norvins. We're going to bob for apples at the party."

I'm looking at the beautiful man; I'm staring at the beautiful man; I'm sending out every vibration I can so he'll know I want him and only him. His hair's red. His cheekbones're high. He's older than me. His right hand's lost in my short black head hairs. His left hand's resting on my cheek. I can feel the hot cum pouring out of my cunt.

The bar swirls and swirls around us.

"Listen you goddamn shitface assbung," I announce, "you've got to fuck me. If you don't fuck me, I'm going to blow up every rat scum tenement in Montmartre. The cops'll shit in their pants. They'll have nothing left to do. If you don't fuck me Mr. Beautiful I'll kick your lousy dick inside out I mean it. You can't treat me like a piece of moldy shit."

"I think you're extremely beautiful."

"Fuck me. Fuck me. Fuck me. Take me to Brazil. Take me to Argentina. Take me to bed. You're the only person or thing who can make me happy. You can make me ecstatic right now." I throw my arms in the air, leap on the table. My crippled legs buckle under me.

"I'm too old for you . . ."

"I'm sick of younger men. They always screw me over."

"I can only screw you three times a day. I know that's not very much, not for a woman of your extreme . . ."

"I'm in love with you. When I'm in love, what do minor things such as screwing, old age, and lack of money matter? D'you have any money? Darling. Will you support me? Can I be your child? I've never had any parents. I love you. I love you. When're you going to fuck me? Now?"

"You must have had a difficult childhood. I can tell by the difficulty you have expressing your desires. Listen, baby, I'm going to fuck you so hard you won't even know what's happening to you. I'm going to shove this hard throbbing piston into your cunt your ass your asshole the holes between your toes your nostrils every microinch of your ears your hands your breasts the space between your flopping breasts your mouth your eyes your sweating armpits your navel at 60 miles per hour 200 miles per hour 2,000,000 miles per hour. So fast, my cock'll never leave you. My cock'll be 24 inches, 36 inches long. And you'll be feeling every inch of it. Baby."

I can see his cock following me everywhere: through the Champs-Élysées, Montmartre, the Seine. A huge golden cock at least 70 inches long. Five feet; no, six feet.

"And when you can stop writhing, my baby, cause I've made you come so much and so hard, you're just coming and coming and coming, all you're doing is coming, I'm going to slowly, more lightly and slowly than's possible, lick every part of your body, so slowly, until my tongue comes to your clit. Your clit sticking out, dripping, from your thick red lips. Tongue will be a point; go dot dot dot hammer a tiny metronome on your clit. Your whole body'll begin to shiver, then . . ."

Wet steaming flesh.

Hot breath shuddering next to me.

His lips kiss me so gently I hardly know I'm being kissed. I don't feel mad passion. I feel he loves me.

I'm not sure he wants to fuck me.

His tongue moves between my lips. Lightly grazes my tongue. My mouth hardly feels his tongue. I figure he wants to fuck me. I feel a lot of tenderness for him. Tenderness that's opening me up physically.

Will I fall in love with him?

His red head's rubbing against my head. I rub my right shoulder against his left shoulder, like friends. I want him to feel love for me. I'll wait until he feels love for me. He's kissing me harder and harder. He's going to love me. He's going to take me into his secret warm cave. I'm slowly licking the inside of his right ear. He's shivering and moaning. I'm open. I want him to love me so badly. His hands're running up and down the tender insides of my legs.

"Baby," he's saying, "I'm going to fuck you and keep you. But not yet. You're going to have to suffer first. You're going to have to learn the meaning of suffering. One day you'll find me; and then, it'll be the end of the world. Fuck. Fuck. Fuck. Fuck. I love you so . . ."

He grabs his pants and rushes out of the bar.

I can't follow him cause I'm a cripple.

"These goddamn cunts." Norvins' towering body's making me ripple and swoon. "Have you seen Giannina around? Now that cunt's gone. She's the only one who knows how to put the apples correctly in the bobbing tub."

"I haven't seen Giannina."

"And what happened to that female twerp who said she had seen a murder?"

"She ran into the back room."

"All she wants is attention. Forget her. There's Theo." He runs out and leaves.

I'm a totally hideous monster. I'm too ugly to go out into the world. If I was living with a man, I would have someone who'd tell me if I'm hideous. Now I have no way of knowing if I'm hideous or not. I'm extremely paranoid. I don't want to see anyone. I'm another Paris art failure. I'm not even anonymous. All I want is to constantly fuck someone I love who loves me. Fuck. Fuck. Fuck. Fuck. Fuck.

No one will ever fuck me because I'm a hideous cripple.

I don't know how to present my image properly. When I'm with people, I act either like a changing wishywashy gook or like an aggressive leather bulldog. That's an image. Obviously nobody wants to fall in love with me. I'm miserable, I'm completely miserable. I've got this hole inside me my work won't fill. I have to work harder. I'm too freaky. Why was I born a cripple?

Maybe some man will love me if I pay him for it.

Here all the women know everything. They know if they don't spread their legs, no man'll notice them; when they spread their legs, they get fucked not loved. They're worn. They know they have to turn to the brothel.

They flock en masse to the brothel in the back of Norvins' bar. All the pretty boys are there, earning their daily bread. Pretty boys; studs; sexy ugly men. Whenever there's a party in Norvins' brothel, it's the talk of the town.

I hate paying for love.

"Well, my dear," Norvins says to Paul, "it's about time you're here. Your costume looks wonderful. You'll have to set up your mirror behind the crystal ball so you can reflect Giannina who's disguising herself as various men. Each time you need to show some horny dame a future boyfriend, Giannina'll appear in the crystal."

Paul Gauguin's the local cleaning woman.

"Is that that female twerp," Norvins whispers to Theo, "who keeps lying? It's immoral for children to be in a brothel. Get her out of here. Better yet: hide her in the library that's opposite the dining room."

"Don't be ridiculous darling. You're just jealous cause you're too old to wear children's drag."

"Carry this." Norvins hands a broomstick to Theo. "I've got to present the prizes for bobbing apples."

All around me're couples. They laugh and kiss. It's disgusting. I can't stand this loneliness. This party. I hobble up to one of the male whores, ask him if he's busy.

Fifty dollars an hour, honey.

I shudder. How disgusting. How painful. Love's the only revolution, the only way I can escape this society's economic controls. I can't pay someone to really truly love me.

Now this sleazy whore thinks I want him. Now he's rubbing the insides of my thighs. I love being touched there. I don't want to give in to this disgusting emotionless touch. I don't want to give in to anything. I'm burning. "Go away," I scream. "Get out of here. You're a creep. I don't want you. Even if I've paid you." Thank god he doesn't listen to me. I'm tough: I can take care of myself. He's putting his arms around me. For at least a moment I'll be able to relax. I'm deliriously happy. I'm thinking about how much and badly I'm going to get hurt. I'm going to get burned. I'm going to get burned all over. His arms hold me in this real warmth that makes the constant pain I feel go away. I'm no longer thinking. I'm in his arms forever and ever.

All I do is feel: His wet soft lips brush my earlobes, my short thick hairs which make my scalp tingle every time they're rubbed. My forehead. My eyebrows. My eyelids. My eyelashes. The skin between my eyebrows. My sideburns. I feel so warm and safe I want to give him everything that's me I want to forget myself: I turn my face trustingly toward his so that my full lips open, longing, feel his lips I can't tell what I feel I. I feel his mouth's wetness. I feel my body ache, and rub against his.

As he takes off his clothes, I curl around his big red cock. His cock's going to make the world change totally. I take his cock in my mouth, as far as it'll go, I'm testing; then out so I can lick its tip, so I can wet my right hand, corkscrew my right hand up and down the lower smooth slippery shaft. Am I pleasing him? His hands clutch my head. Push my head toward his curling red hair. More and more of his cock hits the back of my throat. My fingers are drumming, not rhythmically, light and hard on his cock. My tongue moves not rhythmically, light and hard, on his long hard cock.

"I'm fucking you for money," he tells me. "I'm fucking you for money."

First he lies on top of me and fucks me. Then we both lie on our sides and fuck. Then he lies on top of me and alternately fucks me in my cunt and in my ass. I come and I come and I come and I come. He moves very slowly as he's coming. He never looks at me. He falls asleep while he's holding me.

"Any man'll fuck me," Giannina tells Veronique in total privacy, "once or twice. But it's like fucking the men in the porno movies I'm in. And I get paid to fuck when I make movies."

Veronique sighs.

"The fucking's always terrific. I come once twice lots I come and I come and I come. The guy never gives a shit about me. The only difference between the artists I fuck and the studs in the movies is that I can talk to the studs in the movies."

"I hardly ever come." Giannina gasps amazement. "I need

to fuck guys who fuck really slowly, for a long time, so it just comes over me. I tremble and tremble and tremble."

"Veronique," Giannina says, "I think I'm falling in love with Jim."

"What's the matter with that?"

"He doesn't want to see me again. He doesn't like me. I don't understand why. We love fucking together."

"It's just your paranoia. I've had the worst week I've had in a long time I'm so paranoid. We're both paranoid cause we're Aries."

"I was lying on the couch with Jim. Watching T.V. I felt I was with this warm person in a home. That hasn't happened to me in months: being with a guy and not just fuck fuck fucking."

"Jim's settling down with Linda. He gets more prudish the more married he gets. He's been dropping all his girlfriends."

"Gee William's cute. He's got the continual hots."

"He kept looking like he was about to jump me. He was real drunk, that's why he was letting some emotion show. This life's keeping us lonely, Giannina. What these artists really want are pillows. Nice soft sweet female pillows. We can't be that way. We've got our own work. We're waitresses."

"Each time I get hurt, I close myself up."

"You act like you don't need anyone."

"The more I find I can live alone, the more I don't want to deal with the younger weakly formless men. The older men never have any emotions. Not toward me."

"The trouble is we keep having images of what we want. We don't let our emotions take over."

"At the end of the party," I'm telling Poirot, "she was dead."

"Where'd she die, Toulouse?"

"It was the end of the party. Veronique said, 'Where's that little twerp Norvins hates? The one who keeps saying she saw a murder. She didn't get lost or something?' We all looked for her. Suddenly Paul screeched. A body was hanging out of the bobbing apple tub."

"Do you always bob for apples? Whose idea was that?"

"I don't know. But she must have been killed during the party." We're sitting in Poirot's small flat on the Rue de Ganglia in Paris. Only one man servant, George, attends the flat. Poirot thinks for a moment.

"Tell me, this Norvins, who runs the bar, what's she like?"

"A good person. Efficient. Hard on her girls and her whores, but she has to be. Looks like a society dame. Veronique, Berthe, and Giannina're her waitresses."

"Did Norvins know the victim?"

"Slightly. She thought of her as 'the nuisance.' So did Theo and Paul. You can't let a young girl run in and out of a brothel as she pleases."

"Who exactly was at the party and what was the layout of the place?"

"The people I've told you. Plus Theo, a young teacher; Paul who was dressed as a witch she was telling everyone's fortune; Vincent my friend; and all the male whores Norvins uses they're all the same. It was basically their party. And two other teachers, Rousseau and Seurat. We call them teachers cause they're so good, they show the whores what to do."

"Were any of these people holding any sort of grudge against the young dead girl?"

"How could they? She was so, so full of shit. She did keep saying she had seen a murder, but no one believed her."

"Maybe she had seen a murder." Poirot's stroking his moustaches like a big fat cat. "Did she say when she had seen this murder?"

"I don't know."

"What's the layout of the brothel?"

"Here:

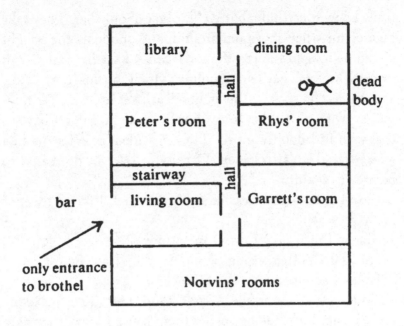

Will I kill myself if I don't get a man?

What do I care who killed that twerp? What's her name? Marie.

Poirot'll figure everything out. He's my father.

I live alone. I've got enough money if my rich mother keeps forking it over. She's sorry for me cause I'm a cripple.

It's better to be a cripple in this world than just a plain ugly creep who writes books.

Every night I lie on my bed and am miserable. I look at the empty spot next to me. When I want to put my head on someone's shoulder, I . . . When I want to find out if I possibly don't look like an ugly cripple, I ask . . . When I want to feel someone's weight pounding into me, bruising me, naked flesh streaming against naked flesh naked flesh pouring wet against naked flesh, I . . . When I ache and ache and ache; I always ache; every day I ache; I . . . I need a man because I love men. I love their thick rough skins. I love the ways they totally know about everything so I don't need to know anything. They don't really know everything, but we'll forget about that. They take hold of me; they shove me around; and suddenly the weight of my own aggression's off me. I can go farther out. I can explore more. They're masculine which means they know about a certain society, this polite-death society which is their society, with which they know how to deal. So I don't have to deal with it. I don't want to. They provide a base for me in a society to which I feel alien. Otherwise I've got no reason to be in this world.

I can't get a man unless money's involved. I found this out in the brothel.

Maybe this is only cause I'm so ugly.

"Should I bother seeing people at all?" I ask Poirot.

Poirot's stumped.

"Whenever I see people, I can't stand them. They make my nerves snap. I can't stand seeing them cause I know they hate me."

"Did you murder the young girl?" Poirot asks.

"I don't like my friends anymore. I don't want to see anyone. I want to sit by myself, and play chess.

"I've got to paint. I've got to paint more and more, make something beautiful, make up for make away with this misery, this dragging . . ."

"You lack the analytical mind. You're too emotional to have planned this murder."

"The cops finally got Norvins' brother," Bethe exclaims. "They gave him the death sentence, and all he was doing was stealing."

"All I ever do is play with myself. I don't care about politics."

"When the cop arrested Clement, Clement hit him over the head with the end of a bottle. What d'you think of that? At his trial Clement said: 'The policeman arrested me in the name of the law; I hit him in the name of liberty.' "

"Berthe, do you think it's better to fuck a man for money, or just to fuck for free?"

"Then Clement said: 'When society refuses you the right to existence, you must take it.' "

"I'll fuck any way I can get it. I love to fuck so much."

"The other day the cops arrested Charles Gallo."

"Huh," says Giannina.

"The anarchist who threw a bottle of vitriol into the middle of the Stock Exchange; fired three revolver shots into the crowd, and didn't kill anyone. When the cops got to him, he said, 'Long live revolution! Long live anarchism! Death to the bourgeois judiciary! Long live dynamite! Bunch of idiots!' "

"That stuff doesn't concern us. We're women. We know about ourselves, our cunts, not the crap you read in the newspapers. Who'd you think murdered the girl?"

"Maybe a person who lives in the same hell we live in. Sure we're waitresses. We're part of the meat market. We're the meat. That's how we get loved. We get cooked. We get our asses burned cause sex, like everything else, is always involved with money."

"I don't like to think and I don't trust people who think." Giannina kisses Bethe on her right ear.

"If we lived in a society without bosses," Bethe says seriously, "we'd be fucking all the time. We wouldn't have to be images. Cunt special. We could fuck every artist in the world."

"I'd like to fuck all the time."

"My heroine is Sophie Perovskaya." Giannina's slowly licking the inside of Berthe's ear. "Five years ago March first The People's Will, a group she was part of, murdered Tsar Alexander II. As she died, she rejoiced, for she realized her death would deal a fatal blow to autocracy." Giannina blows into her ear. "I'd like to have the guts to follow that woman."

"I want to be a whore."

"Don't you understand the world in which we're living?"

Berthe screams. "On Sunday May 21 the first detachment of Versailles troops entered the capital. This entrance caught the Commune unawares. Thiers' army made up of prisoners of war and provincial recruits shot everyone in sight. They killed 25,000 people. The Communards, retreating from Paris, burned as much as they could. Marshal MacMahon of the Versailles army declared order was restored. The death of the Paris Commune was the death of the workers' revolutionary power. Now we have to give up our lives to cause any destruction of this society."

Giannina kisses Berthe again and again. Her tongue slowly enters Berthe's full red mouth.

"We want men!" both women think. "Be a man to me! Fuck me. Fuck me. Lie on top of me. Drive it into me. We want women!"

Their warmth and need for warmth drive them into each other.

They feel confused. They're not sure they want each other, even though sweat's pouring out of their flesh and their cunt muscles're relaxing, opening with the agony of desire.

Naked flesh against naked flesh. Naked lips against naked lips. Naked cunt burning against naked cunt. Naked thighs against naked thighs. Bare shoulders twisting around bare shoulders. Naked tits against naked tits.

"Giannina," murmurs Berthe, "sometimes I hate you. You're so beautiful every man's always creaming in his pants after you. I could never be so beautiful. When I'm with you, sometimes, I feel ugly." Her tongue flickers the aching nipples.

Her whole mouth goes to the nipple, and sucks.

The hair curling above the cunt, between the thighs, around the outer lips, in the red crack of the ass touches the thick pink outer lips touches the tiny red inner lips inside the outer lips touches the red berry at one end of the inner lips whose inside grows if it's grazed lightly enough touches the muscles and nerves spiraling as a canal away from the red inner lips. Berthe's thumb draws a slow pink spiral against the soft yielding breast flesh. Her right hand's fingertips grasp the heavy falling breast. The nipple rubs against the inside of her palm.

"Giannina, I don't want to. I think I'm falling in love with you. Help me not to, or don't let me get burned, I'm scared I'm going to be very very in love with you."

The wide open pink cunt lips. Giannina's fingers touch.

The thin slivers of red membrane.

As Giannina touches the membrane, lightly, very lightly, she sees the membrane move, the whole cunt quiver. Sigh. Lightly she draws her middle finger along the main fold . . .

She hears Berthe scream and scream. Berthe screams and screams. Berthe's in a world composed only of sensations. She doesn't know anything except what she feels. She rolls around on this wonderful mass of flesh and bones, yielding and non-yielding, her nerves rub into warm, wet, rough hairs. She writhes reels quivers shakes turns spins falls rises bounces squirms wiggles pants. Her sense of balance's rolling against Giannina.

Fucking. Fucking. Fucking. Feeling all the possible feelings which are needs in the world.

Giannina's the cat. She throws herself up, against Berthe because she wants Berthe. She wants to throw her body into Berthe's body because she wants to bask in Berthe's heat. Berthe's safety. Berthe's going to do it to her. Berthe looks so huge. Berthe's flaming hair. Berthe's blue eyes. Berthe's huge hands. Berthe'll protect her: she can open herself totally to Berthe . . .

Her cunt opens to Berthe's cunt. To all of Berthe's body which's going to get inside her. Her mouth's open. Her eyes're open. Her arms are open, groping wet heavy flesh. Her legs're open. Wide. Her stomach's rending. Her whole abdomen's opening. Her womb . . .

"I'm frightened. I want you. This's the sun. I want you," Berthe squeals.

"If you were a man, I could love you," says Giannina.

The Paris of 1886 is the Paris of the Conservatives, in spite of the surprising, and painfully short presidency of the Radical René Goblet; of General Boulanger; of the Opportunists who're making Paris and France into an empire whose only rival is Great Britain; of depression due to increasing imports of American and Australian wheat, widespread phylloxera destruction of grapevines, lack of natural sources such as coal needed in this beginning industrial period. An act passed July 1886 forbids the Orleans and Bourbon heirs access to French soil. General Boulanger, the new Minister of War, expels the Duc d'Aumale and the Duc de Chartres from the Army. The general on the black horse's charming! Bismarck, a bit too hastily, incarcerates a prominent unnamable French person. Boulanger gets him released! But people're still starving everywhere: strikes're increasing especially in the mining, iron, and steel industries.

What can we know of such a period?

A particularly brutal strike and murder occurs in the mining town of Decazeville.

The most important incident of the year, at least for us, takes place not in France, but in Chicago, U.S.A. The most industrialized city in the world. A city that's a giant factory. In France the workers still support their bosses. The workers want to be petit bourgeoisie. The new Marxist party, tiny to begin with and composed of intellectuals, splits into the "Possibilists" and the French Workers' Party. In Chicago the workers unite.

May Day, 1886.

The workers celebrate and demonstrate.

A strike's going on at the McCormick harvester works.

Two days later. Chicago cops shoot at strikers during a clash between strikers and blacklegs at the works.

Local anarchists hold a meeting at Haymarket, a large empty spot in Chicago, to protest the cop shootout.

The meeting goes peacefully enough. A heavy storm drives away most of the people. The police order the meeting to close. Samuel Fielden, one of the demonstration leaders, who's still speaking, objects. He tells the cop the meeting's orderly. The police lieutenant insists. Suddenly, a bomb explodes the crowd.

Who threw the bomb?

The day is wet, cold, and windy. One policeman, several other people wounded. The police start to shoot. Demonstrators policemen wounded killed.

The city panics! Bombers terrorists're going to take over! The police arrest nine prominent anarchists. One of the nine, Schnaubelt, disappears.

Another of the nine, Albert Parsons, who's been missing, turns himself in to the cops so he can share his friends' fate.

The defendant anarchists try to use their trial to put the conservative American government on the defensive:

SCHWAB (ONE OF THE ANARCHISTS): I demand the floor in the name of all the defendants.

JUDGE: You can't have the floor!

THE ANARCHISTS: Speak, Schwab, speak!

SEVERAL JURYMEN: Your Honor, tell the defendants to shut up.

THE D.A.: The defendants are to remain seated!

(All the anarchists stand up and scream.)

JUDGE: The court will not permit itself to be intimidated by this uproar. I declare that, if the slightest disturbance is injected into the trial, I shall bring in a verdict of guilt against the defendants.

SEVERAL ANARCHISTS: Cut it short! Judge us now, without letting us be heard! That won't take so long!
THE ANARCHISTS (EN MASSE): Condemn all of us! All! All!

The court sentences four of the anarchists to death.
The court sentences four of the anarchists to long prison terms.
During the appeal sessions, Albert Parsons speaks for eight hours. Samuel Fielden speaks for three. Schwab calls for "a state of society in which all human beings do right for the simple reason that it's right and hate wrong because it's wrong."
Lingg (a true terrorist who has manufactured bombs) expresses contempt for "your ORDER, your laws, your force-propped authority."
The court changes none of the death or prison sentences.
My friends Vincent, Paul, Theo're starving. I'm dying for lack of love. Suddenly I'm also starving because my mother stops giving me money. I move into the brothel.
In the last bedroom of Norvins' brothel, a small dingy room into which a beam of light occasionally filters, Rhys Chatham, a prostitute, lives. Rhys is a tall red-hair, lanky, huge basketball player's chest, broad shoulders, green eyes thin large nose stiff spine. He's an ex-cop. In fact, he used to be Superintendent of the Paris police. He was a good, honest cop, as cops go; he got his desire to work hard and be honest from his religious parents. But he also wanted to find God, and God isn't in the police force. This's the wildness and meanness of Rhys' character.
"Masturbate in front of me," Rhys says to me.

2

longing for better things

"You know that city called San Francisco," Giannina says to Vincent Van Gogh one day in the brothel.

"Huh," says Vincent.

"You know. The place where all the criminals and perverts live. They've got lots of earthquakes there so the U.S.A. government encourages all its misfits to live there so maybe the earthquake'll kill them."

"Huh," says Vincent.

"I want to go there, Vincent. I love this American poet Ron Silliman who lives in San Francisco."

"Giannina, you shouldn't be here, in the brothel. You're only a lowly waitress."

"I'm desperately in love. I'm going to kill myself if I don't get to San Francisco. Maybe I can become a prostitute; earn enough money to get to San Francisco."

"You're too much like a cat. You're not tough enough, and

you don't like people enough. You're good in bed, G., when you love someone and only when you love someone. That's a problem."

"You're not so terrific yourself, big boy, and I've heard that you've turned a few tricks. I've seen you go crazy when you're in bed with me; you love what I do to you; what d'ya mean I'm not any good in bed? And I've never fallen in love with you! You're too young anyway!"

"Does this guy in San Francisco love you?"

"I'm not even sure he knows who I am."

Vincent sighs. These waitresses sure can be stupid. "Giannina," he moans, "don't go to San Francisco. In this city there's no such thing as love. We're all too much into doing our art: when we fuck, we fuck, but really, fucking's not very important . . ."

"All there is is art . . .

"Giannina, we're all friends here . . .

"Giannina, you can't go running half-way across the world . . .

"You can't race to San Francisco after some guy who doesn't even know you or love you . . ."

Giannina the cat's not listening to this claptrap. She's too sensual to be smart. She's not sure what she wants. There's a faint idea in her mind, a kind of shitty goosh feeling. A glimmering knowledge of feeling for someone so strongly nothing else exists. A possibility of living in a world to which she's not always alien. San Francisco!

San Francisco!

"Listen," Poirot tells Rhys the prostitute, "we have to use our brains. If we don't find this murderer, more murders'll occur in this brothel.

"Who could have possibly murdered the girl?"

"I don't know," Rhys replies.

"O.K. According to the coroner's report, the girl was murdered during Norvins' party. Could anyone have gotten from the bar or from the outside street into the party?"

"No."

"Then it was someone at the party . . ."

"It was one of us . . ."

"Who exactly was at the party? Do any of these people dislike the little girl who was murdered?"

"Norvins was at the party. Vincent, you know, Toulouse, Paul, all those artists who hang out at the brothel. And their teacher friends: Theo, who's also Vincent's brother, and Père Tanguy, headmaster of the school Vincent teaches at. Marie, the girl who was murdered, went to that school. Marie's family, her mother brother and sister, were there. They're all prostitutes and older than Marie. Berthe, Giannina, and Veronique. All of us: myself, Peter, Garrett. And Zidler, the whore lawyer."

"Who are these people?"

"Veronique, Berthe, Giannina work as waitresses for Norvins. They're too stupid to murder anyone. Peter Garrett and I are Norvins' boys. Marie's mom, sis, and brother sometimes work for Norvins. Vincent Van Gogh Toulouse Lautrec Paul Gauguin the artists hang around here cause they work so hard, they need to calm down to play hard so they can start working hard again. Theo and Tanguy hang out with them. Zippy Zidler's the family lawyer for this whole neighborhood."

"The murderer must be one of these people."

"Listen, Poirot, you have to stop thinking like that. We all love each other here."

"I hate every one and thing I know," that mad flighty girl Giannina confesses. "All I think about is Ron.

"I think about his blond moustache.

"I think about his uncircumcised cock. I never saw one before.

"I think about how he gets so scared in bed, when he really loves someone, that his cock can't get hard.

"Now he's wearing a red flannel shirt. Thin off-white pants that make his hips look wide. He's got a funny flat kind of heavy body. A hat slung low over his eyes.

"He's so smart.

"He's very male; he goes after whoever he wants. He never pushes.

"He's strong and quiet.

"He knows so much more than me he can teach me stuff I don't know.

"He's so secure, he'll give me some stability. I'm too flighty.

"He doesn't love me which means he'll be mean to me so I can look up to him even more.

"He's less sensual than me."

"I thought you didn't know this guy, G. Maybe you just want to get out of this doom claustrophobic filth city like the rest of us. There must be someplace else besides here."

Giannina scratches her dark head. "I don't think that's the only reason I'm falling in love with Ron, though I certainly hate this city. I have to be totally dull in this city. If I open myself to feeling anything, I'll get totally destroyed."

"Yeah. Paris' a rotting stinking shithole. Every now and then, suddenly, I realize that no person should be able to live in such filth. I ask the person I'm with: "why d'you stay here?" The invariable reply "cause the pressure excitement keeps me working hard" proves my friend's becoming immersed in the filth.

"I don't know. I don't want to think about being here too hard."

"Sometimes I think I'm going crazy: I'm walking down the filthy street to work, and I think I'm going crazy. The skin on my head starts swelling. My fingers, hands, shoulders, legs, feet. My sinuses are pounding. I've got to run. The air's too thick.

There's too many people. Thousands of people're sitting on rows of folding chairs in one tiny filthy room. Water's gushing out of their skins. I'm one of these people. Nobody says a word. Nobody complains. More and more people enter the room. They tell us to go to another room. We go to another room and sit on identical folding chairs. One person says they're about to close off the cities cause our government can't handle the city problems any more and doesn't need the cities.

"We'll never get out again.

"Ron is so wonderful, Vincent."

"Giannina, if you have to fall in love, fall in love with someone who's rich. We need money to get out of here."

"Ron was my closest friend when I lived in San Francisco.

"I never talked to anyone when I loved out there. I was very shy.

"One night I was sitting in a bar in North Beach with my friend Andrei. We were drinking Angels' Clits.

"A friend of Andrei's named Jim walked into the bar.

"After we had drunk a lot of Angels' Clits, we decided to bust up this poetry reading that was happening a few blocks away. Andrei and Jim walked me in a shopping cart into the reading. I jumped out of the cart just as it began to clatter down a series of steep steps . . .

"Andrei wanted to go into the reading cause in the reading people'd come to him and tell him he was famous. Jim and I lumbered into an empty theater right above the reading.

"Jim began to eat me. His jaw dislocated. A guy named Stanley, another friend of Andrei's, punched it back into place. We knew Stanley was a Buddhist genius. People were coming out of the reading, so Andrei, Jim, Stanley and I stood by the door. greeted the people by kissing my nipples. I propositioned the women.

"Suddenly I noticed some man's eyes on me.

"He looked straight. I decided he was a creep.

"He said, 'Excuse me, are you Giannina? I'm Ron Silliman. Bruce Leary told me you're a waitress.'

" 'Yeah,' I said, and ignored him. I went back to kissing Jim.

"I don't remember the next time I saw him. I got to know Rae Armantrout, one of Ron's closest friends, who's bi like me. We hung out together. I guess I got to know Ron gradually. My closest friend at that time, Clay, decided he liked David Melnick and David's friends.

"I remember the first time I wanted to fuck Ron. We were on a bus on Market Street. I asked, 'Do you want to come home with me?' He replied, 'No.' I figured he didn't want to fuck me.

"About a month before I planned to leave San Francisco, I was planning to leave San Francisco temporarily," Giannina rubs her black-haired cat's head. "Ron moved to a house near my house. We started going drinking a lot. One night we were drinking in a bar called The Pub. We spent hours talking about writing and people. When we left, I put my hand on Rob's shirt, told him to button his shirt so he wouldn't catch cold. I figured if he wanted to fuck me, he'd touch my hand.

"He didn't."

Vincent's not even listening anymore to this inanity. He's got to figure out how to get out of Montmartre.

"We drank and talked together twice more. At that time I felt I had more in common with Ron than with anyone else I knew.

"The night before I was going to Paris, I went over to Ron's house to see him once more and say goodbye to him. We talked for hours, again about writing. Also, something about his ex-wife. He was becoming friendly again with his ex-wife. He was tired. About midnight I said, 'I'd better go.' He says, 'You can stay the night if you want.'

"I feel confused. I don't know what to do. I figure I should stay the night because I've been wanting to. I don't know how to approach Ron sexually. There's never been anything sexual between us. I walk into the tiny room in which's his bed, leaf through his new work. It looks terrific. I turn around to him. He's larger than me. Is he as frightened as I am?

"I'm not confused: I'm frightened.

"I don't understand why Ron's face's so close to mine. I'm not used to seeing Ron like this. His face looks strange: his yellow moustache his blue eyes. He looks too familiar and not familiar enough. We take our clothes off. He looks totally strange to me now he's naked. I can recognize his head, but not his body. His head doesn't belong to his body. He's very tender to me.

"I want hot violent passionate sex. That way the intensity of my physical feelings will make me forget, not have to deal with the person I'm with, the total confusion I'm feeling.

"Ron's so gentle with me. I can't handle it. He wants to kiss my lips. I'm committed to going to Paris. I'm feeling crazy. He tells me some woman he's been fucking's great in bed. I should fuck her. I'm wondering if I'm good in bed. I keep licking nibbling at, squeezing, sucking, rubbing his cock so I don't have to look at his face.

"As soon as I can, I'm running out of his house, into the San Francisco night, and home."

"Giannina, do you even know this guy?" Vincent asks.

"I love Ron mainly because I love his work. I always fall in love that way. Ron's a great poet: His varied sensuous language reflects and questions itself. What emerges, finally, is a restless deeply-perceiving consciousness. A consciousness, finally, I don't understand. I adore him."

"We'll get out by going to Tahiti," Vincent says. "We can take a freighter past Morea to Papeete. Then we'll go into the countryside. As far away as we can get from Paris. No one ever works in this countryside. No one does art, for art is a category separate from other activities. No one needs such separations in Tahiti cause no one needs to escape. We don't have to suffer all the time.

"From Tahiti, we'll sail to the Fiji Islands. We're gonna get out of here."

"I want to live with Ron for a while," Giannina decides. "I don't think he wants to live with me. I don't know how he feels. I know he doesn't want to live with me. I know I'm crazy saying this. If I don't say this, if I don't keep throwing myself into the unknown, I'll die. Vincent, Vincent, do you understand what I'm saying?"

3

the desperation of the poor

In Paris, the poor are desperate.

Vincent was born on March 30, 1853, at Zundert, a village of 3,000 inhabitants near the Belgian frontier in Brabant, Holland. His father, Theodore, the pastor of the village, was himself the son of a pastor who had had twelve children. Three of Vincent's uncles're picture-dealers; one of them, also called Vincent, carries on his business at The Hague.

Theodore and his wife, Anna Carbentus, have six children: three sons, Vincent, and Theo who's four years the younger, Cornelis, and three daughters, Anna, Elisabeth, and Wilhelmina. The family's a most united one, like many others in a country where the domestic virtues and adherence to Christian doctrine are the foundations of society. Like so many others too, in Holland, the Van Goghs are middle-class citizens living narrow and monotonous lives, still further restricted by Calvinist austerity. Such families often dread the emergence in their midst of some rebellious member likely at any moment to shatter the rigid framework of the home and destroy its unity, an adventurer destined to carve an empire from the ends of the earth, a scientist who may later revolutionize the laws of physics, a thinker who breaks new ground, or an artist whose turbulent genius will scandalize his native land before it comes to idolize him.

The Calvinism of Holland produced a capitalistic spirit. It's doubtful whether anyone, the preacher Theodore . . . Anna . . . appreciated the child Vincent's virtues and needs. Most poets and artists revenge themselves upon society for their early humiliations. But Vincent always blamed himself alone for his sufferings. A frustrated and misunderstood child, not given its due need of affection, ends as a man without roots, in rebellion or bewilderment, almost always embittered. Such are myself, Gauguin, and Van Gogh: sufferers who make others suffer. "One may have a blazing hearth in one's soul," I remember Vincent wrote, "and yet no one ever comes to sit by it. Passersby only see a wisp of smoke rising from the chimney and continue on their way."

At sixteen Vincent was given a post as salesman in the art gallery formerly managed by his Uncle Vincent at The Hague. He was then transferred by the latter to the Parisian firm of Goupil. The boy stayed in this gallery for four years and left it in May 1873 for the London branch. There he fell in love with his landlady's daughter, Ursula. She rejected him. He returned home. Four months later, he was back in the London Goupil Gallery. Ursula. Ursula. He tried to see her; she told him to get lost. He arrived at the Paris Goupil Gallery on May 15, 1875, in a state of desperation.

"Toulouse," Poirot says to me one day, "we're going to have to visit Marie's family. They live in the poorest section of Montmartre. I hope you won't be disgusted by what you're going to see."

"An artist has to see everything," I loftily reply.

"Are you an artist, mon ami? I thought you were a whore. Grab your crutches if you don't want to trip over the drunken bums."

The streets of Montmartre are filthy. Garbage cans and dogshit lie strewn over the sidewalks. Bums lie under the garbage for warmth. Cats run through the collapsing railings; the buildings landlords have burned down to collect insurance, their tenants can no longer pay rent so why not burn down everything, this's the beginning of socialism; the churchyard graves.

There's only one law: don't stop walking as fast as possible. Not for any reason. Thefts, pushing, kidnappings, tricks, murders: all these crimes take place in the open.

The street.

People die in front of other people on the street. There's very little room. Poirot and I have to rush down the Rue Cailancourt. We don't want to see any murders. If we see any murders, we might have to solve them.

We see a woman vomiting in the street.

"Mrs. Freilicher," Poirot bows, "we've been looking for you."

Her bleary eyes stare at us.

"We're investigating your daughter's murder. We thought you might be able to help us."

The woman vomits again. The vomit's red and green and blue and brown. It adds some color to the street.

"Lady, your daughter Marie died the other day.

"If we can find out who murdered her, we might be able to prevent future murders.

"Did your daughter have any enemies?"

The woman blinks at us. She understands nothing. Obviously poverty's destroyed her mind. "Mrrlrrp," her mouth gurgles.

"Marie said she had seen a murder. What'd she mean by this?"

"Marie's a liar." The old woman looks as dazed as ever.

"Mommy, mommy, mommy."

"Go away, Missia. I'm talking to someone. Goddamn children."

A thin girl wearing black shirt and black pants runs in front of my eyes. She slaps her mother hard across the face. "Mommy. Pull yourself together. Something's happened to Melvyn!"

"Who gives a shit?"

The girl turns to Poirot. "Do ya understand? Melvyn my brother's out there. A brick hit him; we were walking. He fell to the ground. He's dead."

"Where'd he die?" Poirot asks.

"Rue Cailancourt. A few blocks from here."

Right near the brothel.

"Missia, your sister died a few days ago in a house near where your bother just died. We're trying to find out who killed her. Your mother isn't able to help us. Right before your sister died, she said she had just seen a murder. Do you know if she had witnessed a murder?"

The thin girl looks at us as if she's testing us. What can she get out of us? What're we good for? She's got to survive. Her mother's a vomiting nuisance. She wiggles her hips. One of her eyes is lower than her other. "Marie was a liar."

"Then she didn't see a murder?"

"She was stupid." The girl's lower eye winks. Her straggly hair looks like it's wet.

"If Marie had seen a murder, would she have told your brother Melvyn?"

"She never saw any murder. Forget about it."

"Did she talk to Melvyn a lot?"

"Melvyn was like her. Greedy. That's why he died."

In December 1877, without waiting for an appointment—of which he was to be apprised a month later—Vincent went off to the Borinage district of Belgium, intent on revealing the light of the gospel to those who most needed it: miners living in extreme poverty and engaged in the hardest possible work. He flattered himself, with the touching presumption of a novice, that he was capable of bringing consolation and the Christian faith to these outcasts.

Then he began his apostolic career whose distressing episodes are so well known. He spent himself with selfless generosity: teaching the children, tending the sick, distributing his scanty possessions, money, clothing, and furniture. He overflowed with love, less for God if the truth must be told, than for humanity. In spite of his efforts to prove his compassion and devotion to the miners, he didn't succeed in convincing them. Moreover, since he's an indifferent speaker, his preaching had no effect on these unfortunate people whom he had thought the most likely of all to listen to him. Whatever advance and sacrifices he made, the Borain proletariat misunderstood him as had his own family. The repeated rebuffs which met his anxious longing to communicate with and be received by and among the workers threw him back, time after time, into his irremediable solitude. It was even questionable whether these hapless creatures would have agreed to an improvement of their lot. Bernardin St. Pierre used to say he never met any human being who didn't revel in his own misery. Vincent stripped himself of everything he had and made himself the poorest of the poor. He even blackened his face so as to look just like the rest of them. Whatever he did, he remained a stranger among the miners.

On April 12, 1881, Vincent took refuge with his parents at Etten. A cousin named Kee came to spend a holiday at Etten. Vincent fell deeply in love with her and proposed. It was a perfectly natural proceeding. He was 28 and wanted to found a family, to put an end to the loneliness that tormented him. Kee refused him. She said she had promised to remain faithful to the memory of her husband. And her parents were utterly opposed to the idea of a penniless son-in-law, with no settled work, and, of all things, an artist. Vincent persisted. She fled to her father in Amsterdam.

He wrote her again and again. She didn't reply. Desperate, he set off to see her. When he called at her house, she declined to appear. He insisted, with an obstinacy described by his uncle as "disgusting," on seeing her. He held his hand over a lighted lamp on the table and said he would keep it there till she arrived. Her horrified parents saw the flame begin to burn the motionless flesh. At last Vincent fainted.

He reached Antwerp on November 28, 1885, and at once rented a room at 194 Beeldekensstraat. In the daytime, he did his own work and attended courses at the Municipal Academy. From 8 till 10 evenings, he practiced drawing from life at a class in the Grand Marche. From 10 until midnight, he went to another life class. For all this art he needed expensive materials which he bought with the necessarily limited funds provided by Theo. When having to choose between working and satisfying his hunger, he was condemned to exhausting undernourishment. He lived exclusively on bread, a little cheese, and coffee. Consequently, he was in a state of perpetual weakness. He suffered from internal pains, lost about ten of his teeth, and coughed incessantly. One day, when he was feeling ill, he could no longer hide the truth from Theo: "I must tell you that Im literally starving."

He left Antwerp suddenly, for Paris, where he arrived February 28, 1886. Poirot again interrupts my thoughts.

"Toulouse," he growls. "You have to wake up. If you keep dreaming all the time, you're going to get killed. I want you to accompany me to T.T.'s house."

"Who's T.T.?"

"Rhys' brother. He knows everyone in Montmartre. He can tell us which of Norvin's guests at the party knew Marie. If any of them wanted Marie out of the way. Oh, also, if there've been any unsolved murders lately."

"You mean maybe Marie wasn't lying? Everyone says she was a lousy little liar."

"T.T. lives on the Rue des Martyrs. The other side of Montmartre. The only thing I know about T.T.'s that he's supposed to be a hermit . . ."

"I'm miserable. I'm totally miserable. I can't see anyone because everyone hates me. I don't want to see you here!"

"T.T.," Poirot says, "we're not going to hurt you. We have to talk to you about Norvin's brothel. There's been a murder."

"I feel so much, sometimes I think I'm going crazy. You won't hurt me? Where the fuck's my bottle? Come on in." I see a heavy-set man. Small face. Small eyes. Six feet three inches. Businessman's clothes.

"I'm an outsider. I can't talk to anyone. My emotions're so strong, they take me over. They drive me. They totally rule me."

"Listen T.T. Three days ago, someone murdered this twerp at one of Norvins' parties. Today a brick hit the twerp's brother's head and killed him."

"I know all about it," T.T. says. "I was at the party." He picks up a newspaper and starts shredding it. Hands me a bottle of rum.

I started drinking as much rum as possible.

"I've known Norvins for years. She was the last person I used to visit. Now I visit no one. She's a good woman: hard as nails. Every woman who succeeds in the business has to be that tough. It's the only way women survive. No wonder I'm refusing to leave this house, get involved in the violent hustling and desires of my friends."

I silently nod my head.

"I've got just enough money to remain in this prison, erect my own fantasies." He grabs for the bottle. Takes a few swigs. I'm sitting so the massive left side of his body leans against my right shoulder, arm, and thigh. "I sent Rhys to Norvins'. Rhys's young and needs guidance. No place for guidance like a brothel. The money he earns'll help me maintain this hermitage."

"Prostitution's supporting everyone these days," I murmur. I start drinking again.

"As I was saying, I was at Norvins' party. I hadn't seen Norvins for a while. The day after the party, I started being a hermit. I don't think anyone who was at the party really knew the murdered girl. She was just a nuisance. That's all Rousseau and Seurat really knew of her."

"She said she had witnessed a murder?"

"Yes. You know all these young girls'll do anything to get attention. That's all she wanted. She'd do anything. A desperate little girl. Anyway, no one noticed her once the party began. She must have been hiding somewhere. I remembered her when I saw her hanging over the side of the bobbing tub, dead."

"What I really want to know is whether there've been any unsolved murders in Montmartre lately."

"You think that brat was telling the truth . . . No one who's poor cares much about the truth . . ."

Suddenly I realize I want to fuck with this strange heavy man. I don't understand why. I shouldn't be attracted to him cause he obviously thinks I'm ugly. I must be getting desperate. I drink more rum.

"Every day thousands of murders occur in Montmartre. How else can a poor person eat? But what murders would Marie have possibly witnessed? There's the Ganneron shootout. In fact, it took place right outside Marie's building: 11 Rue Ganneron. The landlord of 11 Rue Ganneron tried to burn down the building. He realized he couldn't keep collecting rent from people who had no more money and were going through garbage cans, looking for food. He decided to burn down the building to collect city fire insurance. One of the neighborhood leather boys who lives in the building caught the landlord starting the fire. He rushed at the landlord, shiv in hand. This started the largest gang war that's occurred in years. The landlord's mongoloid son, who lives across the street, sees the leather kid making the death rush. He throws a knife into the kid's right arm. This son and the kid belong to separate, and very important, Montmartre gangs. So before ya' know it, it's an all-out gang war. BOOM BOOM BOOM. I saw one kid step out of 14 Rue Ganneron with a cardboard box containing 14 Molotov cocktails. Stuffed with rags. Ready to go.

"The cops never interfere in Montmartre politics. They're too scared they'll get burned. They don't even clean up the dead bodies: the rates can do that."

"I think I'm looking for another type of murder," Poirot says thoughtfully.

I look at T.T.'s red face. As I see his eyes swerve toward mine, I quickly turn away my face. I'm scared he'll notice me. I'm scared that I feel so strongly. Does he want me?

"There was the Haitian voodoo killing: That happened three days before the twerp got bumped off. This guy and his wife weren't getting along too well. Well, they were getting along like most couples these days. He'd go to some whorehouse, not an uppity one like Norvins', for a quickie. She'd screw the garbageman or the delivery boy every now and then. All clean and sane. Like everyone else, this couple gets poorer and poorer. The poorer they get, the more they take it out on each other. How're poor people supposed to live? The guy starts saving his shit: he smears it on the street outside his house. He probably thinks he's cleaning up the neighborhood. The wife starts screwing every man who'll go down on her. If she can't eat, she might as well screw. White-blonde hair. Luscious breasts. The kind of woman who gets every man hard who sees her and who won't give anything away. Her eyes're cold. She's too hungry. The husband wants to go to Haiti, Mexico City, Acapulco. He disappears. When he returns, he's very quiet. He complains he's got a radio in his head and the radio's getting the wrong channel. The U.S.A. government stuck the radio in his head in Mexico City. He's programmed not to say any more. One day he's going to kill some important political figure. Everyone in Montmartre thinks he's crazy. There's no politics in this slum. He's known as "Baron Murder." One day, on the Champs de Mars, the wife, who's called Connie, is found dead. Her white hair flows on to the sidewalk. A white satin sheath cloaks her huge tits. The huge slit in her throat contains no more blood. She was out walking with some boyfriend: one of the neighborhood brats saw her. But he couldn't tell who was with her. And the husband's gone.

"Connie's friend, Arthur, also got bumped off. Connie and Arthur, when they desperately needed money, would work for this solicitor. Name's Zidler, or something like that. Actually . . . as I remember . . . Arthur was the one working for Zidler. There was a dope war going on at the time. It may still be going on. Zidler's located on the Avenue St. Charles right off the Place de Clichy. Near Rue de Ganneron, ya' know? The Avenue St. Charles people, all Africans, want to clean up their street. The street doesn't want to get cleaned up. The pushers bump off a few residents. So the residents form a vigilante committee: any pusher who comes near the block's gonna get it. Then the cops rush in, full blast! Bang, bang, bang! They've got to help their friends the pushers. Arthur's somehow in the middle of all this. He's using Zidler's office as a pusher-station. On the side, he's doing some forging. That's the theory. He's also screwing this hot number, Clay Fear, who's got a jealous boyfriend. Who knows? One night, Arthur's found stabbed in the back. Right in Zidler's office. What a thing to happen in a respectable solicitor's office! Three days before Connie's slaughter. No one knows why he's been murdered.

"Then there's Mrs. Alexander's death. She's an old rich woman who lives off the Rue de Clignancourt. Anyone could have bumped her off, she's so mean. She lives in Montmartre and she thinks poor people don't exist. One night she dies. Death happens to everyone. Who cares if she died naturally or not? Her will says she leaves everything to some whore who was living in her house and making it with every bit of trash off the street. This whore used to do all Mrs. Alexander's correspondence. Zidler, Mrs. Alexander's lawyer, says the whore forged the will. No money for you, honey. So the whore leaves. She was only trying to survive."

"I've got to get back to the brothel so I can requestion Norvins about these murders. T.T., could you get Toulouse home? She's quite drunk."

"I'm madly in love with you, T.T.," I whisper. "My cunt and womb are flaming so much I think I'm becoming a nymphomaniac. If I want you this much, you must want me."

"I think I want you very much, Tooloose. I've never had a cripple before." I feel my face muscles twitch. I can't move. I see his face muscles twitch.

Suddenly we're kissing. We're kissing like both of us have never kissed before.

It seems to be Vincent's longing for the wholesome and his loathing of shams which makes it hard for him to endure Paris. In this late fall of 1886, he begins to despair. In his fur cap and goatish cloak he tramps the snow-covered streets in deep depression. He has no idea where to go, where to find a trace of warm human feeling. He has no friends to call upon. Anyhow, their paltry rivalries disgust him.

As I fuck T.T., all I think about is my brother Vincent.

the creation of the world

At night, after all our customers have gone home, Peters, Rhys, Garrett, and I lie in the brothel livingroom. We try to forget our weary bodies by telling each other bedtime stories. Stores that'll make us dream and sleep.

Peter's rubbing his sore red cock. "I'm going to tell," he says, "the first story tonight":

THE CREATION OF THE WORLD

A cat who has one green whisker and one white whisker keeps getting drunk. She's in love with a big hairy baboon who won't notice her.

When she gets drunk, she lies next to anyone: an elephant, a rat, a stick, even a human. She rubs and rolls and pounces and roars and shuffles and whimpers and prowls. She then smells all the smells in the world.

"Mr. Baboon," she says, "what can I do to make you love me? I'll do anything for you I want you to know that."

The baboon, barely noticing her, says, "You can't make me love you. But it's a depression this year: the rain won't come down because it's in a bad mood; there're almost no plants; I can't get enough to eat. You can bring me some food to show me how much you love me."

The little cat licks her white whisker then she licks her green whisker she runs rushes pounces leaps saunters everywhere, and she brings the baboon all the food that exists in the world.

The baboon looks at all the food that exists in the world. He smiles. He opens his red mouth so wide he blots out the sun. Into this vast wasteland he throws all the bananas all the plums all the mangoes all the kiwis all the apricots all the eggplants all the sugar cane all the honey all the basil all the edible plants and liquids that exist. He swallows. Now there's no more food left in the world.

The little cat looks up at the big hairy baboon. "Do you love me, baboon, now that you're fat and happy?"

"You can't make me love you," growls the baboon. "But the snakes are giving me trouble this year. They want me to pay taxes on the trees I use as my home. I want to have power over the snakes."

The little cat sighs. She'll do anything so the big hairy baboon'll love her. She catches all the mice and rats in the world, plays with them until they're dead. Then she ties them to her tail, one after the other. A long string of mice and rats. All the snakes that exist start following this one little cat.

The cat gives her mice-and-rat tail to the baboon. Now the baboon controls all the snakes in the world.

"Do you love me, darling?" murmurs the shy little cat.

"You can't make me love you, stupid!" the baboon growls. "All I care about is power. I want to control everyone in the world."

The little cat shivers. She doesn't want to help the big hairy gross baboon control everyone. She runs into an old falling-apart house, and hides.

There're no more plants and liquids in the world, so all the animals are forced to eat each other. This is known as scarcity and depression. The lizards alligators crocodiles eat the fish. The hippos snap up the crocodiles. The red ants nibble at the hippos. The anteaters yump up the ants. The wild black hairy boars swallow the anteaters. The hungry black leopards attack the boars. The wild antelopes' horns pierce through the hungry black leopards. The elephants gobble up the wild antelopes. Huge hungry bones-sticking-out tigers drive their jaws into the elephants. The big fish who are left, cause all the little fish are in their bellies, the big sharks snap up the huge hungry bones-sticking-out tigers.

And what about the humans? They were all eaten up long ago. They never did know how to survive.

The big hairy baboon, whose stomach is as big as his head, eats every animal he can get his hands on.

All the fish go into his stomach. All the insects go into his stomach. All the birds, the pretty little parakeets who fall in love with whatever animal they're around and who think they are that animal, the doves who're constantly committing sui-cide because they're so stupid, go into his stomach. All the plant-eating grass-eating animals, the giraffes, and the horses, and the zebras, the water buffalo who loves to fuck go into his stomach. Now the gross baboon's stomach is bigger than his head.

The baboon's so big, the huge hungry bones-sticking-out tigers and the lean sleek black leopards, the crocodiles alligators and piranhas of the big-teeth jaws can't figure out how to sink their teeth into him. The baboon's stomach is too full. So the baboon eats all the animals with huge teeth. Now the gross baboon's stomach's as big as a tent.

The huge elephant tries to kick the baboon. He starts running at this monstrosity of a baboon. There are no plants no rivers to cut down the elephant's speed. Thump, thump, thump! The huge elephant feet. Tramp, Tramp, Tramp. Huge holes left in the surface of the world. Closer . . . Closer . . . The elephant's almost next to the hairy baboon. The elephant's almost on top of the hairy baboon. The baboon can no longer see the elephant: the elephant's running so fast. He sees a grey mist cover the flat barren surface of the earth.

WHOOMP! The baboon's stomach is so huge and hard, it's harder than the hardest rock in the world because there're so many animals plants and liquids in this stomach, this stomach is so dense and immense; the elephant falls right over it. PLUMP! The elephant falls flat on his long sensitive nose. Before he can tell what's happened to him, the horrible evil gross baboon has eaten him up.

Now the horrible baboon's stomach is so huge, it rubs against the white moon. This stomach is so dense, it weighs as much as the earth. So there exist three balls: earth, baboon, and moon.

The little cat's been watching everything.

She's been watching everything from her hide-out in the old dilapidated house.

She's starving. She has to find food so badly she comes crawling out of her hiding-place.

The only being who exists besides her is the gross hairy baboon.

The baboon sees this skinny, crawling, purring creature. He wants her so badly that, finally, after all this time, he's in love with her. He wants her more than anything else in the world!

He sings the following song to make her come purring to him:

> *Finally I've found you love*
> *I realize I have to open up*

The shy little cat doesn't move. She's much too weak. The baboon sings another song:

> *I'm scared you'll hurt me*
> *I've never let myself love anyone*
> *I don't want you to hurt me and I*
> *don't want to stop being this open*

The cat doesn't move. She's too hungry to love anyone.

The baboon sings another heart-rending song:

> *I don't understand love*
> *it's not rational*

The little cat doesn't move. She just doesn't care.

All existence's silent.

The little cat's dreaming: She's dreaming of a forest where white leopards lie down among the free-floating giraffes black rivers run silently by tiny bears graze in the low bushes the wind smells of shit and grass and crushed leaves and cinnamon bark huge hippos yawn and catch flies in their mouths a human staring at his long red prick he doesn't know what to do with it a wasp lands on it and stings while the black rain liquid drips on the shiny plants down in the black soil and up through the thick green shining plant black liquids coursing through the forest grounds coming out of the animals the crocodiles who wait to snap at the stupid deer the wolves who talk to each other the little car plays with everyone by rubbing against the hot skin then running just slightly faster than the other animal, teasing coming small white bears rise up bat their paws against each other's face. The little cat's not dreaming anymore. This is how the world came to be.

And now that the world exists . . .

" 'STOP IT, TED,' I SCREAMED WHEN HE FINALLY RELEASED ME. BUT HE DIDN'T HEAR. HE WAS LIKE A MADMAN: OVERCOME WITH LUST. I WAS TOTALLY IN HIS POWER, COMPLETELY HELP-LESS."

Fear, like an electric shock, ran through my body as Bill turned the car onto the deserted country road. I knew what was coming, the grand finish toward which the events of the evening had been leading. I hadn't tried to stop it. Deep down inside I knew that it was what I really wanted, and as the car bumped down the old dirt road I prayed inwardly that this time everything would work out, that I would be able to go through with it. Bravely I tried to fight down the familiar feeling of terror, but the attempt was useless. Slowly, surely, it began to take control of me, increasing as we rocked closer and closer to the end of the road.

I watched Bill as he drove, wondering if he had any idea of the way I felt. No. Of course not. He thought I was just another girl, maybe prettier than most, but basically like everybody else. He had no idea of the struggle going on inside my head or the dark secret that lay in my past. But I knew that all too soon he would find out what I was really like. Then he would be gone also, just like all the others.

We were near the end of the road and Bill slowed the car

to a stop along the side. He switched off the lights. Then, stretching his arms above his head, he gave a long, contented sigh.

"Wow," he said, "it's a terrific night! Listen to the birds."

"I am," I said, trying to sound calm even though my heart was beating so violently I could hardly even speak.

Bill turned his face to me and smiled. It was dark and I could barely make out his features. His light brown hair looked black. The moonlight glittering in his eyes hid their blue and turned his freckled face ash-white. Although I knew he was good-looking, the darkness made him seem more a monster than a man. Without wanting to, I started to shake. Bill reached out and put his hand lightly on my leg.

"What's the matter? Are you cold?"

"Yes, a little," I answered quietly, even though my inner voice was screaming, "No, I'm not cold, you fool: I'm scared half to death."

"Come here, baby. I'll warm you up."

I wanted to go to him and I didn't want to go to him. I wanted him to love me like I wanted to eat. I didn't want him to turn me away. Then I'd be out in the cold again. Like I always was.

I was scared. I was more scared than I'd been before. I had done this. I had gotten myself in this situation. I could have been stronger. "Baby," his hot breath was rasping my flesh. I could feel his hand play with the tips of my breasts under my bra. I jumped back.

"What's the matter, baby. Scared of daddy? Come to daddy, baby, o baby . . ." He started moaning again and put his arms around me to draw me into him. His huge lips descended on my lips and I felt his tongue, his tongue in the middle of my mouth.

Something in me clicked. I wrenched myself out of his arms.

"What's the matter with you?" Bill looked at me queerly. "You sick or something."

"I, I can't, Bill. I wanted to, I wanted to do everything with you, but I can't."

"You've been coming on hot and heavy all night. You couldn't keep your hands off me until we got out here. What d'you think I am? I'm not going to let you tease me and control me." His eyes looked mean and heavy. I had never seen him like this before. Now he made me really frightened. He put one hand on the opening of my shirt. "You're going to give, girl, you're going to give me what you've been promising. I don't take teasing from no one."

"Bill," I gasped, "I just can't. Please don't be angry with me. I can't stand it when people are angry with me. I can't explain. Just drive me home . . ."

He almost hit me, and then he stopped. I could feel him make the decision. He put his foot on the gas pedal and the car started up. All the way home I felt miserable. I couldn't say anything to him. I couldn't give him what he wanted. When he said good-night in a cold mechanical voice, all I could do was murmur good-night and get out of the car.

I stood looking at the moon for a few moments before unlocking the front door and going inside. The evening had started out so beautifully, so romantically. But I had managed to ruin it. Like so many times before, I had become terrified at the thought of physical intimacy with a man. It seemed like I would never be able to keep a fellow of my own. The once lovely night had become a melancholy symbol of everything my life had ever been . . .

As I lay down on my bed, my future lay bleakly before me, that of a lonely old maid, yearly growing more sour and miserable. I had hoped Bill would save me from such a life.

Somehow I made it through work the next day. I was nervous and irritable. I'm always like that when I get upset because I'm angry at myself and don't know how to handle my anger.

Finally, when I got home, I fell into a soft armchair. I collapsed. Since the livingroom lights were out, I knew my parents weren't home. Finally, I could let myself go and I sobbed and sobbed.

I don't know how long I lay sobbing in the dark. The doorbell rang, but it was in the distance, and I didn't want to answer it. "Go away," I said as loudly as I could.

"Claire, it's me, Bill. Please let me in."

I didn't want to. I dried my eyes and let him in. He looked sheepish, and a bit scared. I could tell that even though I was trembling so hard I could barely stand up.

"What do you want, Bill?"

"I want to apologize for my actions last night. I didn't mean, to treat you like that. I wanted to be good to you and I loused everything up."

I understood that he wanted to save his sexual pride and still adjust to what I wanted. How could I tell him that I didn't want anything? That I would never let a man touch me because of my hideous past?

"Bill," I said, "I thought that with you it'd be different. I really liked," I couldn't say 'love,' "you and I wanted you. All night I was trying to get you to make love to me and when you did, I just couldn't . . . uh . . . You're in the right, Bill, not me."

"It doesn't matter who's right and who's wrong, Claire," he said gently. "We're not playing power games. I love you. I want to know why you wouldn't let me make love to you."

He was so gentle to me and so loving. I couldn't keep myself closed, and dark and hideous, even though I knew my dreadful secret would drive him away from me forever. "Bill. Bill.

"It was a Sunday morning, Bill. Mother and Dad had gone to church but I stayed home so I could cook a huge Sunday brunch for the whole family.

"As I was mixing the eggs and milk in a bowl my brother Ted came into the kitchen. Ted had just gotten back from Nam and he hadn't quite adjusted yet to our peaceful home. He seemed unable to talk and he seemed real scared, like everything was just about to attack him. I knew he didn't sleep well at nights cause I heard him screaming at night through the wall that separated our two bedrooms.

" 'Hi Ted,' I said. I wanted to show him that home was okay. Friendly. I wasn't going to attack him.

"He didn't answer me. After a while he said, 'Come upstairs. I've got something to show you.' He had a strange glassy look in his eyes.

"I wanted to talk with him so I went upstairs eagerly.

" 'Look, Claire,' he said, pulling a pair of red silk pajamas out of his suitcase. 'This is what the Vietnamese girls wear.'

" 'Gee, Ted, they're beautiful.'

" 'Why don't you try them on? You can pretend you're a little Vietnamese girl.'

"I grabbed them and ran into my room. When I returned, Ted was sitting on his bed. 'What d'you think, Ted? Am I O.K.?'

" 'Come here,' he said.

"At first I didn't know what he was saying.

" 'Come here you little bitch yellow girl. Come here pussy. Come here gook twat. Come here, come to Teddy-boy.'

"I couldn't come. I was shocked and frightened. As I started to run out of the room, his hand caught my arm and yanked me back to him and under him so that his heavy body was crushing mine.

" 'That's right, baby. I'm no enemy. I'm going to give you what you want, what all of you yellow bitches want, I've got the thing that's going to conquer your country.' His huge lips bore down on my lips and his hands began to crush my shoulders.

"I shoved his face away. 'Ted, I'm your sister. I'm your sister! Let me go!'

"He grabbed my head with his hands and his right hand covered my mouth. As he shoved my head back against the bed, his other hand tore off the red silk pajamas. His eyes were glazed and drool was coming out of his mouth. He looked cruel and he was hurting me badly.

"I kept struggling as much as I could, hoping, hoping for anything.

" 'Baby, that's the way I like you. The more you move, the hotter you make me. You're so little and delicate, I just want to feel you. I want to feel you all over me.' Then he started to pant. His breath was hot and fetid. I was about to faint. His demanding mouth bit down on my tongue and then on my unformed breasts. He was hurting me.

"His right hand unzipped his pants and he lowered himself into me. Lowered his hardened manhood into me so that I thought he was tearing my skin, thrusting an iron-hot cleaver into the most secret part of my body. He kept forcing himself into me until he began to shudder, and shudder harder. Finally he bore into me so hard, some part of me, burning, gave way. I felt no relief.

"He rolled off of me. Suddenly he began to see me. A look of horror replaced the dazed grin on his face.

" 'O my god,' he gasped. 'What have I done?'

"I grabbed my clothes and ran. I locked myself in my bathroom and turned on the bathtub. Frantically, I kept trying to clean myself.

"Later that night I learned that Ted had rushed out, taken the car, and driven off a cliff."

When I finished talking, I realized that Bill was still in the room. He was shivering.

"What have I done to you, Claire? I should have known. Look," his hand gently took my hand, "do you think you'll ever be able to trust me?"

"Yes," I said. "But I'll have to go slowly. I'm still very scared of men."

"It'll take a long time," Bill said. "But one day you'll want me to touch you and hold you and do all those other things. As for now, I love you, I love the real you because I know everything about you.

"Everything else will happen."

Now I think I must be one of the luckiest girls alive. Every night I thank God for sending me my Bill. If it hadn't been for him, I would have gone through life a lonely and bitter old maid. Instead, with the help of the man I love, I have become at last a real woman. The past few months have been a dream, and I know that there are even greater things in store. Next week, Bill and I are getting married, and with all that we have going for us we can't help but be happy.

"If you're nice to me and send me presents, especially money so I can get this trash printed," I exclaim, rolling drunkenly over my matchstick legs, "I'll tell you another story":

the true story of a rich woman:

I WANT TO BE RAPED EVERY NIGHT!

I was walking along the street. I wasn't doing anything. I was looking for some action.

It was night, late at night, Times Square. The blue yellow green red white and violet neon lights were still blinking. They wouldn't stop blinking for another two hours. And it would still be dark. It's always dark on Times Square: only rats live there, rats and some of those creepy insects that only come out at night.

My name is Jacqueline Onassis.

I kept walking down the slightly wet shining street. The neon lights were blinking at me, winking, inviting hot desires

I had never known existed. In one dark alleyway, seven naked women are waiting to slowly peel off my clothes. One has her tongue under my left arm. One has her hand buried in the soft flesh of my thigh. Hot. There's a woman waiting for me who's madly in love with me. In fact she can't live without me. Every waking minute of the day she sees my face, my face twice its normal size hovering in front of her eyes, my hands tangled in, pressing, messing her wet cunt hairs. She dreams that I'm wet: my thighs are pillars. Joined at the top. Water streaks down their insides. I'm so wet and anxious that sweat's pouring out of me. "Come get me," I whisper to her. "Come get me and handle me."

The street was still wet and shiny. I felt a hand lightly touch my shoulder.

I quickly turned around.

"Look," a young dark-haired man said to me, releasing his erect cock from his pants. "See what you do to me? Every moment I see you. Three nights I've been following you. Three times I had to relieve myself."

I laughed. "Didn't anyone tell you that was bad for you? You could stunt your growth doing it so much."

He didn't laugh. "When are you going to spend a whole night with me? Just one time that we could make love . . ."

I laughed again. "You're too greedy. I'm a married woman with responsibilities. I must be home every night so that I see my children when I wake up in the morning."

"What would be so terrible if you did not?" He pouted.

"Then I'd be remiss in the one duty that my husband demands of me," I said. "And that I would not do."

"Your husband does not care. Otherwise he would have come to see you and the children at least once these past three months," he said.

My voice went cold. "How do you know that? What my husband does or does not do is none of your business."

He sensed instantly he had said too much. "But I love you. I am going crazy for wanting you."

I nodded slowly. Relaxing. "Then keep things in their proper perspective," I said. "And if you're going to keep playing with your cock, you'd better get to the nearest bar before a cop arrests you."

"If I do, will you suck me?"

I was high. The private section of the Metropole was packed. The strobe lights were like a stop-motion camera on my eyes. The heavy pounding of the rock group tortured my ears. I took another sip of wine and looked down at the crowd.

I was annoyed with the black-haired man. He seemed to take too much for granted. In some ways he was like a woman, only in his case he seemed to think that the world revolved around his cock. I was beginning to be bored with him but I didn't see any other possibilities. It was the boredom that led me to smoke a joint. Usually I never smoke in public. But when the Englishwoman offered me a toke in the ladies' room, I stayed.

After that I didn't mind the evening at all. It seemed that I had never laughed so much in my life. Everyone was excruciatingly bright and witty. Now I wanted to dance, but everyone was too busy talking.

I got out of my chair and went to the dance floor alone. Pushing my way into the crowd, I began to dance. I gave myself to the music, happy that I was in the middle of New York City where no one thought it strange that a woman or man wanted to dance alone. I closed my eyes.

When I opened them, the tall good-looking black man was dancing in front of me. He caught my eye but we didn't speak. He moved fantastically well, his body fluid under the shirt, which was open to his waist and tied in a tight knot just over the seemingly glued-on black jeans.

I began to move with him.

After a moment, I spoke. "You're from the South, aren't you?"

"How did you know?"

"You don't dance like the men up here. They jerk up and down."

He laughed. "I never thought of that."

"Where are you from?"

"Cracker country," he said. "Georgia."

"I've never been there."

"You're not missing anything." He looked at me. "I like it better here. We could never do this down there."

"Still?" I asked.

"Still," he said. "They never change."

"My folks sent me up here to a private school when I was eight. I went back when my father was killed—I was sixteen then but I couldn't take it. I headed right back to New York the minute I got enough bread together."

I knew what New York City private schools cost and they weren't cheap. His family had to have money. "What did your father do?"

His voice was even. "He was a pimp. He had a finger in every pie. But he was black and the honkies didn't like that, so they cut him up in an alley an' blamed it on a passing nigger. Then they hung the nigger an' everything was cool."

"I'm sorry."

He shrugged. "My father said that was the way they would do it someday."

The music crashed to a stop and the group came. The record player began a slow number. "Nice talking with you," I said, starting back to the table.

His hand on my arm stopped me. "You don't have to go back there."

I didn't speak.

"You look like a fast-track lady and there's nothin' but mud-
ders back there," he said.

"What've you got in mind?" I asked.

"Action. That's something I got from my father. I'm a
fast-track man. Why don't you meet me outside?"

Again I didn't speak.

"I saw the way you looked," he said. "You gotta be turned
off that black-haired man over there." He smiled suddenly.
"You ever make it with a black man before?"

"No," I answered. I never had.

"I'm better than they say we are," he said.

"Okay." I said. "But we'll have only about an hour. I have
to leave then."

"An hour's enough," he laughed. "In one hour I'll have you
to the moon and back."

When I came out he was on the street opposite the disco-
theque, watching the last of the stores close up for the night.
He turned when he heard the sound of my high-stacked shoes
on the sidewalk. "Any trouble gettin' out?" he asked.

"No," I answered, "I told him I was going to the ladies'."

He grinned. "Mind walking? My place is just up the street
past the Paradise."

"It's the only way to get to the moon," I said, falling in step
beside him.

Despite the hour there were still hookers walking back and
forth. They were engaged in their principal form of amuse-
ment, looking at each other and trying to dodge the cops who
cruised by. For many it was the only thing they had to do for
they were fourteen years old or older and too old for the
streetwalker trade. When most of the people in a city have no
money and no source of money, they live without mercy.

We turned up the street past the Paradise with its smell of

dried cunt juice and piss stains and began to see the cold, now deserted, sidewalk. Halfway up the block he stopped in front of the dirtiest apartment building. He opened the door with a huge key. "We're six flights up."

I nodded and followed him up the old wooden staircase. His apartment was at the head of of the seventh flight. There were no lights in the hall.

I stepped inside the apartment. The room was dark. I heard a click. The room was filled with a soft red light which came from two lamps, one on either side of the bed against the far wall. I looked at the room curiously.

There was no other furniture besides an armless metal chair. A bathtub covered by a wooden board served as a table. I didn't see a toilet, only a sink.

He went over to the bed and reached under a pillow. He took out a joint. Lit it. The sweet acrid smell reached my nostrils as he held it toward me. "I don't have anything to drink."

"That's O.K.," I said, taking a toke from the reefer. "This is good grass."

He smiled. "A friend of mine just in from Istanbul dropped it off. He also laid some righteous coke on me. Ever use it?"

"Sometimes," I said, passing the joint back to him. I put down my bag and moved toward him. I felt the buzzing in my head and the wetness between my legs. It was really good grass if one toke could do that. I pulled at the knot of his shirt. "I have an hour."

Deliberately, he placed the joint in an ashtray and then pushed the see-through blouse down from my shoulders, exposing my naked breasts. He cupped one in each hand, squeezing the nipples between a thumb and forefinger until the pain suddenly flashed through me. "White bitch," he said, smiling.

My smile was as taunting as his own. "Nigger!"

His hands pressed me to my knees in front of him. "You better learn to beg a little if you want some black cock in your hot little pussy."

I had the shirt untied. I pulled at the zipper on his jeans. He wore nothing underneath and his phallus leapt free as I pulled the pants down around his knees. I put a hand on his shaft and pulled it toward my mouth.

His hand held my face away from him. "Beg!" he said sharply.

I looked up at him. "Please," I whispered.

He smiled and relaxed his hands, letting me take him in my mouth while he reached to the bed and lifted up a small vial filled with coke. The tiny gold spoon was attached to the cap with a small bead chain. Expertly he took a spoonful and snorted it up each nostril. Then he looked down at me. "Your turn," he said.

"I'm happy." I was kissing him and licking at his testicles. "I don't need any."

"White bitch!" He pulled at my hair, snapping my head back. He lifted me to my feet, filled a spoon, and held it under a nostril. "You do as I say. Snort!"

I sniffed and the powder lifted from the spoon into my nose. Almost at the same second he had the filled spoon under the other nostril. This time I snorted without his saying a word. I felt the faint numbness in my nose almost immediately. Then the powder exploded in my brain and I felt the strength pouring right into my genitals. "God!" I exclaimed. "That's wild. I came just sniffing it."

He laughed. "You ain't seen nothing yet, baby. I'm goin' to show you some tricks my pappy taught me with that stuff."

A moment later we were naked on the bed and I was laughing. I had never felt so good. He took another spoonful and rubbed it on his gums, making me do the same. Then he licked my nipples until they were wet from his tongue and sprinkled a little of the white powder on them and began to work them over with his mouth and fingers.

I had never felt them grow so long and hard. After a few moments I thought they were going to burst with agonizing pleasure. I began to moan and writhe. "Fuck me," I said. "Fuck me!"

"Not yet," he laughed. "We only beginning."

The next moment the lights were extinguished, and this wild cannibal sprang into bed with me. I sang out, I could not help it now; and giving a grunt of astonishment he began feeling me.

After a moment I was screaming as I had never screamed before. Each orgasm seemed to take me higher than I had ever been. I reached down for his phallus and finding it, pulled myself around so that I was able to take him into my mouth. Greedily I sucked at him. I wanted to swallow him alive, to choke myself to death on that giant beautiful tool.

"O, cut the shit," Norvins says, dragging her huge body into the room. "The boys are snorting away, Toulouse, and you're still talking."

"Norvins," I've got tears in my eyes. "Do you think Peter committed the murders?"

"Peter? Peter the whore?"

I nod yes.

"Don't be ridiculous. Peter's a lamb."

"Peter had this really weird childhood: His father did propaganda work for the American government. His mother was a member of the Young Socialist Party and a headshrinker. His younger brother raised rats. He grew up in the U.S.A. and in Germany. No stability. Plus he was fat. Unattractive. He was always unsure of himself. Since he was a musical genius, he trusted himself implicitly. That sort of thing often leads to murder."

"Why would he have murdered the twerp?"

Suddenly I realize I don't know what I'm saying. I'm too tired to think. All these stories are whirling around in my head, my head's whirling like a moon gone crazy, I'm going to stop thinking. Marcia . . .

A ten-year-old kid who's beautiful, innocent, and unworldly. Suddenly a door closes behind me.

I'm left alone. The men I know have been mistreating me. They all think, because I like to fuck, they can do what they want with me. Step on me. Beat me. Never give me presents. They only fuck me when they have no one else to fuck 'cause they know I'm always ready to fuck. If I fall in love with a ten-year-old brat, maybe I'll find the road to happiness.

Marcia . . .

What would it be like if Marcia one day doesn't resist—if, as my fingers caress the creamy inner surface of one thigh, slightly above the knee, she relaxes, allowing her thighs to open like a book with smooth pages. What then? There comes a softness at the tips of my fingers, a wet, breaking softness under a mat of fragile hair. What does she have deep there, at her pit, between her legs, like a furry animal? Does it have a life of its own? Is it a strange beast lying in wait, with its heaped softness simply bait for the unwary? I'd give anything to know.

I fall asleep, a curtain of softness descending over my senses. My last image is of Marcia, her head tilted back, her chest erect, and, like a vast portal at which I'm longing to prostrate myself, the soft yet muscled forward thrust of her dusky white thighs.

In another part of Montmartre, in an old crumbling deserted house on the corner of the Rue de Clignancourt and Rue Picard, a section of Paris that's still country due to the slight patches of grass, lives a couple a man and a wife who've been together, god willing, for the past thirty years.

These two old people are the only survivors of the once powerful Alexander family. They are not even Alexanders, to tell the truth, for the last Alexander, the rich old beautiful bitch Mrs. Alexander, has died, but they have been servants to the Alexanders for so long that they have inherited, or kept alive, the mysterious Alexander attributes. These two people influence peoples' dreams. Rhys, Peter, Norvins, Poirot, haughtily as they bear themselves in the noonday streets of Montmartre, are no better than slaves to these servant Alexanders, on entering the topsy-turvy commonwealth of sleep.

Two other people live in this rusty wooden house. A young architect who built the house and surrounding garden and who now cares for this living tangle of trees bush and water, and Marcia, the young daughter of Vincent Van Gogh and a clap-ridden sleaze-hag prostitute Vincent fell in love with in The Hague around 1881. Marcia's one of the most innocent of all creatures. She's very pretty; as graceful as a bird, and graceful much in the same way: floppy; as pleasant about the house as a gleam of sunshine falling on the floor through a shadow of twinkling leaves, or as a ray of firelight that dances on the wall while evening is drawing nigh. She gilds all with an atmosphere of love and joy.

The architect is quite another sort of person. He considers himself a thinker, and is certainly of a thoughtful turn, but, with his own path to discover, has perhaps hardly yet reached the point where an educated man begins to think. The true value of his character lies in that deep consciousness of inward strength, which makes all his past vicissitudes seem merely like a change of garments; in that enthusiasm, so quiet that he scarcely knows of its existence, but which gives a warmth to everything that he lays his hand on; in that personal ambition, hidden—from his own as well as others' eyes—among his more generous impulses, but in which lurks a certain efficacy, that might solidify him from a theorist into a champion of some practicable cause. Altogether, in his culture and want of culture—in his crude, wild, and misty philosophy, and the practical experience that counteracts some of its tendencies; in his magnanimous zeal for man's welfare, and his recklessness of whatever the ages had established in man's behalf; in his faith, and in his infidelity; in what he has, and in what he lacks—the artist might fitly enough stand forth as the representative of many compeers in his native land.

The sun's beating down on the tangled branches, the long-waving grass, the weeds, the rock piles, the strange mazes of the garden. Marcia's standing in front of a stream, her back to the house, clad in a halter and pair of underpants. The sun beats down on her. She reaches behind her and unfastens the halter, then, half turning, steps out of the underpants. She steps into the stream, bathes herself, then she puts on her underpants. Slowly she pulls the halter around her chest and ties the neck strap.

The young artist feels faint beads of perspiration across his forehead. This is the first time he's ever seen a ten-year-old girl completely naked. He never thought they could be so beautiful and exciting.

Walking quietly, he passes into a thicker part of the woods where he can no longer see her. He closes his eyes, and sinks, still trembling, to the soil. For a long moment he sits there, the pain of the heat surging inside him bending him almost double.

Slowly he reasons with himself. No. He mustn't. Not again. If he gives into it now, he'll always give into it. At last, he begins to feel better. He puts the French pictures Norvins gave him on the ground, so he can bury them.

All you need is a little self-control and determination. He places the pictures face-down on a tree-stump. He begins to feel proud of himself. He's not going to look at those pictures ever again.

He lies down, on his back, on the earth. The sun beating

down on him makes his mind wander. He forgets the pictures.

As he's about to fall asleep, he hears footsteps. He doesn't want to wake up. He remembers. He freezes. Dazed from the sun, he lurches toward the tree-stump.

She's standing by the tree-stump, the pictures in her hand. She looks up at him in surprise. "Scott, where'd you get these pictures?" she asks, a curious excitement in her voice.

"Give them to me!" he demands, walking toward her.

"I will not!" she retorts, turning her back to him. Her left leg kicks up into the air. "I haven't finished looking at them yet."

Lithely she spins away from his outstretched hand, across the grass, to the far side of the stump. "Let me finish," she says calmly. "Then you can have them back."

She turns to avoid his heavy grasp but his hand catches her shoulder. The pictures fly from her hand as she falls against him. She reaches for the pictures. His hand catches at her halter strap to keep her from getting them, and the strap breaks in his hand. He freezes and stares at her white chest.

"You broke my strap," she says quietly. She makes no move to cover herself. Her eyes watch his face.

He doesn't answer her.

She smiles slowly and raises her hand to her breast, rubbing her palm gently across the nipple. "Im just as pretty as any of the girls in those pictures, aren't I?"

He's fascinated, unable to speak. His eyes follow the movement of her hand. "Aren't I?" she asks again. "You can tell me. I won't tell anyone Why do you think I let you watch while I was bathing?"

"You knew I was watching?" he asks in surprise.

She laughs. "Of course, stupid. I could see you in the water. I almost burst out laughing. I thought your eyes would pop out of your head."

He can feel the tension begin to build up inside him. "I don't think that's funny."

"Look at me," she says. "I like you to look at me. I wish everyone could." She swivels around so that her knees stick away from her thighs.

"That's not right," he says.

"Why not?" she demands. "What's wrong with it? I like to look at you; why shouldn't you look at me?"

"But you never did," he quickly replies.

A smile comes to her lips. "Oh, yes I did."

"You did? When?"

"The other afternoon when you came back from Norvins'. I know what you do there. There was no one home and I watched you through the bathroom keyhole. I saw everything you did."

"Everything?" The word escapes his mouth like a caress.

"Everything," she says smugly. "You were exercising your muscle." Her eyes look into his. "I never knew it could get so long. I always thought it was little and kind of droopy like it was in the beginning."

There's a tightness in his throat. He can hardly speak. He begins to get up from the tree-stump. "I think you'd better get away from here," he says hoarsely.

She looks up at him. Smiling. "Would you like to see all of me?"

He doesn't answer.

Her hand reaches up and unties the neck strap of the halter. Half turning, she steps out of the underpants. He stares at her naked body, feeling his legs begin to tremble. He sees her eyes move down on him. His shirt hangs open. He looks at her again.

"Now take off your clothes and let me see all of you," she says.

As if in a daze he lets his shirt, then his pants slip to the earth. He groans and sinks to his knees in the earth, holding himself.

Quickly she moves to him and looks down at him. A faint

sound of triumph comes into her voice. "Now," she says, "you can do it for me."

His hand reaches up to touch her chest. She lets it rest there a moment, then suddenly moves away from him. "No!" she says sharply. "Don't touch me!"

He stares at her dumbly, the agony pouring through him in waves.

Her heavy-lidded eyes watch him.

"Do it for me," she says in a husky voice. "And I'll do it for you. But don't touch me!"

how love can lead
youngsters to murder

Scott's, the young artist's, real name is James Dean.

Marcia's real name is Janis Joplin.

James and Janie fell madly in love when James, or Jimmy, was still working on *Rebel Without a Cause*. They were children and not yet hardened, frightened into feelinglessness by the Hollywood scene: still able to fall in love. Fall in love frantically, desperately, without any reservation. With all the insane hopes, fantasies, myths, and desires children have. Jimmy was 24 years old. Janis was only 9. They were unhappy, scared. They didn't understand the world they had been thrown into. Not only could they escape into each other; they also were able to reinforce each other's fantasy that the constant loneliness and paranoia of the world no longer existed for them.

Theirs was the perfect American love affair.

Rebel Without a Cause tells a story as old as *Tom Brown's*

School Days: a boy's adventures, travails, and triumph on his first day at a new school. Jim Dean plays the part of the fledgling Jim Stark, a new boy at Dawson High. What makes *Rebel* different from traditional schoolboy adventures is that school is no longer the only relevant field of action. Most of *Rebel* takes place away from Dawson High, late at night, in a teenage underworld of violence, romance, and death. There are also new, more powerful authority figures: parents and the police.

In *Rebel Without a Cause* Jimmy Dean plays himself. He's victim and hero: the kid who learns to be bad cause he can't be good in a society whose goodness stinks. The kid who keeps his innocence and vulnerability while he learns. The corrupted society. Jimmy not only played in this film, he also helped director Nicholas Ray create the film. Jimmy did this while he was lonely, overwhelmingly lonely, confused by his homosexuality and the sudden success he was having. The Hollywood world in which he made the film was, as is reality, far more complexly corrupt than the society in *Rebel Without a Cause*. Everyone in Hollywood carries hell in his or her heart.

If Jimmy was lonely, Janis was even more lonely. She had fled the boredom and the hostility of her hometown, Port Arthur, Texas, to find a place that was like her: bubbling and wild. Venice, Hollywood, all that part of southern California at that time was full of freaks, but Janis was too insecure, too unsure of herself to talk to anyone.

One day, when Jimmy was sitting in the Warner Brothers' cafeteria, he met Janis. He noticed a young girl sitting at the table across from him. She was so young she should have been with her parents, but she wasn't. She seemed so innocent Jimmy was intrigued. "Hey," he said to the long-haired kid, "what are you doing around here?"

"What d'you mean 'what am I doing around here'?" she pugnaciously replied. "I have as much right to be here as you do." Janis noticed how good-looking Jimmy was, but she wasn't going to show she noticed.

"You're just a kid."

"I am not." She pushed up her filthy shirt sleeve and showed him the tracks covering the lower part of her arm.

Jimmy sneered. "So what. Only brats who want to act grown-up do that. Real actors have to take care of themselves."

Janis felt put-down. "Fuck it up your ass. Star." She tossed her long brown hair. "Anyway I'm not an actress. I'm a singer. I sing the blues."

"Hey, Jimmy, you're on," Natalie Wood's voice rang out. Natalie was playing Judy, the main girl in *Rebel Without a Cause.*

Jimmy decided he wanted to see this brat again. She wasn't like any other girl he had ever met. "Listen." His finger pointed at her face. "Wait here, I'll be back in three hours."

When Jimmy drove his MG right up to the door of the Warner Brothers' cafeteria, Janis' heart began to flutter in her chest. What a wild thing to do, Janis thought to herself. Here's a man whom I want to be able to tell what to do. He's tough and he's wild and he's mean. I need a mean man cause I'm mean and wild myself. I'm too intelligent for a woman. I need a man who can help me a little cause this death society doesn't like intelligent women. A man who can teach me something. I need a man who can step on me a little. A woman's gotta be stepped on, otherwise she stops being hard and mean and she can't deal with society anymore. I mean, I've got to make it and I've got to keep on making it. Dum, dum, dum.

This man isn't like those Port Arthur creeps. Those jocks and rednecks who made fun of me and told their children to stop associating with me, cause I wasn't feminine enough and pretty enough and I didn't DO THINGS RIGHT.

This guy probably doesn't like me. Hard men never go for powerful chicks, the ones like me, who got visions. They got their own visions and they just want some pretty chickie who'll say yes to them and make life easier for them. That's all they want.

But I gotta get loved and I gotta get love from a guy who's real to me. I need a tough leather guy. So I'll just take whatever this boy offers, Janis decided, I'll do whatever he wants, as much as I can, so that he'll love me a little. If he kicks me in the groin, and throws me away, so what, at least I'll have gotten a little bit of good loving. When it's over, it's over.

As soon as Janis got in the car, Jimmy stopped noticing her. He wanted her to reject him. As if alone, he began to race his red 53 MG down Santa Monica Boulevard, Venice Boulevard, right on to a deserted portion of the Venice beach. He pulled the car up to an old, old for California, ramshackle beach house.

He got out of the car and, hands in his pockets, started slouching toward the ocean.

Janis wasn't going to be put off like this. Goddamnit, he was going to notice her. Notice me! Notice me! her body cried. She ran into Jimmy and started punching him.

"Just cause you're some fuckin' MOVIE STAR," her eyes, skin, and hair seemed to light up and explode, "you think you can ignore me. You're just like all the other creepy men I've ever known." She was trying hard not to cry.

Jimmy smiled. He looked shy and childlike. "O.K. Let's see if we can become friends." They grabbed hands and fell down in the sand. Jimmy's body was thin and muscular. Janis was already in love with him.

"I'll tell you everything," Janis said. "I want to sing, man. That's all there is to me. I got this vision and it's driving me crazy. Like Zelda Fitzgerald.

"You're not going to understand cause you're a man."

"I understand what it is to be driven. My mother died when I was 9 years old. She just left me like that. Then my father sent me away. I knew I was bad and I knew I had to create my own world. Really. Not just fantasize. Create my own world."

"You still don't understand." Suddenly Janis didn't care anymore if she was impressing him. She was caught up in her own pain. "Men can do what they want. Those who got visions can try to follow them. Women in show business, man, they sing their fuckin' insides out cause they give up more than you'd ever know. If they got kids, they give them up; any woman gives up a home life, an old man, probably, a home and friends; you give up an old man and friends; you give up every constant in the world except music. That's the only thing you got, man."

"It's the same for a man," Jimmy said thoughtfully. "An actor doesn't even have a constant like music. Everything in the world is simply a tool for him, nothing more."

"But you can get laid, man! Every movie star gets laid! But I'm a woman: I don't want an ass-kisser, I want a guy who's bigger and stronger and ballsier than me. When I'm on the road, where am I going to find a man like that? Men like that want ass-lickers. They don't want women they're constantly going to have to fight. I'm always going to be alone, man."

Jimmy looked at Janis seriously. She was being honest and, like him, she sensed her own badness. "I'm lonely too, Janis. I'm trying to make myself be someone else, be JAMES DEAN, but I'm killing myself, I don't know who and where I am. As for sex," he looked at her closely, "I haven't been to bed with anybody. I've told all the girls I've met to kiss my ass because they're sterile, spineless, stupid prostitutes. What d'you think of that?"

"I think we're going to be friends, man." They looked at each other for a long time.

Both of them felt they had found something they had lost a long time ago, before they could remember. Now they could relax. They started playing with each other and giggling, just like kids.

Often they talked about themselves and their problems,

about movies and acting, about life and life after death. Then they'd walk side-by-side, not actually speaking, but communicating their love silently to each other.

They were beginning to have a complete understanding of each other.

They were like Romeo and Juliet, together and inseparable. Sometimes on the beach they loved each other so much they just wanted to walk together into the sea, holding hands, because they knew then that they would always be together.

It wasn't that they wanted to commit suicide.

They loved their lives, and it was just that they wanted to be that close to each other always.

They didn't want to be seen together at film premieres and nightclubs.

They didn't want to be in the gossip columns or be seen at the big Hollywood parties.

They were kids together and that's the way they both liked it.

They began to see a great deal of each other when they weren't making films or singing. They were young and wanted to enjoy life together and they did.

More than any other person Henry Kissinger is determining our lives in the 1970's.

On January 20, 1969, the government of the United States fell into the hands of a group of men who were undistinguished in intellect, personality, or vision. Swept into power at the end of a tormented decade, they were chosen not so much out of admiration or enthusiasm as out of fear, hatred, and desperation. No one would deign to bestow upon them the superficial accolades that had frequently adorned their predecessors, even in the worst hours of poverty and cruelty and war; in these administrations there are no Thousand Days, no New Frontier or Great Society. It was as if everyone had instantly grasped their obvious inferiority, and hoped only that the country could somehow muddle on until a time in the future when, refreshed and reinvigorated, it would catch hold of itself and produce leadership where a simple void had existed before.

In this bleak and unpromising setting, for those who think they know or presume to judge, one figure stands out. Unlike the rest, he is sharp, determined, relentlessly intellectual—one of the brightest men, some say, this country has ever produced. Open-minded and pragmatic, he is not tied to the mistakes of the past, even to those he himself had once spoken for. Brash and impenetrable, yes, but there is still a humility about him that his steelier and more arrogant predecessors clearly lacked: he possesses a stark recognition of America's and his own limitations, and he has promised again and again that neither will be tested at its extreme. The days when America would pay any price, would bear any burden, would meet any hardship, would fight any foe to achieve the defense of liberty had made for a certain public spirit and élan; but, in retrospect, they led to overcommitment, to useless loss and destruction around the world. And in those hours of crisis, the President of the United States was surrounded by men largely lacking in open-mindedness and critical perspective, men who blindly insisted that the country continue on the same futile course of action that they themselves had launched. But now, it would be different: there would be a sense of proportion. One often wonders, in fact, how he emerged in this crowd of banal and mediocre men, and more important yet, how influential he will be and how long he will last.

The main question of our age is: how can all-out war and total nuclear destruction be avoided? Kissinger's answer is: by limited war. Kissinger was led to believe in limited war through his faith in the universal applicability of Metternich-style diplomacy, a diplomacy that presupposed an area of common interest and understanding, as well as one of conflict, between the contending parties. "In seeking to avoid the horrors of all-out war by outlining an alternative, in developing a concept of limitation that combines firmness with moderation, diplomacy can once more establish a relationship with force even in the nuclear age."

What are the requisites of such a diplomacy?

A diplomat, to be effective, must possess a certain degree of credibility. Under the circumstances of America's worldwide commitment—a commitment that, by its very scope, would seem to defy belief—and of the general unstable world condition due, among other causes, to the advanced nuclear technology many nations now possess, Washington's and Washington's international representatives' credibility must be total and constant. Washington's diplomats must have the freedom and the power to handle incredibly subtle and difficult tactical maneuvers. That means that diplomats must not be harassed by public opinion or the necessities of domestic policy.

According to Kissinger, ". . . it is the President who decides and he, therefore, has to feel comfortable with the way his choices are presented to him or indeed whether he wants any choices." The Presidency is necessary only for decisions on America's role in international affairs. As the chief diplomat, the President is his own Secretary, his own adviser, his own deskman. One of the consequences of Kissinger's "diplomacy"

The story of *Rebel Without a Cause* played a large part in Jimmy's and Janis' romance and so must be told:

Rebel Without a Cause is the story of Romeo and Juliet. Jimmy is the first person we see in *Rebel Without a Cause*, lying dead drunk on the sidewalk, curled up next to a toy monkey he is whimsically trying to cover with a piece of paper, while credits and title flash by in flaming letters.

Without being introduced or identified, Jimmy acts out his own prologue to the movie. He plays an isolated, defenseless child, deliriously enclosed in his own protective fantasy, stranded like some inhabitant of another world on a grimy concrete ledge. Jimmy modeled his pose on one of his favorite paintings, Manet's *Dead Bullfighter*, and in his slow, deliberate actions, the hero is introduced to us almost in embryo, a child with his mechanical toy who wishes nothing more than to be left alone with his dreams.

In the course of this night journey Jimmy (Jimmy Dean) is hauled into Juvenile Hall—a cold, sterile maze with glass partitions and jangling phones, gloomy and bizarre, with endless forms and mechanical procedures. These wards are the result of parental indifference and inability to understand their children. Despondently, the "juvenile delinquents" wait for the real culprits to collect them.

Jim's been hauled in because he's suspected of having beaten up some man. Society sends all its youngest casualties to Juvenile. Plato's (Sal Mineo's) also in this decompression chamber because he's shot a puppy. Judy (Natalie Wood), in searing red coat and lipstick, has been picked up for wandering around late at night.

> RAY (THE JUVENILE DETECTIVE): Why were you out walking the streets at one o'clock in the morning, Judy? You weren't looking for company, were you? (She starts to cry.)
>
> JUDY: He hates me.
>
> RAY: What?
>
> JUDY: He doesn't like anything about me. He calls me . . . He calls me . . .
>
> RAY: He makes you feel pretty unhappy?
>
> JUDY: He calls me a dirty tramp—my own father!

When Ray calls Jim in, he immediately recognizes Jim's act: "You don't kid me, pal. How come you're not wearing your boots?" When Jim tries to take a swing at Ray, Ray invites Jim to "blow your wheels . . . take it out on the desk." Jim blurts out, "If I could have just one day when I wasn't all confused . . . I wasn't ashamed of everything. If I felt I belonged some place." Ray releases Jimmy for lack of evidence.

The next day, the students of Dawson High sit in a darkened auditorium, confronted with a giant replica of the heavens, listening to the dry, droning voice of a lecturer as insectlike as his projector, and they watch this artificial show, a Hollywood projection of the universe! As the lecturer says,

> FOR MANY DAYS BEFORE THE END OF OUR EARTH, PEOPLE WILL LOOK AT THE NIGHT SKY AND NOTICE A STAR, IN-CREASINGLY BRIGHT AND INCREASINGLY NEAR,

Jim enters and says in a stage whisper to the teacher checking names at the door, "STARK, Jim STARK." Jim's the new boy in school. The class turns; the lecturer hesitates; Jim slithers to a seat.

Jim tries to make himself part of Buzz' (Corey Allen's) gang:

> LECTURER'S VOICE: . . . and Taurus, the bull . . .
>
> JIM (IN GOOD IMITATION): Moo! (He waits for approval.)

But Jim's attempt to horn in on the gang has the opposite of the desired effect: it provokes them and they taunt Jim with the idea that he may be a coward:

> SCENE: Angle shot of Judy, Buzz, and group (seen from Jim's angle). He is in the foreground. They are staring at him. Nobody laughs.
>
> CRUNCH (FLAT): Yeah, moo.
>
> BUZZ: Moo. That's real cute. Moo.
>
> GOON: Hey, he's real rough.
>
> CRUNCH: I bet he fights with cows.
>
> BUZZ: Moo.

PLATO, WHO'S TRYING TO MAKE FRIENDS WITH JIMMY, WHIS-
PERS SOME ADVICE:

PLATO: You shouldn't MONKEY with him.

JIM: What?

PLATO: He's a wheel. So's she. It's hard to make friends with
them.

JIM: I don't want to make friends. (He turns back, unhappy
at having revealed himself.)

LECTURER'S VOICE: Destroyed as we began, in a burst of gas
and fire.

The lifeless professor who manipulates the cosmos with his
dumbbell projection ends the world:

LECTURER: The heavens are still and cold once more. In all
the complexity of our universe and the galaxies beyond,
the earth will not be missed . . .
    Through the infinite reaches of space, the problems of
man seem trivial and naive. Indeed. And man, existing
alone, seems to be an episode of little consequence . . .
That's all. Thank you very much.

PLATO: What does HE know about man alone?

Outside the school, Buzz jabs his knife into Jim's whitewall
while Judy's nylon-stockinged leg dangles suggestively in front
of the tire. Jimmy, sitting on the parapet with his back to the
gang, lets out a slow, painful breath of air. There's no way he
can avoid the trouble behind him. He climbs down and moves
toward the group. Goon, then the rest of the gang, and finally
Buzz start clucking at Jim.

Jim asks if they're calling him chicken. He'd had to leave
another school for "messin' up a guy" who called him chicken.
He tries to refuse the knife Buzz forces on him, but the gang
knows he really has no choice and eggs him on.

The two boys circle each other, like wolves vying for territory. Buzz seems to snarl, thoroughly enjoying the encounter, while Jim hesitates, then lunges and gets jabbed in the stomach. Buzz grins. Jimmy makes another quick leap and is cut again.

Jimmy wins the knife fight, but he still can't get into the gang. Now Jimmy has to win Buzz in a chickie run.

Jimmy takes his dilemma home. Can his father help him? Jimmy's father's wearing an apron,

JIM: Can you answer me NOW?

FATHER: Listen, nobody should make a snap decision—this isn't something you just—we ought to consider the pros and cons—

JIM: We don't have TIME.

FATHER: We'll make time. Where's some paper? We'll make a list . . .

JIM (SHOUTING): WHAT CAN YOU DO WHEN YOU HAVE TO BE A MAN?

FATHER: What?

JIM: You going to stop me, Dad?

FATHER: You know I never stop you from anything.

(Jim suddenly makes his decision and sheds his jacket for the red one.)

Believe me—you're at a wonderful age. In ten years you'll look back on this and wish you were a kid again. When you're older, you'll laugh at yourself for thinking this is so important.

Jimmy runs out of the house to meet his next battle, incredulously repeating, "Ten years . . . ten years . . ."

Wind shrieks over the exposed plateau which is several hundred yards long. It cuts into the darkness like the prow of a ship and ends in empty air. Several cars are scattered about defining a sort of runway in the center. There are several kids present but very little talk . . . They stand in small clots, murmuring and smoking.

BUZZ (QUIETLY): This is the edge, boy. This is the end.

JIM: Yeah.

BUZZ: I like you, you know?

JIM: Buzz? What are we doing this for?

BUZZ (STILL QUIET): We got to do SOMETHING. Don't we?

It's the last time they speak, for during the run Buzz catches his sleeve on the door handle and can't get out. Trapped in his car, he careens over the side, and his life ends in a "burst of gas and flames." Jim, looking over the cliff, realizes he's lost his first friend.

Buzz' girlfriend, Judy, rides home with Jim.

Jimmy slips into his parents' home. To cool his overheated brain and heal his frayed nerve ends, he rolls the cool glass of milk bottle across his forehead.

Jimmy sees his father watching T.V. His father (Jim Backus) doesn't want to notice him. Jimmy can't leave: he can't let go of his father.

Jimmy's mother enters the room. Jimmy tells them he got in trouble out at the bluff. His parents tell him they've seen a "bad accident" on the T.V. Jimmy tells them this accident was real and involves him. His parents don't understand. Jim puts his hands around his father's throat, drags him down the stairs, pushes him over his easy chair and onto the floor. His mother runs after them, shrieking, "STOP IT! YOU'LL KILL HIM. JIM! DO YOU WANT TO KILL YOUR FATHER?"

Jim runs away from his parents. He looks for the only other adult he believes can help him—Ray, the juvenile officer. Ray isn't at the precinct, but the gang is. They think Jim's going to tell all so Crunch decides they'd better take care of him.

Jim doesn't want to go home. He has nowhere else to go. He finds Judy waiting in his parents' driveway. She's run away too:

JIM: I swear sometimes, you just want to hold on to somebody! Judy, what am I going to do? I can't go home again.

JUDY: Neither can I.

JIM: No? Why not? (no answer) You know something? I never figured I'd live to see 18. Isn't that dumb.

JUDY: No.

JIM: Each day I'd look in the mirror and I'd say, "What? You still here?" Man! (They laugh a little.)
Like even today. I woke up this morning, you know? Then the first thing that happens is I see you, and I thought this is going to be one terrific day so you better live it up, boy, cause tomorrow maybe you'll be nothing.

As Jimmy gets to kiss Judy—their first kiss

There's a place where Jimmy and Judy can hide: an old mansion Plato knows about. An abandoned villa, with its sunken gardens, waterless foundations, stone balustrades, and rococo candelabra.

This is the new world:

PLATO (HE HOLDS UP THE CANDELABRA): What do you think?

JIM: Wow! Well, now, then, there . . . Let's take it for the summer.

JUDY (LAUGHING): Oh, Jim.

JIM: Should we rent or are we in a buying mood, dear?

PLATO: . . . Only three million dollars a month!

JIM: Why don't we just rent it for the season?

JUDY: You see, we've just . . . oh, you tell him, darling. I'm so embarrassed I could die!

JIM: Well, we're newlyweds.

Judy hums a little lullaby to Plato and he falls off to sleep, but his dreams of the future become nightmares. As the gang members arrive, Plato, as frightened as a child and he is a child, shoots one, screams "You're NOT my father!" at Jim, and rushes off into the bush as the police arrive. Judy and Jim run down the hill after Plato, who has broken into the planetarium and hidden himself in its dark, empty space. The cops arrive at the planetarium door. There are light, bullhorns, Officer Ray, Jim's parents, Plato's maid, and cops.

Cops with guns surround the planetarium. Officer Ray tells the boy in the planetarium to come out with his hands up.

PLATO (SHIVERING LIKE A PUPPY): Do you think the end of the world will come at night, Jim?

Jim tells Plato he'll trade Plato's gun for his jacket. Then he'll unload the gun and give it back to Plato.

JIM (HANDING PLATO THE EMPTY REVOLVER): Friends keep promises, don't they?

Jim walks with Plato to the planetarium door. Plato hesitates when he sees the menacing searchlights and the faceless crowd outside. Plato runs away from Jim and Judy and sobs, "They're not my friends!" The police open fire and the child falls dead.

"But I've got the bullets!" Jim shouts to everyone and no one. Jim goes over to Plato, the second friend he's lost today, and zips up Plato's jacket.

"He was always cold."

The dumbbell professor who gave the astrology lecture walks up to the planetarium and doesn't understand anything,

is that the Presidency has gained more power in decision-making, and Congress and the Pentagon, among others, have lost power.

The second requisite of Kissinger's "diplomacy" is that diplomatic decisions are made according to historical necessities. A diplomat has to follow a course of action which is manifestly correct, rather than give in to the transitory whims of public opinion. A diplomat thinks conceptually because he thinks in terms of wide-range even visionary historic goals.

What are the pragmatic consequences of this conceptual thinking?

Above all, Kissinger fears any power who, for the sake of an idea, as did Hitler, will deny and try to destroy the area of common interest and understanding the other powers have set up. Kissinger most fears ideology. He sees America as the defender of the free world simply because America is still the main nonideological power. Since the Soviet Union is the main ideological power, the fundamental priority of Kissinger's policy is to convince Moscow that it is fruitless to conduct international business on ideological grounds. And the clearest expression so far of Kissinger's opposition to the idea of an ideologically oriented foreign policy is Washington's rapprochement with the People's Republic of China.

Another consequence of Kissinger's conceptual thinking besides his hatred of ideology and revolution, for Kissinger is the arch-conservative, is the concept of "linkage." The rationale of linkage is that all the world's trouble spots exist on a single continuum which connects the Soviet Union and the United States. In this context, the resolution of an individual issue depends not so much on the merits of the specific case as on the overall balance of power in the world. Kissinger's tendency has been to link Europe, the Mideast, and Vietnam without much regard to political or conceptual subtleties. Seeing no viability in modified linkage, he has chosen total linkage over no linkage at all.

Given this situation, America needs a sturdy and dependable group of allies. Kissinger's main disagreement with President Kennedy was Kissinger's assertion that America could not limit the Soviet Union's power by itself. For this reason America has had to militarily and psychologically overcommit itself.

At the same time Kissinger is trying to reduce America's military presence and the power of the Pentagon. So more and more, the United States, to maintain its credibility, must use threats. Threats tough enough to work. Kissinger and Ford would like to avoid nuclear war, but the excessive political commitments of their regime are edging them closer in that direction.

Kissinger is the intellectual. Kissinger himself, philosophically influenced by Hegel, believes that individual men can make real decisions that affect the world: ". . . on co-operating the intellectual has two loyalties: to the organization that employs him and to values which transcend the bureaucratic framework and provide his basic motivation. It is important for him to remember that one of his contributions to the administrative process is his independence, and that one of his tasks is to prevent routine from becoming an end in itself. . . . It is essential for him to retain the freedom to deal with the policy-maker from a position of independence, and to reserve the right to assess the policymaker's demands in terms of his own standards."

Kissinger moved from Harvard, via Rockefeller and Henry Cabot Lodge, to Washington. Yet Harvard University had been, and will continue to be, the focus of Kissinger's life: he had been launched on his fortune there, and his most enduring friendships and personal associations are still there. Harvard has trained many men including Schlesinger, Bundy, and Galbraith for the White House; there has always been a beeline from Harvard to the White House.

Kissinger is an individual who has always been obsessed, even before his arrival in government, with making his mark on history. It would not be at all surprising if, besides seeing Nixon and Ford administration foreign policy as a historical turning point, and besides conceiving of himself as a notable historical figure—which, no doubt, he does—Kissinger imagines, in his moments of greatest personal self-esteem, that he is one of Hegel's great men, one of those rare individuals, those carriers of mankind's historical spirit, about whom Kissinger's favorite philosopher once speculated so long ago.

Both Kissinger and Kissinger's policies, according to Kissinger, above all must reflect the historical conditions we see today and the historic possibilities we see for tomorrow. They are moving with history and moving history themselves. But a

policy and a man who speak not to concrete realties or to
contemporary concerns, but merely to what the man sees as the
vindication of history, are a policy and a man who harshly
excludes those human beings who are not living with the histo-
rians of the future in mind, and who completely disregard
whatever torment and anguish happen to be generated at this
time.

"There's a new woman in the life of James Dean," Kandid
Kendris wrote in her column:

> —a wild youngster who's putting a new sparkle in
> his eyes.
>
> For the first time since he came to Hollywood,
> Jimmy's dating in public—and the woman he loves
> being seen with is Janis Joplin, one of America's new-
> est blues singers.
>
> His dates with this excitable 9-year-old make
> Jimmy glow. The couple has been seen gazing into
> each other's eyes at cozy, exclusive Topanga Canyon
> restaurants and laughing and whispering cheek-to-
> cheek on Jimmy's motorcycle. On one date—in an
> unprecedented public display of affection—Jimmy
> kissed her.
>
> "I was only a few feet away when it happened,"
> said a photographer who's been observing Jimmy's
> new dating game since it began in August. The pho-
> tographer, who asked not to be named, said he's never
> seen Jimmy looking more relaxed and radiant. "He
> doesn't even avoid the camera when he's gone out
> with her."
>
> The new woman in Jimmy's life is a former key-
> punch operator with the Los Angeles Telephone
> Company and the most exciting new singer on the
> scene. She lives on the Venice beach.

Janis, who's made no effort to hide her friendship with Jimmy, had her first known date with him on August 20. She met him at the Warner Brothers' studio. They went to a drive-in to see *The Sun Also Rises.*

After the movie, they spent a lingering evening on Sunset Boulevard, in the pool halls, and left around 3 A.M.

Jimmy and Janis dated several times after that in August and September.

A pool hustler who saw them together told *The Enquirer:* "They would talk together in hushed tones in the back, and once I overheard them having a conversation about leaving Hollywood. They really seemed to have a good time together."

Everywhere the couple went, they left an impression of warmth, even heat. At Schwab's Drugstore, a soda jerk told *The Enquirer:* "Jimmy and the girl had dinner here recently. They chatted and laughed a lot, and seemed to know each other very well. Jimmy Dean looked very happy."

At another drugstore, Googie's, a manager identified photos of Janis and admitted: "The girl was with Jimmy Dean. She didn't give her name, but she was very loving and pleasant to him, and obviously a pal."

Janis is well-known in rock-and-roll circles. It's difficult to determine whether her family is wealthy or not, for Janis looks like a beatnik.

Hollywood, all its evil, was beginning to destroy Jimmy's and Janis' love. Every word these two youngsters whispered to each other in public, every word of trust and affection, every gesture of trust and desire, was immediately reported in the gossip columns, the scandal sheets, the teenage heartthrob mags.

Reported and distorted. Were Jimmy and Janis beginning to believe these distortions of their feelings and of themselves?

JANIS and DRUGS. Janis Joplin, the gutsy, raunchy, and very vulnerable singer that everyone's talking about, a psychiatric social worker from Venice told *Photoplay*, is taking drugs. A lot of drugs.

"According to Janis," said the social worker, "she's having a nervous breakdown. Her parents are psychotics, and she's been trying to break away from them. 'I don't want parents,' she told me. 'I was born from nothing.' Even though she's told her parents to stop calling her, they now call her and hang up the phone when she answers.

"At the same time the enormous amount of publicity Janis has been receiving on account of her affair with JAMES DEAN has made Janis feel more unstable. Janis has to flee to something, and she's fleeing to what's easiest for her: drugs."

Janis refused to talk seriously about her use of drugs. The only thing she said to us was: "I never wanted to sing publicly, man. Much less be a STAR! I just came to Hollywood and sang cause that way, I thought, I could get LAID a lot and get a lot of drugs."

One of Janis' friends, who wants to remain nameless, told *Photoplay* that she had the impression that Janis is now receiving insulin shock.

Janis was too young and too vulnerable to battle Hollywood's glamorizing dehumanizing death machine. And drugs were destroying whatever chance she had to toughen up and keep her love for Jimmy, her ability to love anyone, in a private fortress. Drugs were making her duller and, finally, even more vulnerable.

The evil of Hollywood. The coldness of Hollywood. The other side of Hollywood: if someone wants to become a really good actor or actress, that person has to become someone else, in fact become everyone he or she plays. Actors have to destroy themselves. They don't have time for love.

Jimmy began to realize that his affair with Janis was forcing him to remain human. Remain stuck on the ground when he wanted to soar into the air, a myth. As he put it, "Up here, I hate all earthlings."

But love is strong. Stronger than the desire for immortalization. Stronger than the desire for death. Jimmy and Janis had to flee Hollywood. They went to Montmartre, Paris, France and changed their names.

the future

Being wet and dark with someone.

Being touched and being able to know the person will touch you again. Being in a cave you don't want to leave and don't have to leave. Being in a place in which you're able to be open and stupid and boring.

You're open and wet and your edges are rough and hurt. You remember that you've always been this: totally vulnerable. You don't want to forget who you are. Being with someone has made you remember that you're totally vulnerable.

Marcia and Scott now always felt these ways. Being out of control and not knowing it. Being in total danger and believing that you're safer than you've ever been in your life, you're inside and so you can open yourself and make yourself raw to the other person.

Suddenly seeing something you've never seen before. You're willing to compromise yourself for this person. Forget what you've just thought. You don't have any more thoughts of yourself. You want to know everything about the other person:

What was your childhood like?

What do you like to do the most?

Have you ever fucked any weirdos?

When did you start being an adult?

You think you are the other person. You begin to forget what you feel.

Scott and Marcia now were living on the street cause they didn't have any money. Caught between the devil and the deep blue sea: The other person's frightened of you. He's scared if he lets you into his wetness and heat, you'll disrupt everything. You want him wet and hot so badly, you act so heavy, he gets more scared. you put him out of your head. You want nothing to do with him. Finally you can think one thought which isn't about him. The second you see him again and his hand barely grazes your hand, your heart flops over, you almost faint, you feel like you're turning inside out. When he holds you, you forget the room exists. You can't act like he's the most casual fuck in the world. You can't tell him you're madly in love with him cause then he'll never see you again. You're screwed.

Marcia and Scott didn't even notice they didn't have any money. You're a man. You're not going to take anything from anyone cause you're a man. When you see her, your mouth dries up and your eyes can't leave her face. You want her so much you can't handle it. You flee. You tell her you don't want her warmth. You tell her to go fuck herself. You can't let her go because you and she are, at one point, one. The more she wants you, the crazier you get. You have to let her go and you want to sink into her body.

You tell her you're in love with other women. When you wake up in the morning, holding her warm sleeping body in the curve of your body, you tell her you want to fall in love with someone.

Marcia and Scott hardly had enough money to eat and they were sleeping on the streets. They'd lie on top of one blue blanket and place newspapers over their huddling bodies. Being at ease and in paradise. Every person you see looks proud and interesting. Every person you meet gives you information you want to hear. Every object in the store windows looks beautiful and yet doesn't drive you crazy with desire. Doesn't torment you with the knowledge of how poor you are. Every new street, every alleyway you see is a new stage of the voodoo ritual you're part of: A series of rooms. In each room a new magic event which changes you takes place. You're fascinated and scared. One room contains swamps and alligators and floating moss and voodoo doctors. In another room your sex is cut open and you become a third weird sex. You feel freaked. In another room, a little table, covered with a white cloth, serves as an altar upon which offerings are placed, and a candle burns on the dirt floor as its base, where the vevers are drawn. For the greater part of the time, Ogoun, and then Ghede mount the houngenikon. You place your hand on the heads of lions and wolves whom you're now equal to and who stand next to you. You find yourself outside: in a green green grassy world, outside the wooden building.

Marcia and Scott knew that if the cops ever noticed they were people and not pieces of garbage strewn on the street, the cops would beat them up and put them in jail. The cops would forcibly separate them. Being so happy that you forget everything. You don't know whether you love or don't love. Forget you ever felt anything. Forget you can feel anything. You sleep cause you have to sleep and you piss in the streets. You're learning to know everything a new way.

Marcia and Scott now lived off Marcia's scant earnings as a street chanteuse. Feeling so strongly you're at the edge of a cyclone or huge hurricane. You're about to go over, if you don't constantly fight, into some new territory where the winds are whirling madly and there's no stability and your head bursts open. You still can't contain yourself, the feeling's so strong, your heart's pumping too fast and your flesh is burning: your only sense of yourself is that the world's sky has turned over inside you and that churning air is rushing out in every direction into the rest of the world and you can't fight it and the churning air becomes a force, a demonic force that exists outside of you as do all the forces of the world. All you can do is learn. Maybe, gradually, you can learn to control this force: to keep it open so that you don't destroy the other person and/or the other person doesn't destroy you which is how most love affairs end. But all you do is stupidly and obviously unsuccessfully fight the force that is tearing all of you apart.

Capitalism as a world system had its origins in the late fifteenth and early sixteenth centuries when Europeans, mastering the art of long-distance navigation, broke out of their little corner of the globe and roamed the seven seas, conquering, plundering, and trading. Ever since then capitalism has consisted of two sharply contrasting parts: on the one hand a handful of dominant exploiting countries and on the other hand a much larger number of dominated and exploited countries.

In the beginning the relations between the developed and underdeveloped parts of the world capitalist system were based on force. The stronger conquered the weaker, plundered their resources, subjected them to unequal trading relations, and reorganized their economic structures (e.g., by introducing slavery) to serve the needs of the Europeans. In the course of these predatory operations vast colonial empires were built up and fought over by the Spanish, Portuguese, Dutch, French, and British; and the wealth transferred from the colonies to the metropolises was an important factor in the economic development of the latter.

Gradually the element of force receded into the background

to be replaced by "normal" economic relations of trade and investment—without, however, in any way weakening the basic development/underdevelopment pattern, or stopping the transfer of wealth from the periphery to the center. Adam Smith was one of the first economists who tried to describe, order, and further this new society of trade, this society in which, for the first time in the world, all men could attempt to determine their own economies without the regulations of kings or traditions.

After its victory in the Napoleonic Wars and the related dissolution of the Spanish and Portuguese empires in the Americas, Britain—which was already industrially far ahead of the other developed countries—moved into a position of virtual monopoly of world trade in manufactured goods. The simple laissez-faire capitalism had developed, seemingly from necessity for competition causes expansion, into imperialism.

Around 1885, A. F. Mummery, a successful British businessman, was speculating as to the cause of those periodic slumps in trade which had worried the business community as far back as the early eighteenth century. He decided that the cause of depression lay in the fact of excessive saving, in the chronic inability of the business system to distribute enough purchasing power to buy its own products back.

A shy and retiring economist named John A. Hobson agreed with Mummery. Together the two men wrote *The Physiology of Industry*, setting forth their heretical notion that savings might undermine prosperity.

Hobson continued to worry about the problems of capitalism, and in 1902, he wrote *Imperialism* which is a critique of the profit system. In *Imperialism* Hobson claimed that capitalism faced an internal and insoluble difficulty and that it was forced to turn to imperialism, not out of pure lust for conquest, but as a means of ensuring its own economic survival.

The inequality of incomes, the rich and the poor, the developed and the underdeveloped countries, said Hobson, led to the strangest of dilemmas: a paradoxical situation in which neither rich nor poor could consume enough goods. The poor don't have any money. The rich lack the physical capacity for that much consumption.

So, as a consequence of an inequitable division of wealth, the rich—both individuals and corporations—are forced to save.

This savings leads to trouble. The automatic savings of the rich strata of society had to be put to use, unless the economy was to suffer from the disastrous effects of a steady withdrawal of purchasing power. The question was how to put the savings to work. The classical answer was to invest them in even more factories and more production and thus to ascend to an even higher level of output and productivity.

But, said Hobson, if the mass of people were already having trouble buying all the goods thrown on the market because their incomes were too small, how could the capitalists sell their new products?

Overseas. Imperialism is "the endeavor of the great controllers of industry to broaden the channel for the flow of their surplus wealth by seeking foreign markets and foreign investments to take off the goods and capital they cannot use at home."

All the developed nations are in the same boat. They all need new markets. Imperialism necessarily becomes the road to war.

Out of this situation arose the First World War (1914–1918) which had as major consequences for the global capitalist system: (a) extensive reshuffling of colonies and dependencies in favor of the victorious countries; (b) emergence of the United States as economically the strongest capitalist country; (c) socialist revolution in Tsarist Russia, the weakest of the imperialist powers; (d) birth and/or vigorous growth of national liberation movements in many underdeveloped countries, for the most part strongly influenced by the Russian

Revolution. Thenceforth the dominant capitalist powers had to cope not only with their own internecine struggles but also with challenges from the rival socialist system and from increasingly militant liberation movements in their dependencies.

The Second World War and its outcome faithfully reflected these realities. Started as a war by the "have-not" imperialist powers (Germany, Japan, Italy) to redivide the world, it soon acquired, with the Nazi invasion of the USSR, a capitalism-versus-socialism character as well. For reasons of survival the threatened capitalist powers and the invaded Soviet Union made common cause, defeating the Axis challenge. But there was not and could not be a return to the status quo ante bellum. America, enriched by the war while all the other imperialist powers were severely damaged, became the undisputed leader of world capitalism.

At this point many of the largest American corporations are located, at least in part, outside the USA. By 1970, more than 25% of all these corporations' workers lived outside the USA. By 1970, according to Commerce Department statistics, foreign sales accounted for almost 13% of the total sales of all US manufacturing corporations. By 1971, the American global giants, determined to avoid the high American taxes and make higher profits, were diverting a quarter out of every dollar of new investment to foreign expansion.

More specifically, what does it mean for Americans and for the American federal regulatory process when the economic environment created by America's largest companies is increasingly beyond the control of the American government?

The more the corporate giants locate their production centers outside the USA, the more unemployment in the USA increases. Money becomes tighter. When money is tight and there's an intense competition for funds to lend, big banks obtain such funds when small banks cannot. Thus in 1973, according to the Federal Reserve, nine New York City banks, six of which belonged to the Rockefeller-Morgan group, accounted for more than 26% of all commercial and industrial lending by banks in the US. About half of all the money lent by these New York superbanks goes to global corporations—with the result, as George Budzeika of the New York Federal Reserve Bank has noted, that about 90% of the entire indebtedness in the United States petroleum and natural gas industry, two-thirds in the machinery and metal-products industry, and three-fourths in the chemical and rubber industries are held by these same nine New York banks.

It is the big banks, the very ones whose lending policies must be controlled if the government is to manage the economy successfully, that have the resources to escape control. Because large banks can evade mild credit restrictions, serious efforts to cool the economy by means of monetary policy must be so Draconian as to create even higher unemployment and idle factories. Heavy unemployment is not politically desirable.

For Americans, this situation means inflation because the corporations' current borrowings are permanently accelerating much faster than the corporations' increase in current holdings. Given the international status of the multinational corporations, the American government has no way to control the increasing inflation.

We're being crunched between rising unemployment and increasing inflation.

If employment possibilities increase, so will wages—not only because there are more jobs for more people to fill but also because employers in a time of labor scarcity must pay more. So we're experiencing increasing inflation, increasing unemployment, and decreasing wages.

Meanwhile there's less and less chance for the American worker or the American bum to get a share of the wealth that exists. Because the industrial giants such as I.T.T. have absorbed thousands of smaller companies in the last generation, a share of stock in these corporations represented a much larger portion of America's productive wealth in 1970 than it did in 1950—and a significant part of the stock of the largest corporations is going to their own top managers. The managers are becoming owners, deriving an ever-larger proportion of their income not from their managerial skills but from the stock they own in their own corporations.

You don't give a damn if he never comes around. Your never want to see him again. Fuck his round face and his blonde hair and his five feet ten inches lean body. Fuck him in shit. Fuck his screwed-up mouth and his skinny legs. Fuck him in piss. Fuck his broad shoulders fuck his "good-guy" manner fuck his 155 pounds fuck him with a needle fuck his filthy toes and his feet and his red nose fuck his hicksville manner and fuck that lousy cynicism that covers his naiveté that's totally fake fuck his sexual uptightness fuck his scaredness fuck his egotism fuck everything he's ever done fuck everything he's ever said everything he's ever said is false stick it in a barrel and send it to me. I'll stick dynamite in it and up his ass and light 'em all. *KERPOW!* Fuck him in my blood.

Marcia woke up one morning and realized that Scott no longer loved her. I'm free. Singing and dancing on the streets in the bars they don't make me pay to get into, get as drunk as I want whenever I want. If I pass out someone will pick me up, or I'll just lay there I won't know the difference. Fuck everyone alive cause I'm so high: I'm zooming with the winds. Do ya' see me? I'm the wind cause I just go by what I feel. That's all I care about. And what other people feel. I can sense their feelings more and more strongly it's like my skin touches different kinds of air and knows what these kinds of air are. I'm always sensing and shaking and shivering and knowing the future. Long as I don't get too near anyone. I want to get too close

She realized that Scott was no longer satisfied with a bum's life. What I wanna do is fuck every man in sight. Fuck every man who comes near me and fuck every man who looks at me like he wants to fuck me. Go into some bar, fuck three men in the bathroom, then lie down on the dance floor and wiggle out of my rags. Let every man do to me what he wants. Men will spit on me and piss on me. Women will shoot liquids up my cunt. People become shadows. Then I'll stand up and walk over to these famous businessmen, the Duponts, and put my arms around one of their necks. He'll lift me up and fuck me while I'm naked on the street. Someone else will take me home. I won't even look to see his face. I'll walk into a bums' bar, slowly take off my clothes. Slowly they'll notice me. They won't believe what's happening. I'll love watching the drool and vomit dribble out of their mouths. I turn on watching them remember they have cocks. Their hands slowly reach into their bums' clothing. Their hands are shaking so hard they can't even get it together to touch themselves. As soon as I see this happening, I'll begin to moan. I'll sleep with some bum, with some bum who graduated from the Sorbonne and who made $700,000 a week as a Marseilles gigolo, just to find out how it feels.

Scott wanted to get his own work known. Turn your head toward me gently. That's right. I'm looking at your face. It's almost touching mine. It's right next to me on the pillow. I feel very soft. As if something's just touching me, beginning to smooth away the rough edges and granite boulders in my skin. Do you want to touch me? I'm always amazed anyone wants to touch me cause I'm always feeling these granite blocks and roughness and my ugliness. I have to be able to touch you and keep my distance from you. You're lying partly on top of me and you're falling asleep in my arms. You must've come. I feel you like me and I like you. I'm not thinking about Scott now. For the first time I've calmed down cause I know what to expect with you.

Scott wanted fame and fortune. I live totally by my emotions. That's who I am. Today someone told me I move like a little animal. She doesn't know how I survive. Yesterday someone told me I'm conventionally moral because I'm not fucking three guys at the same time. The same person who told me I'm conventionally moral told me I need endless shots of valium. Today this old lady told my closest friend that I'm getting more and more violent. She's worried about my work. I don't know what my work is. All this stuff passes over my head. I feel a lot of pain most of the time because I act on my feelings and I barge into other people's feelings, opinions, beliefs, whatever they act on, and I scare and hurt them.

Scott wanted beautiful Parisian women to drool over him because he was the guy who was making the most powerful architecture in Paris. If someone doesn't kiss me goodbye, I think the person hates me. If someone I'm fucking doesn't tell me he loves me, I'm sure he hates me. If someone I want doesn't show me constant physical affection, I'm sure that person wants nothing to do with me. If I'm living with someone and he goes away, I refuse to speak to him when he returns. If he goes away again and again, I leave him. Once a man's fallen in love with me, I tell him I don't want to fuck him anymore. I insult my friends to their faces and to other friends. Sometimes I refuse to see the people I'm closest to and I feel I hate them.

Marcia realized she was a bum and didn't belong in this picture of Scott's success. Please tell me whether you love me or not. WHY DO YOU WANT TO KNOW? I can't fuck anyone else cause I'm always thinking about you and I'm getting too horny. I'M NOT IN LOVE WITH YOU AND I DON'T WANT A HEAVY RELATIONSHIP. I'M MORE OFF THAN ON. I understand what's going on. THIS IS CRAZY. WHY SHOULD I DEFINE MY FEELINGS FOR YOU? I DON'T HAVE TO TELL YOU WHAT I FEEL. YOU'RE SO CONVENTIONALLY MORAL:

YOU CAN ONLY FUCK ONE GUY AT A TIME. All I said
was that I was stuck on you. HOW CAN YOU BE IN LOVE
WITH ME? YOU'VE ONLY KNOWN ME FOR A FEW
MONTHS AND YOU'RE JUST A KID. I DON'T BE-
LIEVE YOU WHEN YOU TELL ME YOU LOVE ME.

She began to go crazy. A glance at the annual earnings of
220 men in charge of some of America's largest corporations
(there are no women) shows them to be at the very top of the
income pyramid.

Even though we no longer experience a laissez-faire, or even
a free market, economy, the multinational conglomerate corporations that control the world's wealth need, as did the capitalists of nineteenth-century Britain, markets for their products.
Due to increasing inflation unemployment and tightening of
money, even the corporations are experiencing increasing stagnation. The state can counteract stagnation by suitably large
expenditures on welfare and/or warfare, both of which are
indispensable to monopoly capitalism for other reasons: welfare
as a way of placating the masses and dissuading them from
turning to revolutionary politics, and warfare as a means used
by each leading capitalist power to maximize its economic
"living space" and to control undeveloped and potentially rebellious dependent countries.

Since ours isn't a welfare economy, America is not going
socialist god forbid, it has become a war economy. The military
market supports the largest single industry in the country
today, providing more than 40 billion dollars in sales each year
and involving in total over 20,000 firms. The industry is re-
markably concentrated, with the 100 largest contractors receiving two-thirds of the total contract funds, and the top 25
receiving half these funds.

Negotiated contracts are the rule rather than the exception
in the defense industry, accounting for 58% of all military
prime contracts in 1968, with advertised competitive bidding

accounting for only 11.5% of the total procurement dollars. This industry is one of our least competitive. Firms seldom if ever suffer a financial loss in their defense business. The Defense Department acts to insure that the firms which do business with it remain financially healthy. In fact, the large defense firms often win and/or maintain government contracts by suggesting new systems and new systems improvements and establishing in the minds of the government the special competence of their firms to carry out the job. Peter Schenck, an official of the Raytheon Corporation and former president of the Air Force Corporation, put it in this way: "Today it is more likely that the military requirement is the result of joint participation of military and industrial personnel, and it is not unusual for industry's contribution to be the key factor. Indeed, there are highly-placed military men who sincerely feel that industry is currently setting the pace in the research and development of new weapons systems."

What are the economic results of this dependence upon arms production and maintenance? That wars are engines of inflation is well known: in fact, every substantial war in U.S. history has been accompanied by inflation. And the wildest inflationary periods in other countries have been associated with wars. For 30 years the United States has had a permanently militarized economy. The same applies, in a lesser degree, to other major capitalist powers and, to an even greater degree, to certain small capitalist states.

Militarization provides corporations with a cushion of high-profit business, enabling them to set and maintain higher profit margins in civilian markets. Fantastic markups of four or five times factory cost are applied to the sale of products originally developed for military use, for example, electronics. Efficiency in production for the military is a fraction of that in civilian production, and the corresponding multiplication of costs inevitably is transmitted, at least in part, to civilian sales of armament manufacturers.

How does the rising inflation affect the large American, if they can still be called American, corporations and the United States government?

The multinational corporations are more and more, as has been said, depending upon bank loans. The U.S. is the Debt Economy without peer. One trillion dollars in corporate debt. Six hundred billion dollars in mortgage debt. Five hundred billion in U.S. government debt. Two hundred billion in state and local government debt. Two hundred billion in consumer debt. To fuel nearly three decades of postwar economic boom at home and export it abroad, this nation has borrowed an average net two hundred million dollars a day, each and every day, since the close of World War II.

The American government and the huge corporations took on their enormous burden of debt with the expectation that personal income (buying power) and corporate profits would continue to grow year after year and that government economic policy would remain essentially expansionary. But inflation, while adding greatly to the need to borrow, has slashed the share of income—corporate and personal—available to pay off debts, and an expansionary government economic policy would only add to the inflationary pressures.

So now the nation's burden of debt is like a string drawn very taut: 2.5 trillion dollars in debt outstanding and more money needed to keep the economy growing, while the ability of borrowers to repay what they owe and to find more money is very much in question. The string has not broken, and it may not. The energies of every economist, of every government official, of every lender and borrower will be directed in the weeks and months ahead to keeping that string from breaking. Yet no one knows the precise breaking point and, while there are schemes and theories galore, no one really knows how to ease the tension either.

As unwilling as economists are to admit it, the string has to break.

Keynesian economics, as a system of pushbutton monetary and fiscal policies designed to finely tune the economy and create full or near-full employment with zero or mild inflation, has seen its day (if it ever had a day). Economists can no longer describe what's happening. Economically we're going through a period of transformation.

So what are we to expect?

Capitalism has always been based on a certain relation between two living entities. There are the dominant exploiting countries and a much larger number of dominated and exploited countries. These two groups are indissolubly linked together, and nothing that happens in either part can be understood if it is considered in abstraction from the system as a whole. The principal contradiction in the system, at least in the present historical period, is not within the developed part but between the developed and the underdeveloped parts. The relations of the one to the other (and the policies which grow out of these relations) are fundamentally exploitative: they perpetuate and deepen the development/underdevelopment pattern. Keynesian economics has failed because of its politics and not its techniques—in broadest terms, because it attempted to paper over the class conflicts present in a capitalist society.

The transformation of American capitalism is now becoming manifest. The reversal in the historical (Keynesian) belief that profits are the outcome of high volume or mass production spells disruption for the ordinary processes of production and consumption. There will be frequent manipulated shortages of almost everything that is bought and sold. The notion that inflation can be stemmed by government action has one central defect: the government is subject to the political domination of the large corporations. The penetration by corporations of government agencies charged with regulating business activity vitiates the idea that the state is separate from the marketplace and independent of ruling class control.

There are no effective mechanisms for controlling inflation within a highly centralized and monopolistic economy. Corporate and government decision makers will be constrained to find some solution to the crisis. The chance of stemming inflation depends on finding ways to expand war industries and other forms of public expenditures. The worsening economic situation within the U.S. will probably result in the widening of military influence.

There are substantial problems in implementing this option. First, the United States lacks an available external enemy. Second, the outcome of the Vietnam War has certainly dampened popular enthusiasm for military action.

Which raises the distinct probability of the emergence of new forms of authoritarian rule at home. We are on the road to what Bertram Gross has called "friendly fascism." Unlike its European predecessors, American fascism may not be marked by an "open terroristic dictatorship." The foundation of fascism has already been laid in the consolidation of political and economic power in incredibly few hands.

One night, as she was lying on the street, Marcia dreamt that she returned home. It seemed to her she stood by the iron gate leading to the drive, and for a while she couldn't enter for the way was barred to her. There was a padlock and a chain upon the gate. She called in her dream to her parents, and had no answer, and peering closer through the rusted spokes of the gate, she saw that the house seemed uninhabited.

No smoke came from the chimney, and the little lattice windows gaped forlorn. Then, like all dreamers, she was suddenly possessed with supernatural powers and passed like a spirit through the barrier before her. The drive wound around in front of her, twisting and turning as it had always done, but as she advanced she was aware that a change had come upon it: it was narrow and unkempt, not the drive that she had known. At first she was puzzled and did not understand, and it was only when she bent her head to avoid the low swinging branch of a tree that she realized what had happened. Nature had come into her own again and, little by little, in her stealthy, insidious way had encroached upon the drive with long tenacious fingers. The woods, always a menace even in the past, had triumphed in the end. They crowded, dark and uncontrolled, to the borders of the drive. The beeches with white, naked limbs leant close to one another, their branches intermingled in a strange embrace, making a vault above her head like the archway of a church. And there were other trees as well, trees that she did not recognize, squat oaks and tortured elms that straggled cheek by jowl with the beeches, and had thrust themselves out of the quiet earth, along with monster shrubs and plants, none of which she remembered.

The drive was a ribbon now, a thread of its former self, with gravel surface gone, and choked with grass and moss. The trees had thrown out low branches, making an impediment to progress; the gnarled roots looked like skeleton claws. Scattered here and again amongst this jungle growth she could recognize shrubs that had been landmarks of her childhood, hydrangeas she had touched and seen as her friends. No hand had checked their progress, and they had gone native now, rearing to monster height without a bloom, black and ugly as the nameless parasites that grew besides them.

On and on, now east now west, would the poor thread that had once been the drive. Sometimes she thought it lost, but it appeared again, beneath a fallen tree perhaps, or struggling on the other side of a muddied ditch created by the winter rains. She hadn't thought the way home was so long. Surely the miles had multiplied, even as the trees had done, and this path led but to a labyrinth, some choked wilderness, and not to the house at all. She came upon it suddenly; the approach masked by the unnatural growth of a vast shrub that spread in all directions, and she stood, her heart thumping in her breast, tears behind her eyes.

This was her home, secretive and silent as it had always been, the grey stone shining in the moonlight of her dream, the mullioned windows reflecting the green lawns and the terrace.

Feeling lonely. Feeling lonely, and crazy all the time cause so lonely. Always wanting and wanting and the wanting's never satisfied. Hate myself for wanting so much and for feeling lonely cause it's disgusting and lowering to need someone else and to feel lonely. Hate everyone in the world cause they're all potential lovers and they don't love me. I hate them cause they hate me. Feeling envy and resentment and fear.

If no one bothers me I'll be O.K. As long as I don't have to see anyone and deal with their feelings. Walk the streets alone. Don't let anyone touch me, cause if someone touches me I might want him or her to touch me again.

Don't want anything to do with anyone anymore. Them coming too close to me, wanting to touch me, my skin's gone, wanting something from me, can't figure out what they want. They want me to smile and touch them, but not to smile and touch them too hard. Can't do that cause want affection so desperately. Am not in control.

Feeling almost cut to the bone. Part of me hates, snaps, wants to destroy, wants to cut out the part of other people that hurts me. This part's out of control. This part frightens me. Hurt other people and quiver and shake cause hurt them and run away. Two parts running away from each other. The string has to break. Feeling gentle and soft (the second part). Feeling incapable of doing anything except reaching in this totally soft way. Feeling big large eyes opening wider and wider. This part is all defense. Feeling can have power over my life. Can prevent myself from being hurt by snapping and by being defensive. Feeling I'm so special if I'm hurt I should stop being hurt.

Feeling like a thing rather than living. Knowing that wanting a lover, wanting Scott back, is wanting to be dead again, wanting one feeling so much that feeling becomes a thing, my possession. Knowing this but not feeling it all throughout my body.

7

the life of johnny rocco

She couldn't take it anymore.

She was just a cheap gun moll. He approached her sexually.
But she was too scared of him and she didn't come through.
He didn't want anything to do with her anymore. Sexually. He
was punishing her.

He told her he was fucking a lot of women and he didn't
want to fuck her. All the women he was fucking were taking
away his energy. He needed energy for his business. He wanted
to establish a relation with her that wouldn't sap his energy.
She agreed with him.

In the beginning it was murder for the woman because he
wouldn't show her any love. One day she slashed her wrists, not
seriously, to make him notice her. A few days later she got
seriously sick; her body had taken over her search for love.

The man told her she should look into herself for love.

The moll made a decision: This was the first man she had

ever met in her 28 years of living to whom she was completely opening herself. She told the businessman she'd do anything for him. Would he just let her in. She'd be his secretary, his gun boy, his cook, anything despite her 28 years of increasing independence. He told her he didn't need anything from her.

Nonetheless the woman and the man were becoming closer and closer. They were slowly beginning to tell each other everything.

One day, over breakfast, they reached the height of their friendship. They both agreed that they weren't in love with anyone. The woman told the man who (she knew) tended to be dishonest, that he shouldn't pretend he was in love with the women he was fucking when he wasn't. The man told the woman she needed to be loved. She trusted him so much she openly agreed with him.

The next day the businessman said to the moll, "My love, I want to take you places you've never been . . ." The moll made her third mistake.

First mistake: fucking with the guy that one time he approached her.

Second mistake: thinking the guy might be falling in love with her when he said "My love . . ."

Third mistake: She said to the man, "Do you love me? I want to know because I could fall in love with you very deeply."

"I don't love you," the businessman replied. "However, I feel affectionately toward you. Right now you matter to me more than all the other women I know. Why don't you call me tomorrow?"

The next day she called him and he told her that he was exhausted because he had been fucking around. Then he lied to her, like she was another of those women who were chasing him only she was lower because he wouldn't even fuck her, she was no longer his friend because she had admitted to him she could fall in love with him, about his plans for that night.

When she got off the phone, she felt a lot of pain. She wrote him the following letter: I'VE GOT TO SPLIT. HERE'S THE OPIUM I OWE YOU AND A GOING-AWAY PRE-SENT. GOOD KNOWING YOU. Then she realized that she had cut off, purposely, willingly, the only person she had ever been able to talk to completely and learn from. She was more and more in pain. She didn't want to stay where people could reach her so she went outside. It was snowing, snowing so hard you couldn't see the hand you stuck out in front of your body. She was being even more stupid when she threw herself in front of a moving car.

The name of the businessman was Johnny Rocco.

What does being a man mean? The only thing you trust is the
edge your own loneliness makes. You make your decisions
according to this edge. You trust other perceptions and other
people only partially. No matter how deeply you may love some
man or how closely you may be working with some man, you'd
cut that person dead if your loneliness demanded it.

"Have you got the guns?"

"Just got the shipment in from Vito. I don't trust that guy."

"Nobody cares whether you trust him or not."

"I care whether I live or die."

"Sure. Get the crates open. We've got to get the guns out
of here soon."

"What about the dame?"

"What d'ya mean: 'What about the dame'?"

"The last time I saw the crates, there was a dame sitting on
them."

"You're seeing things. No dame's ever come into this warehouse. Dames aren't part of the business.' "
"I said, 'Dames aren't part of our business.' "

"You said, 'Dames aren't part of the business.' "

"All we've got are ourselves and our blood. Dames, dope,
ideas—they don't matter."

"The dame says she wants to talk with you."

"Get rid of her."

"How should I do that?"

"Try killing her."

Johnny and I were children together. I can remember running around with him on the Brooklyn streets. Looking up to him like he was God. When I got old enough to go into business, he helped me open my first business. Gave me money and never questioned me. I try to keep my life clean, American; Johnny's the only person I'm friends with.

I went into my office to talk to her to see what kind of trouble she was bringing.

Her back was sticking in my eyes. She must have heard footsteps cause she turned around.

"I don't like women," I told her. "You don't concern me and you don't belong here. Tell me your business and then get out of here as quickly as possible."

"I'm not a woman," she replied.

"You look like a woman to me."

"That's your problem." She told me that the guns she was sitting on, the ones my brother had just sent me, were hot. The minute my boys used the guns, the cops would be on to me. I asked her why Vito had sent me hot rods. She said she didn't know anything else.

I stopped looking at her. "Get out of here."

She walked away like she was walking down Park Avenue. She wasn't running and she wasn't looking. I couldn't tell if she had been lying to me or not.

The years of pretense in my soul are nothing compared to the years the business for which they had hired me had been going on.

The Dominican Republic was going to hell. The economy was at an all-time low, for their President, Rafael Trujillo, was fleecing all of the industries and making treaties according to his personal needs. Censorship was absolute. No one in the country had any personal rights. Not that the United States minded any of this.

Unfortunately in March of 1960 President Romulo Betancourt of Venezuela asked the Organization of American States to censure Trujillo for "flagrant violations of human rights." Trujillo blew his cool and decided to off Betancourt. The assassination didn't work and the United States got worried that Trujillo was losing his touch.

31 years of Trujillo's fleecing and now the United States decided they needed a new fleecer. Trujillo had gotten so paranoid that he was controlling the Dominican military bases and weaponry. The United States decided they had to import some guns into the Dominican Republic.

On December 28, 1960, a man named Plato Cox told me he needed my trucks to ship some groceries to the supermarkets in the Dominican Republic. The Dominican Republic was having trouble getting food because Trujillo was appropriating all of the food. The groceries would consist of specially marked and packed food cans. Once the trucks reached the Dominican Republic, a man named Lorenzo Berry would meet each truck and show each truck where to go.

I wasn't sure these were the facts and I wasn't sure who was fleecing whom. All I knew was I was legitimate because I was powerful and power causes legitimacy in this country.

"The guns're packed."

"What're you bothering me for? Did you put a tail on that dame?"

"The dame disappeared."

"She disappeared? Who'd you put on her?"

"She knew what she was doing."

"Then she must have had a reason for telling me what she did."

"Dames never do anything for reasons. You can never tell why they do what they do."

"I mean that she must be working for someone. Someone who has a business of his own."

"I tell you you can never tell why dames do what they do. Forget whatever she told you, boss: she was probably hallucinating like all dames do. I never should have let her in here. You can never trust what they say."

"Oh yeah?" There was ice in my soul. "The dame doesn't matter. Nobody matters to me."

All my consciousness has ever been is I love and adore Johnny. One man shouldn't feel this way about another man. But Johnny's my brother. I don't feel like I've given myself away to Johnny. I don't feel I've tried to escape my own loneliness. My business is the outpouring, the continuation of my loneliness, and my business is separate from Johnny's business. I supply guns and other tools to businesses in need. This isn't the truth. The truth is I exist according to the blood, the strength of the blood, I was born in. Johnny's the only family I have left. To the extent he'll stick to me, I'll doubly and triply try to give him what he wants, his muscle, because that's where one of my centers is.

The trouble's always been that Johnny isn't as simple as I am and doesn't support me the way I support him. Johnny says to me: "You're my brother. The only relations between people that can possibly exist in this world are blood relations. If it wasn't for blood, it'd be every man for himself."

"Yeah, Johnny," I say. He looks at me and walks away. He's forgotten what he's been saying. Johnny offers me 40 grand if I ever want it. A month later I'm in a jam. Johnny can't lend me the money cause he just bought too many racing horses. I figure Johnny hates me. Johnny calls me up, almost crying: Why am I acting so paranoid? Won't I have dinner with him at Teddy's? He's got a business engagement. He has to go now.

Johnny's ambivalence affects everything. His ambivalence makes him charming. I don't know whether to trust him or not.

Johnny doesn't kill because he's ambivalent and I'm a killer.

I had forgotten about the dame and, by chance, I met her again. It was a dimly lit street, the polluted air was so thick you could see it at the edge of the lights. Somewhere below Houston on the Bowery. I'm not usually found in such a filthy neighborhood. The dame was walking up the street, slightly ahead of me.

I increased my pace and caught up with her. "Hello," I said to her.

"Hello," she murmured. She increased her walking pace.

The light from a bum bar sign cast a diagonal of purple light across her face. "I want to find out why you told me Vito's guns are hot."

"Why do you want to know?"

By now the purple light had left her face. "Either Vito sent me hot guns and someone wants me to know that. In that case I'd like to find out who my unknown friend is. In this business friends don't exist for no reason. Or else someone sent you with a phony story to break up Vito and me. So tell me who you're working for."

She didn't look like she minded my questions. "I won't even

try the story that Vito loved me, discarded me, and I'm trying to get revenge. Let's just say I decided to squelch on Vito for personal reasons."

"Meaning you have a business of your own. That's the only personal reason I know of. That won't help you. Dames don't have businesses of their own."

"Do you want to hear lies?"

I was getting sick of her toughness. It was a stupid toughness because it didn't make sense. "Listen, honey. You're going to tell me who you're working for whether you like it or not. So you might as well start telling me now before I start giving you trouble."

She had started walking again, as fast as she could. There was no one on the streets. There was no one she could run to. There was nowhere she could run to. "Get out of my life before I call the cops."

It was dark. I put my arms around her and pinned her to the building. My hands held her wrists and my legs were stuck between her legs. The typical rapist's position. "Tell me who you work for, why he hired you, why he sent you over to me. I'm sick of fooling around."

"I told you already. I don't work for any man. I work for myself."

"I'll try again. Tell me who you work for, why he hired you, and why he sent you over to me. If you don't tell me, I'm going to beat you to a pulp."

She didn't say anything. I slapped her face a few times.

"I told you: I'm in business for myself. I went with Vito for a while. I learned the ropes, and when he dumped me, I decided to use what I'd learned.

"I thought you'd be nicer to me than Vito."

I almost puked. What did she want me to do? Make love to her like I was daddy with his new little girl? I hit at her again and again. Then I realized how tough she was. She didn't even try to give me a believable lie. She just told me the stupidest thing she could think of, the sex line, and I fell for it. She was never going to tell me anything. I beat her up some more and left her there. I didn't know whether she was alive or dead.

I guess I didn't kill her outright cause I was hoping she'd remember who I was.

I got back to the office. It looked like nothing had changed. A big, empty warehouse with a few dollies shoved against the wall to my left. I walked into my office in the back of the warehouse. It was pitch black.

"Mr. Rocco."

I didn't move. The lights were on all around me.

"I hope you don't mind I let myself into your office. I don't like to stand on the street. I can cause unnecessary attention."

"I'm a private man, Mr. Cox, and I get nervous easily. Why d'you break into my office?"

"Mr. Rocco, you're one of the most intelligent men it's been my privilege to deal with. Our business is almost over with. I'm sure you're going to understand what I'm going to tell you."

His voice sounded like it was coming out of a machine. I looked at his pig face and held my breath.

"Because we live in a complex world, unfortunately we're forced to act one way and say we're acting another. Let me give you an example: A few months ago Castro allowed the Russkies to enter Cuba, build missile sites on the island, flood Havana with technicians. Naturally we couldn't allow this. We acted directly. We invaded Cuba and, when that failed, threatened to bomb Cuba. Castro successfully called our bluff."

"You wanted Batista back so you could keep splitting the profits with him and Meyer Lansky. Who're you kidding?"

He brushed my words off him with his fingertips. "Of course the world no longer accepts our credibility. We're no longer able to act directly. But we still have to get rid of Castro."

"So why don't you hire Lansky to off Castro? Lansky's a better businessman than you are."

"Let's take another example:
"The horrendous situation of the people of the Dominican Republic. We'd like to help certain Dominican Republic patriots recover—"

"Their beloved homeland. Your business is democracy. You want to ask Trujillo to resign."

"You don't understand, Mr. Rocco. Because of the Bay of Pigs fiasco, we can't risk another assassination at this time. We have to abandon our plans for Rafael Trujillo.
"We'd like you to remain quiet, Mr. Rocco. Very very quiet about your dealings with us."

"I don't care what your fuckin' plans are as long as you pay me for the business I've done for you. But if you ever break into my office again or in any way disturb my business operations, I'll blast this secret wide open."

"Of course we'll do you any favors you need. Because we're friends, Mr. Rocco. Let's both observe each other's privacy." I picked up my hat and left.

■

I dreamed I was in this plane. The earth was turning away from me as if it were running away from itself at 100 miles per hour. The sky's getting darker and darker. The winds are howling around me. When I come down to earth, I learn that two new mailplane pilots, Les and Joe, have entered the Dutchman's premises. Joe's girlfriend is Bonnie Lee. As head pilot of the Dutchman service, successful landings and continuing flying are my business. Joe's up in a plane. The air changes to fog. I try to bring Joe down but I can't. The fog's too thick. Joe insists on landing, against his own rational knowledge, because he's supposed to have dinner with Bonnie. Grey haze. I'm sitting in the restaurant with some other flyers and Bonnie. Bonnie asks me if Joe's death is her fault. "Sure it was your fault. You were going to have dinner with him, the Dutchman hired him, I sent him up on schedule, the fog came in, a tree got in the way. All your fault." The steaks Bonnie ordered for her and Joe arrive. I take Joe's steak. Bonnie says, "Are you going to eat it?" I say, "What do you want me to do, have it stuffed?" Bonnie says, "It was Joe's steak." "Who's Joe?" I look at the steak. Then Bonnie and I sing the "Peanut Vendor" to signal her initiation into and acceptance of our living on the edge of death. We haven't forgotten Joe's death. We're shouting our defiance of the face of darkness surrounding human life and the chaos of the universe. Then Kid, my closest friend whose eyesight's been failing but who won't stop flying, fatally crashes his plane. I go crazy. In my craziness I realize I love Bonnie: I need her world of out-of-control feelings and personal commitment.

"Johnny."

"Huh?"

"What are you doing here?"

"I'm having this bad dream. Do you ever get worried?"

"Huh? I trust your boss. You run a powerful family. I came back to clean up."

"You came back to clean up. I think I'm going to die soon."

"You worried about that Vito business, boss? Why don't you just give him a vacation?"

"I'm not worried about anyone. The dame. Vito. That lousy gun-running business that just fell through. I just think that things are over. I think Johnny Rocco has no more use."

"My brother-in-law told me this great joke. There's this lady, see, who lives in Brooklyn. Her backyard's been smelling worse and worse. She sees a skunk run into her kitchen so she captures the skunk in a brown paper bag and takes the paper bag to the nearest bus stop. She says to the bus driver of the first bus which comes along, 'Listen, driver. Tell me when we get to the end of the line. In this bag I've got a skunk who's been smelling up everything so I want to get him as far away from my house as possible.' The driver tells the lady to sit in the back of the bus. She sits in the back of the bus. Some time goes by. The bus driver yells out, 'Will the lady with the stinkin' pussy please get off the bus?' All the women on the bus cross their legs as tightly as they can. Six women run out the rear door."

"I think that I'm dead. I don't care who I beat up anymore. I don't care if I beat anyone up anymore. I can sit on my ass and I can do nothing, I can destroy the world, and I don't know the difference. I'm a ghost wandering about in a ghost land that's made up of all my own garbage."

"You don't look dead to me boss. We're gonna have two new trucks coming tomorrow."

"I've got guns and knives. I can do anything I want. I've got men who are guns and knives. I can tell them to do anything. I've got all the money I need. I planned it this way. I figured out the steps. I can make any move I want cause I've got the know-how to create reality the way I want it so all the others accept it as reality."

"The trucks're gonna be the biggest we've ever had. The boys'll want to celebrate."

"How can I fight myself? How the hell can I start the real death battle of all time? I'm sick of the pretense. Maybe I'm going crazy like Joey Gallo went crazy when he took Profaci's four top men."

I was standing at the doorway to my private office. I saw a line of bullets rip through the windows. Bits of glass flying. A body throws me down to the floor.

"You wanna get killed?"

"Stay still." I watch the line of bullets go back and forth until the windows are wide open. I see a gun on the floor.

After a long quiet I walk to the gun. A note around the gun tells me I have to watch how I act: I'm forgetting my manners. I shouldn't have beat up the girl.

I guess the girl's still alive and has protectors.

"Looks like you've been asking for trouble Johnny."

I had to find the girl. I figured she was with Vito or she was with those thugs who had hired me for the Dominican Repub-

lic job. When I had gotten about three blocks from the warehouse, I saw her lurking next to the corner of a building.

"I've been waiting for you."

I looked at her. Bandages practically covered her face. I liked
what I saw. "I don't want to be seen with you in public. We'll
go to my place."

"I have to tell you something important," she said. "I'm
scared."

I let her into my place and motioned her to sit down on the
rickety armchair facing the leather sofa. Then I went to get us
coffee.

"I've decided to tell you who I'm working for."

I brought out the coffee. "What happened after I beat you
up?"

"One of my bosses had been following me. He picked me
up and asked why you had been knocking into me."

"You mean he didn't try to stop me."

"Don't be a fool. I told him you were trying to find out who
I was working for. Since I didn't tell you, you beat me up. He
didn't believe me."

"Uh-huh. So now you're scared. You come running to me."
There was something strange in her eyes.

"He said he was going to murder you cause you weren't
obeying orders and he was going to murder me."

"I'm not obeying orders? You must be working for those
government guys who hired me to run guns to the Dominican
Republic. They sent you with that story about Vito to try to
bust up me and Vito so they could get a tighter hold on me."

"I just did what they told me. I was working for them."

"You seemed so tough. And now you come running to me
just cause your boss threatens to kill you. Even with all your
bandages on, I still don't like you."

"You've got to believe me. We're up against people who are
much stronger than us. After I told the boss my story, he left

me. I was lying there in the dark. I overheard two men talking about Giancana. Giancana was the top Chicago boss no one had been able to do in for 30 years. The bosses hired him to help them assassinate Castro. When he didn't succeed, cause they couldn't trust him, they shot him in the throat, mouth, and back of the head.

"I came here."

I didn't like the parallel she was drawing between me and Salvatore Giancana.

"You can't fight them, Johnny. The only thing you can do is run. You must have enough friends who'll help you take a semi-permanent vacation."

"And you'll go with me cause you need protection." I started talking to myself out loud. "And what about Vito? I need Vito's help." I looked at her bandaged face. "Were your bosses trying to break up Vito and me, or were they working in collusion with Vito?"

"I don't know. I never even saw Vito."

"I have to find out about that. I have to know if I can use Vito's help."

I turned to her. "Now I'm putting myself in your hands. I want you to return to your bosses and learn if they're working with Vito." I thought for a minute. "That'll show me I can trust you and take you with me."

"I don't have a choice."

"You can sleep here. I have to speak to Vito now." I threw her a blanket. "As soon as you wake up, go back to your bosses."

"Mommy always loved you more than she did me."

I was startled a grown man would speak to me this honestly. "I don't think that's true. She used me as a whipping-post to get you to do what she wanted."

"She wanted me to be exactly like you. You were smart and tough and handsome. You knew what you were doing. I was stupid."

"She was just using who you thought I was to control you. You were so stupid you accepted whatever she said."

"She cared more about you than she did about me."

"The truth is she hated me. You don't know any of this. When she was 19, she was a wild kid. She used to escape from her strict parents at night, secretly, and fuck every guy in sight. She fell madly in love with this one guy. Maybe they got married. When she was three months pregnant, he split."

"You were the kid?"

"According to her, he split because she was pregnant. He never sent her any money or wanted to see me. So when I was a year old, she married a guy she despised."

"She must have loved you too. You were all she had left of the guy she loved. I was the son of that good-for-nothing lazy vegetable she had to support. No wonder she despised me."

"She might have loved me when I was a kid. Remember I look exactly like her 'cept I'm a man, and you look like your stupid father. But once I started fucking around, she hated me."

"I don't understand, Johnny."

"She actually tried to kill me. I had run away from her to be with another woman."

"I thought you hated women."

"That was before I decided women were so stupid, they were only interested in their own comforts. She hired some class-C private dick, gave him some knock-out drops to give me so he could stick me in his car and bring me home. I tested those drops. They were poison."

"She's crazy cause she's always wanted a man and never got one. You can't blame her for the ways she's acted."

"You still adore her. I do too. She's a totally beautiful woman."

I was surprised to hear Johnny say that. I've always known my brother's a bit cold and has trouble feeling things. Whereas I'm stupid, but I feel strongly.

"Vito, I came to ask you about the guns you sent me."

"Huh? Didn't you get them yet?"

"Yeah. A dame came with them."

"I didn't know you had girlfriends, Johnny."

"The dame told me the guns you sent me were cop-registered. Then I found out the dame was working for the feds."

"You think I'm working for the fed? I wouldn't do that."

I saw the hurt in his eyes. "You're my brother. I don't think you'd work against me unless you thought you'd become Capo di Tutti Capi. I'm in trouble, Vito. I've got to get out of town tonight and no one can know about it."

"You know I'll help you Johnny. Meet me at the store tonight at 8:00. Everything'll be set up. I'll be at my warehouse all day if you need me."

I put my hand on his cheek and kissed him.
When I got outside, the sun was coming up.
Most of my men were already in the warehouse when I entered it.

"Johnny, there's some guy here from the United Fruit Company."

"Tell him to wait. Did the new trucks come in?"

"Yeah, and they're beauts. We've never had bigger and they handle like happy prostitutes."

"The bigger they are, the bigger I am." I was feeling good. "And now the United Fruit Company, the only banana company who's been using free labor, comes to me.
"You know why they come to me? I know how to make the moves. I started off with nothing. I was a creep on the street like all of you are still creeps on the street. When I was still a kid, I saw everything clearly: If I didn't go ahead and make it for myself, no one would make if for me. It was black, nothing, a hole. I just made some moves. I wasn't smarter than you guys, I just had more guts. I saw it didn't even matter what moves I made, because everyone else was so stupid, they were just sitting on their asses and gawking.
"I'm the real bourgeoisie cause I'm one of the people who makes the paths everyone in this society follows."

"The United Fruit guy says he'd like to speak with you soon, if it's O.K. with you, cause he has to get back to the docks . . ."

"Sure there are other guys who know enough to make paths that work. Their paths aren't my paths cause they aren't me. But no one and no family's ever crossed me and won. My territory works and remains untouched cause I know how to deal with the world. I'm a complex guy and I work as complexly as I see. That's what power really is."

"Hey, boss, go talk to that banana guy. He thinks you're offending him cause his prick's not long enough."

"You can't impose your will on the world. You can't go out and shoot some people and expect to get what you want. That's being a muscle-man. The only reason Anastasia lasted so long is cause Frankie backed him. I've studied all this. You've got to know how the world works. You've got to know exactly what the forces are you're dealing with so you know when to bend a little, even when to hide, and when to kill. The Feds are a strong group so I have to take a little vacation. I know when to bend. I also know that in the long run the Feds are dependent on me cause I can do the work they can't do.

"A conscious man can absolutely make his way in the world."

"Boss, someone on the phone says he's sending over a present for you."

"Why d'ya have to tell me about crank phone calls, stupid?" I slapped him across the face. "I'm getting everything I ever wanted. Now the big importers are coming to me."

"The banana guy's waiting in your private office."
As I reached the office door, I heard a crash. I saw one window paneless and the broken glass scattered on the floor. A round object, partly white and partly red, lay on the floor.

I knew what it was before I saw it close. It was the dame's head. The one who had worked for the Feds. Better her head than my head.

I heard a voice behind me. It sounded like Cox.

"It looks like you were stupid. We asked you to keep your mouth shut and you went in search of that girl. Maybe you had a crush on her and couldn't resist your manly ardor."

"So she told you she was working for me."

"I guess you were just a little stupid Johnny and we're more powerful than you."

I heard some shots behind me and some thuds. Screams of agony.

"You've been a good businessman, Johnny. You're getting sloppy taking care of business so we have to take care of your business for you."

I turned around. Now blood, flesh, and guts covered the floor instead of broken glass. I didn't see any of my men who were alive.

"We're going to do our own shipping instead of hiring people like you. Strong individualism is the American ideal."

"Have you killed Vito?"

"Let's clean up this mess." I threw down my gun and walked over to the nearest dead body. I ordered one of my men to pick up a broom and begin to sweep.

They weren't even going to kill me. I ran out of that warehouse. I had no idea where to go. I kept on running.

the end